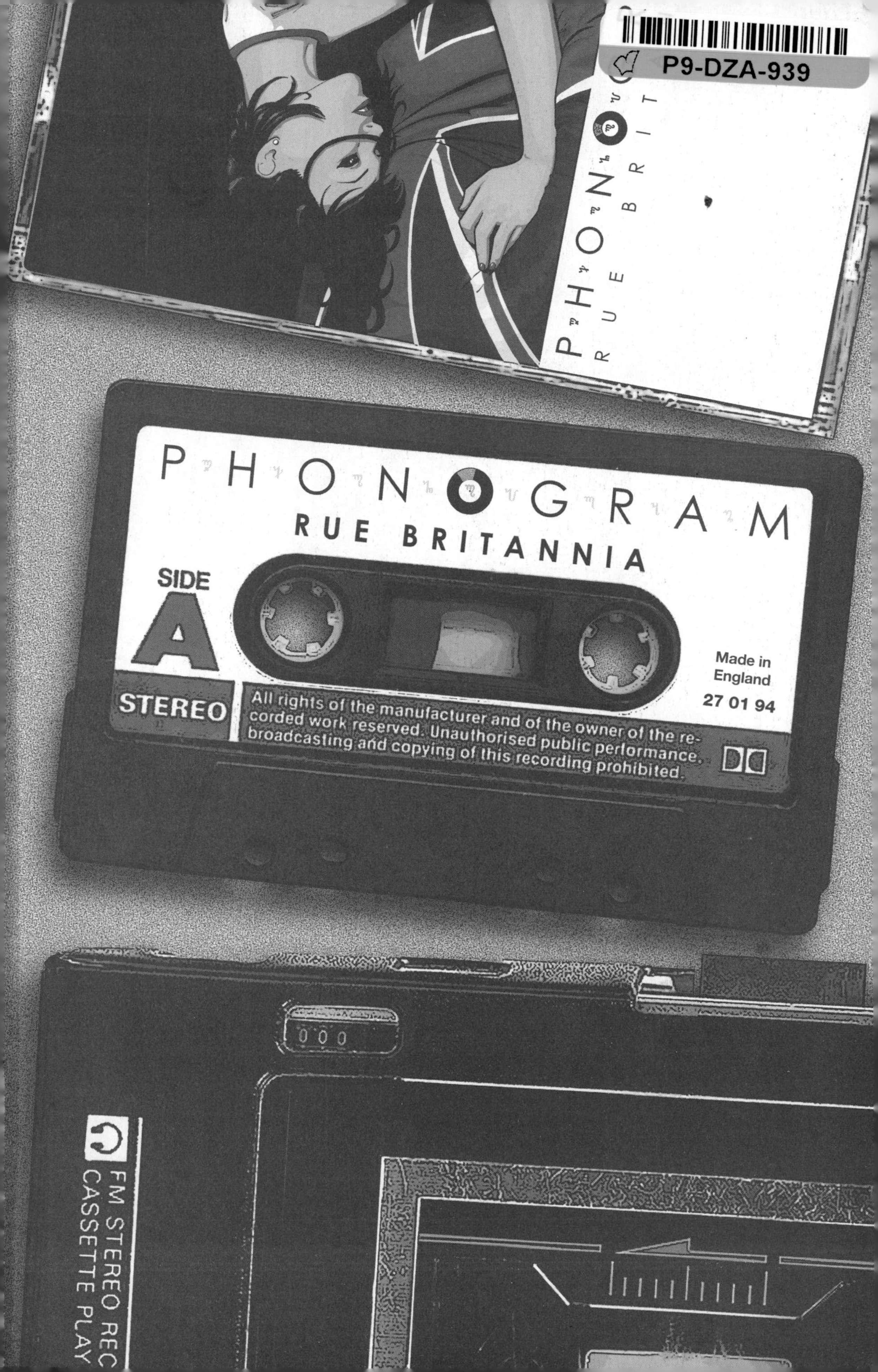
PHONO
RUE BRIT
PHONOGRAM
RUE BRITANNIA
SIDE
A
Made in England
27 01 94
STEREO
All rights of the manufacturer and of the owner of the recorded work reserved. Unauthorised public performance, broadcasting and copying of this recording prohibited.
0 0 0
FM STEREO REC
CASSETTE PLAY

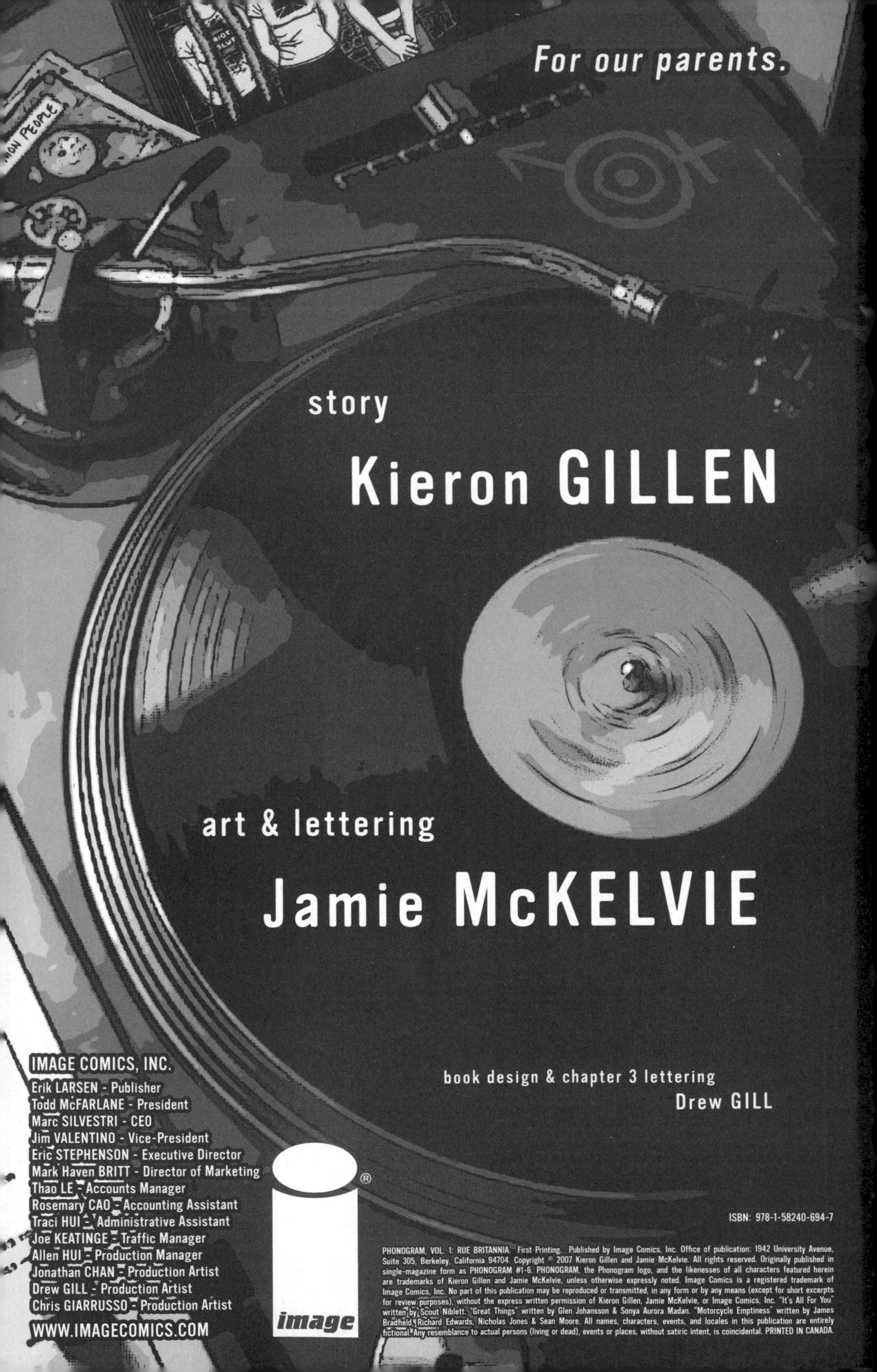

For our parents.

story
Kieron GILLEN

art & lettering
Jamie McKELVIE

book design & chapter 3 lettering
Drew GILL

IMAGE COMICS, INC.
Erik LARSEN - Publisher
Todd McFARLANE - President
Marc SILVESTRI - CEO
Jim VALENTINO - Vice-President
Eric STEPHENSON - Executive Director
Mark Haven BRITT - Director of Marketing
Thao LE - Accounts Manager
Rosemary CAO - Accounting Assistant
Traci HUI - Administrative Assistant
Joe KEATINGE - Traffic Manager
Allen HUI - Production Manager
Jonathan CHAN - Production Artist
Drew GILL - Production Artist
Chris GIARRUSSO - Production Artist
WWW.IMAGECOMICS.COM

ISBN: 978-1-58240-694-7

INTRODUCTION

I may not be giving too much away if I tell you that the pages you are about to read contain a thought or two on the late 20th century phenomenon they called – whisper it – Britpop. Oh, you remember (Kieron Gillen and Jamie McKelvie certainly do) Marion, Kenickie, Echobelly (thanks for that. I am so grateful to you for reminding me of the true horror that is Great Things). Damon and Justine, ah happy days.

But it's not as simple as all that. I suspect that *Phonogram* is a highly subjective meta romp. A meta romp through nostalgia. The writer's nostalgia for a long lost youth. A youth populated with old flames, cigarettes, drink, (did you see what I didn't do just then? Lesser writers would have succumbed to the glaringly obvious) and drugs. Oh and some people that I knew.

So now another highly subjective piece of meta. My own. Variously I have been accused of being a pioneer, the forgotten man and Godfather of what they called Britpop ('90s version, let's not start tracing it back, it's not cost effective and always ends up with a caveman banging a rock with the tusk of a woolly mammoth). So in 1992 there were two new bands; Suede and the Auteurs. Suede had the bum-boy androgyny and I had the songs. One song "American Guitars". That was the one that they thought started it. Taken by the NME and Melody Maker as a rallying call for a new wave of English guitar bands to rise up and destroy the U.S. hegemony. Actually a total misunderstanding of the songs lyrics, still it gave people an idea, and the seeds were sown. Then there was that 1993 Select cover with Brett looking like a ninny in front of a Union Jack. The improbable headline; "Yanks Go Home". Inside were Suede and the Auteurs and a couple of other groups too long in the tooth to be at the vanguard of anything new. So the press had the blueprint of their new cash cow, all they needed were some groups to fit the bill. And for Kurt Cobain to die.

I like to think that Suede and the Auteurs softened up the nation for what was about to come. This once proud nation weak and effete. Begging for mercy, submissive to the horrors of... oh, you get the picture.

Aside from all this talk of subjectivity is the fact, I said *fact*, that *Phonogram* reads like old-school journalism, redolent of the time when there were only four music papers, and the only lists were on the back pages and were called The Charts.

A joke to cheer you up:

1997, the day of Princess Diana's funeral. I am living in Camden Town, I decide to take a walk around the manor to see if I can catch a bit of national mood from the throng of provincial mourners. Up Parkway towards Regents Park and Primrose Hill and over the railway bridge at Chalk Farm, I end up outside the Roundhouse about to cross over the road. On the other side of the road I spot Noel Gallagher eating an ice cream. I have met Noel once before a few years earlier, he came up to me in the street, hugged me and said "top tunes man". Sweet of him. Embarrassing but sweet. So, just as I am looking across at Noel a white van pulls up beside me.
"Oi, Noel," yells the van driver. "Fookin' mad for it!"
The lights change and the van speeds off. Noel Gallagher looks across the road, spots me, smiles and waves.

— LUKE HAINES

Over the last fifteen years or so Luke Haines has had chart hits with The Auteurs and Black Box Recorder, recorded film soundtracks and generally played agent provocateur in an increasingly dull pop landscape. His latest solo album, Off My Rocker at the Art School Bop, *is available on Degenerate Records. He must be on the short list for Greatest Living Englishman by now, surely.*

CHAPTER ONE

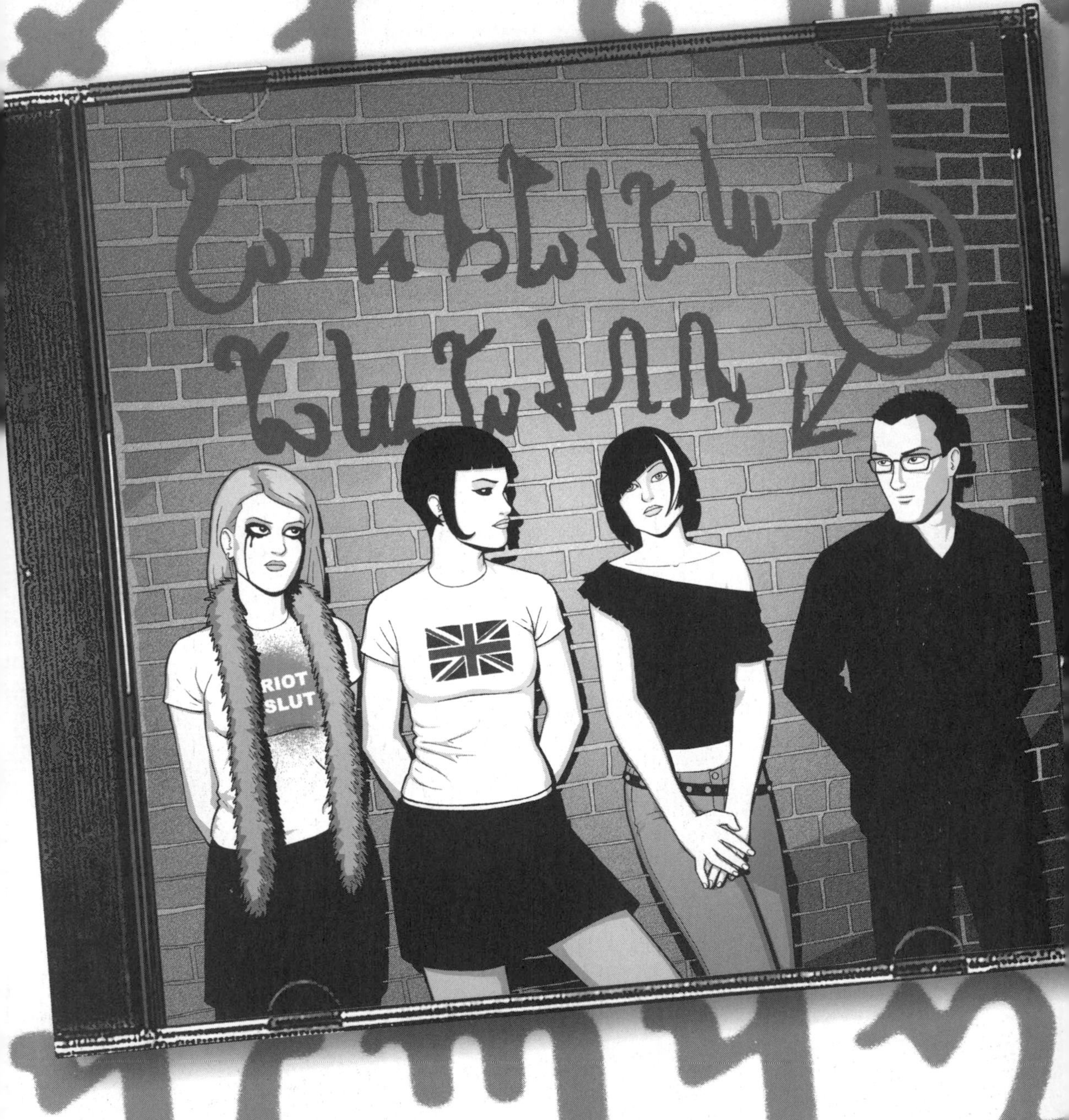
RIOT
SLUT

WITHOUT YOUR PERMISSION

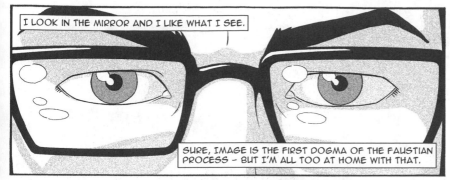

I LOOK IN THE MIRROR AND I LIKE WHAT I SEE.

SURE, IMAGE IS THE FIRST DOGMA OF THE FAUSTIAN PROCESS — BUT I'M ALL TOO AT HOME WITH THAT.

BUZZCUT LIKE A SQUADDIE ON THE TOWN.

GLASSES LIKE AN EXISTENTIALIST POET.

BLACK. BLACK. MORE BLACK.

STILL THIN ENOUGH, JUST.

AND A TOUCH EXTRA, ESPECIALLY FOR THIS EVENING'S FESTIVITIES.

A BOOTLEG POP-ICON T-SHIRT I PICKED UP ON A FESTIVAL SITE BECAUSE IT WAS TOO DAMN COLD.

PLASTIC COAT PACKED WITH SILVER FLUID. ARTIFICIAL ENOUGH TO MAKE YOU THINK IT'S FILLED WITH CHERNOBYL WASTE.

TOXIC AND MALE. UTTERLY NOXIOUS. TOTALLY PERFECT.

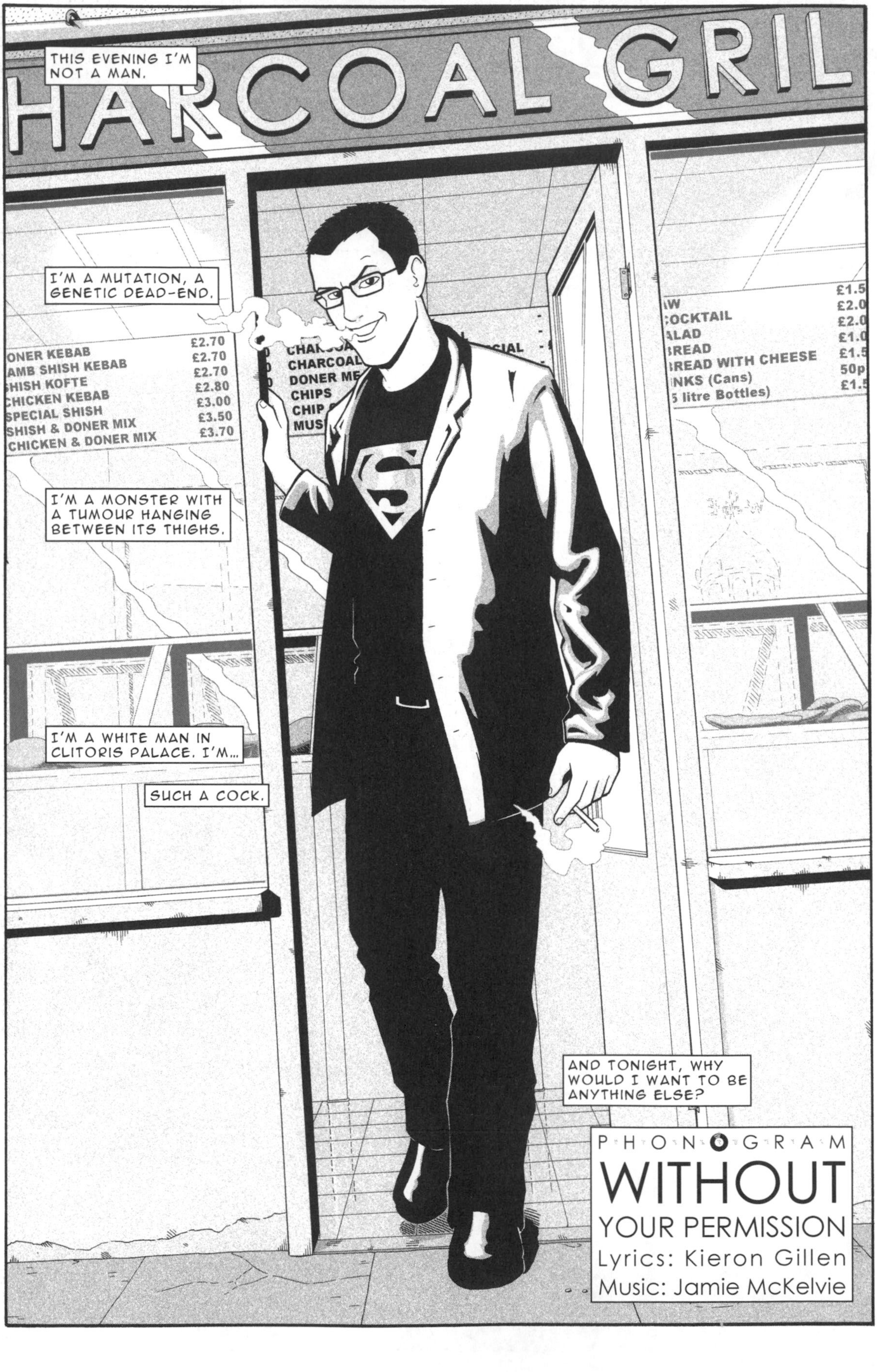
HARCOAL GRIL
THIS EVENING I'M NOT A MAN.
I'M A MUTATION, A GENETIC DEAD-END.
ONER KEBAB £2.70
AMB SHISH KEBAB £2.70
SHISH KOFTE £2.70
CHICKEN KEBAB £2.80
SPECIAL SHISH £3.00
SHISH & DONER MIX £3.50
CHICKEN & DONER MIX £3.70
CHIPS
COCKTAIL
ALAD
READ
READ WITH CHEESE
NKS (Cans)
5 litre Bottles)
I'M A MONSTER WITH A TUMOUR HANGING BETWEEN ITS THIGHS.
I'M A WHITE MAN IN CLITORIS PALACE. I'M...
SUCH A COCK.
AND TONIGHT, WHY WOULD I WANT TO BE ANYTHING ELSE?
PHONOGRAM
WITHOUT YOUR PERMISSION
Lyrics: Kieron Gillen
Music: Jamie McKelvie

THE EVENING'S ENTERTAINMENT IS LADYFEST, BRISTOL ITERATION. THE LADYFESTS ARE WHAT EARLY NINETIES RIOT-GRRL GREW UP INTO.

"FEST" AS IN FESTIVAL. "LADY" AS IN "FEMALE ORIGINATED ART, POLITICS, FILMS AND THE REST". AND OF SPECIFIC INTEREST TO YOURS TRULY, "MUSIC".

THE FIRST ONE TOOK PLACE IN – OOOH – OLYMPIA, PROBABLY. BUT THEY'RE A PRODUCT OF GLOBALISATION AS MUCH AS A BABUSHKA SCOFFING DOWN A BIG MAC IN MOSCOW.

THE SISTERHOOD HAS IT A LOT EASIER WHEN THE SEWING CIRCLE STRETCHES AROUND THE GLOBE ON ELECTRIC THREAD.

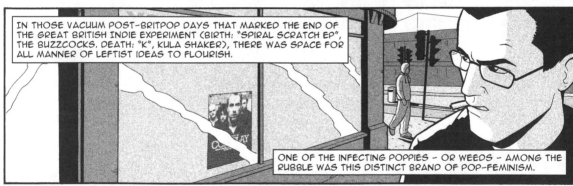

IN THOSE VACUUM POST-BRITPOP DAYS THAT MARKED THE END OF THE GREAT BRITISH INDIE EXPERIMENT (BIRTH: "SPIRAL SCRATCH EP", THE BUZZCOCKS. DEATH: "K", KULA SHAKER), THERE WAS SPACE FOR ALL MANNER OF LEFTIST IDEAS TO FLOURISH.

ONE OF THE INFECTING POPPIES – OR WEEDS – AMONG THE RUBBLE WAS THIS DISTINCT BRAND OF POP-FEMINISM.

IT'S A WOMAN-ENHANCING POSITIVE-ROLE-MODELLING HAIR-CLIP DYKE-FRIENDLY YES-I-LIKE-DANCE-MUSIC-I'VE-GOT-A-LE-TIGRE ALBUM MELANGE.

IT'S GOT PRECISELY *NOTHING* TO DO WITH ME.

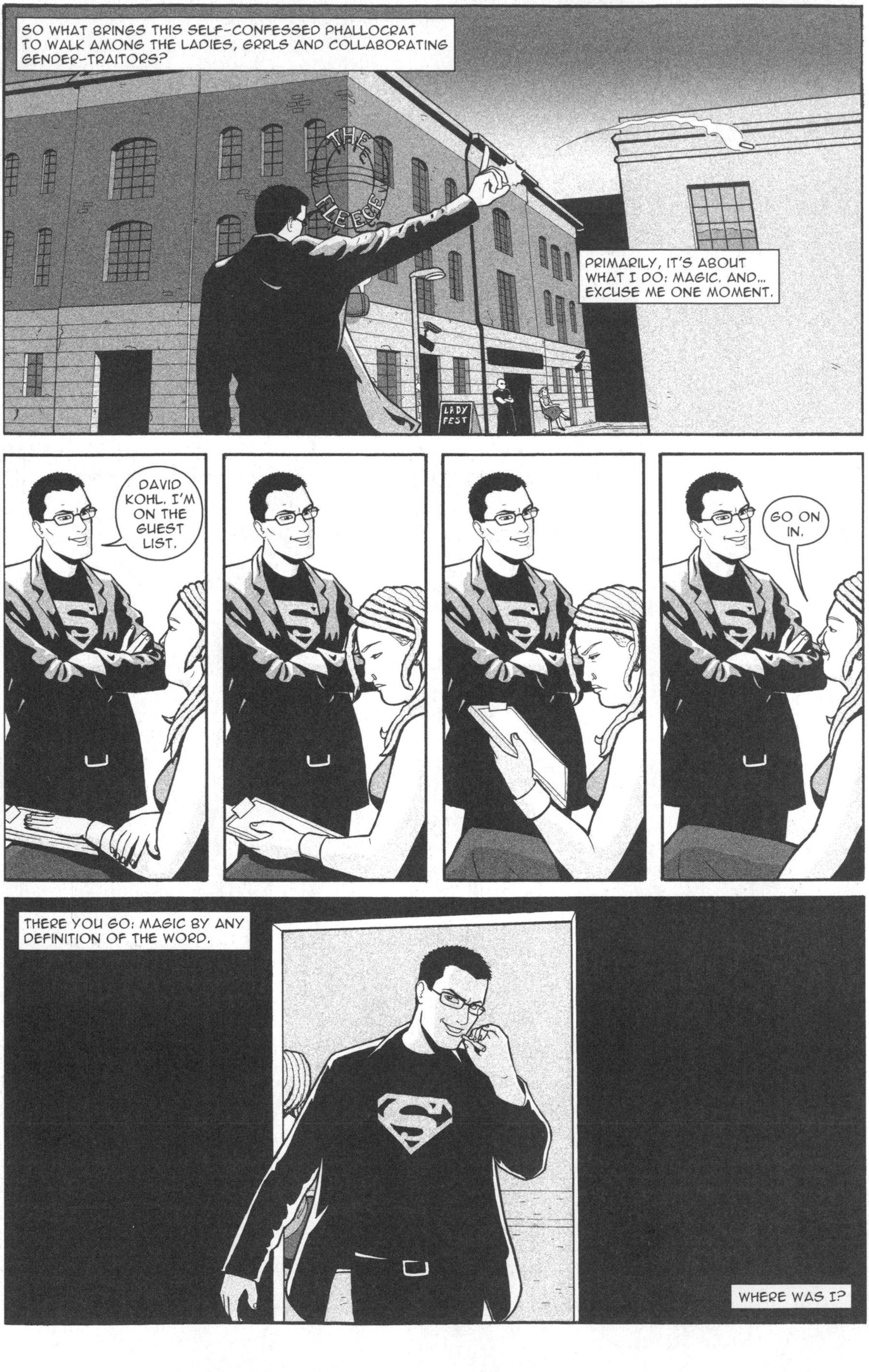
SO WHAT BRINGS THIS SELF-CONFESSED PHALLOCRAT TO WALK AMONG THE LADIES, GRRLS AND COLLABORATING GENDER-TRAITORS?
THE FLEECE
PRIMARILY, IT'S ABOUT WHAT I DO: MAGIC. AND... EXCUSE ME ONE MOMENT.
LADY FEST
DAVID KOHL. I'M ON THE GUEST LIST.
GO ON IN.
THERE YOU GO: MAGIC BY ANY DEFINITION OF THE WORD.
WHERE WAS I?

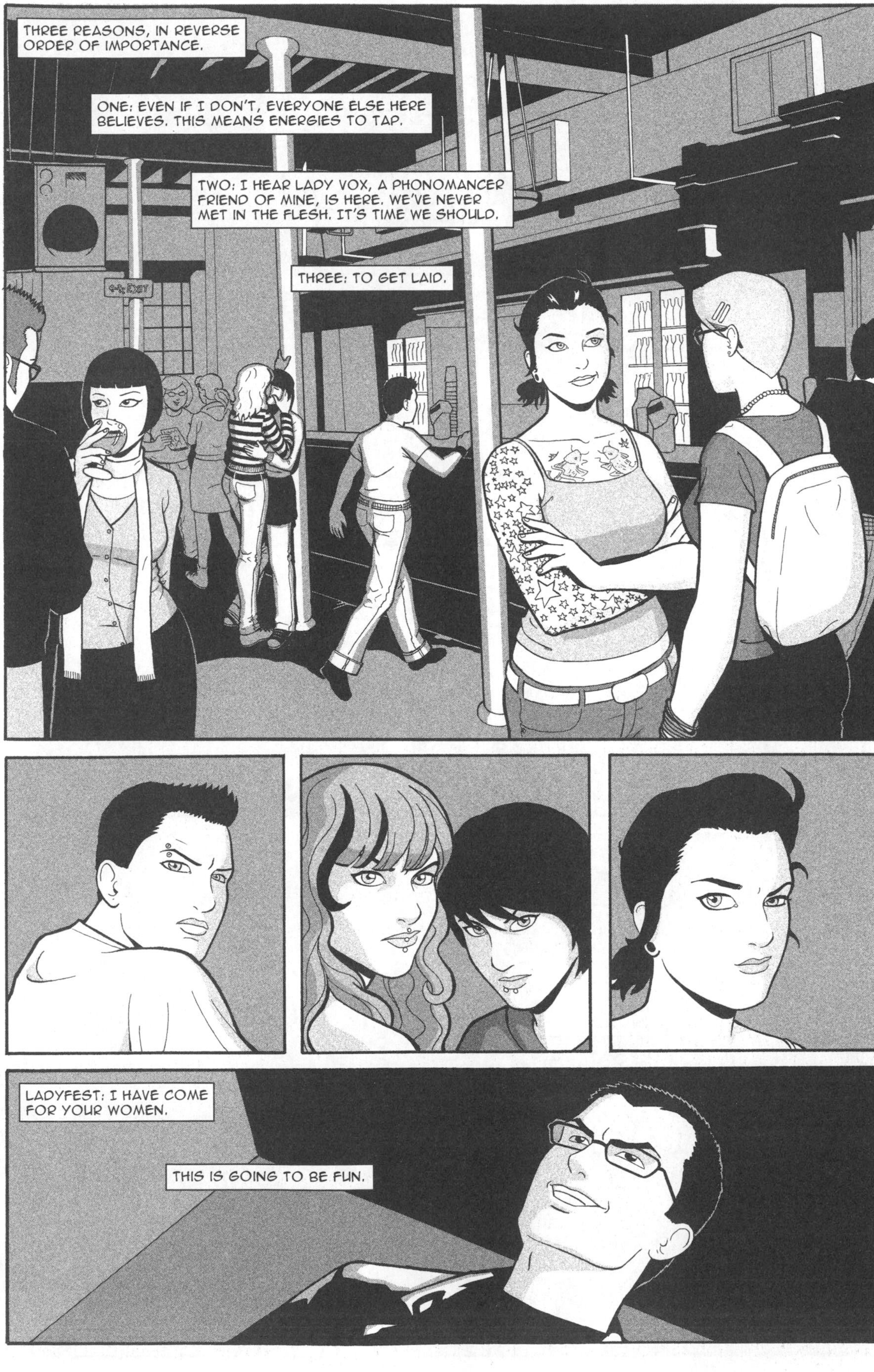
THREE REASONS, IN REVERSE ORDER OF IMPORTANCE.
ONE: EVEN IF I DON'T, EVERYONE ELSE HERE BELIEVES. THIS MEANS ENERGIES TO TAP.
TWO: I HEAR LADY VOX, A PHONOMANCER FRIEND OF MINE, IS HERE. WE'VE NEVER MET IN THE FLESH. IT'S TIME WE SHOULD.
THREE: TO GET LAID.
LADYFEST: I HAVE COME FOR YOUR WOMEN.
THIS IS GOING TO BE FUN.

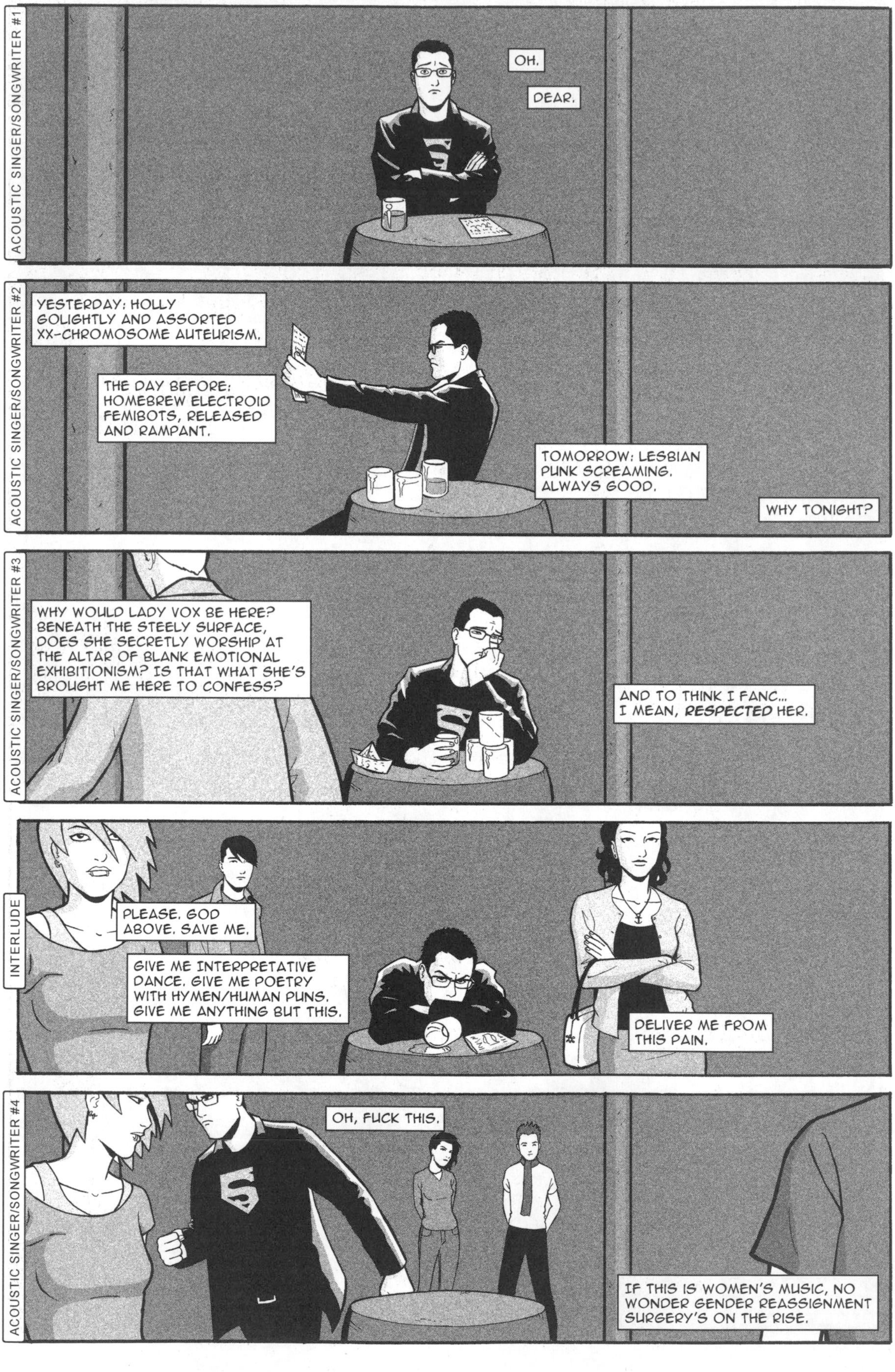
ACOUSTIC SINGER/SONGWRITER #1
OH.
DEAR.
ACOUSTIC SINGER/SONGWRITER #2
YESTERDAY: HOLLY GOLIGHTLY AND ASSORTED XX-CHROMOSOME AUTEURISM.
THE DAY BEFORE: HOMEBREW ELECTROID FEMIBOTS, RELEASED AND RAMPANT.
TOMORROW: LESBIAN PUNK SCREAMING. ALWAYS GOOD.
WHY TONIGHT?
ACOUSTIC SINGER/SONGWRITER #3
WHY WOULD LADY VOX BE HERE? BENEATH THE STEELY SURFACE, DOES SHE SECRETLY WORSHIP AT THE ALTAR OF BLANK EMOTIONAL EXHIBITIONISM? IS THAT WHAT SHE'S BROUGHT ME HERE TO CONFESS?
AND TO THINK I FANC... I MEAN, ***RESPECTED*** HER.
INTERLUDE
PLEASE. GOD ABOVE. SAVE ME.
GIVE ME INTERPRETATIVE DANCE. GIVE ME POETRY WITH HYMEN/HUMAN PUNS. GIVE ME ANYTHING BUT THIS.
DELIVER ME FROM THIS PAIN.
ACOUSTIC SINGER/SONGWRITER #4
OH, FUCK THIS.
IF THIS IS WOMEN'S MUSIC, NO WONDER GENDER REASSIGNMENT SURGERY'S ON THE RISE.

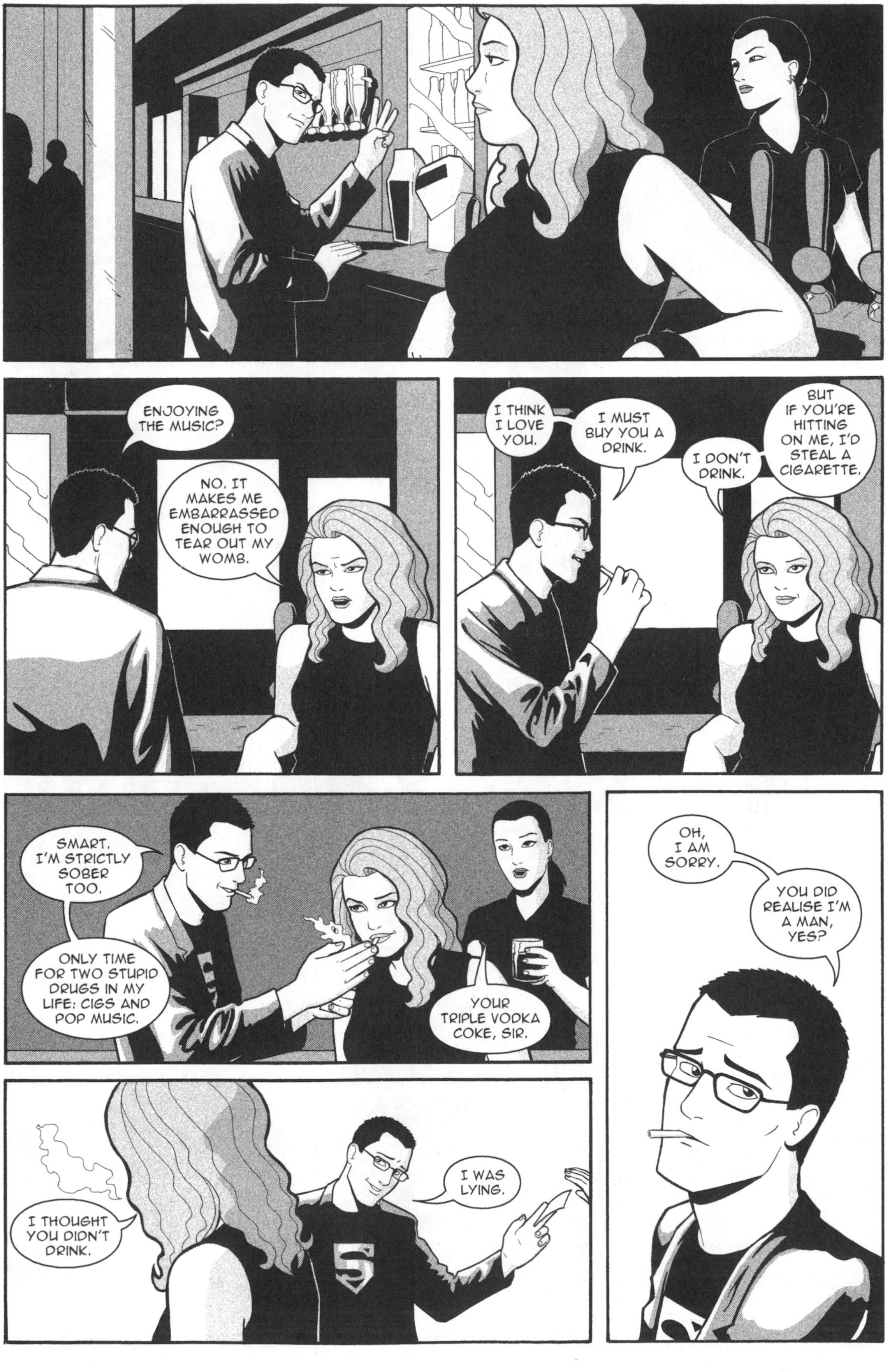
ENJOYING THE MUSIC?
NO. IT MAKES ME EMBARRASSED ENOUGH TO TEAR OUT MY WOMB.
I THINK I LOVE YOU.
I MUST BUY YOU A DRINK.
I DON'T DRINK.
BUT IF YOU'RE HITTING ON ME, I'D STEAL A CIGARETTE.
SMART. I'M STRICTLY SOBER TOO.
ONLY TIME FOR TWO STUPID DRUGS IN MY LIFE: CIGS AND POP MUSIC.
YOUR TRIPLE VODKA COKE, SIR.
I THOUGHT YOU DIDN'T DRINK.
I WAS LYING.
OH, I AM SORRY.
YOU DID REALISE I'M A MAN, YES?

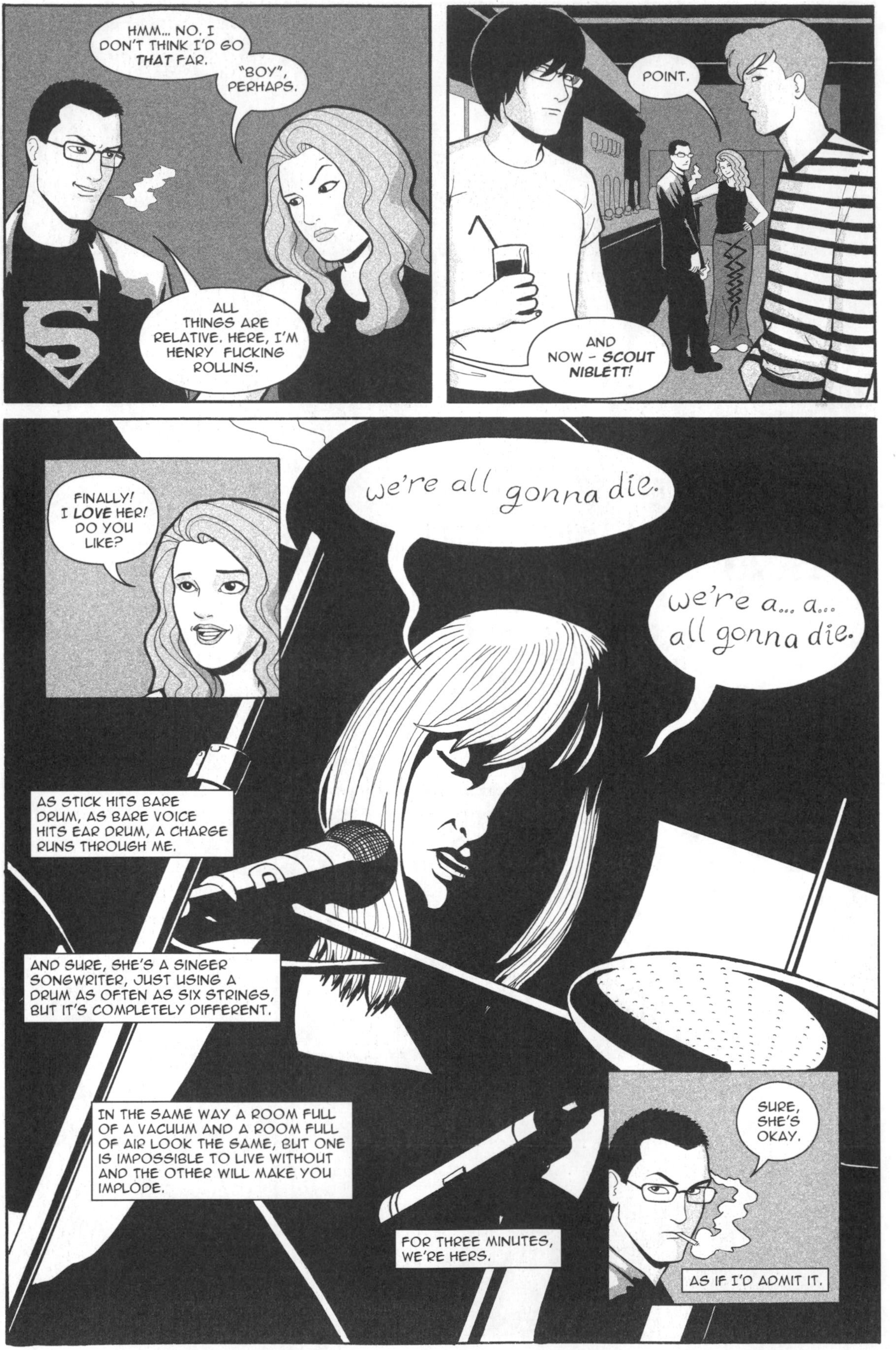
HMM... NO. I DON'T THINK I'D GO **THAT** FAR.
"BOY", PERHAPS.
ALL THINGS ARE RELATIVE. HERE, I'M HENRY FUCKING ROLLINS.
POINT.
AND NOW - **SCOUT NIBLETT!**
FINALLY! I **LOVE** HER! DO YOU LIKE?
we're all gonna die.
we're a... a... all gonna die.
AS STICK HITS BARE DRUM, AS BARE VOICE HITS EAR DRUM, A CHARGE RUNS THROUGH ME.
AND SURE, SHE'S A SINGER SONGWRITER, JUST USING A DRUM AS OFTEN AS SIX STRINGS, BUT IT'S COMPLETELY DIFFERENT.
IN THE SAME WAY A ROOM FULL OF A VACUUM AND A ROOM FULL OF AIR LOOK THE SAME, BUT ONE IS IMPOSSIBLE TO LIVE WITHOUT AND THE OTHER WILL MAKE YOU IMPLODE.
FOR THREE MINUTES, WE'RE HERS.
SURE, SHE'S OKAY.
AS IF I'D ADMIT IT.

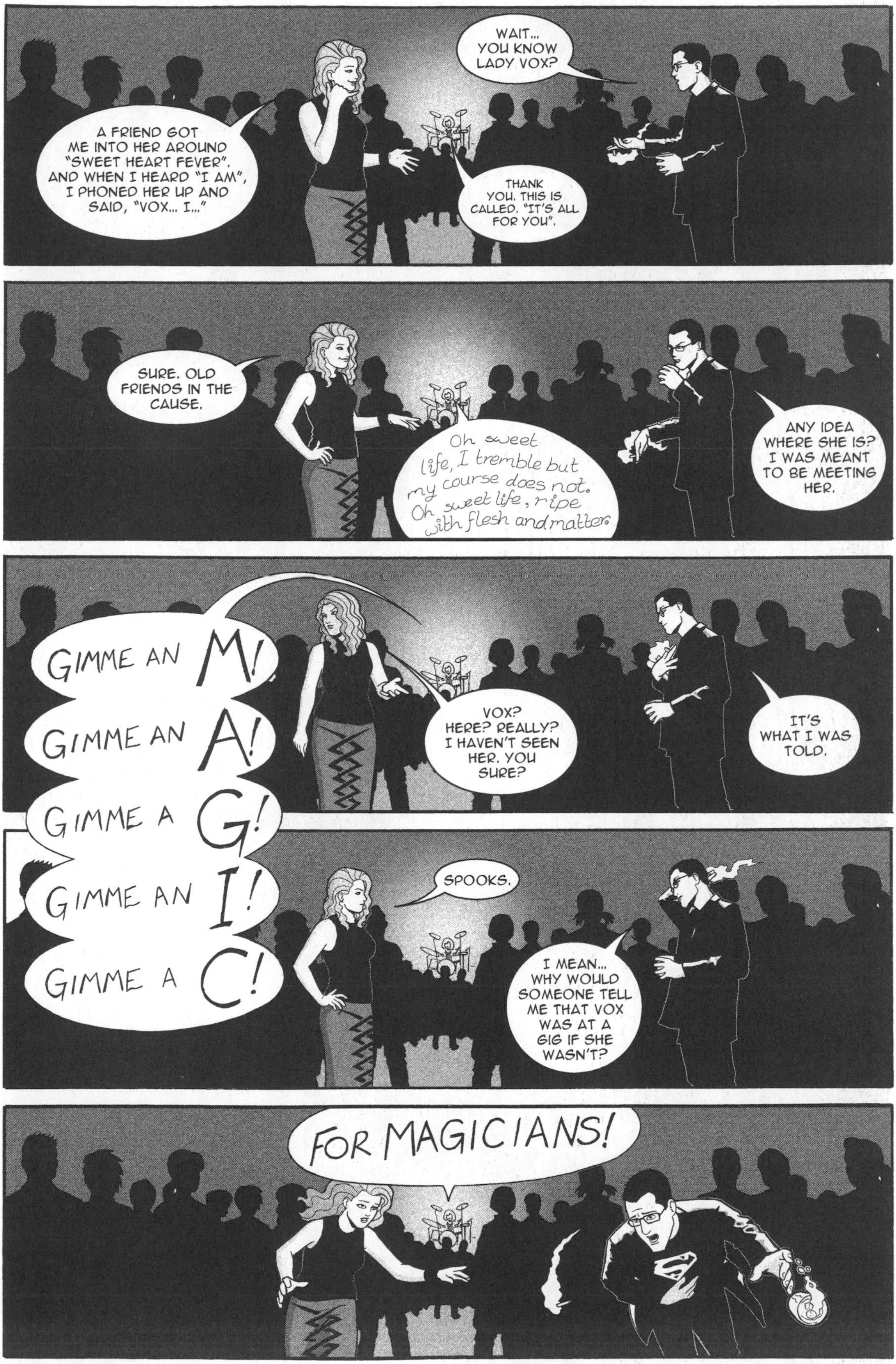
WAIT... YOU KNOW LADY VOX?
A FRIEND GOT ME INTO HER AROUND "SWEET HEART FEVER". AND WHEN I HEARD "I AM", I PHONED HER UP AND SAID, "VOX... I..."
THANK YOU. THIS IS CALLED, "IT'S ALL FOR YOU".
SURE. OLD FRIENDS IN THE CAUSE.
Oh sweet life, I tremble but my course does not. Oh sweet life, ripe with flesh and matter.
ANY IDEA WHERE SHE IS? I WAS MEANT TO BE MEETING HER.
GIMME AN M!
GIMME AN A!
GIMME A G!
GIMME AN I!
GIMME A C!
VOX? HERE? REALLY? I HAVEN'T SEEN HER. YOU SURE?
IT'S WHAT I WAS TOLD.
SPOOKS.
I MEAN... WHY WOULD SOMEONE TELL ME THAT VOX WAS AT A GIG IF SHE WASN'T?
FOR MAGICIANS!

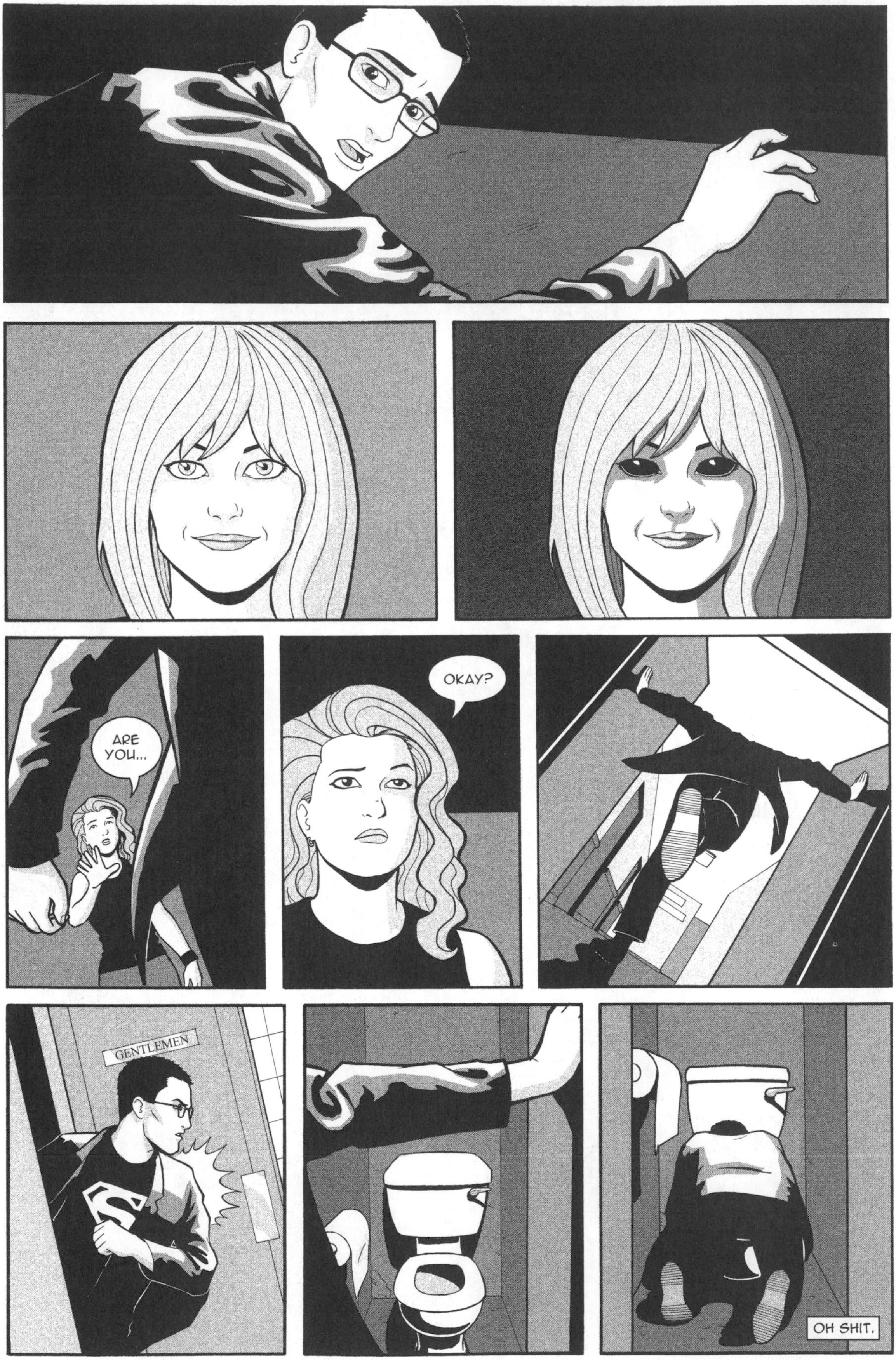
ARE YOU...
OKAY?
GENTLEMEN
OH SHIT.

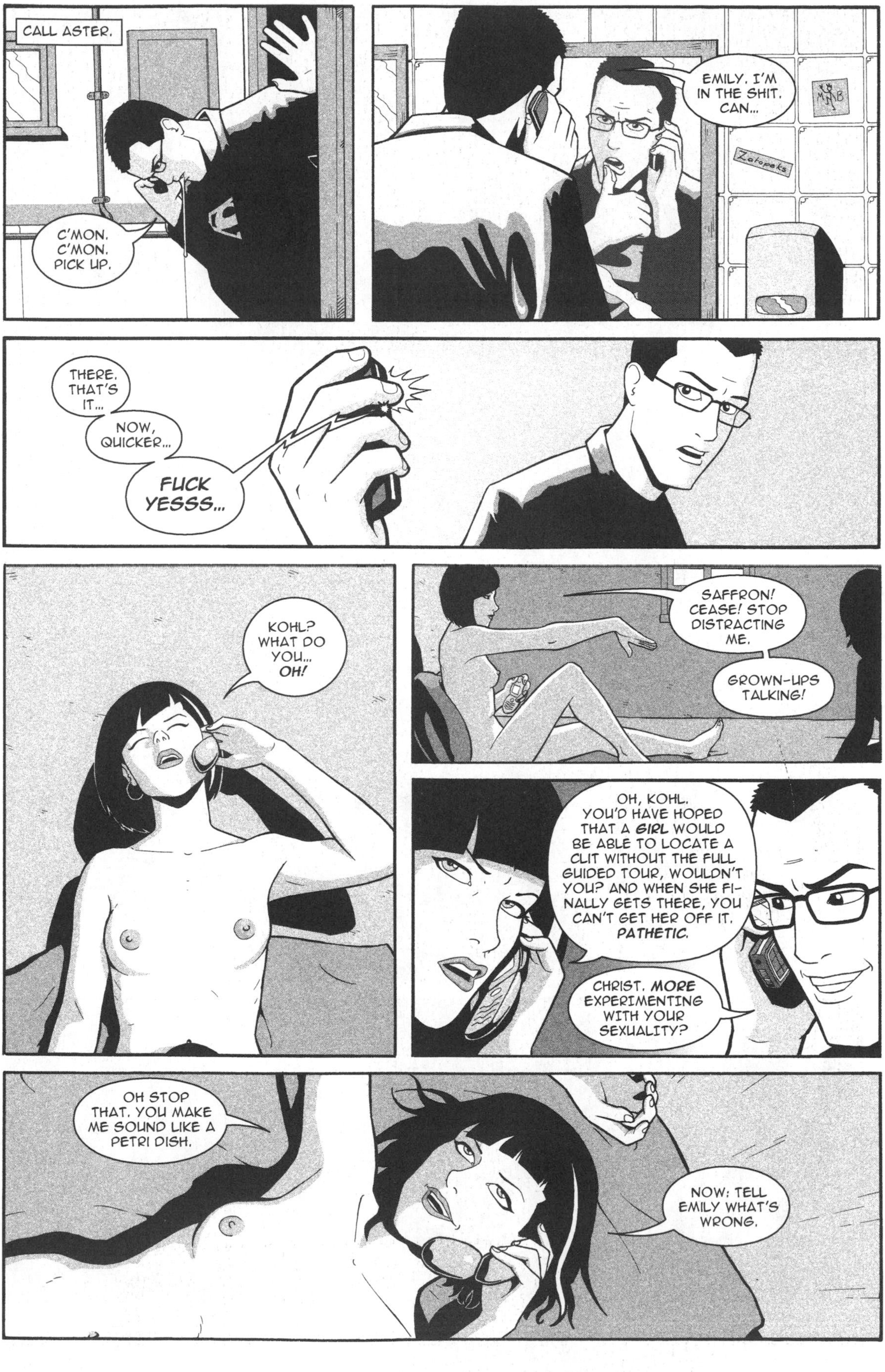
CALL ASTER.
C'MON. C'MON. PICK UP.
EMILY. I'M IN THE SHIT. CAN...
Zatopeks
THERE. THAT'S IT...
NOW, QUICKER...
FUCK YESSS...
KOHL? WHAT DO YOU... **OH!**
SAFFRON! CEASE! STOP DISTRACTING ME.
GROWN-UPS TALKING!
OH, KOHL. YOU'D HAVE HOPED THAT A **GIRL** WOULD BE ABLE TO LOCATE A CLIT WITHOUT THE FULL GUIDED TOUR, WOULDN'T YOU? AND WHEN SHE FINALLY GETS THERE, YOU CAN'T GET HER OFF IT. **PATHETIC**.
CHRIST. **MORE** EXPERIMENTING WITH YOUR SEXUALITY?
OH STOP THAT. YOU MAKE ME SOUND LIKE A PETRI DISH.
NOW: TELL EMILY WHAT'S WRONG.

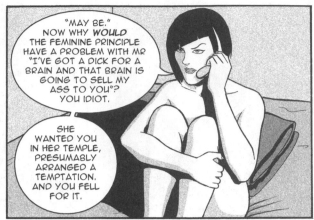

I'M AT LADYFEST. *THE GODDESS* HAS JUST INCARNATED.

I THINK I MAY BE IN TROUBLE.

"MAY BE." NOW WHY *WOULD* THE FEMININE PRINCIPLE HAVE A PROBLEM WITH MR "I'VE GOT A DICK FOR A BRAIN AND THAT BRAIN IS GOING TO SELL MY ASS TO YOU"? YOU IDIOT.

SHE WANTED YOU IN HER TEMPLE, PRESUMABLY ARRANGED A TEMPTATION. AND YOU FELL FOR IT.

WHICH IS WHAT HAPPENS WHEN YOU LET LITTLE DAVID KOHL DO ALL YOUR THINKING.

WHAT SHOULD I DO?

HONEY, GET THE HELL OUT OF THERE.

YOU'VE BEEN SPEAKING WHEN YOU SHOULD HAVE BEEN RUNNING.

JUST RUN.

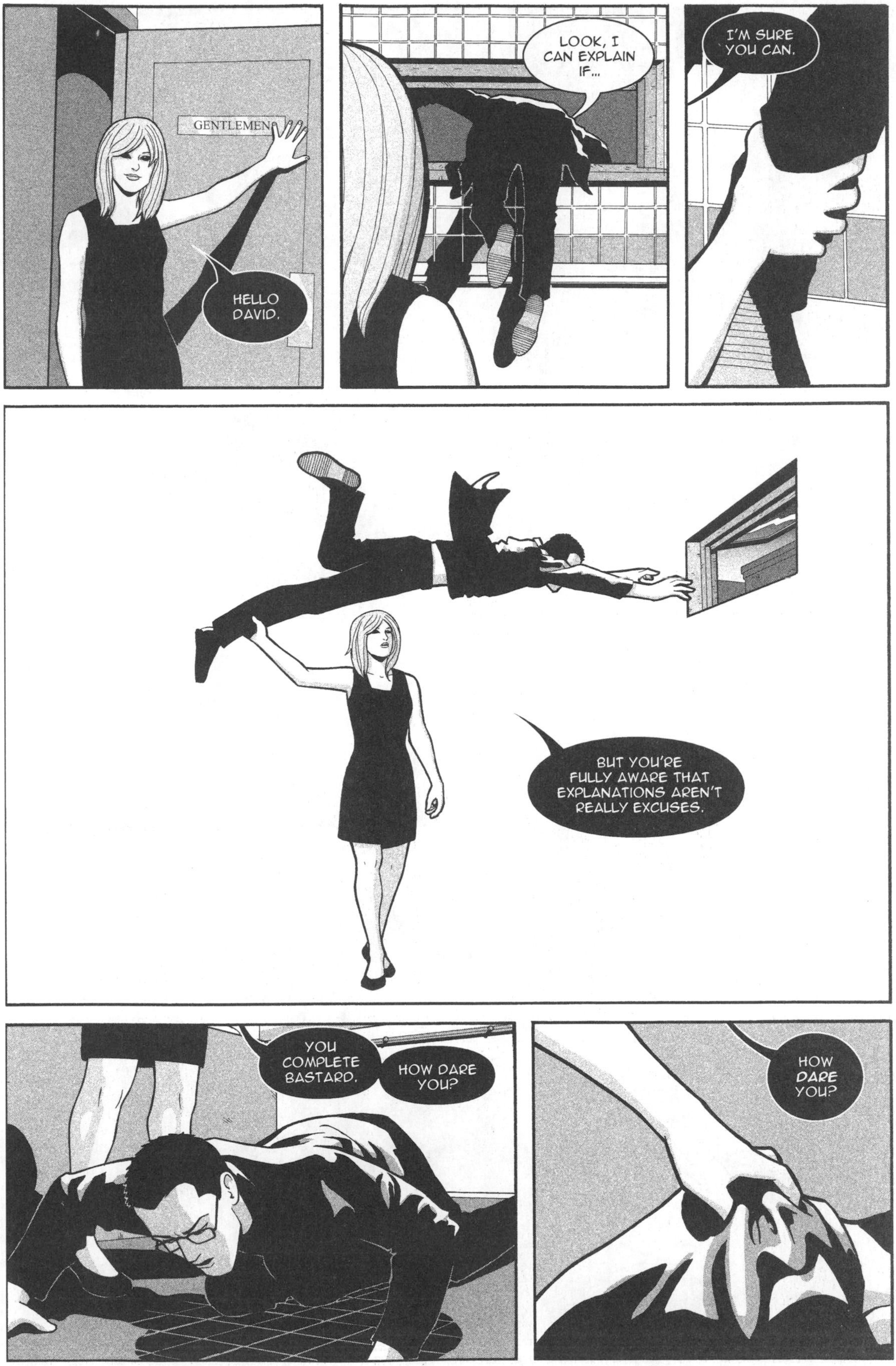
GENTLEMEN
HELLO DAVID.
LOOK, I CAN EXPLAIN IF...
I'M SURE YOU CAN.
BUT YOU'RE FULLY AWARE THAT EXPLANATIONS AREN'T REALLY EXCUSES.
YOU COMPLETE BASTARD.
HOW DARE YOU?
HOW DARE YOU?

YOU COME TO MY TEMPLE WITH YOUR *PHALLIC* PRIDE AND YOUR *EMPTY* SYMBOLS?

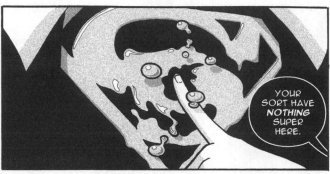

YOUR SORT HAVE *NOTHING* SUPER HERE.

SO... WHAT? BECAUSE IF YOU LURED ME HERE TO KILL ME, I CAN MAKE YOU A BETTER OFFER.

SHUT UP, DAVID. I'M NOT GOING TO KILL YOU.

YOU'RE NOT AN ENEMY. IF YOU WERE, I'D HAVE *SURGICALLY* PRICKED YOU LIKE A PIMPLE RIPE WITH PUS.

BUT YOU, KOHL... YOU *BETRAYED* ME.

I BROUGHT YOU HERE TO *HURT* YOU.

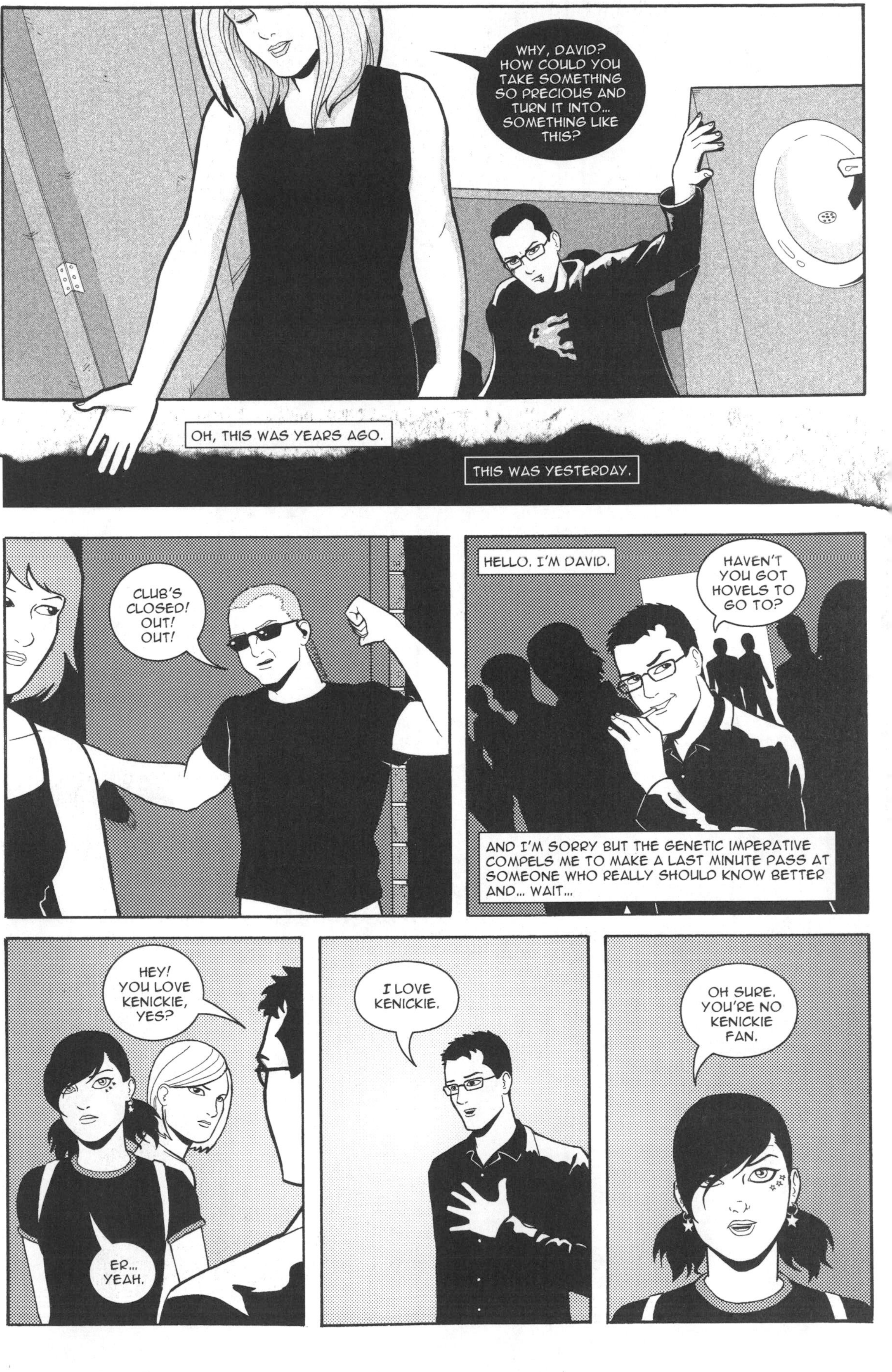
WHY, DAVID? HOW COULD YOU TAKE SOMETHING SO PRECIOUS AND TURN IT INTO... SOMETHING LIKE THIS?
OH, THIS WAS YEARS AGO.
THIS WAS YESTERDAY.
CLUB'S CLOSED! OUT! OUT!
HELLO. I'M DAVID.
HAVEN'T YOU GOT HOVELS TO GO TO?
AND I'M SORRY BUT THE GENETIC IMPERATIVE COMPELS ME TO MAKE A LAST MINUTE PASS AT SOMEONE WHO REALLY SHOULD KNOW BETTER AND... WAIT...
HEY! YOU LOVE KENICKIE, YES?
ER... YEAH.
I LOVE KENICKIE.
OH SURE. YOU'RE NO KENICKIE FAN.

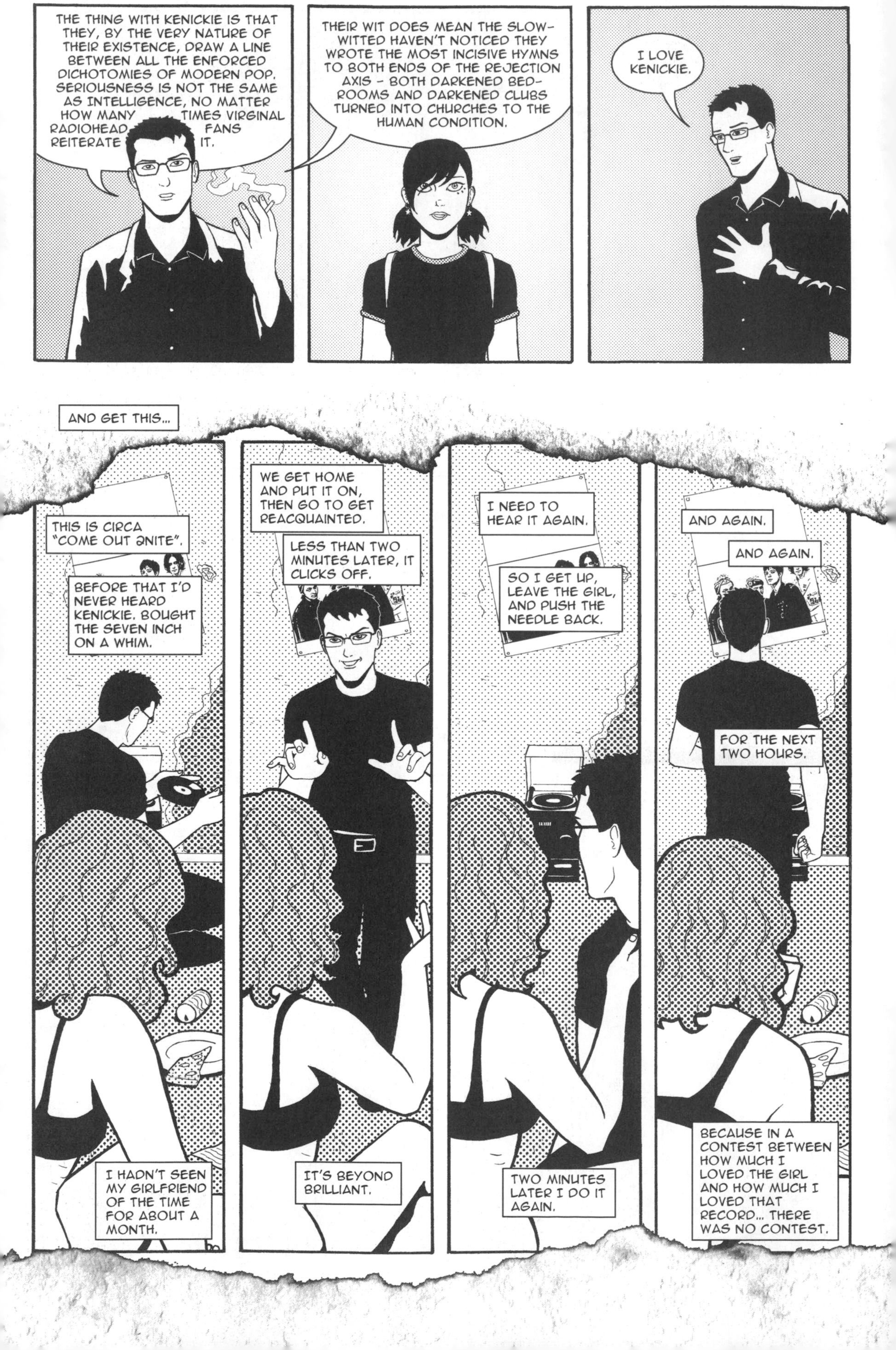
THE THING WITH KENICKIE IS THAT THEY, BY THE VERY NATURE OF THEIR EXISTENCE, DRAW A LINE BETWEEN ALL THE ENFORCED DICHOTOMIES OF MODERN POP. SERIOUSNESS IS NOT THE SAME AS INTELLIGENCE, NO MATTER HOW MANY TIMES VIRGINAL RADIOHEAD FANS REITERATE IT.
THEIR WIT DOES MEAN THE SLOW-WITTED HAVEN'T NOTICED THEY WROTE THE MOST INCISIVE HYMNS TO BOTH ENDS OF THE REJECTION AXIS - BOTH DARKENED BED-ROOMS AND DARKENED CLUBS TURNED INTO CHURCHES TO THE HUMAN CONDITION.
I LOVE KENICKIE.
AND GET THIS...
THIS IS CIRCA "COME OUT 2NITE".
BEFORE THAT I'D NEVER HEARD KENICKIE. BOUGHT THE SEVEN INCH ON A WHIM.
I HADN'T SEEN MY GIRLFRIEND OF THE TIME FOR ABOUT A MONTH.
WE GET HOME AND PUT IT ON, THEN GO TO GET REACQUAINTED.
LESS THAN TWO MINUTES LATER, IT CLICKS OFF.
IT'S BEYOND BRILLIANT.
I NEED TO HEAR IT AGAIN.
SO I GET UP, LEAVE THE GIRL, AND PUSH THE NEEDLE BACK.
TWO MINUTES LATER I DO IT AGAIN.
AND AGAIN.
AND AGAIN.
FOR THE NEXT TWO HOURS.
BECAUSE IN A CONTEST BETWEEN HOW MUCH I LOVED THE GIRL AND HOW MUCH I LOVED THAT RECORD... THERE WAS NO CONTEST.

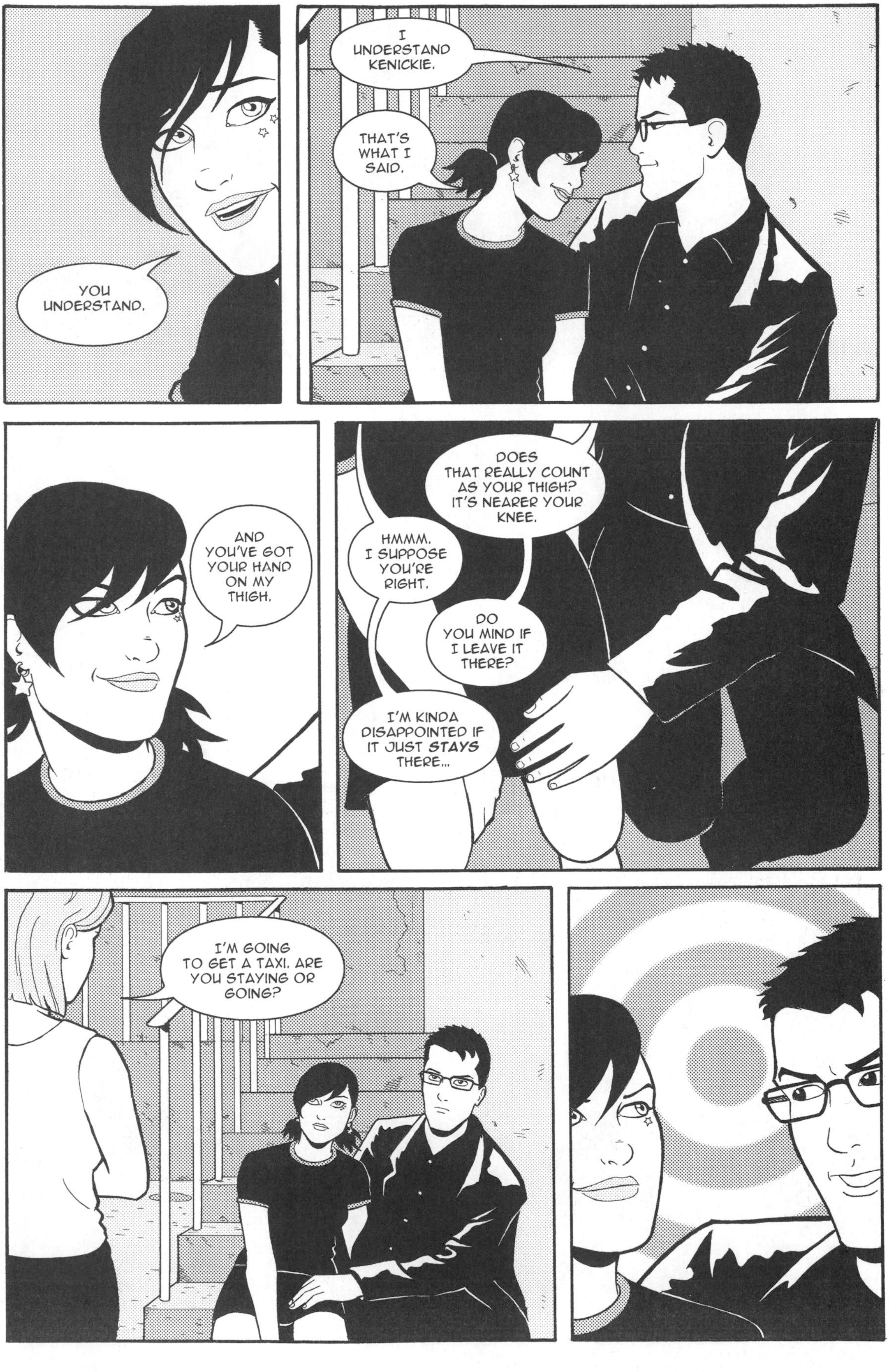
YOU UNDERSTAND.
I UNDERSTAND KENICKIE.
THAT'S WHAT I SAID.
AND YOU'VE GOT YOUR HAND ON MY THIGH.
DOES THAT REALLY COUNT AS YOUR THIGH? IT'S NEARER YOUR KNEE.
HMMM. I SUPPOSE YOU'RE RIGHT.
DO YOU MIND IF I LEAVE IT THERE?
I'M KINDA DISAPPOINTED IF IT JUST STAYS THERE...
I'M GOING TO GET A TAXI. ARE YOU STAYING OR GOING?

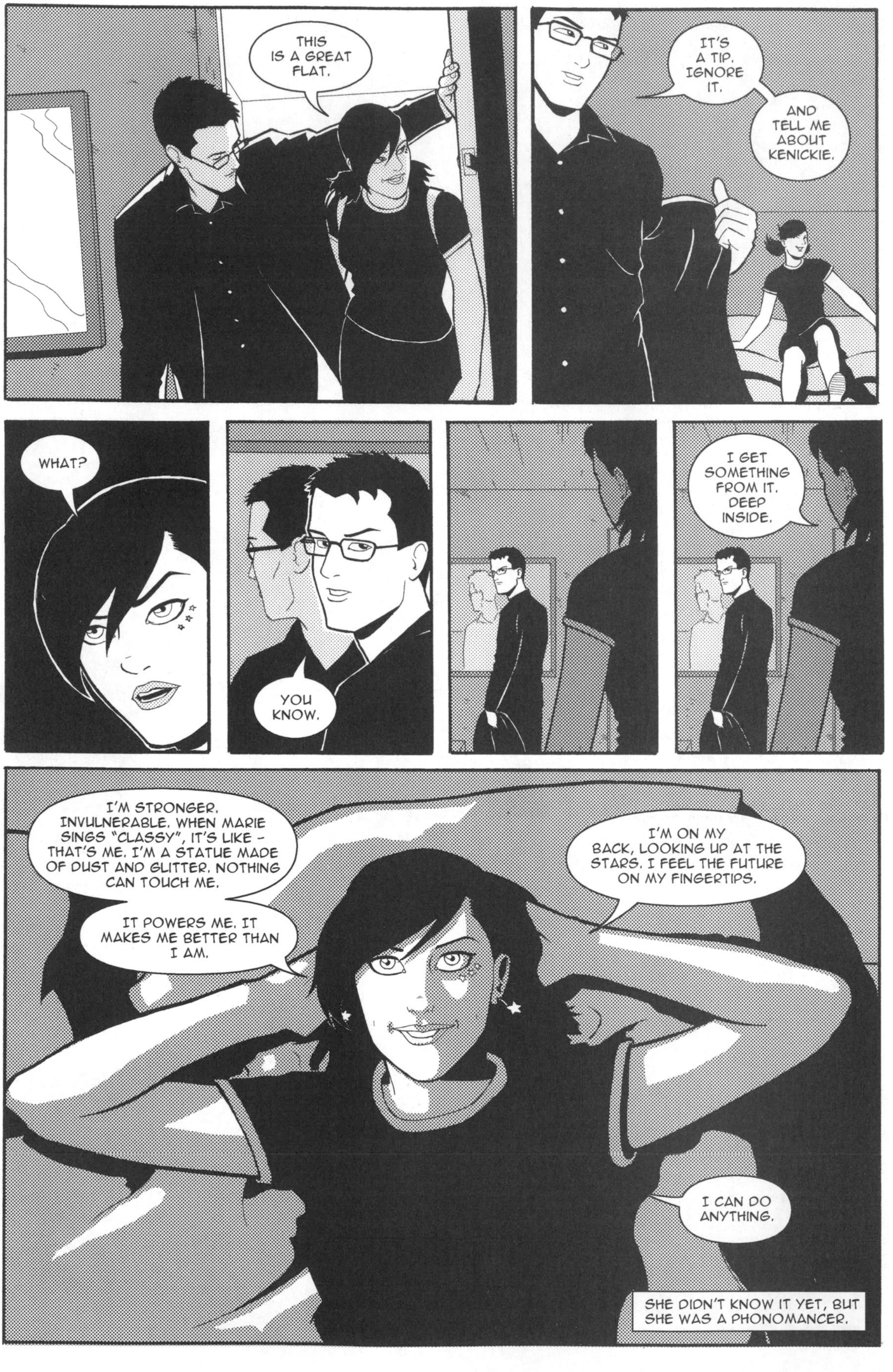
THIS IS A GREAT FLAT.
IT'S A TIP. IGNORE IT.
AND TELL ME ABOUT KENICKIE.
WHAT?
YOU KNOW.
I GET SOMETHING FROM IT. DEEP INSIDE.
I'M STRONGER. INVULNERABLE. WHEN MARIE SINGS "CLASSY", IT'S LIKE - THAT'S ME. I'M A STATUE MADE OF DUST AND GLITTER. NOTHING CAN TOUCH ME.
IT POWERS ME. IT MAKES ME BETTER THAN I AM.
I'M ON MY BACK, LOOKING UP AT THE STARS. I FEEL THE FUTURE ON MY FINGERTIPS.
I CAN DO ANYTHING.
SHE DIDN'T KNOW IT YET, BUT SHE WAS A PHONOMANCER.

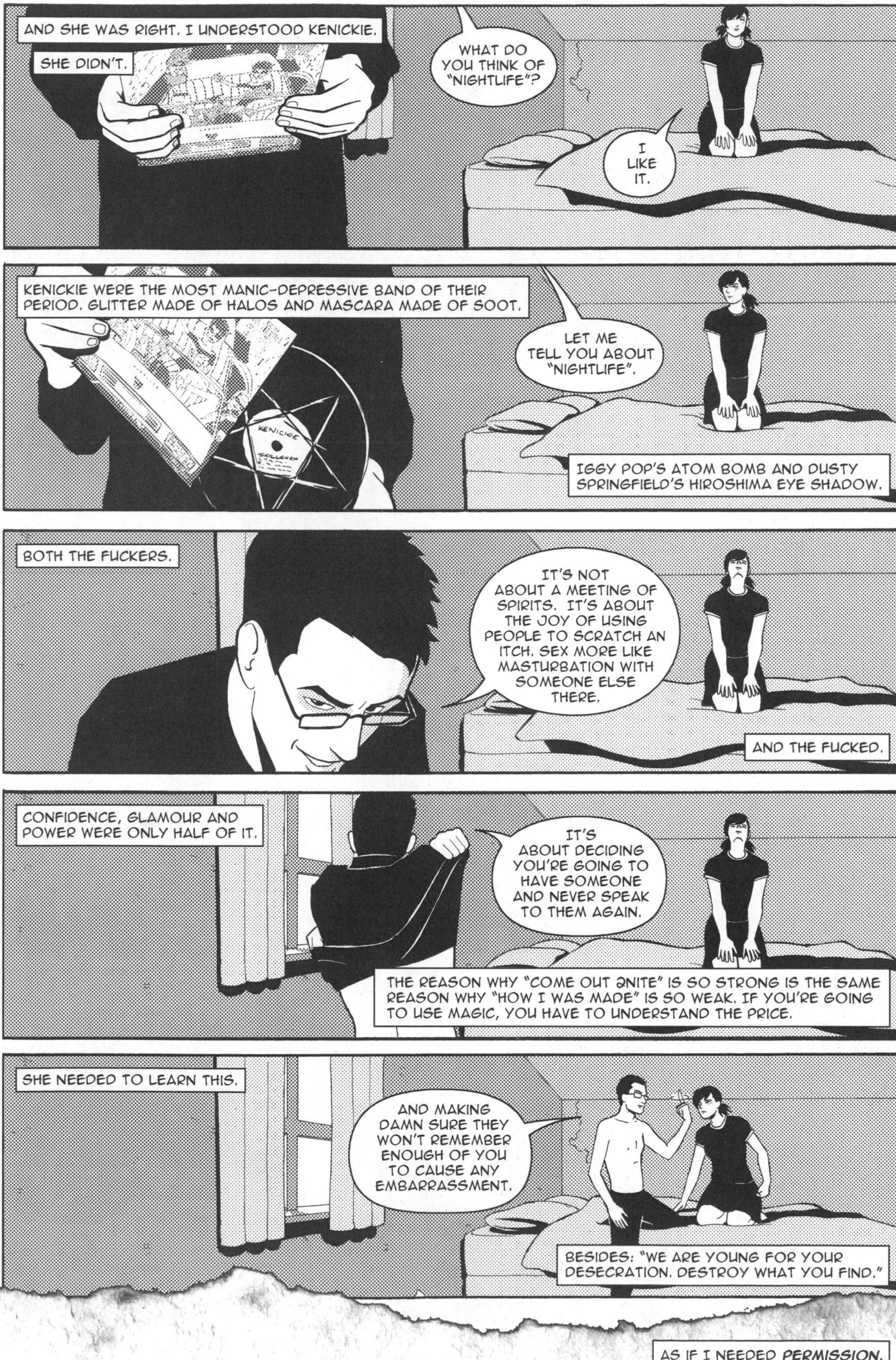

AND SHE WAS RIGHT. I UNDERSTOOD KENICKIE.
SHE DIDN'T.
WHAT DO YOU THINK OF "NIGHTLIFE"?
I LIKE IT.
KENICKIE WERE THE MOST MANIC-DEPRESSIVE BAND OF THEIR PERIOD. GLITTER MADE OF HALOS AND MASCARA MADE OF SOOT.
LET ME TELL YOU ABOUT "NIGHTLIFE".
IGGY POP'S ATOM BOMB AND DUSTY SPRINGFIELD'S HIROSHIMA EYE SHADOW.
BOTH THE FUCKERS.
IT'S NOT ABOUT A MEETING OF SPIRITS. IT'S ABOUT THE JOY OF USING PEOPLE TO SCRATCH AN ITCH. SEX MORE LIKE MASTURBATION WITH SOMEONE ELSE THERE.
AND THE FUCKED.
CONFIDENCE, GLAMOUR AND POWER WERE ONLY HALF OF IT.
IT'S ABOUT DECIDING YOU'RE GOING TO HAVE SOMEONE AND NEVER SPEAK TO THEM AGAIN.
THE REASON WHY "COME OUT 2NITE" IS SO STRONG IS THE SAME REASON WHY "HOW I WAS MADE" IS SO WEAK. IF YOU'RE GOING TO USE MAGIC, YOU HAVE TO UNDERSTAND THE PRICE.
SHE NEEDED TO LEARN THIS.
AND MAKING DAMN SURE THEY WON'T REMEMBER ENOUGH OF YOU TO CAUSE ANY EMBARRASSMENT.
BESIDES: "WE ARE YOUNG FOR YOUR DESECRATION. DESTROY WHAT YOU FIND."
AS IF I NEEDED PERMISSION.

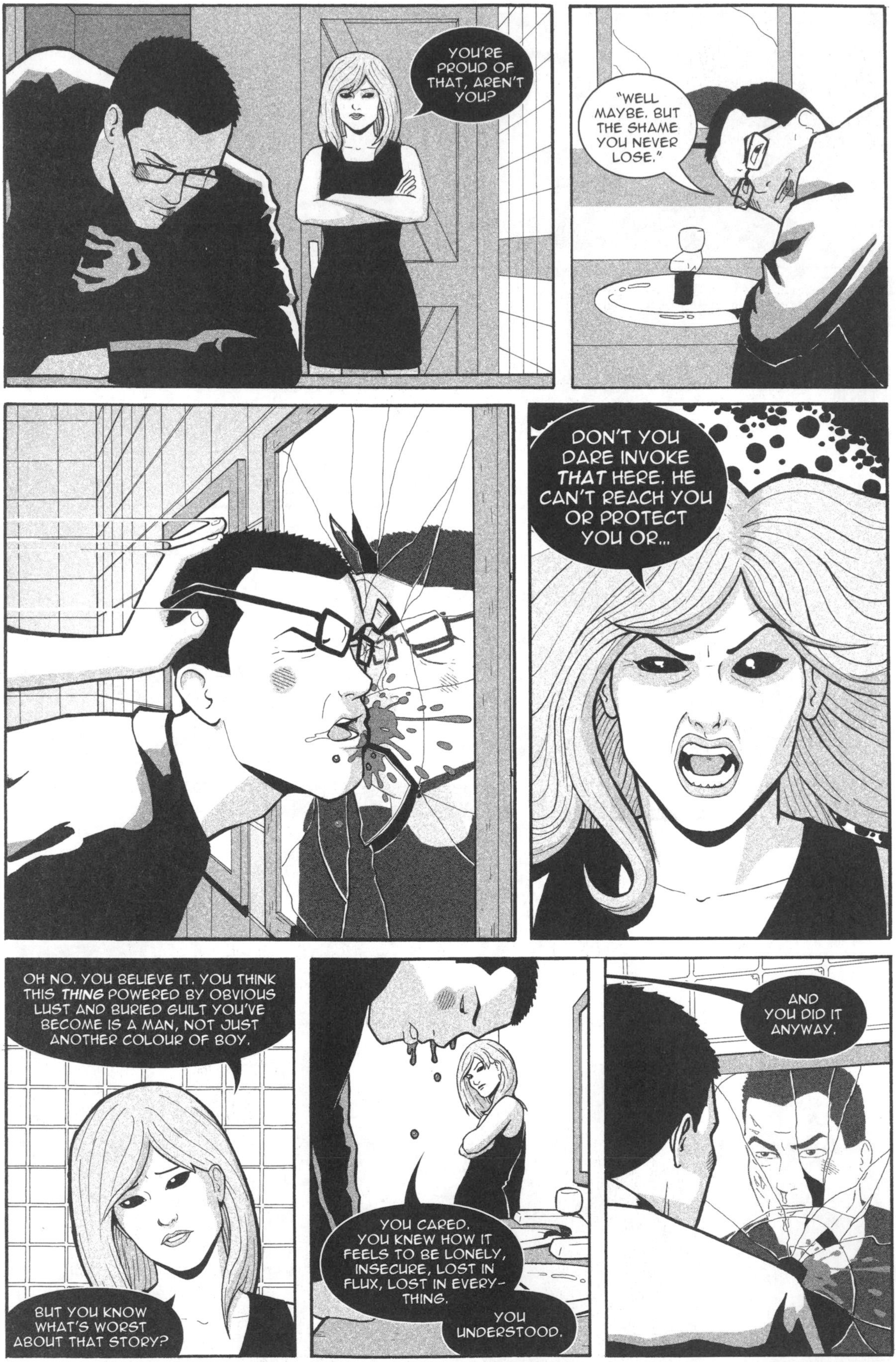
YOU'RE PROUD OF THAT, AREN'T YOU?
"WELL MAYBE. BUT THE SHAME YOU NEVER LOSE."
DON'T YOU DARE INVOKE *THAT* HERE. HE CAN'T REACH YOU OR PROTECT YOU OR...
OH NO. YOU BELIEVE IT. YOU THINK THIS *THING* POWERED BY OBVIOUS LUST AND BURIED GUILT YOU'VE BECOME IS A MAN, NOT JUST ANOTHER COLOUR OF BOY.
BUT YOU KNOW WHAT'S WORST ABOUT THAT STORY?
YOU CARED. YOU KNEW HOW IT FEELS TO BE LONELY, INSECURE, LOST IN FLUX, LOST IN EVERY-THING.
YOU UNDERSTOOD.
AND YOU DID IT ANYWAY.

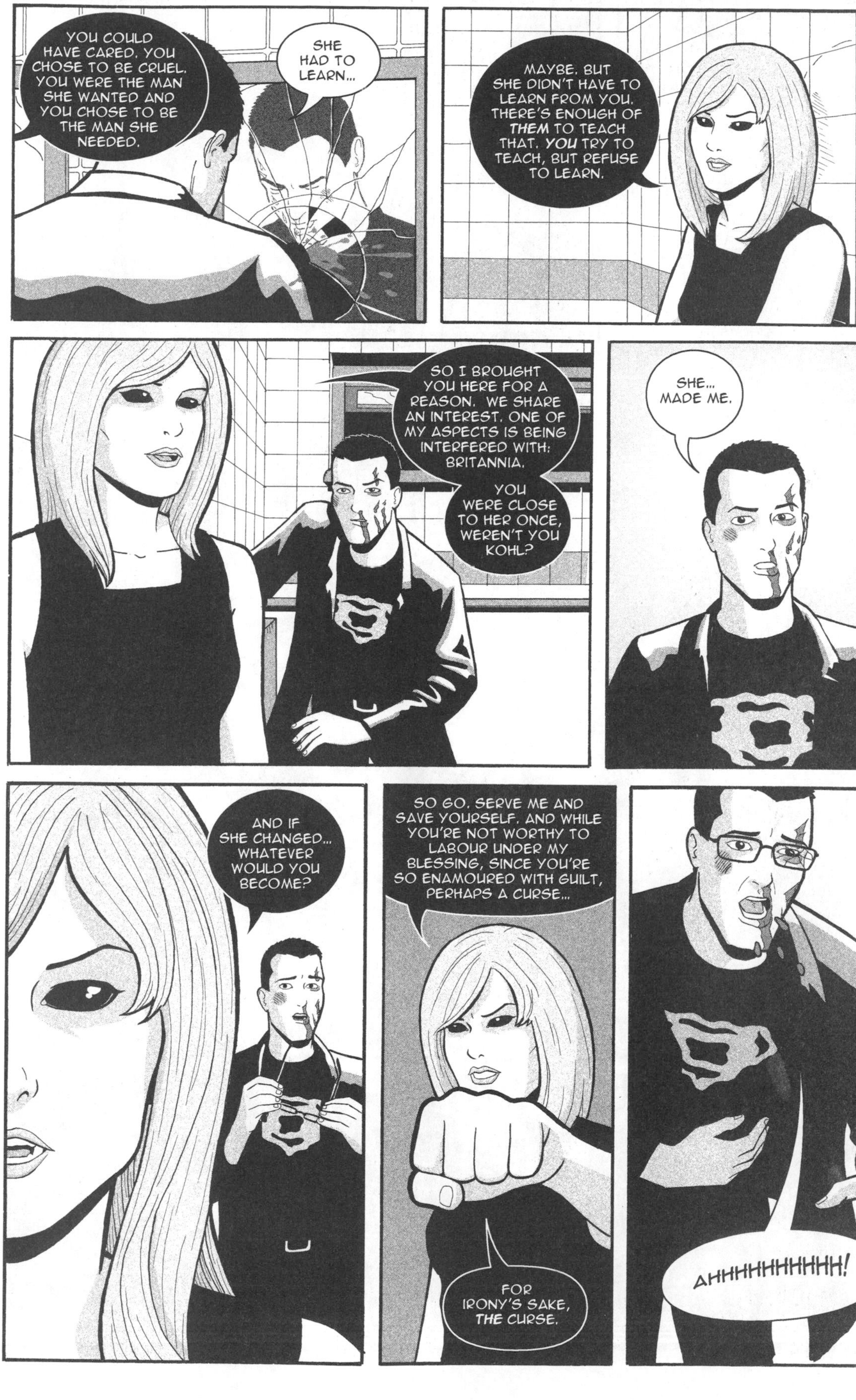
YOU COULD HAVE CARED. YOU CHOSE TO BE CRUEL. YOU WERE THE MAN SHE WANTED AND YOU CHOSE TO BE THE MAN SHE NEEDED.
SHE HAD TO LEARN...
MAYBE. BUT SHE DIDN'T HAVE TO LEARN FROM YOU. THERE'S ENOUGH OF **THEM** TO TEACH THAT. **YOU** TRY TO TEACH, BUT REFUSE TO LEARN.
SO I BROUGHT YOU HERE FOR A REASON. WE SHARE AN INTEREST. ONE OF MY ASPECTS IS BEING INTERFERED WITH: BRITANNIA.
YOU WERE CLOSE TO HER ONCE, WEREN'T YOU KOHL?
SHE... MADE ME.
AND IF SHE CHANGED... WHATEVER WOULD YOU BECOME?
SO GO. SERVE ME AND SAVE YOURSELF. AND WHILE YOU'RE NOT WORTHY TO LABOUR UNDER MY BLESSING, SINCE YOU'RE SO ENAMOURED WITH GUILT, PERHAPS A CURSE...
FOR IRONY'S SAKE, **THE** CURSE.
AHHHHHHHHHH!

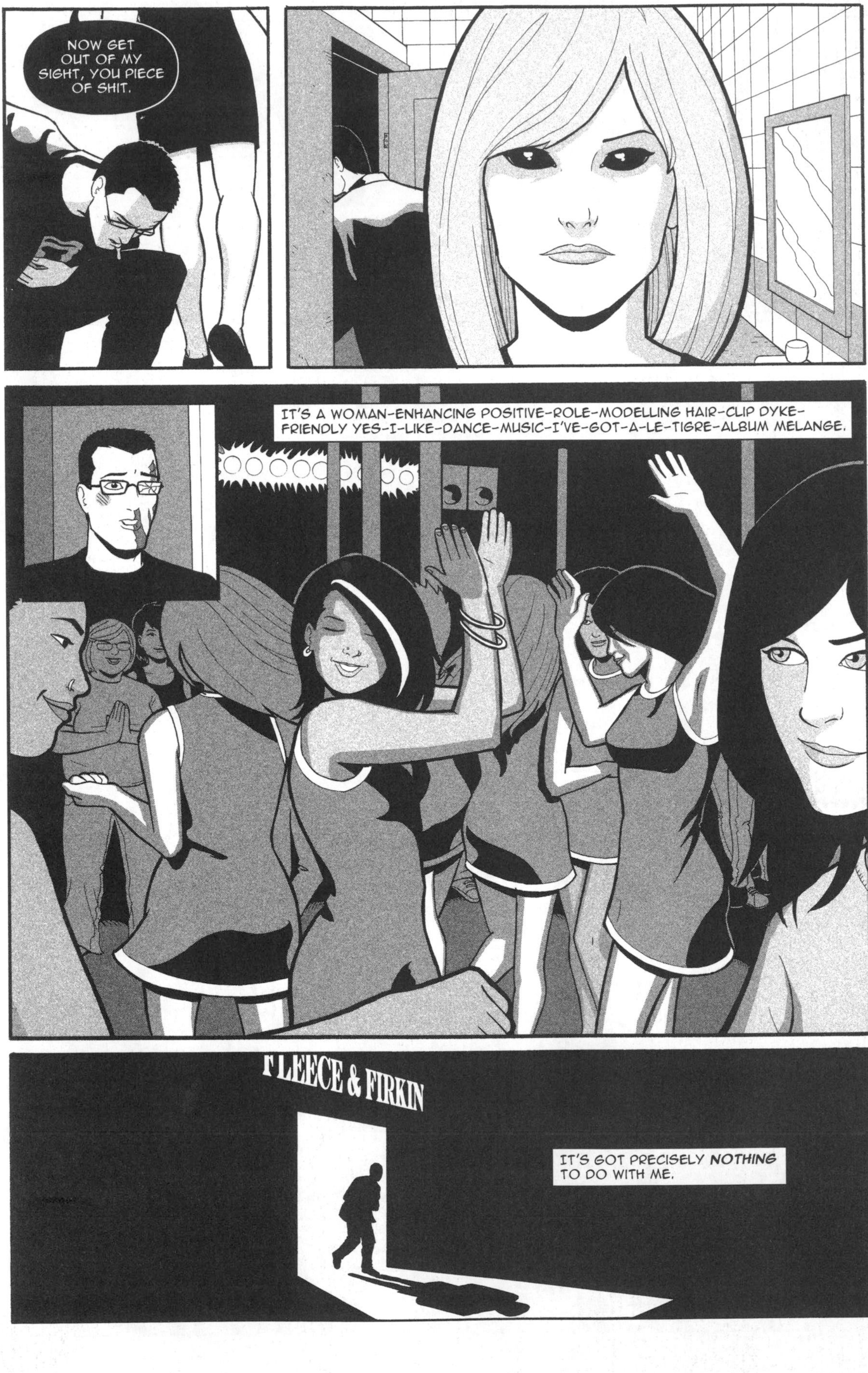
NOW GET OUT OF MY SIGHT, YOU PIECE OF SHIT.
IT'S A WOMAN-ENHANCING POSITIVE-ROLE-MODELLING HAIR-CLIP DYKE-FRIENDLY YES-I-LIKE-DANCE-MUSIC-I'VE-GOT-A-LE-TIGRE-ALBUM MELANGE.
F LEECE & FIRKIN
IT'S GOT PRECISELY **NOTHING** TO DO WITH ME.

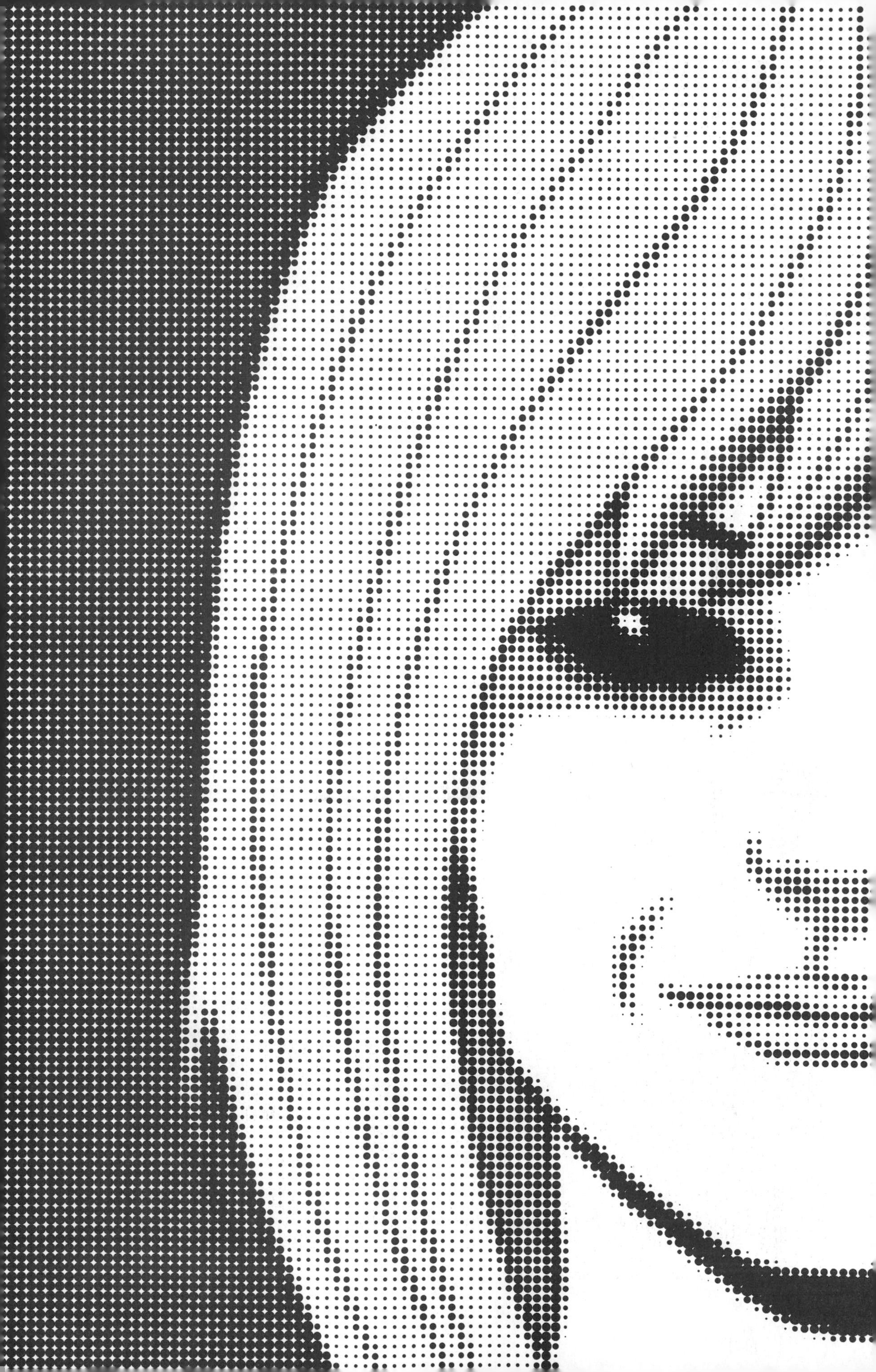

CHAPTER TWO

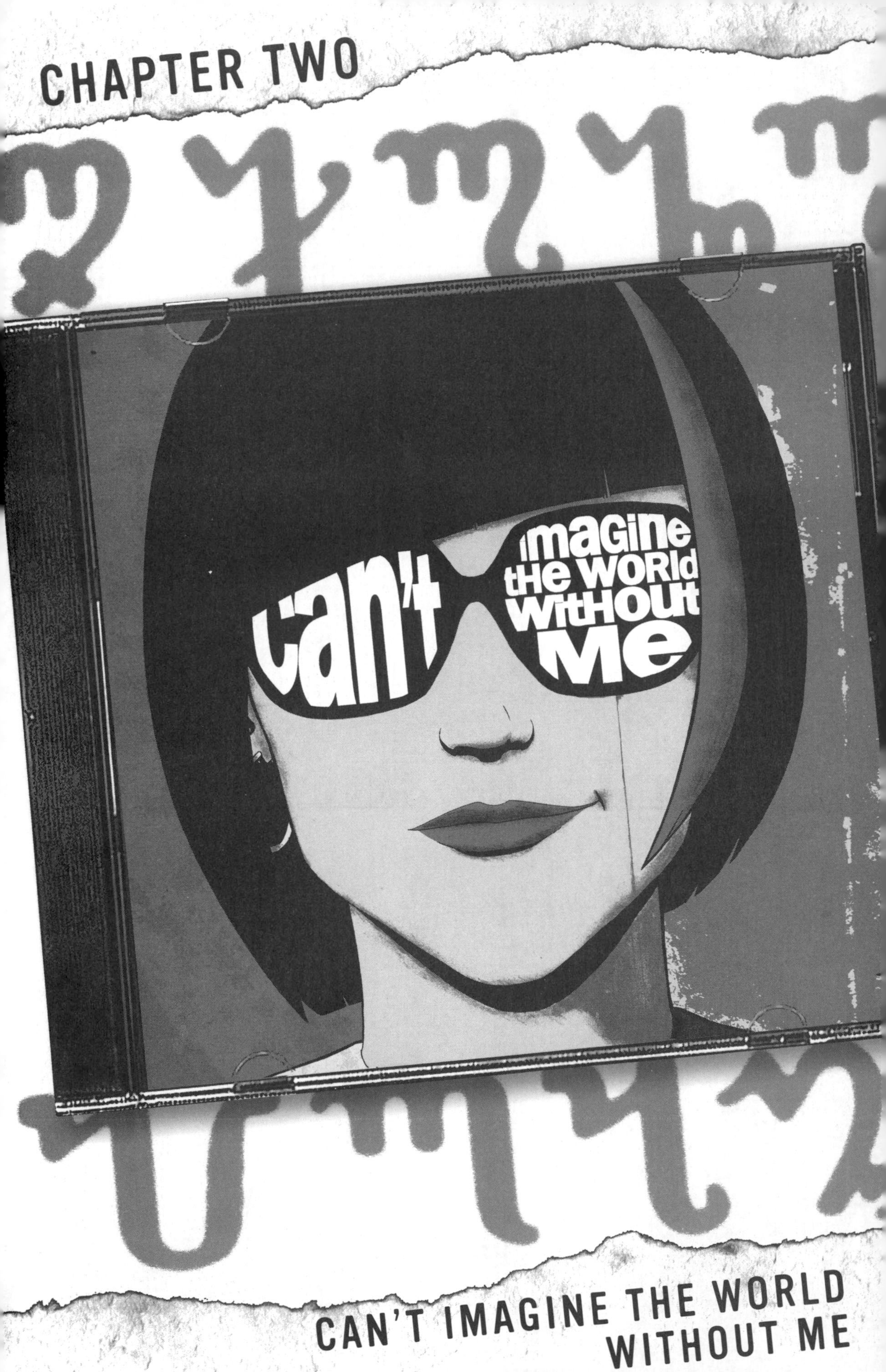
can't
imagine the world without me

CAN'T IMAGINE THE WORLD WITHOUT ME

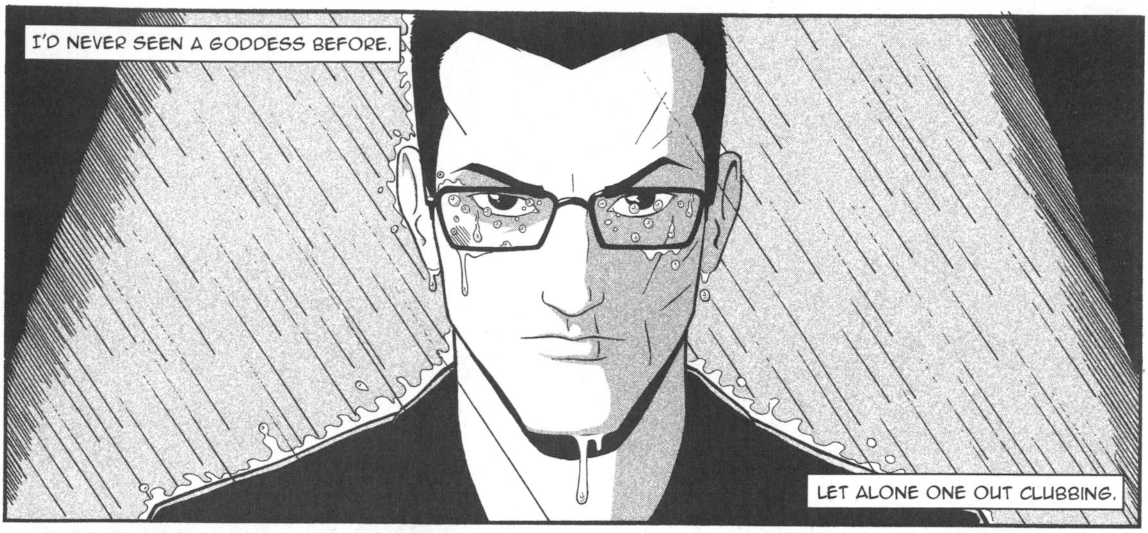
I'D NEVER SEEN A GODDESS BEFORE.
LET ALONE ONE OUT CLUBBING.

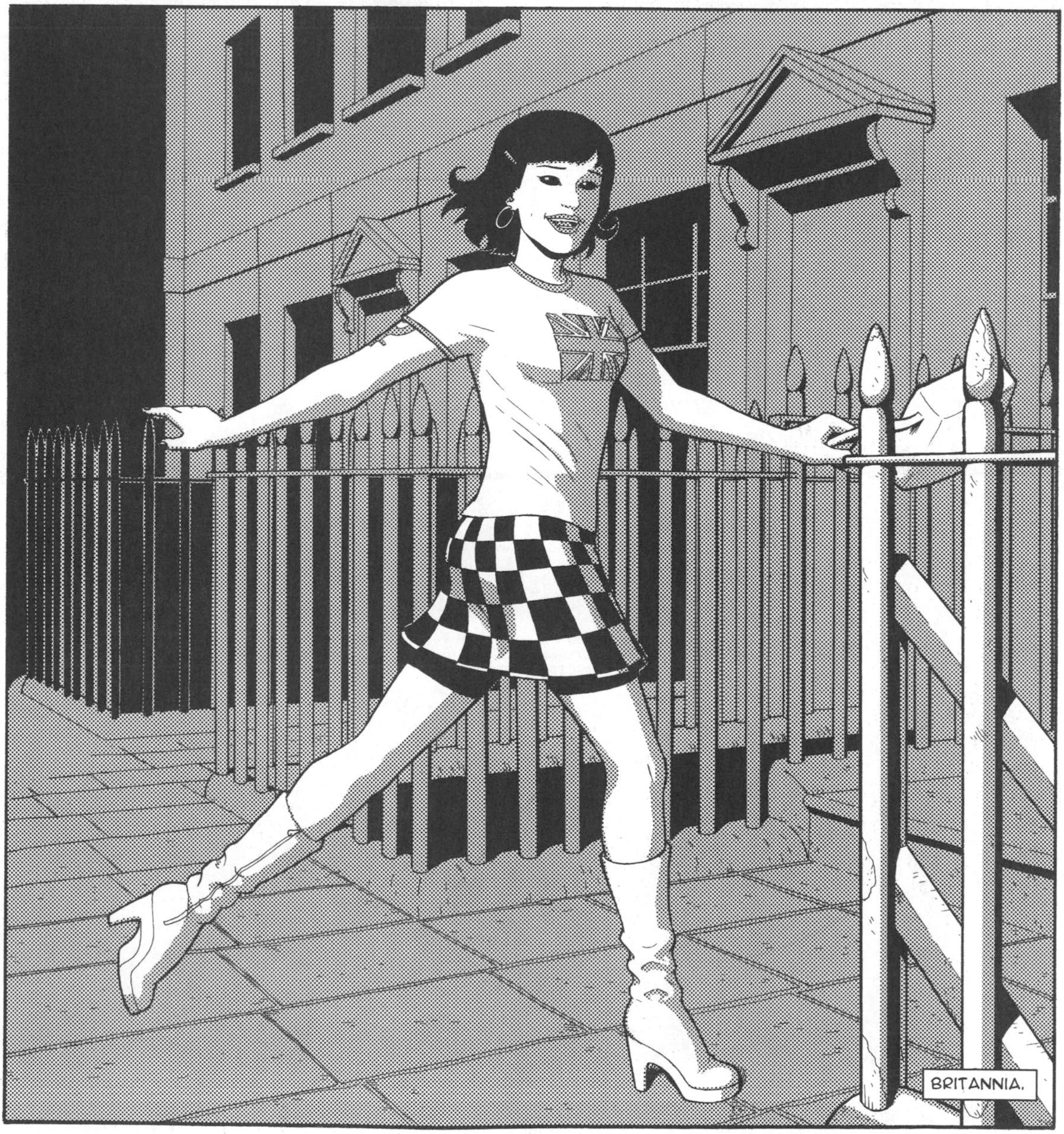
BRITANNIA.

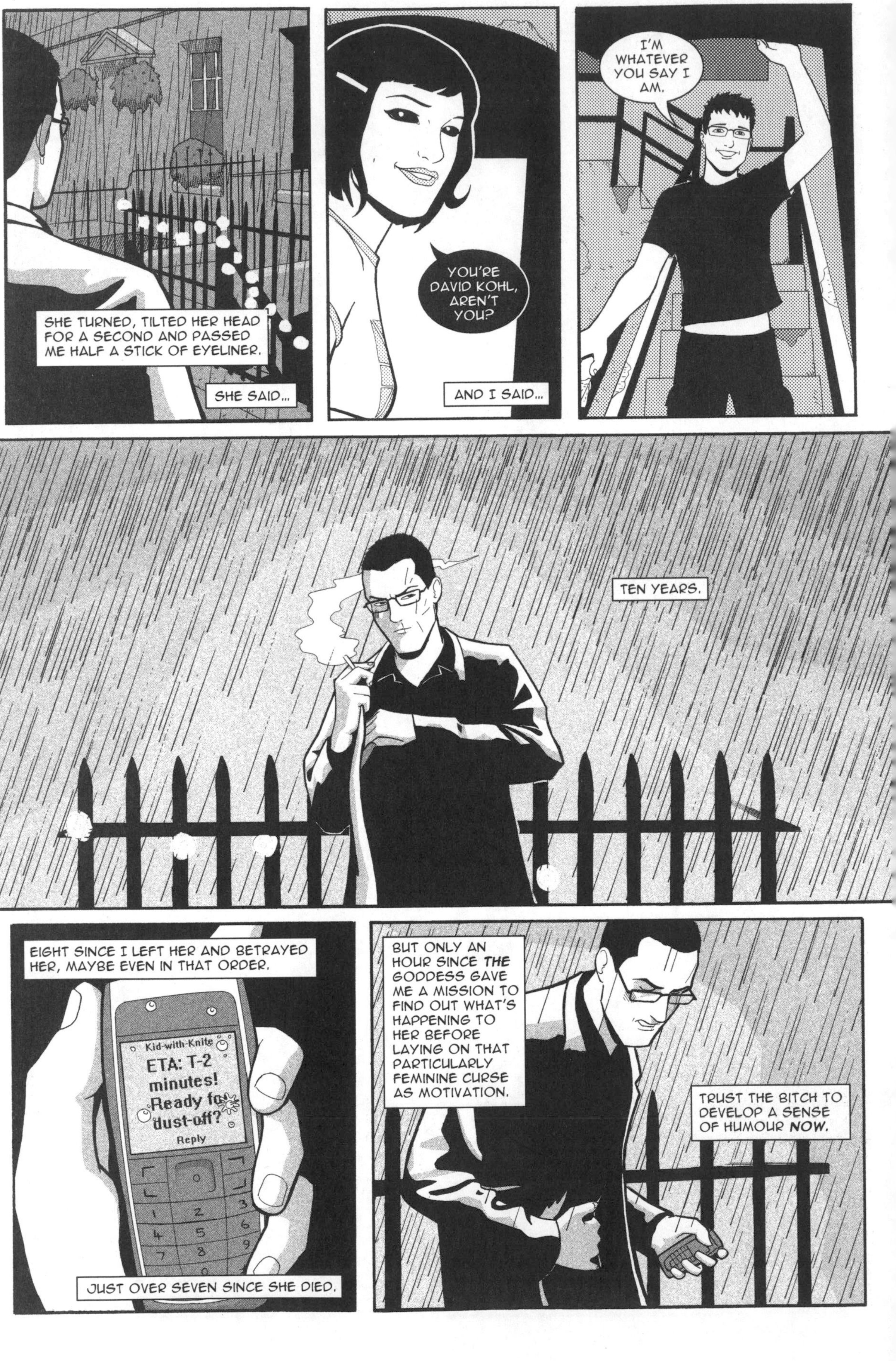
SHE TURNED, TILTED HER HEAD FOR A SECOND AND PASSED ME HALF A STICK OF EYELINER.
SHE SAID...
YOU'RE DAVID KOHL, AREN'T YOU?
AND I SAID...
I'M WHATEVER YOU SAY I AM.
TEN YEARS.
EIGHT SINCE I LEFT HER AND BETRAYED HER, MAYBE EVEN IN THAT ORDER.
Kid-with-Knife
ETA: T-2 minutes! Ready for dust-off?
Reply
JUST OVER SEVEN SINCE SHE DIED.
BUT ONLY AN HOUR SINCE THE GODDESS GAVE ME A MISSION TO FIND OUT WHAT'S HAPPENING TO HER BEFORE LAYING ON THAT PARTICULARLY FEMININE CURSE AS MOTIVATION.
TRUST THE BITCH TO DEVELOP A SENSE OF HUMOUR NOW.

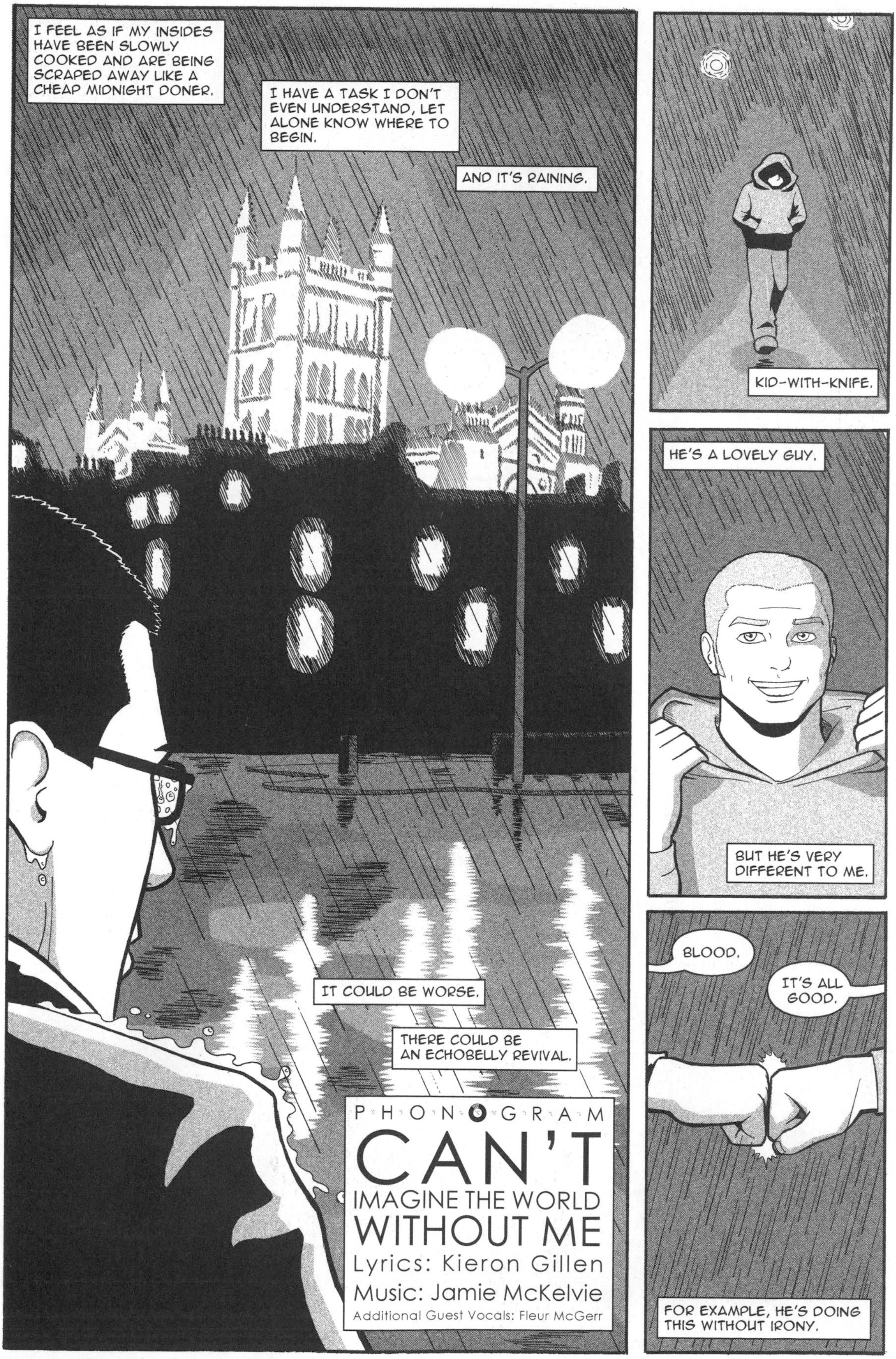
I FEEL AS IF MY INSIDES HAVE BEEN SLOWLY COOKED AND ARE BEING SCRAPED AWAY LIKE A CHEAP MIDNIGHT DONER.
I HAVE A TASK I DON'T EVEN UNDERSTAND, LET ALONE KNOW WHERE TO BEGIN.
AND IT'S RAINING.
IT COULD BE WORSE.
THERE COULD BE AN ECHOBELLY REVIVAL.
PHONOGRAM
CAN'T IMAGINE THE WORLD WITHOUT ME
Lyrics: Kieron Gillen
Music: Jamie McKelvie
Additional Guest Vocals: Fleur McGerr
KID-WITH-KNIFE.
HE'S A LOVELY GUY.
BUT HE'S VERY DIFFERENT TO ME.
BLOOD.
IT'S ALL GOOD.
FOR EXAMPLE, HE'S DOING THIS WITHOUT IRONY.

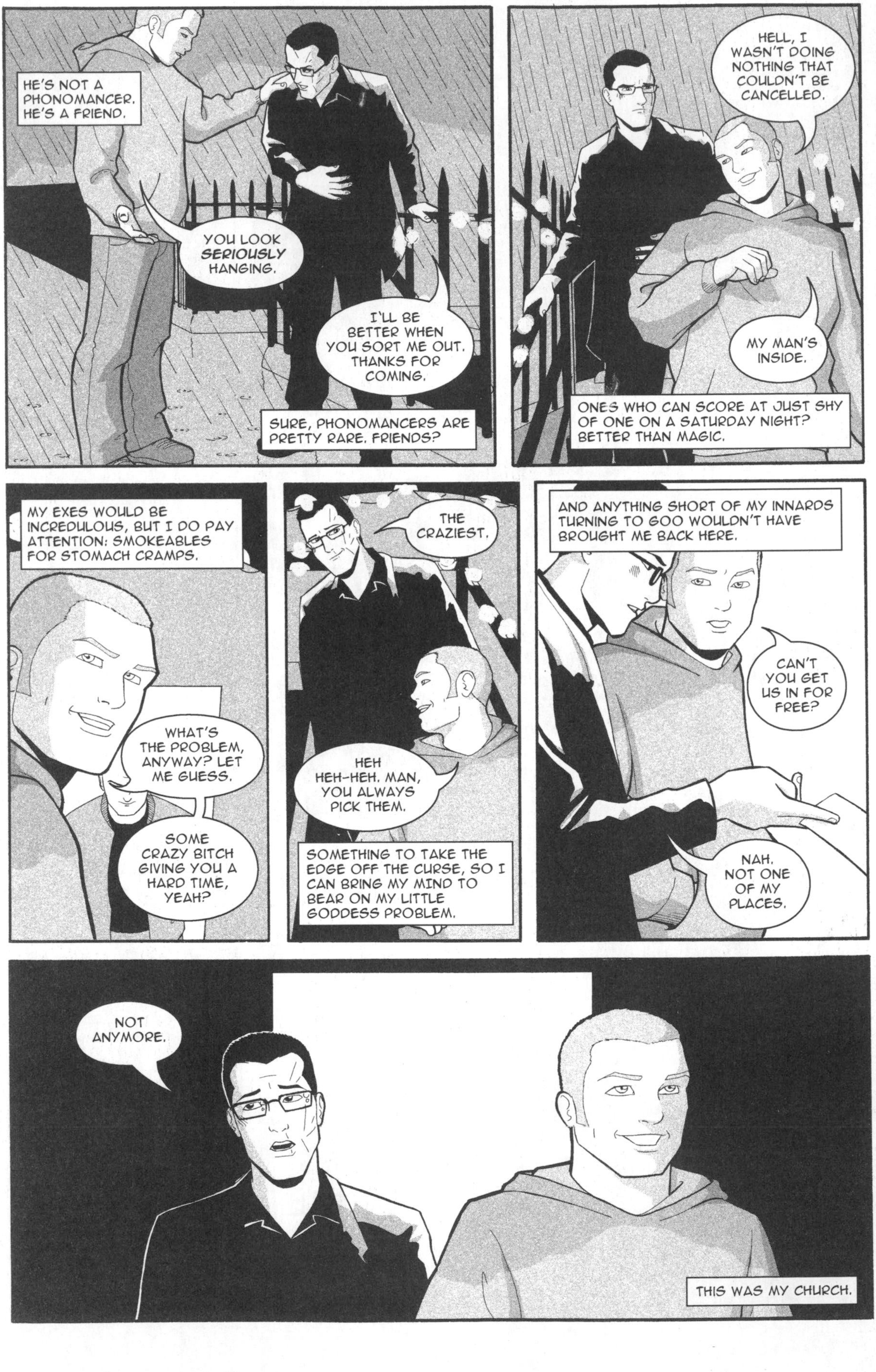
HE'S NOT A PHONOMANCER. HE'S A FRIEND.
YOU LOOK SERIOUSLY HANGING.
I'LL BE BETTER WHEN YOU SORT ME OUT. THANKS FOR COMING.
SURE, PHONOMANCERS ARE PRETTY RARE. FRIENDS?
HELL, I WASN'T DOING NOTHING THAT COULDN'T BE CANCELLED.
MY MAN'S INSIDE.
ONES WHO CAN SCORE AT JUST SHY OF ONE ON A SATURDAY NIGHT? BETTER THAN MAGIC.
MY EXES WOULD BE INCREDULOUS, BUT I DO PAY ATTENTION: SMOKEABLES FOR STOMACH CRAMPS.
WHAT'S THE PROBLEM, ANYWAY? LET ME GUESS.
SOME CRAZY BITCH GIVING YOU A HARD TIME, YEAH?
THE CRAZIEST.
HEH HEH-HEH. MAN, YOU ALWAYS PICK THEM.
SOMETHING TO TAKE THE EDGE OFF THE CURSE, SO I CAN BRING MY MIND TO BEAR ON MY LITTLE GODDESS PROBLEM.
AND ANYTHING SHORT OF MY INNARDS TURNING TO GOO WOULDN'T HAVE BROUGHT ME BACK HERE.
CAN'T YOU GET US IN FOR FREE?
NAH. NOT ONE OF MY PLACES.
NOT ANYMORE.
THIS WAS MY CHURCH.

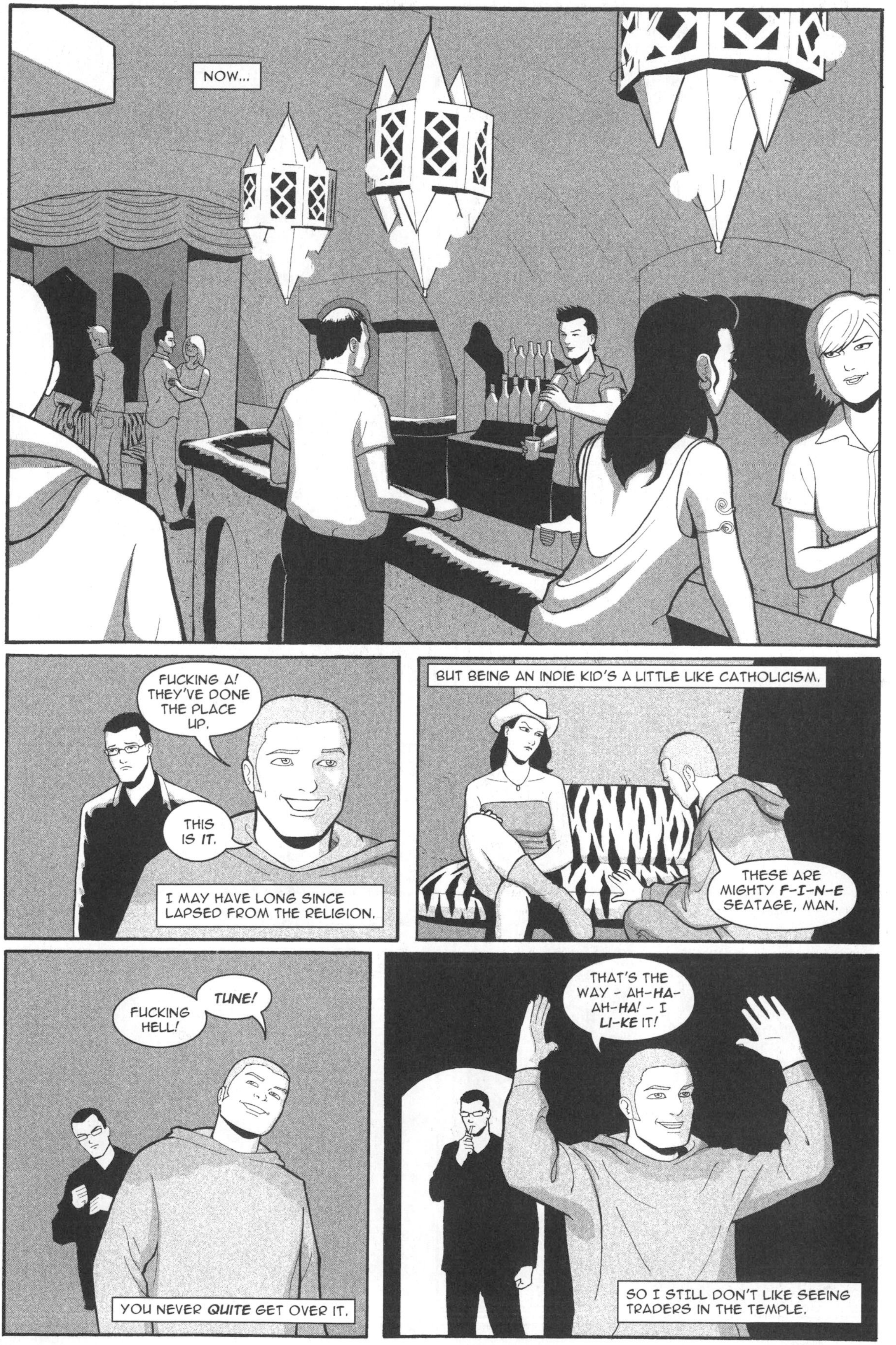
NOW...
FUCKING A! THEY'VE DONE THE PLACE UP.
THIS IS *IT*.
I MAY HAVE LONG SINCE LAPSED FROM THE RELIGION.
BUT BEING AN INDIE KID'S A LITTLE LIKE CATHOLICISM.
THESE ARE MIGHTY **F-I-N-E** SEATAGE, MAN.
FUCKING HELL!
TUNE!
YOU NEVER **QUITE** GET OVER IT.
THAT'S THE WAY - AH-**HA**-AH-**HA**! - I **LI-KE** IT!
SO I STILL DON'T LIKE SEEING TRADERS IN THE TEMPLE.

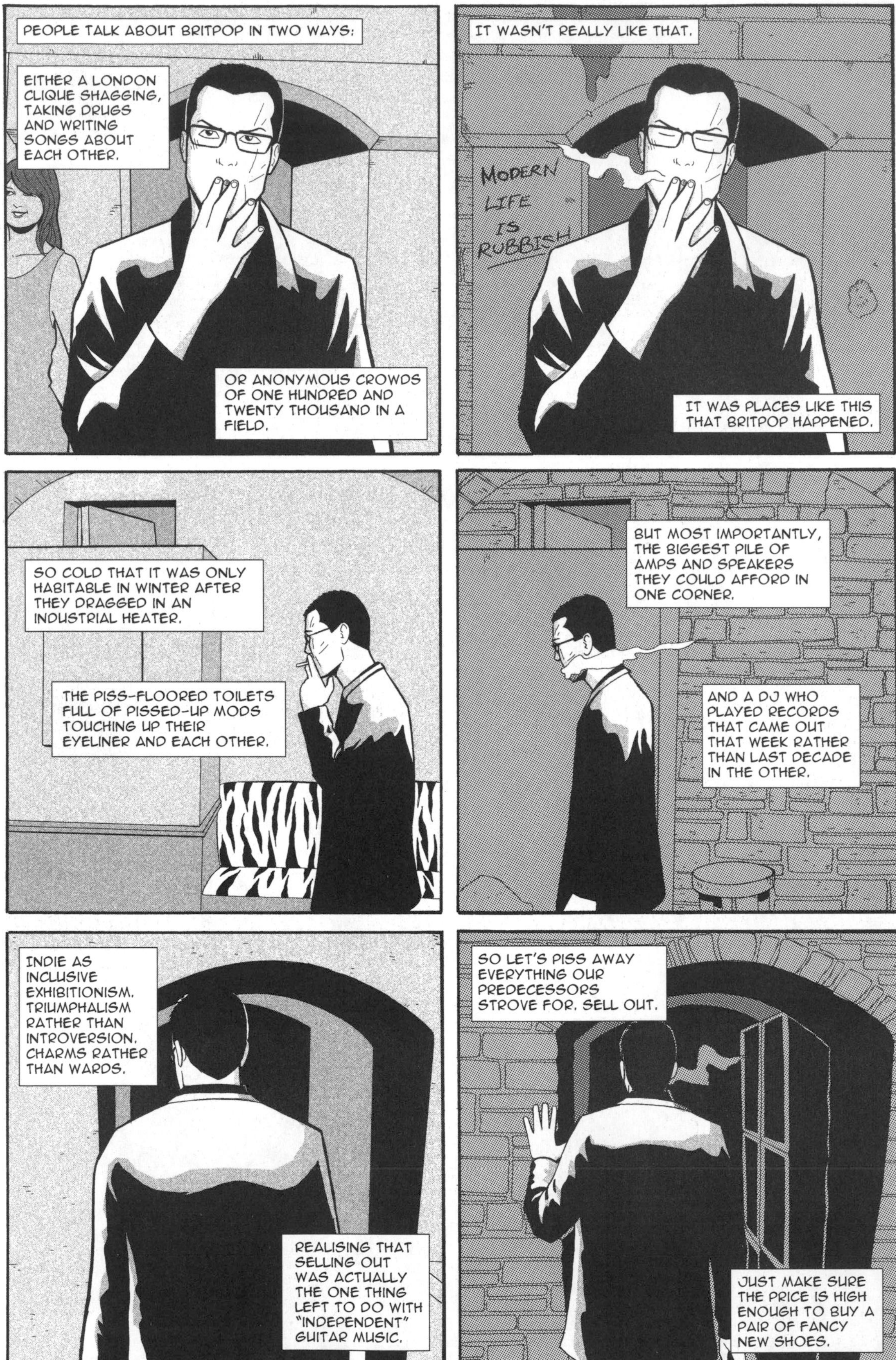
PEOPLE TALK ABOUT BRITPOP IN TWO WAYS:
EITHER A LONDON CLIQUE SHAGGING, TAKING DRUGS AND WRITING SONGS ABOUT EACH OTHER.
OR ANONYMOUS CROWDS OF ONE HUNDRED AND TWENTY THOUSAND IN A FIELD.
IT WASN'T REALLY LIKE THAT.
MODERN LIFE IS RUBBISH
IT WAS PLACES LIKE THIS THAT BRITPOP HAPPENED.
SO COLD THAT IT WAS ONLY HABITABLE IN WINTER AFTER THEY DRAGGED IN AN INDUSTRIAL HEATER.
THE PISS-FLOORED TOILETS FULL OF PISSED-UP MODS TOUCHING UP THEIR EYELINER AND EACH OTHER.
BUT MOST IMPORTANTLY, THE BIGGEST PILE OF AMPS AND SPEAKERS THEY COULD AFFORD IN ONE CORNER.
AND A DJ WHO PLAYED RECORDS THAT CAME OUT THAT WEEK RATHER THAN LAST DECADE IN THE OTHER.
INDIE AS INCLUSIVE EXHIBITIONISM. TRIUMPHALISM RATHER THAN INTROVERSION. CHARMS RATHER THAN WARDS.
REALISING THAT SELLING OUT WAS ACTUALLY THE ONE THING LEFT TO DO WITH "INDEPENDENT" GUITAR MUSIC.
SO LET'S PISS AWAY EVERYTHING OUR PREDECESSORS STROVE FOR, SELL OUT.
JUST MAKE SURE THE PRICE IS HIGH ENOUGH TO BUY A PAIR OF FANCY NEW SHOES.

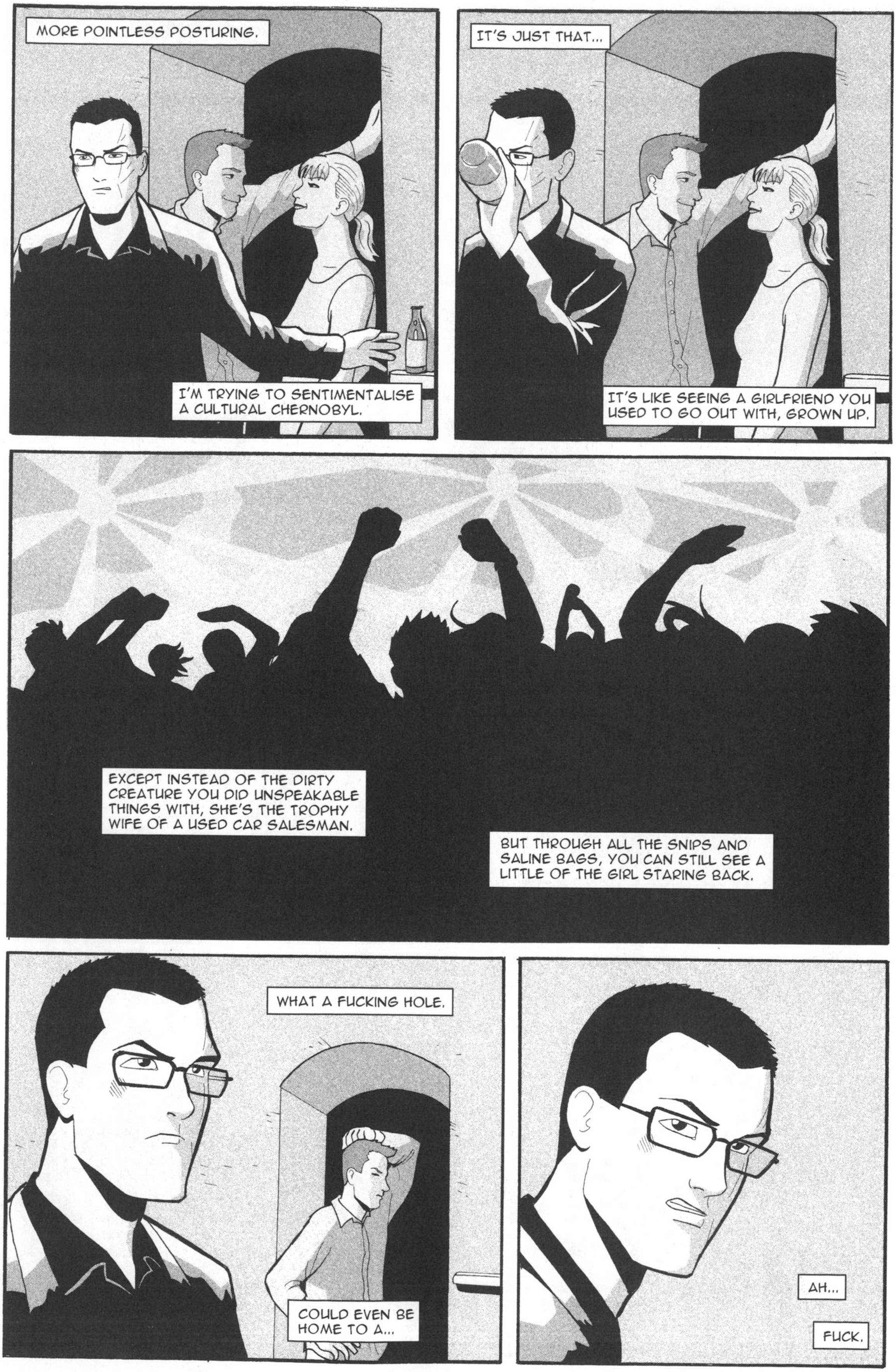
MORE POINTLESS POSTURING.
I'M TRYING TO SENTIMENTALISE A CULTURAL CHERNOBYL.
IT'S JUST THAT...
IT'S LIKE SEEING A GIRLFRIEND YOU USED TO GO OUT WITH, GROWN UP.
EXCEPT INSTEAD OF THE DIRTY CREATURE YOU DID UNSPEAKABLE THINGS WITH, SHE'S THE TROPHY WIFE OF A USED CAR SALESMAN.
BUT THROUGH ALL THE SNIPS AND SALINE BAGS, YOU CAN STILL SEE A LITTLE OF THE GIRL STARING BACK.
WHAT A FUCKING HOLE.
COULD EVEN BE HOME TO A...
AH...
FUCK.

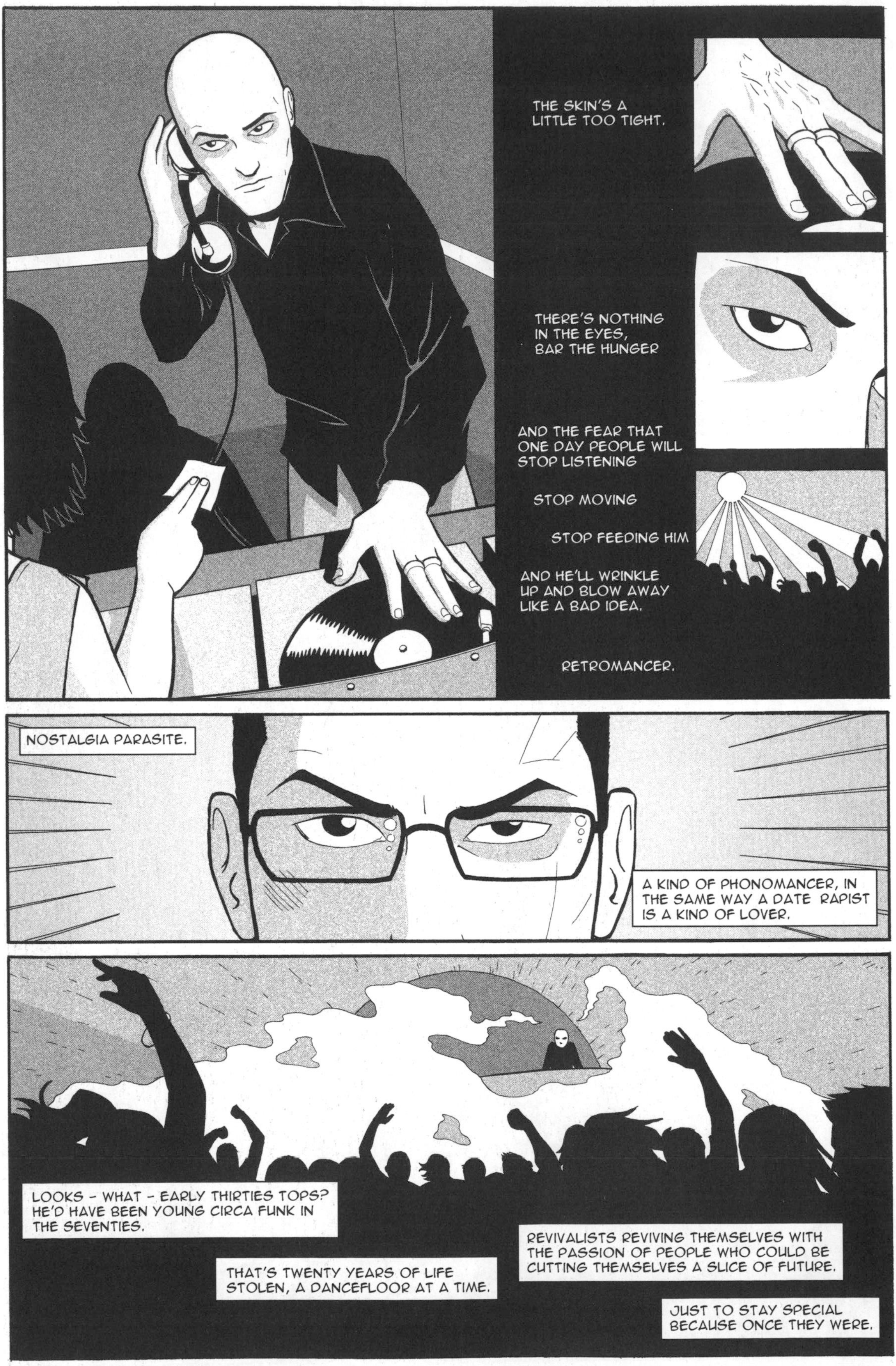
THE SKIN'S A LITTLE TOO TIGHT.
THERE'S NOTHING IN THE EYES, BAR THE HUNGER
AND THE FEAR THAT ONE DAY PEOPLE WILL STOP LISTENING
STOP MOVING
STOP FEEDING HIM
AND HE'LL WRINKLE UP AND BLOW AWAY LIKE A BAD IDEA.
RETROMANCER.
NOSTALGIA PARASITE.
A KIND OF PHONOMANCER, IN THE SAME WAY A DATE RAPIST IS A KIND OF LOVER.
LOOKS - WHAT - EARLY THIRTIES TOPS? HE'D HAVE BEEN YOUNG CIRCA FUNK IN THE SEVENTIES.
THAT'S TWENTY YEARS OF LIFE STOLEN, A DANCEFLOOR AT A TIME.
REVIVALISTS REVIVING THEMSELVES WITH THE PASSION OF PEOPLE WHO COULD BE CUTTING THEMSELVES A SLICE OF FUTURE.
JUST TO STAY SPECIAL BECAUSE ONCE THEY WERE.

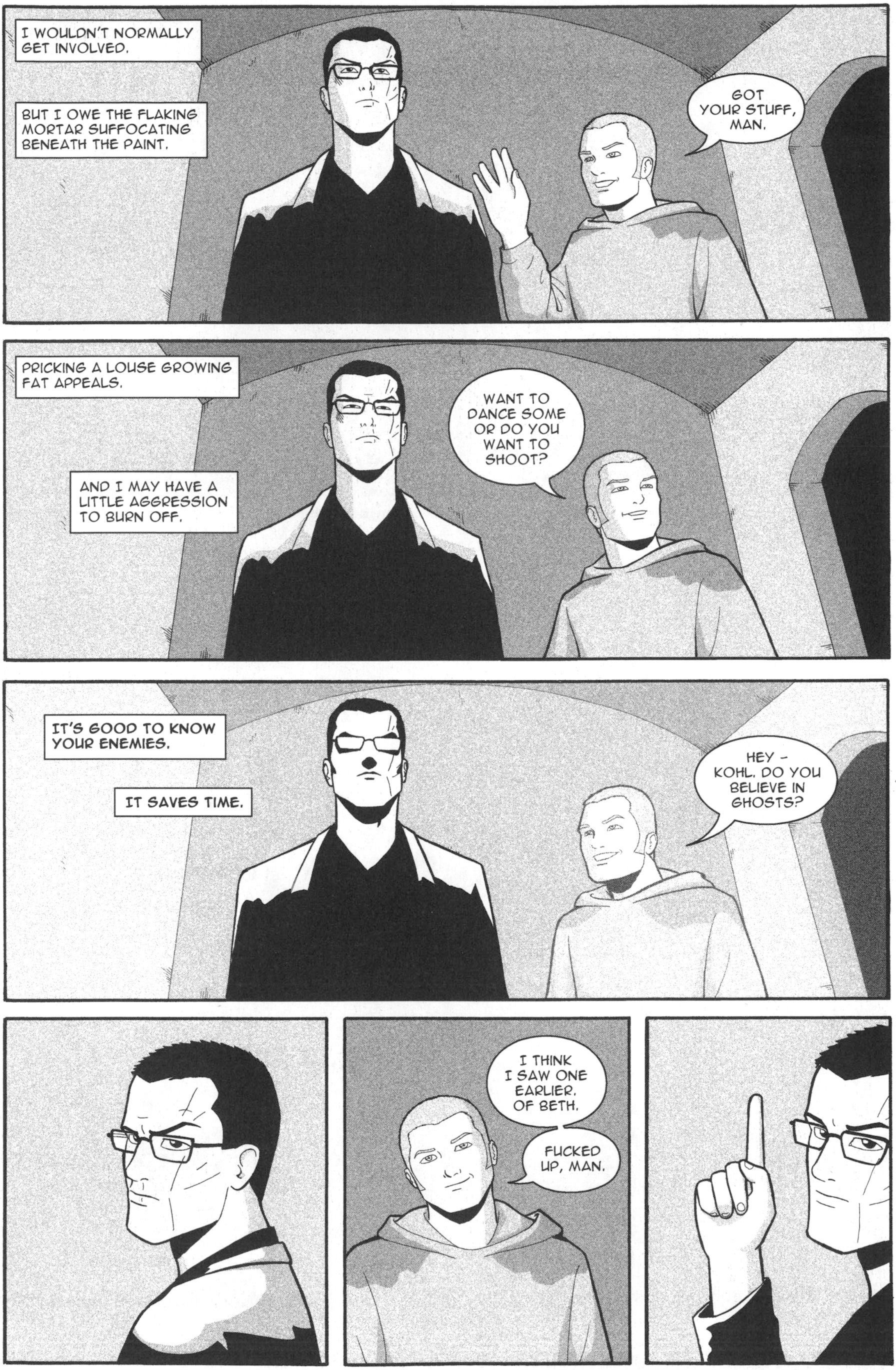
I WOULDN'T NORMALLY GET INVOLVED.
BUT I OWE THE FLAKING MORTAR SUFFOCATING BENEATH THE PAINT.
GOT YOUR STUFF, MAN.
PRICKING A LOUSE GROWING FAT APPEALS.
AND I MAY HAVE A LITTLE AGGRESSION TO BURN OFF.
WANT TO DANCE SOME OR DO YOU WANT TO SHOOT?
IT'S GOOD TO KNOW YOUR ENEMIES.
IT SAVES TIME.
HEY - KOHL. DO YOU BELIEVE IN GHOSTS?
I THINK I SAW ONE EARLIER. OF BETH.
FUCKED UP, MAN.

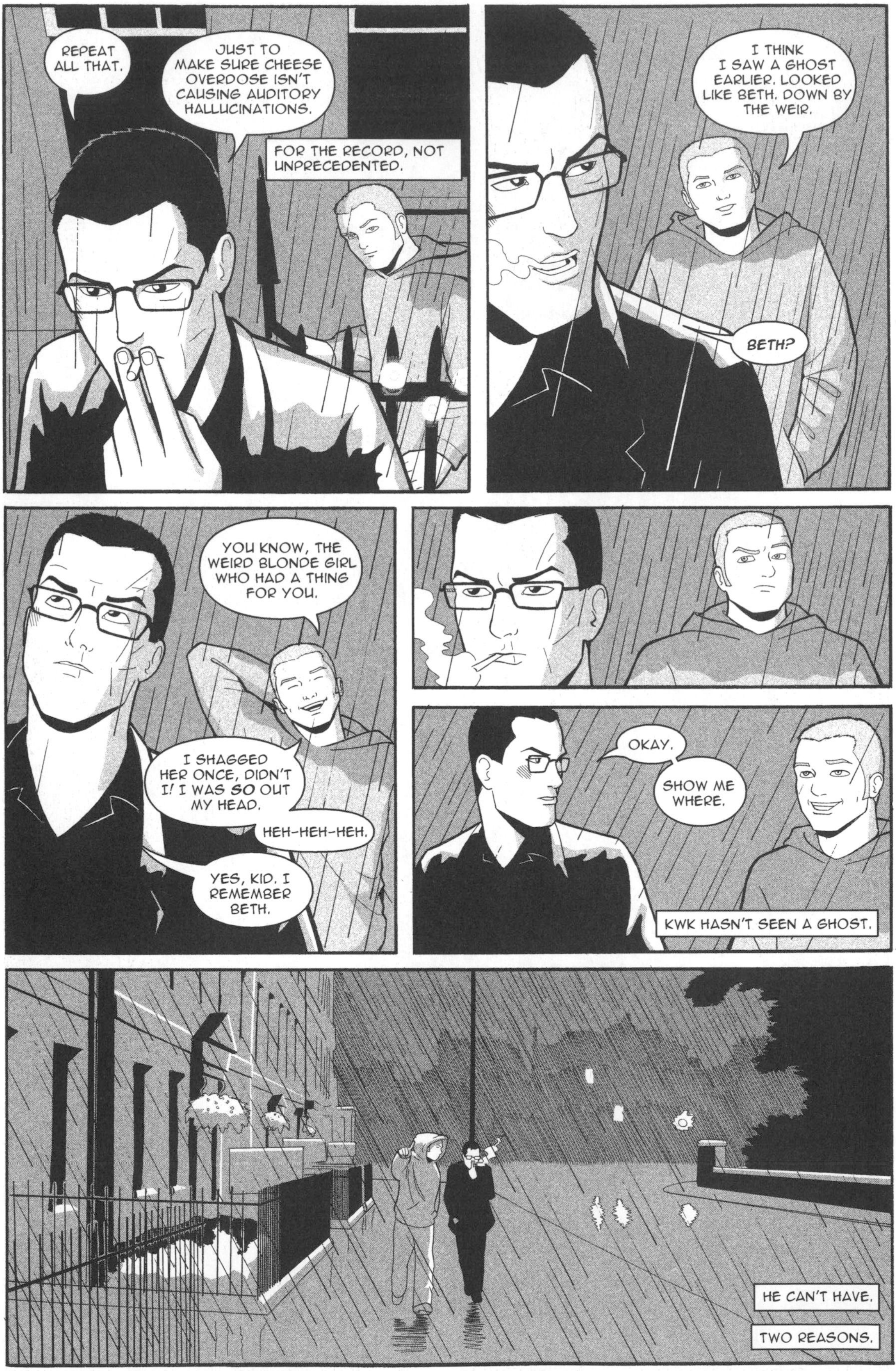
REPEAT ALL THAT.
JUST TO MAKE SURE CHEESE OVERDOSE ISN'T CAUSING AUDITORY HALLUCINATIONS.
FOR THE RECORD, NOT UNPRECEDENTED.
I THINK I SAW A GHOST EARLIER. LOOKED LIKE BETH. DOWN BY THE WEIR.
BETH?
YOU KNOW, THE WEIRD BLONDE GIRL WHO HAD A THING FOR YOU.
I SHAGGED HER ONCE, DIDN'T I! I WAS SO OUT MY HEAD.
HEH-HEH-HEH.
YES, KID. I REMEMBER BETH.
OKAY.
SHOW ME WHERE.
KWK HASN'T SEEN A GHOST.
HE CAN'T HAVE.
TWO REASONS.

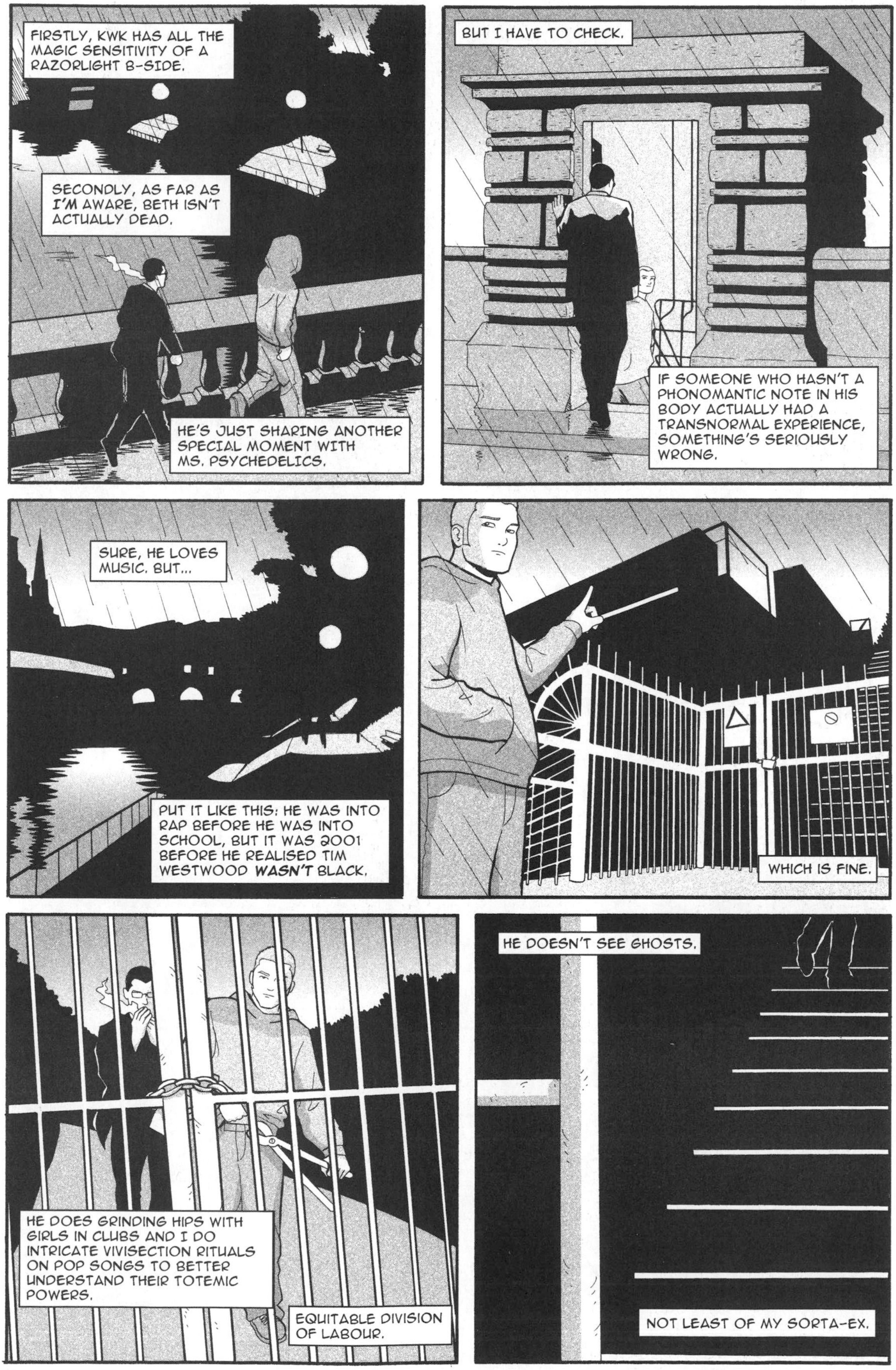
FIRSTLY, KWK HAS ALL THE MAGIC SENSITIVITY OF A RAZORLIGHT B-SIDE.
SECONDLY, AS FAR AS *I'M* AWARE, BETH ISN'T ACTUALLY DEAD.
HE'S JUST SHARING ANOTHER SPECIAL MOMENT WITH MS. PSYCHEDELICS.
BUT I HAVE TO CHECK.
IF SOMEONE WHO HASN'T A PHONOMANTIC NOTE IN HIS BODY ACTUALLY HAD A TRANSNORMAL EXPERIENCE, SOMETHING'S SERIOUSLY WRONG.
SURE, HE LOVES MUSIC. BUT...
PUT IT LIKE THIS: HE WAS INTO RAP BEFORE HE WAS INTO SCHOOL, BUT IT WAS 2001 BEFORE HE REALISED TIM WESTWOOD **WASN'T** BLACK.
WHICH IS FINE.
HE DOES GRINDING HIPS WITH GIRLS IN CLUBS AND I DO INTRICATE VIVISECTION RITUALS ON POP SONGS TO BETTER UNDERSTAND THEIR TOTEMIC POWERS.
EQUITABLE DIVISION OF LABOUR.
HE DOESN'T SEE GHOSTS.
NOT LEAST OF MY SORTA-EX.

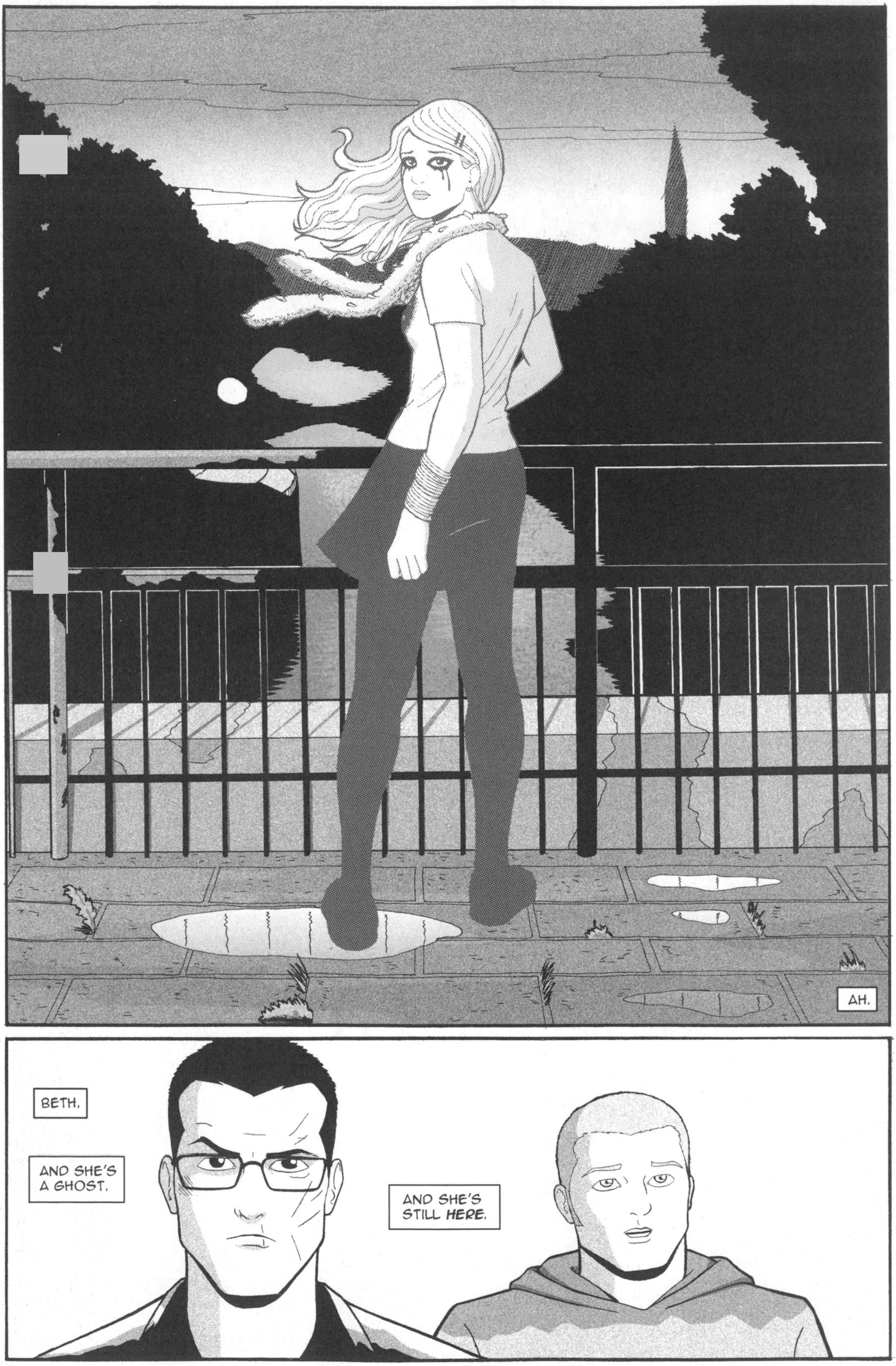
AH.
BETH.
AND SHE'S A GHOST.
AND SHE'S STILL HERE.

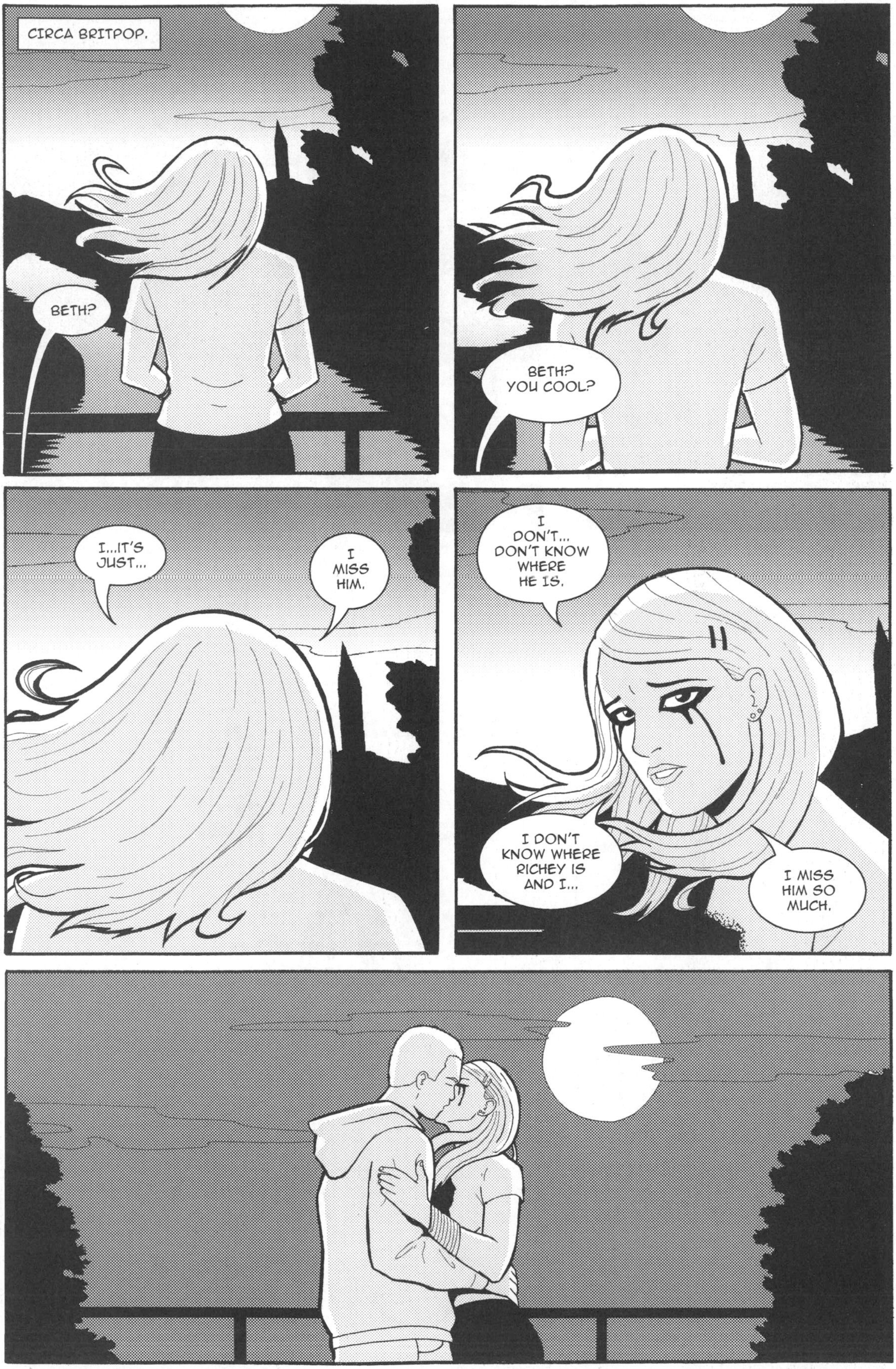
CIRCA BRITPOP.
BETH?
BETH? YOU COOL?
I...IT'S JUST...
I MISS HIM.
I DON'T... DON'T KNOW WHERE HE IS.
I DON'T KNOW WHERE RICHEY IS AND I...
I MISS HIM SO MUCH.

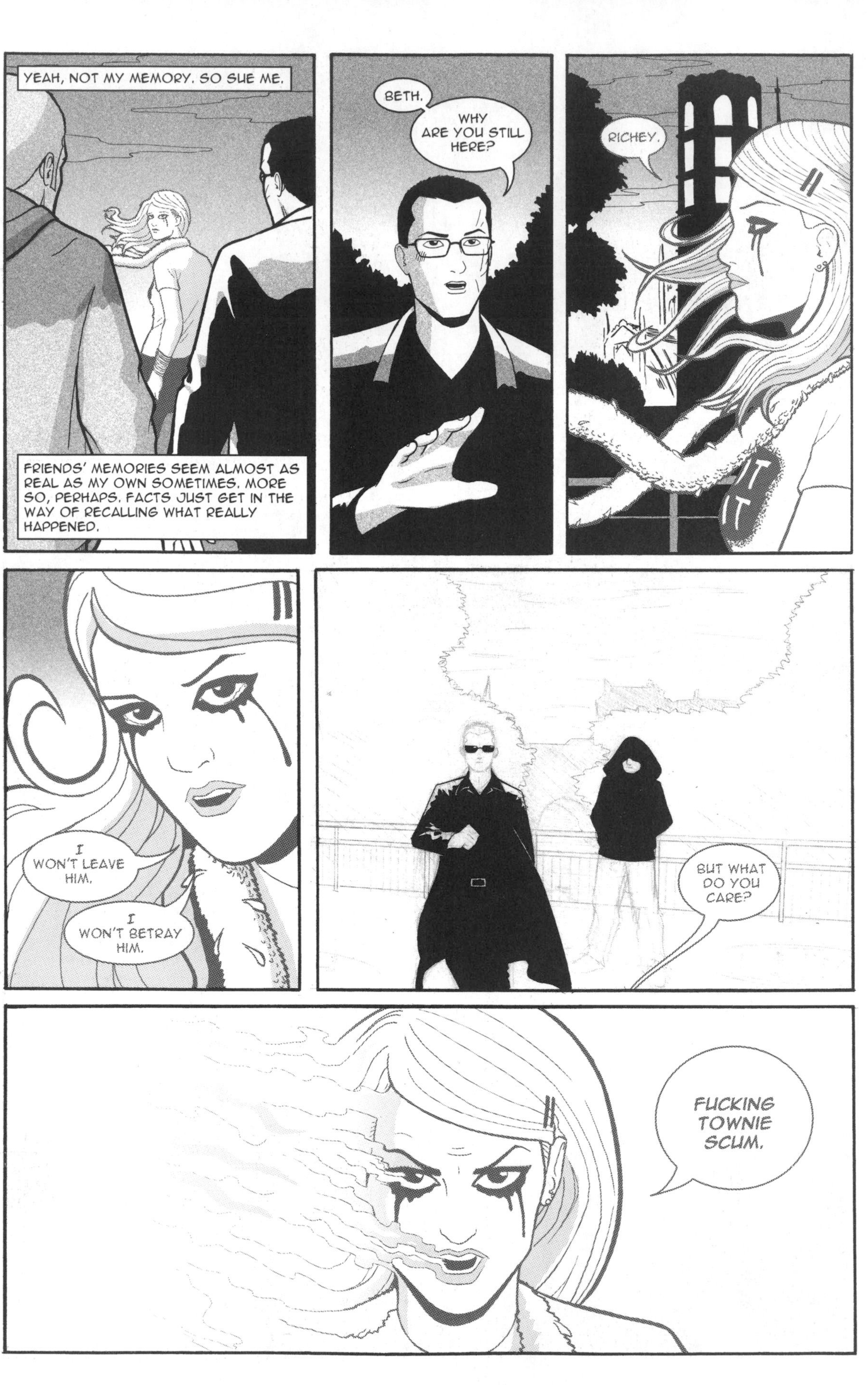
YEAH, NOT MY MEMORY. SO SUE ME.
FRIENDS' MEMORIES SEEM ALMOST AS REAL AS MY OWN SOMETIMES. MORE SO, PERHAPS. FACTS JUST GET IN THE WAY OF RECALLING WHAT REALLY HAPPENED.
BETH.
WHY ARE YOU STILL HERE?
RICHEY.
I WON'T LEAVE HIM.
I WON'T BETRAY HIM.
BUT WHAT DO YOU CARE?
FUCKING TOWNIE SCUM.

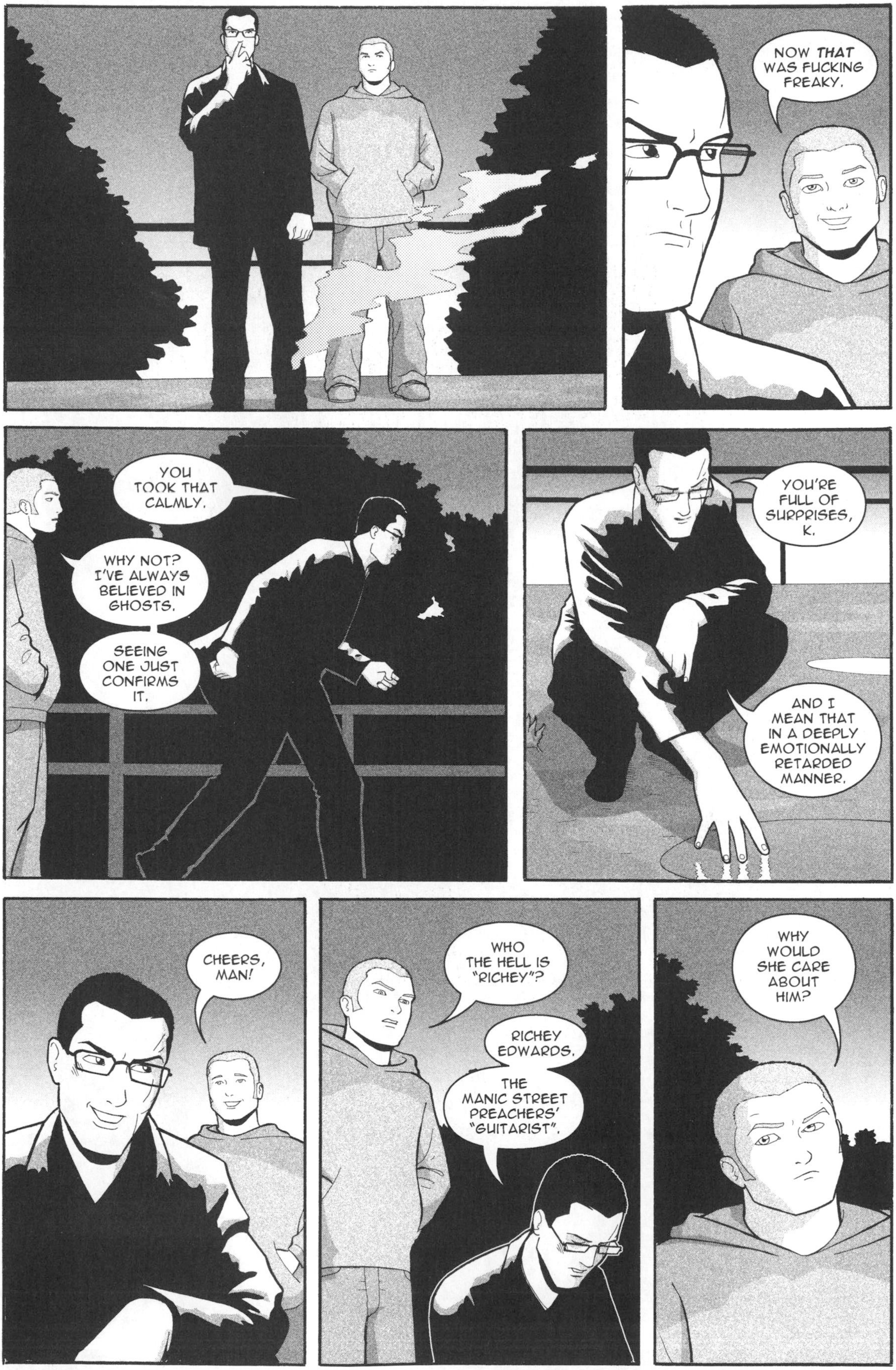
NOW THAT WAS FUCKING FREAKY.
YOU TOOK THAT CALMLY.
WHY NOT? I'VE ALWAYS BELIEVED IN GHOSTS.
SEEING ONE JUST CONFIRMS IT.
YOU'RE FULL OF SURPRISES, K.
AND I MEAN THAT IN A DEEPLY EMOTIONALLY RETARDED MANNER.
CHEERS, MAN!
WHO THE HELL IS "RICHEY"?
RICHEY EDWARDS.
THE MANIC STREET PREACHERS' "GUITARIST".
WHY WOULD SHE CARE ABOUT HIM?

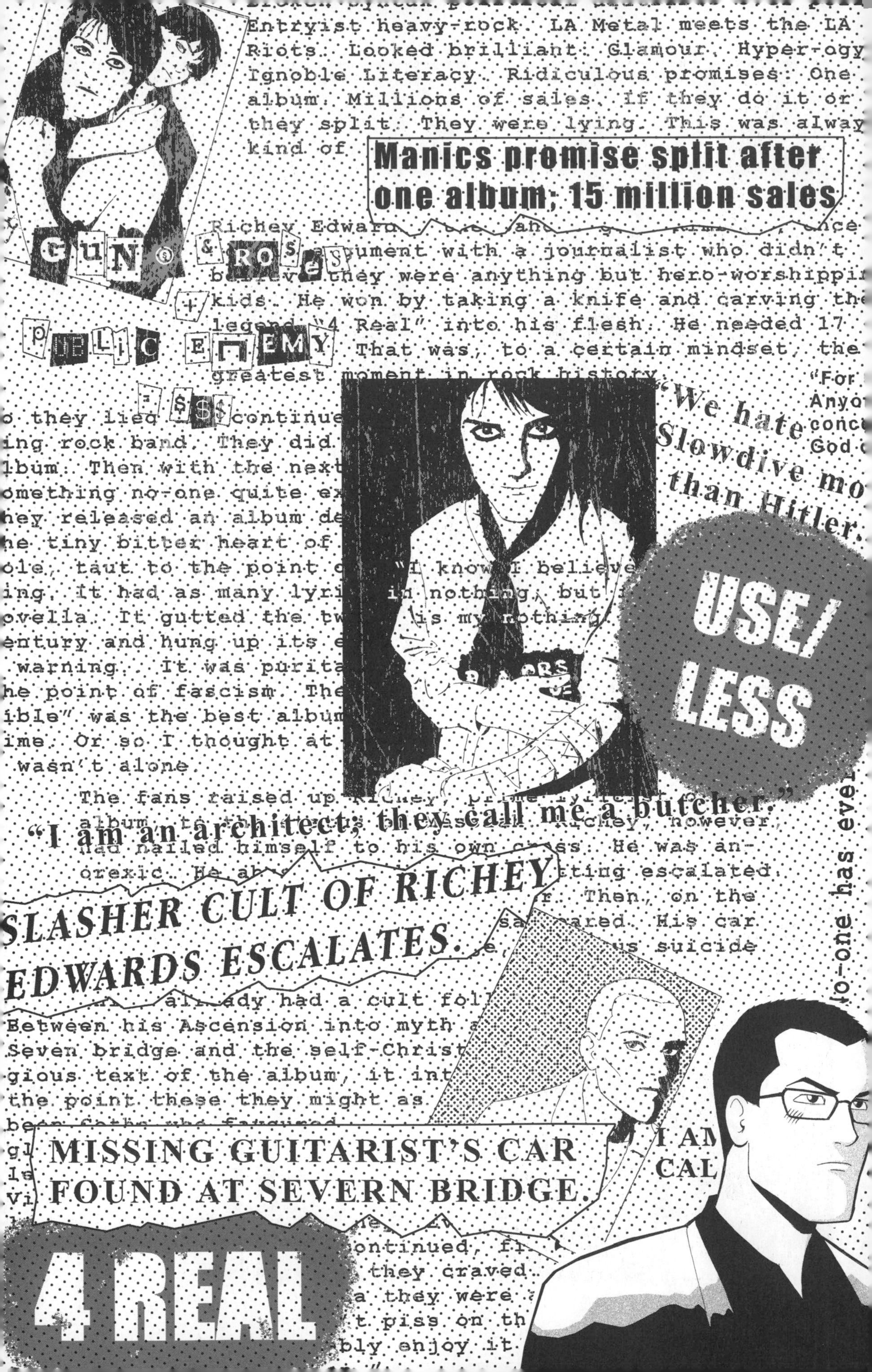
Entryist heavy-rock. LA Metal meets the LA
Riots. Looked brilliant. Glamour. Hyper-ogy
Ignoble Literacy. Ridiculous promises: One
album. Millions of sales. If they do it or
they split. They were lying. This was alway
kind of
Manics promise split after one album; 15 million sales
GUNS & ROSES + PUBLIC ENEMY = $$$
Richey Edward
argument with a journalist who didn't
believe they were anything but hero-worshippi
kids. He won by taking a knife and carving the
legend "4 Real" into his flesh. He needed 17
That was, to a certain mindset, the
greatest moment in rock history.
o they lied continue
ing rock band. They did
lbum. Then with the next
omething no-one quite ex
hey released an album de
he tiny bitter heart of
ole, taut to the point o
ing, it had as many lyri
ovella. It gutted the tw
entury and hung up its e
warning. It was purita
he point of fascism. The
ible" was the best album
ime. Or so I thought at
wasn't alone.
"I know I believe in nothing, but it is my nothing."
"We hate Slowdive more than Hitler."
"For Anyo conce God
USE/LESS
The fans raised up Richey, prime lyricist
"I am an architect; they call me a butcher."
had nailed himself to his own cross. He was an-
orexic.
escalated.
Then, on the
His car
suicide
SLASHER CULT OF RICHEY EDWARDS ESCALATES.
already had a cult foll
Between his Ascension into myth a
Seven bridge and the self-Christ
gious text of the album, it int
the point these they might as
No-one has ever
MISSING GUITARIST'S CAR FOUND AT SEVERN BRIDGE.
I AM
CAL
4 REAL
continued,
they craved.
a they were
t piss on th
bly enjoy it

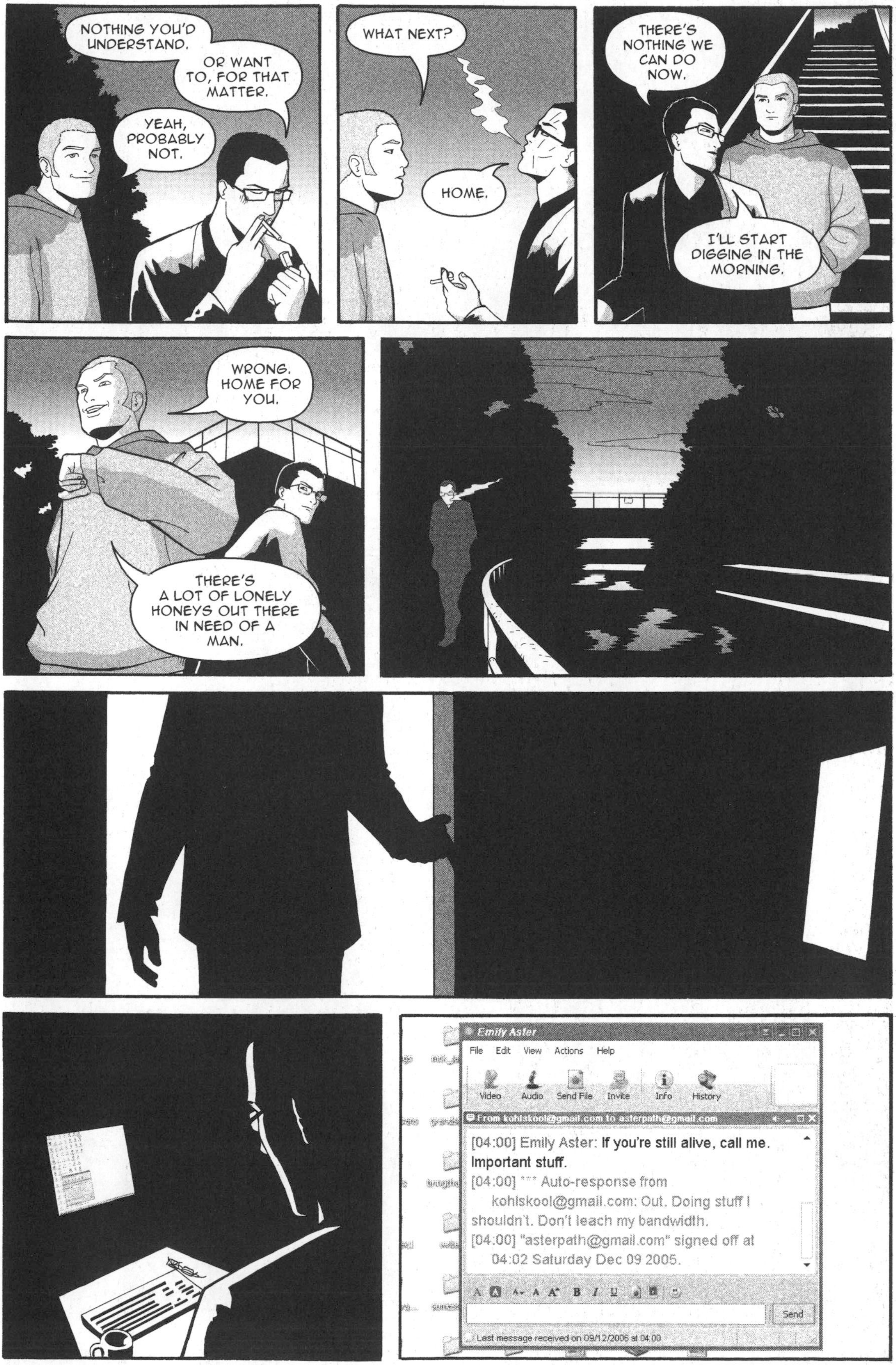

NOTHING YOU'D UNDERSTAND.
OR WANT TO, FOR THAT MATTER.
YEAH, PROBABLY NOT.
WHAT NEXT?
HOME.
THERE'S NOTHING WE CAN DO NOW.
I'LL START DIGGING IN THE MORNING.
WRONG. HOME FOR YOU.
THERE'S A LOT OF LONELY HONEYS OUT THERE IN NEED OF A MAN.
Emily Aster
File Edit View Actions Help
Video Audio Send File Invite Info History
From kohlskool@gmail.com to asterpath@gmail.com
[04:00] Emily Aster: If you're still alive, call me. Important stuff.
[04:00] *** Auto-response from kohlskool@gmail.com: Out. Doing stuff I shouldn't. Don't leach my bandwidth.
[04:00] "asterpath@gmail.com" signed off at 04:02 Saturday Dec 09 2005.
Send
Last message received on 09/12/2006 at 04:00

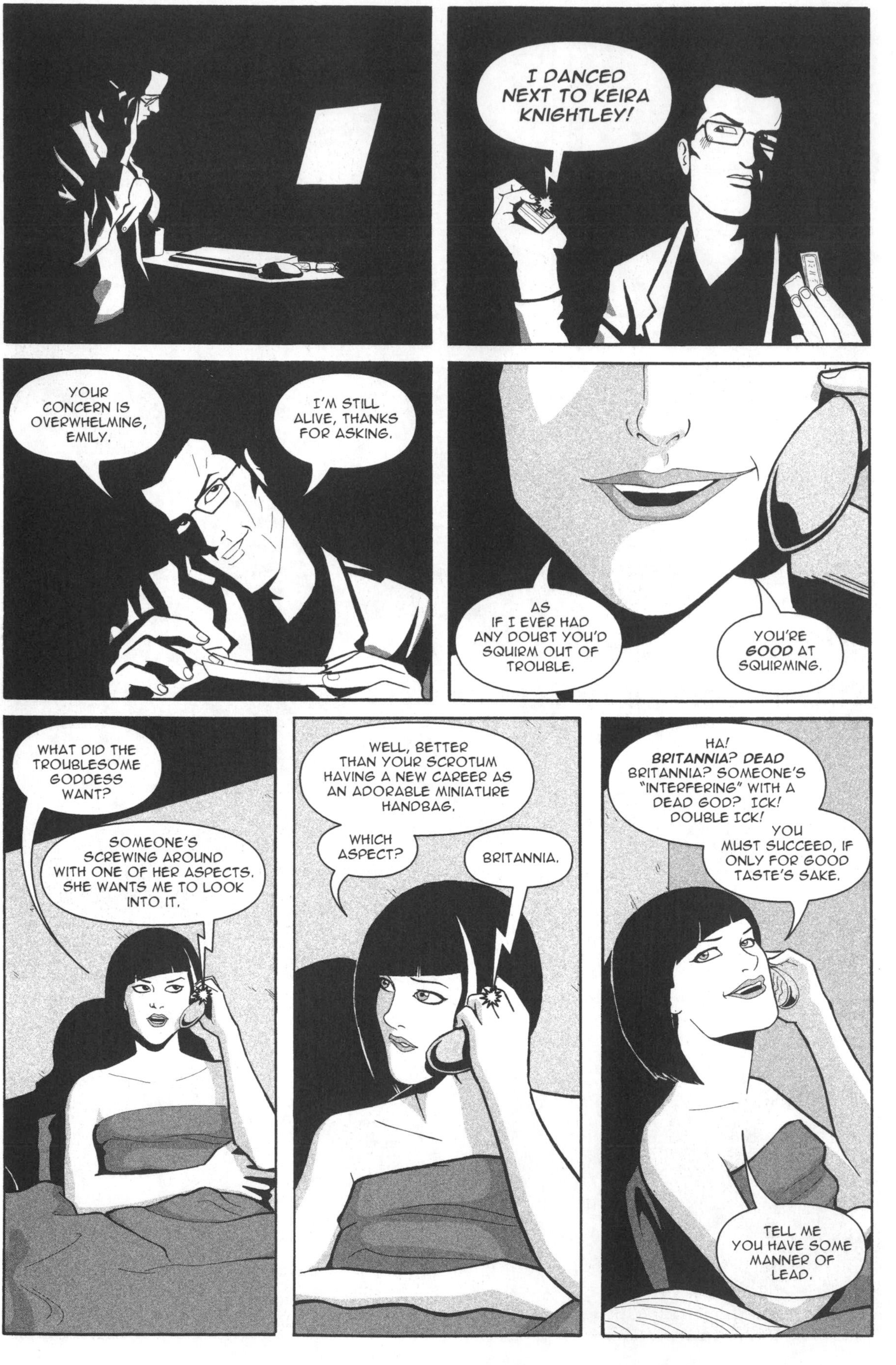
I DANCED NEXT TO KEIRA KNIGHTLEY!
YOUR CONCERN IS OVERWHELMING, EMILY.
I'M STILL ALIVE, THANKS FOR ASKING.
AS IF I EVER HAD ANY DOUBT YOU'D SQUIRM OUT OF TROUBLE.
YOU'RE GOOD AT SQUIRMING.
WHAT DID THE TROUBLESOME GODDESS WANT?
SOMEONE'S SCREWING AROUND WITH ONE OF HER ASPECTS. SHE WANTS ME TO LOOK INTO IT.
WELL, BETTER THAN YOUR SCROTUM HAVING A NEW CAREER AS AN ADORABLE MINIATURE HANDBAG.
WHICH ASPECT?
BRITANNIA.
HA! BRITANNIA? DEAD BRITANNIA? SOMEONE'S "INTERFERING" WITH A DEAD GOD? ICK! DOUBLE ICK!
YOU MUST SUCCEED, IF ONLY FOR GOOD TASTE'S SAKE.
TELL ME YOU HAVE SOME MANNER OF LEAD.

MAYBE. I JUST SAW A GHOST OF BETH, LOOKING LIKE SHE DID BACK THEN.

EXCEPT BETH'S NOT DEAD. I HOPE SHE ISN'T, ANYWAY.

WAIT... *DAVID*. IS THIS THE BETH WHO STALKED YOU FOR A WHOLE YEAR THEN SLEPT WITH YOUR BEST FRIEND IN A FUTILE ATTEMPT TO MAKE YOU JEALOUS?

...YEAH.

SO WHY ARE YOU A MEMBER OF THE GIVING A FUCK CLUB?

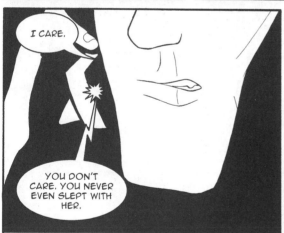

I CARE.

YOU DON'T CARE. YOU NEVER EVEN SLEPT WITH HER.

I DO CARE. SHE WAS A FRIEND.

I JUST DIDN'T LIKE HER VERY MUCH.

BESIDES; SEEING HER LIKE THAT... IT'S NOT RIGHT.

EVEN IF IT'S NOTHING TO DO WITH THIS, I'D LIKE TO HELP HER.

NOT ALL OF US ARE MONSTERS.

OH, DAVID.

YOU *ALMOST* SOUND AS IF YOU ACTUALLY BELIEVE THAT.

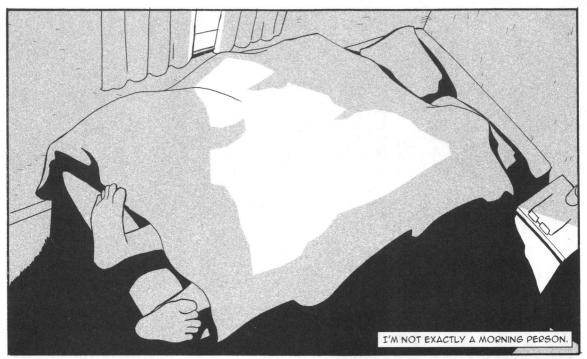
I'M NOT EXACTLY A MORNING PERSON.

EXCUSE ME WHILE I GET MYSELF...

WHAT'S THE WORD?

TOGETHER.

Echobelly - On
Track 4 - Great Things

YEAH, TOGETHER. THAT'S IT.

I WANNA DO GREAT THINGS

DON'T WANNA COM!PROM!ISE!

I WANNA KNOW WHAT LIFE IS IS IT SOMETHING I DO! TO! MYSELF!

DUM-DE DE-DUM SOMETHING I DO TO MY DUM-DE...,

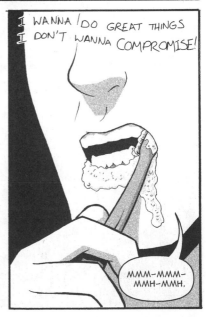
I WANNA / DO GREAT THINGS I DON'T WANNA COMPROMISE!

MMM-MMM-MMH-MMH.

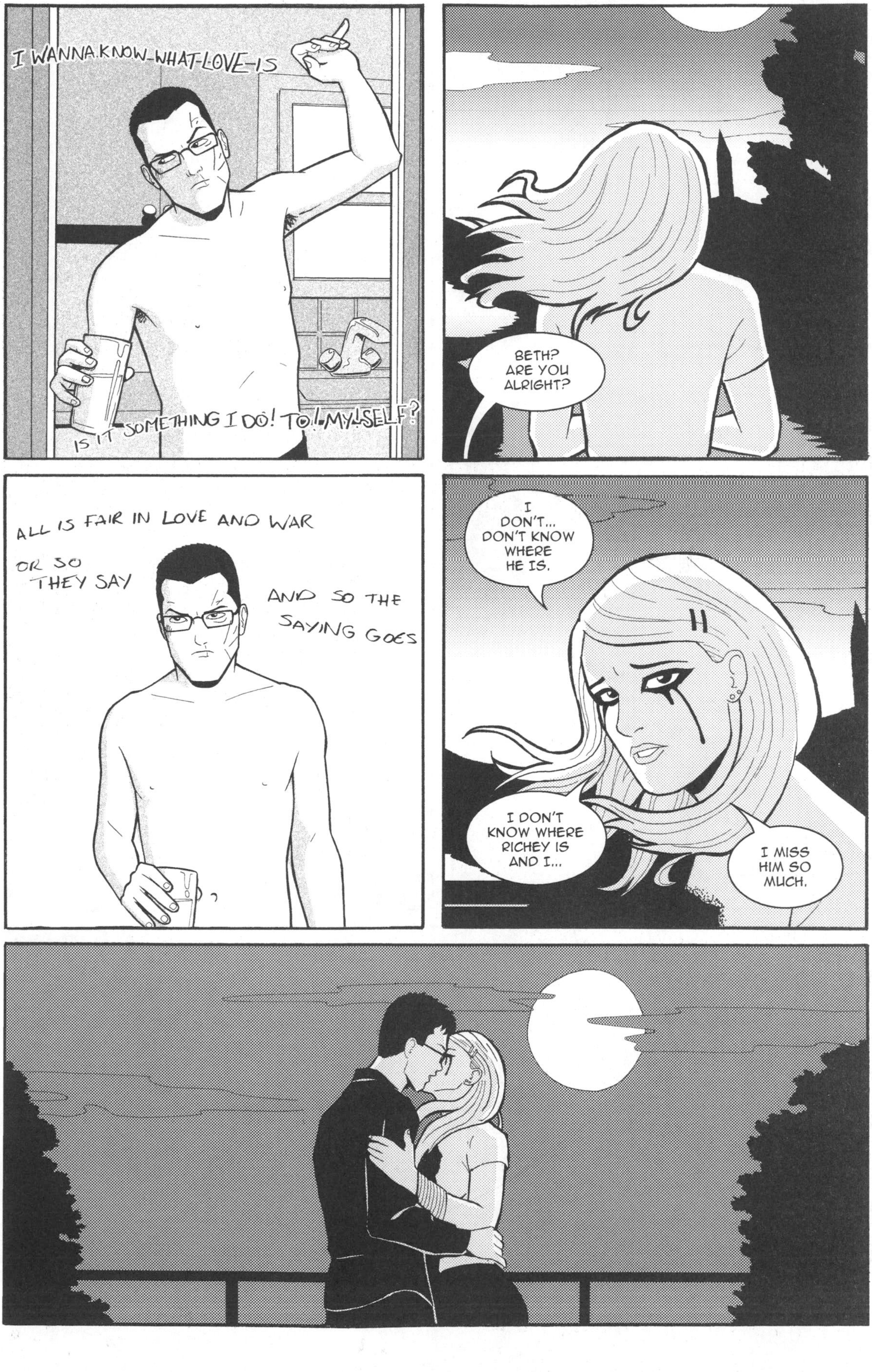
I WANNA KNOW WHAT LOVE IS
IS IT SOMETHING I DO! TO! MY SELF?
BETH? ARE YOU ALRIGHT?
ALL IS FAIR IN LOVE AND WAR
OR SO THEY SAY
AND SO THE SAYING GOES
I DON'T... DON'T KNOW WHERE HE IS.
I DON'T KNOW WHERE RICHEY IS AND I...
I MISS HIM SO MUCH.

OR SO THEY SAY OR SO THE SAYING GOES

STOP.

WRONG, DIDN'T HAPPEN...

NO,

WE NEVER...

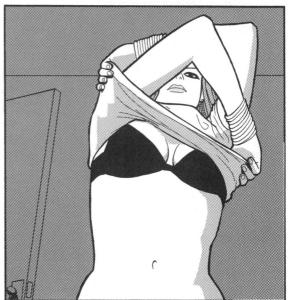

WHAT IS LIFE APART FROM MEMORIES OR DREAMS AND FRIENDSHIPS WE HAVE KNOWN?

AND SINCE WHEN DO I LISTEN TO *ECHOBELLY* RECORDS?

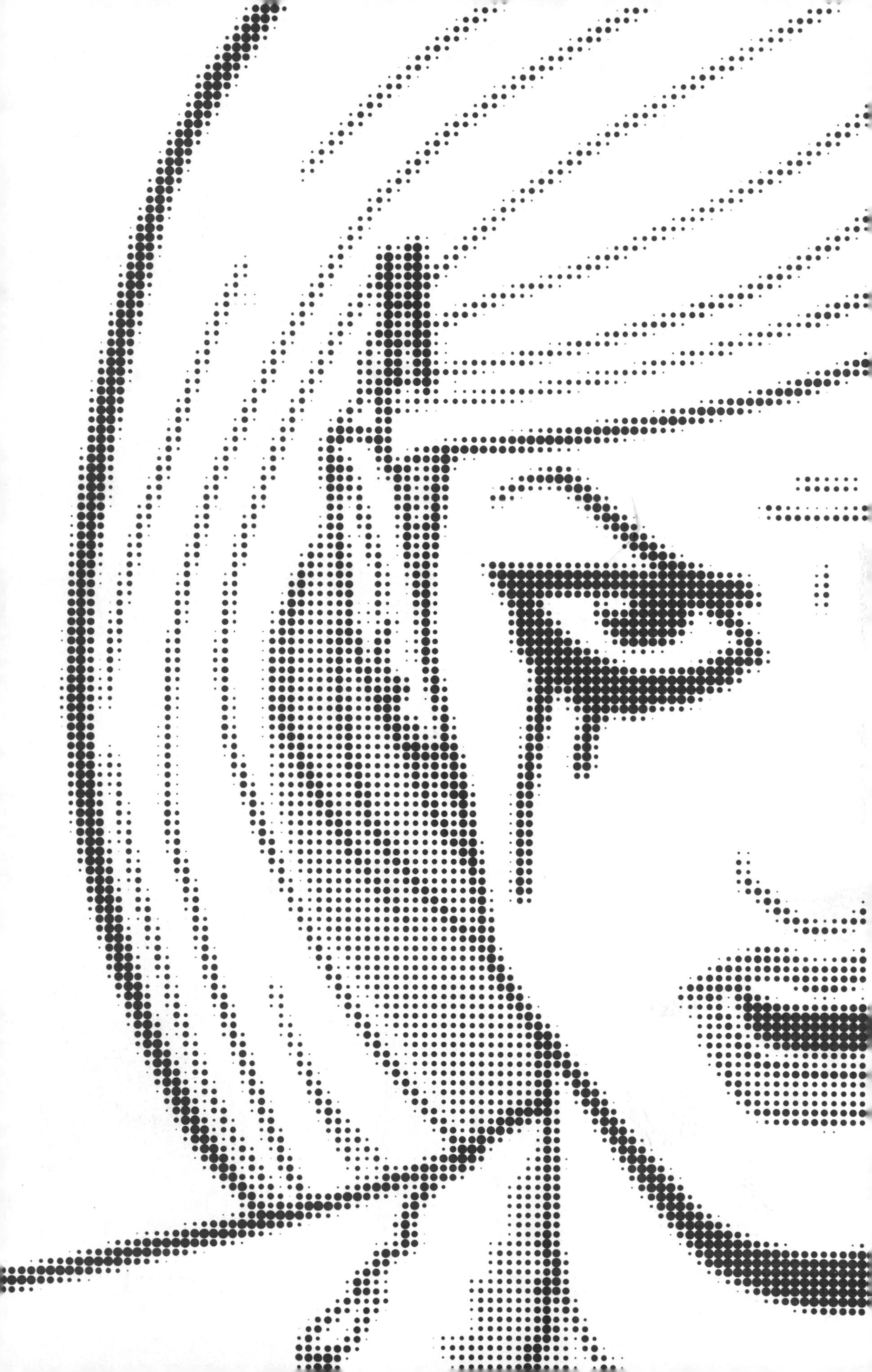

CHAPTER THREE

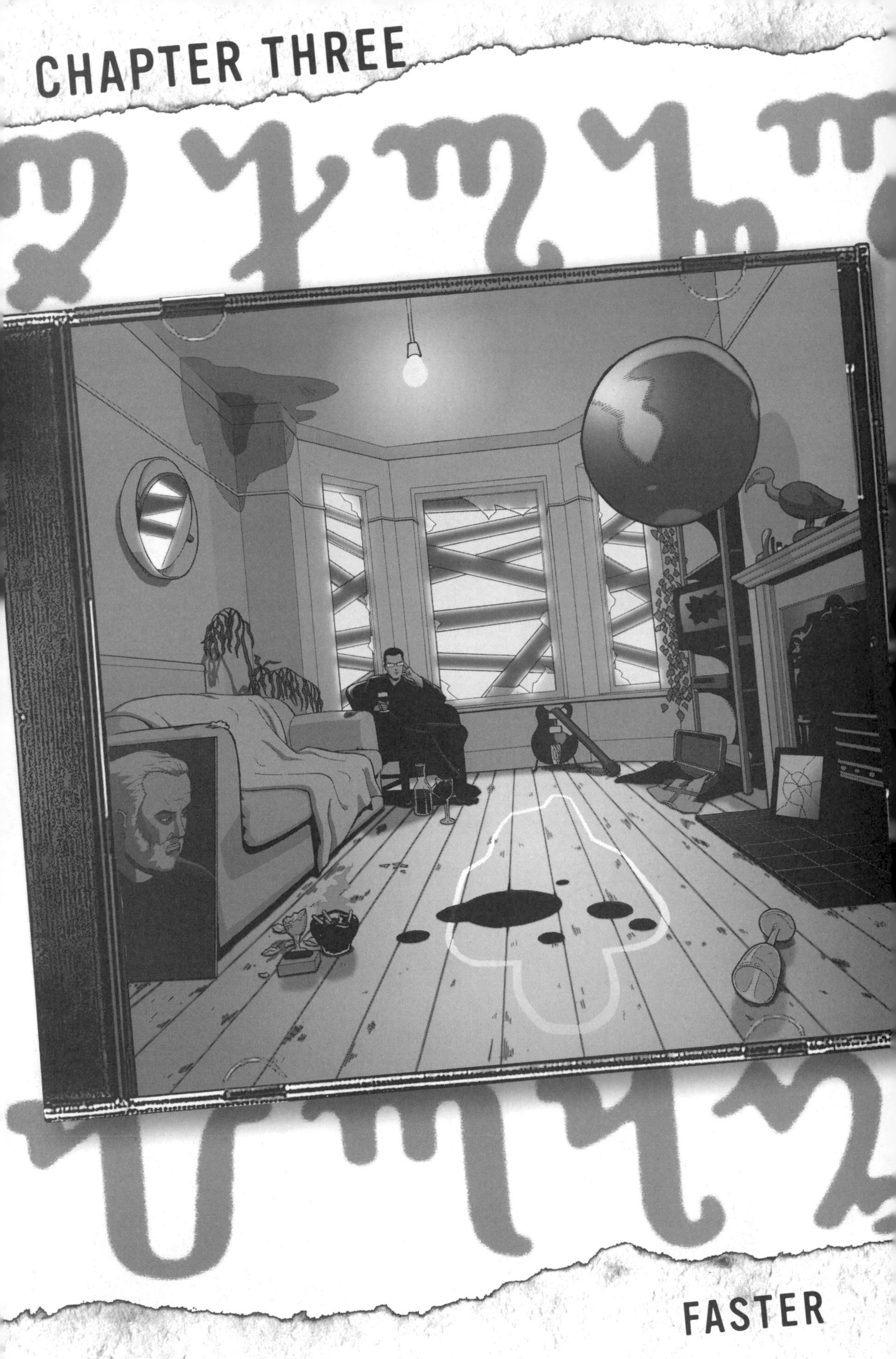

FASTER

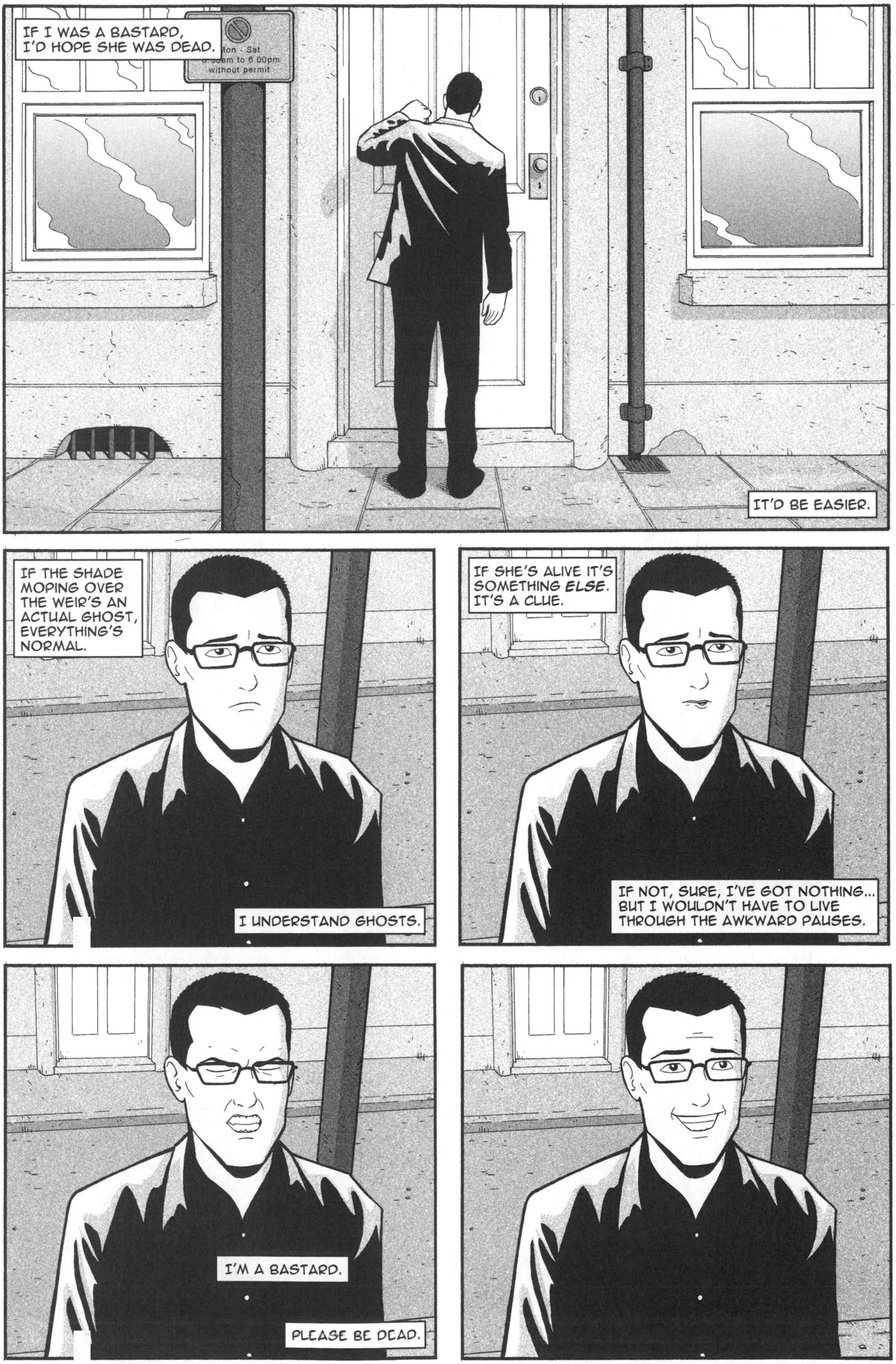
IF I WAS A BASTARD, I'D HOPE SHE WAS DEAD.
IT'D BE EASIER.
IF THE SHADE MOPING OVER THE WEIR'S AN ACTUAL GHOST, EVERYTHING'S NORMAL.
I UNDERSTAND GHOSTS.
IF SHE'S ALIVE IT'S SOMETHING ELSE. IT'S A CLUE.
IF NOT, SURE, I'VE GOT NOTHING... BUT I WOULDN'T HAVE TO LIVE THROUGH THE AWKWARD PAUSES.
I'M A BASTARD.
PLEASE BE DEAD.

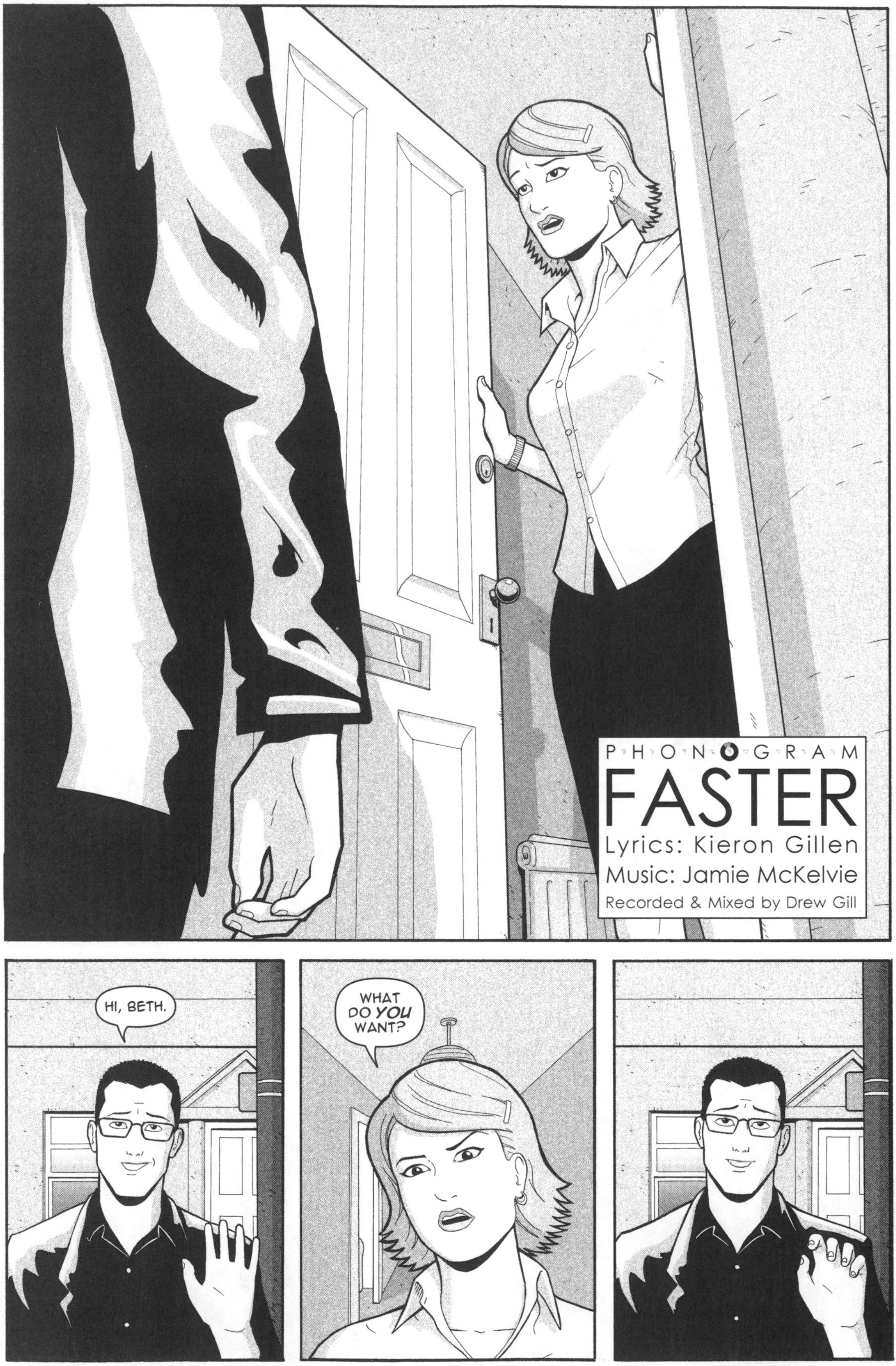
P H O N O G R A M
FASTER
Lyrics: Kieron Gillen
Music: Jamie McKelvie
Recorded & Mixed by Drew Gill
HI, BETH.
WHAT DO YOU WANT?

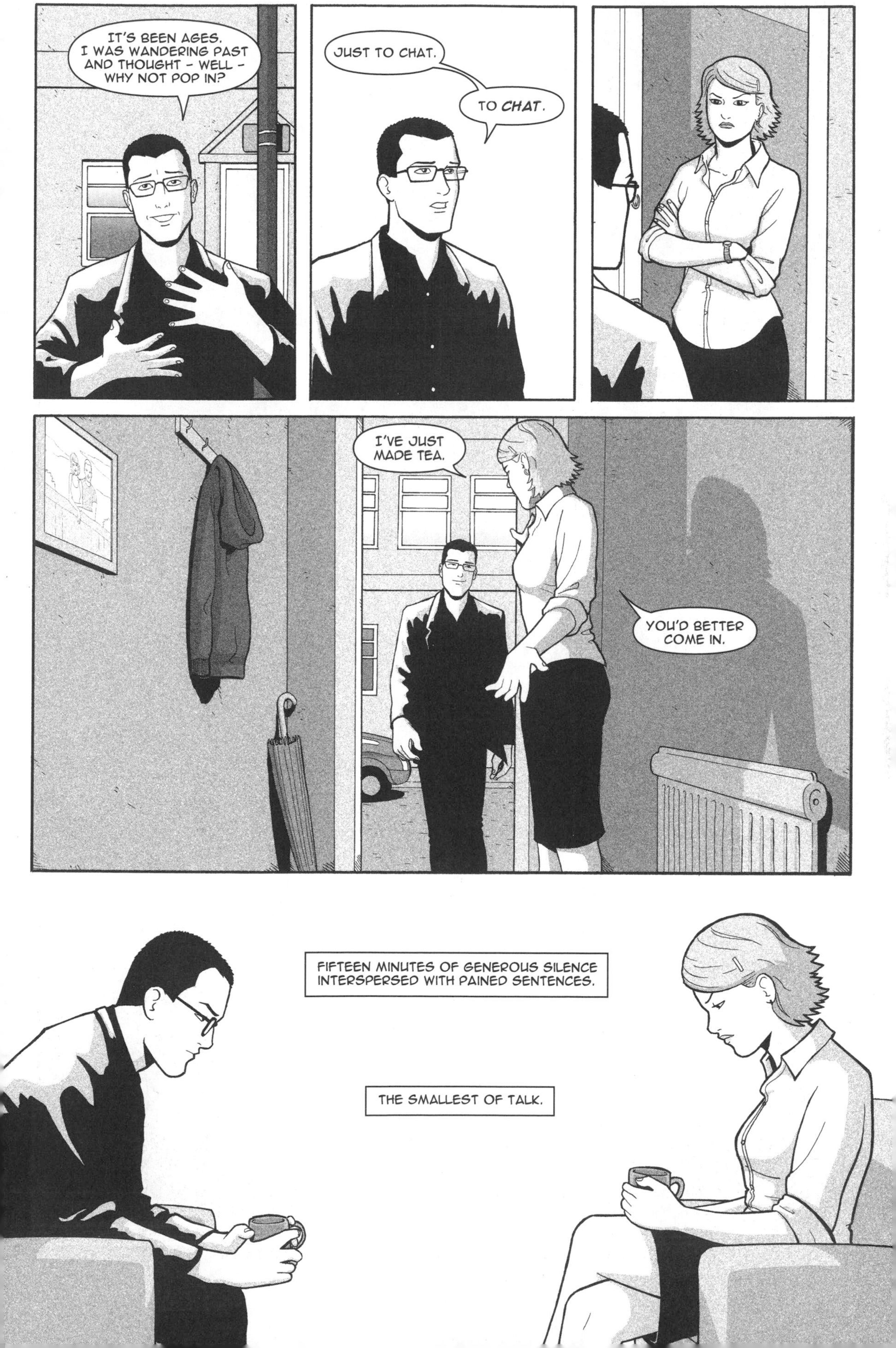
IT'S BEEN AGES. I WAS WANDERING PAST AND THOUGHT - WELL - WHY NOT POP IN?
JUST TO CHAT.
TO CHAT.
I'VE JUST MADE TEA.
YOU'D BETTER COME IN.
FIFTEEN MINUTES OF GENEROUS SILENCE INTERSPERSED WITH PAINED SENTENCES.
THE SMALLEST OF TALK.

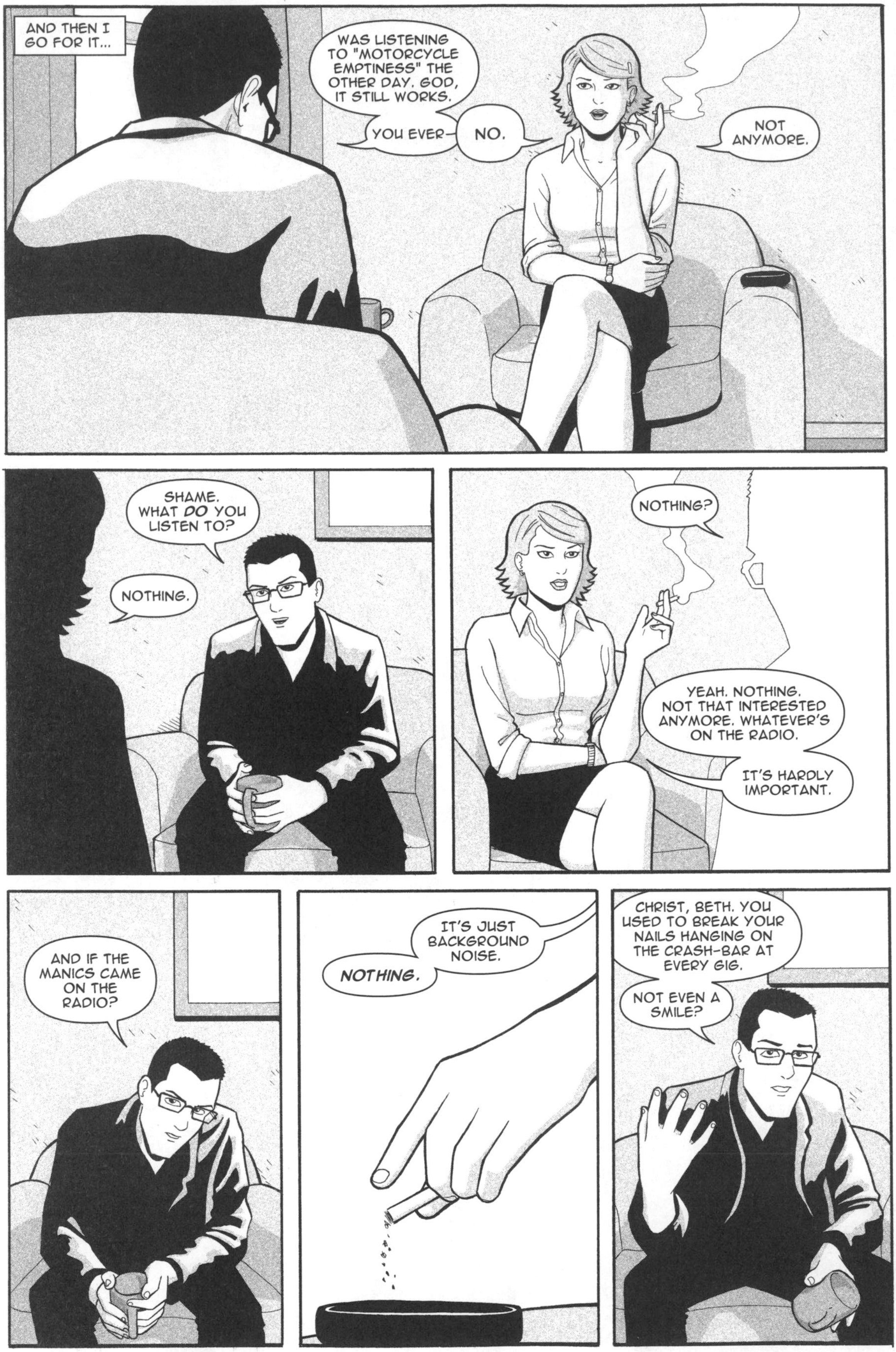
AND THEN I GO FOR IT...
WAS LISTENING TO "MOTORCYCLE EMPTINESS" THE OTHER DAY. GOD, IT STILL WORKS.
YOU EVER-
NO.
NOT ANYMORE.
SHAME. WHAT *DO* YOU LISTEN TO?
NOTHING.
NOTHING?
YEAH. NOTHING. NOT THAT INTERESTED ANYMORE. WHATEVER'S ON THE RADIO.
IT'S HARDLY IMPORTANT.
AND IF THE MANICS CAME ON THE RADIO?
IT'S JUST BACKGROUND NOISE.
NOTHING.
CHRIST, BETH. YOU USED TO BREAK YOUR NAILS HANGING ON THE CRASH-BAR AT EVERY GIG.
NOT EVEN A SMILE?

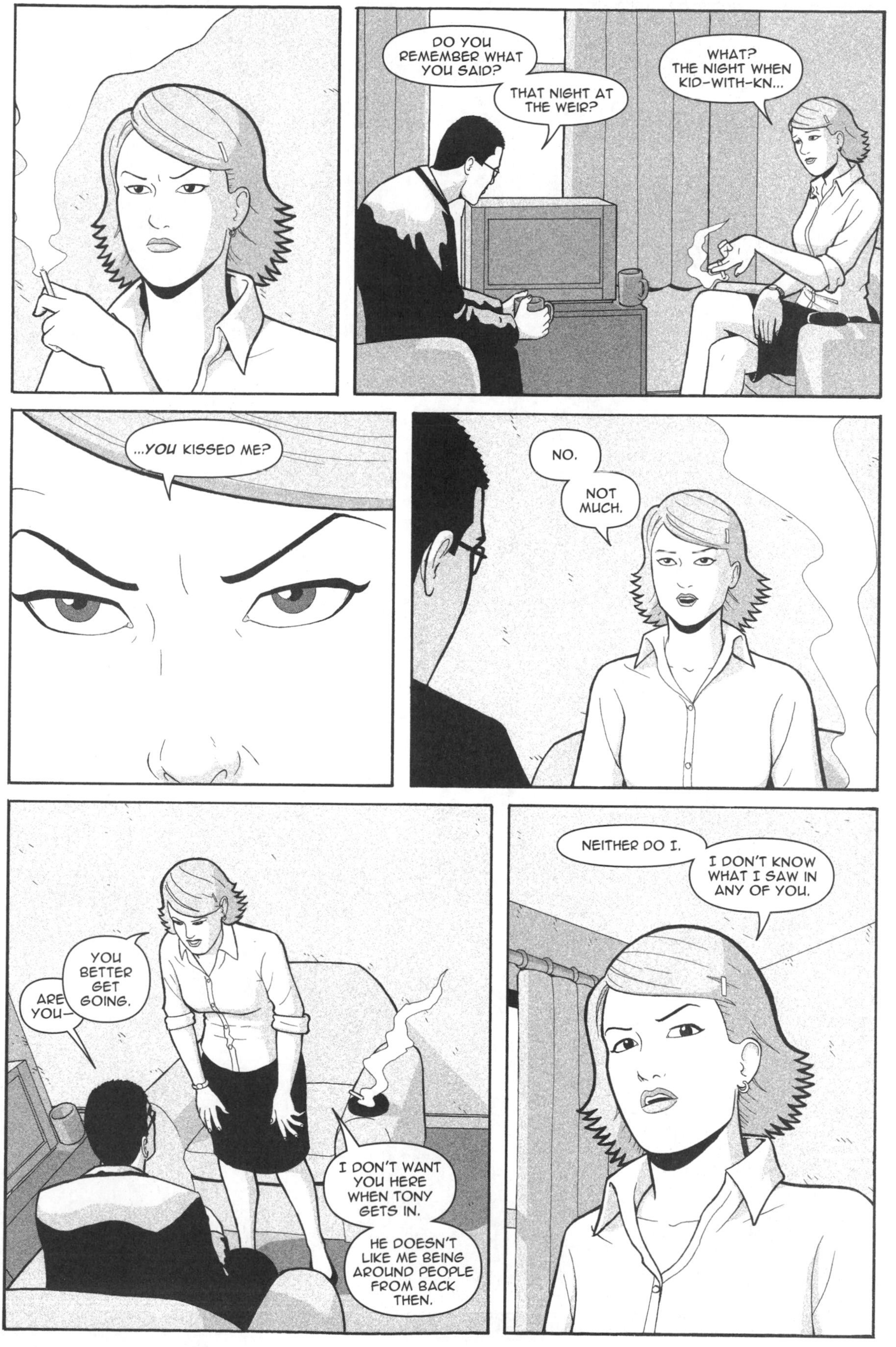
DO YOU REMEMBER WHAT YOU SAID?
THAT NIGHT AT THE WEIR?
WHAT? THE NIGHT WHEN KID-WITH-KN...
...YOU KISSED ME?
NO.
NOT MUCH.
YOU BETTER GET GOING.
ARE YOU—
I DON'T WANT YOU HERE WHEN TONY GETS IN.
HE DOESN'T LIKE ME BEING AROUND PEOPLE FROM BACK THEN.
NEITHER DO I.
I DON'T KNOW WHAT I SAW IN ANY OF YOU.

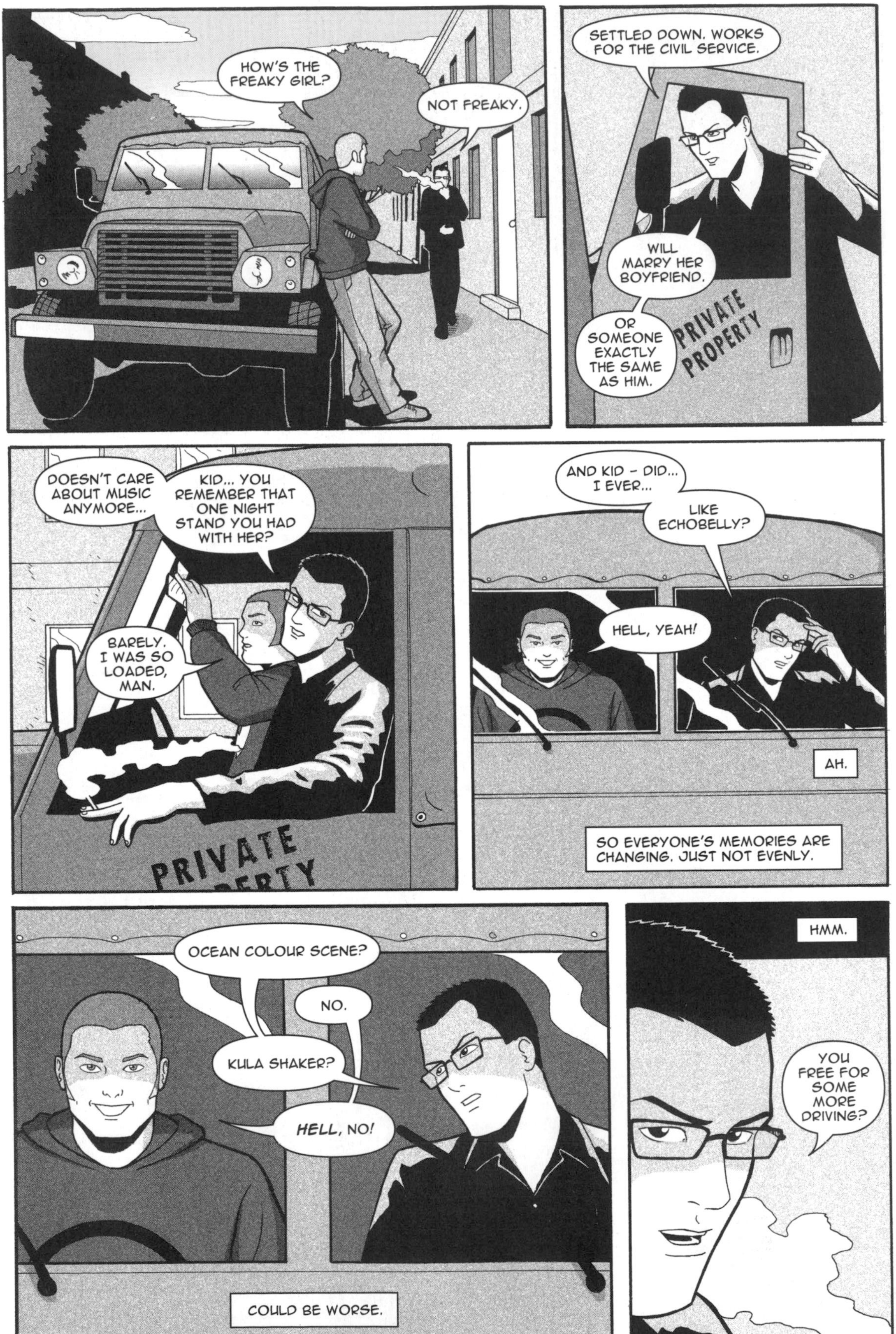
HOW'S THE FREAKY GIRL?
NOT FREAKY.
SETTLED DOWN. WORKS FOR THE CIVIL SERVICE.
WILL MARRY HER BOYFRIEND.
OR SOMEONE EXACTLY THE SAME AS HIM.
PRIVATE PROPERTY
DOESN'T CARE ABOUT MUSIC ANYMORE...
KID... YOU REMEMBER THAT ONE NIGHT STAND YOU HAD WITH HER?
BARELY. I WAS SO LOADED, MAN.
PRIVATE
AND KID – DID... I EVER...
LIKE ECHOBELLY?
HELL, YEAH!
AH.
SO EVERYONE'S MEMORIES ARE CHANGING. JUST NOT EVENLY.
OCEAN COLOUR SCENE?
NO.
KULA SHAKER?
HELL, NO!
COULD BE WORSE.
HMM.
YOU FREE FOR SOME MORE DRIVING?

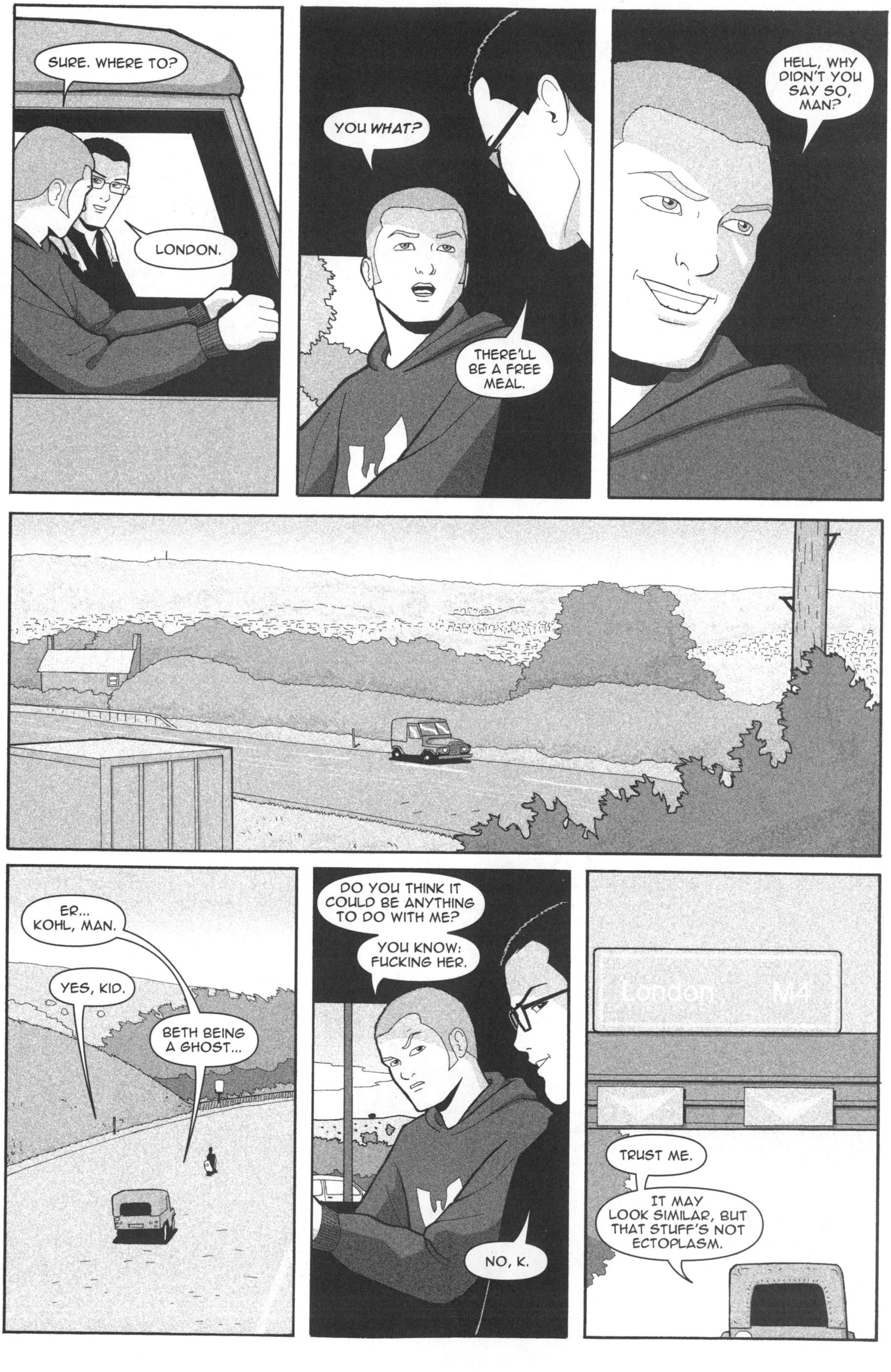
SURE. WHERE TO?
LONDON.
YOU WHAT?
THERE'LL BE A FREE MEAL.
HELL, WHY DIDN'T YOU SAY SO, MAN?
ER... KOHL, MAN.
YES, KID.
BETH BEING A GHOST...
DO YOU THINK IT COULD BE ANYTHING TO DO WITH ME?
YOU KNOW: FUCKING HER.
NO, K.
London
M4
TRUST ME.
IT MAY LOOK SIMILAR, BUT THAT STUFF'S NOT ECTOPLASM.

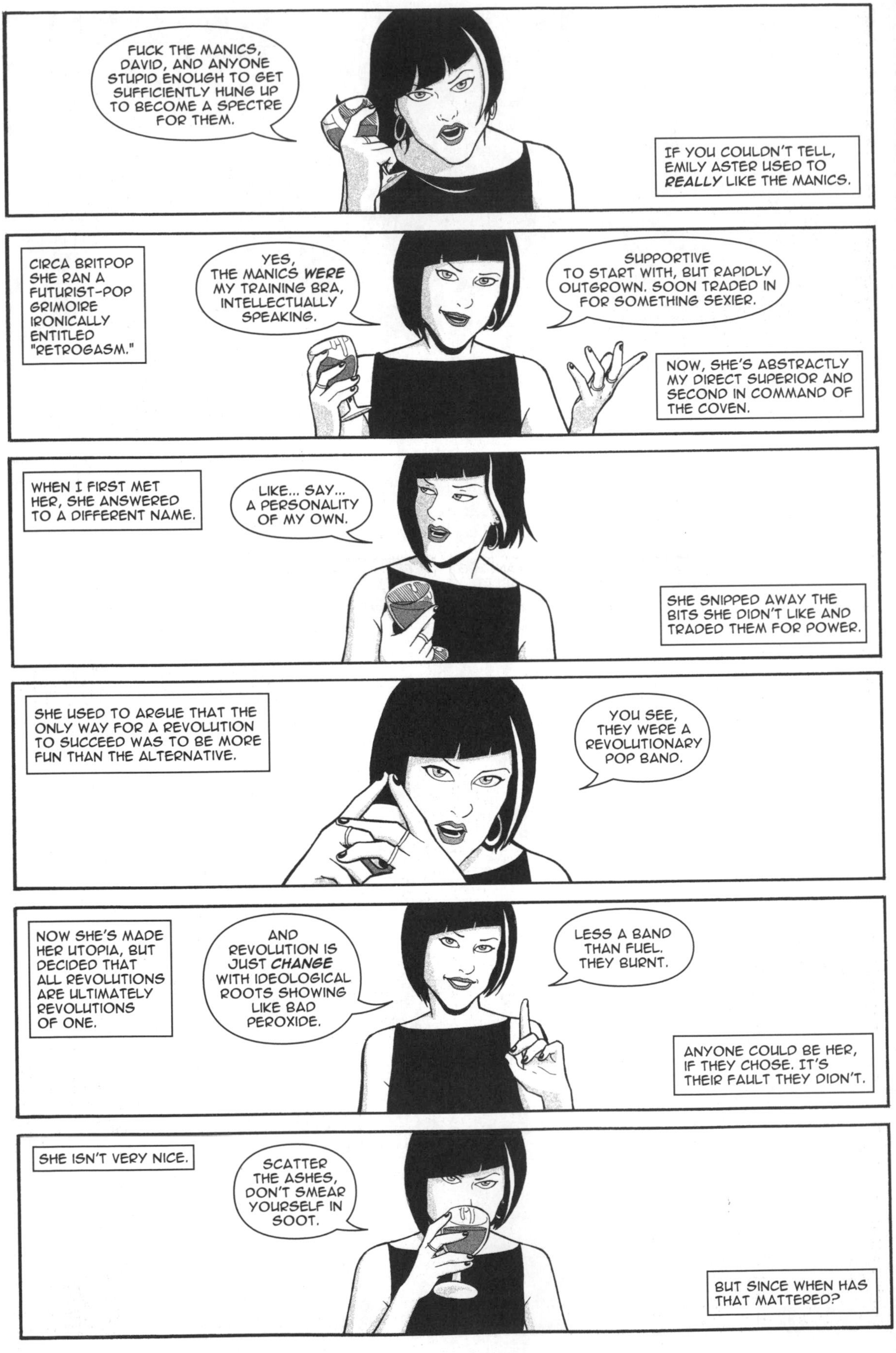
FUCK THE MANICS, DAVID, AND ANYONE STUPID ENOUGH TO GET SUFFICIENTLY HUNG UP TO BECOME A SPECTRE FOR THEM.
IF YOU COULDN'T TELL, EMILY ASTER USED TO *REALLY* LIKE THE MANICS.
CIRCA BRITPOP SHE RAN A FUTURIST-POP GRIMOIRE IRONICALLY ENTITLED "RETROGASM."
YES, THE MANICS *WERE* MY TRAINING BRA, INTELLECTUALLY SPEAKING.
SUPPORTIVE TO START WITH, BUT RAPIDLY OUTGROWN. SOON TRADED IN FOR SOMETHING SEXIER.
NOW, SHE'S ABSTRACTLY MY DIRECT SUPERIOR AND SECOND IN COMMAND OF THE COVEN.
WHEN I FIRST MET HER, SHE ANSWERED TO A DIFFERENT NAME.
LIKE... SAY... A PERSONALITY OF MY OWN.
SHE SNIPPED AWAY THE BITS SHE DIDN'T LIKE AND TRADED THEM FOR POWER.
SHE USED TO ARGUE THAT THE ONLY WAY FOR A REVOLUTION TO SUCCEED WAS TO BE MORE FUN THAN THE ALTERNATIVE.
YOU SEE, THEY WERE A REVOLUTIONARY POP BAND.
NOW SHE'S MADE HER UTOPIA, BUT DECIDED THAT ALL REVOLUTIONS ARE ULTIMATELY REVOLUTIONS OF ONE.
AND REVOLUTION IS JUST *CHANGE* WITH IDEOLOGICAL ROOTS SHOWING LIKE BAD PEROXIDE.
LESS A BAND THAN FUEL. THEY BURNT.
ANYONE COULD BE HER, IF THEY CHOSE. IT'S THEIR FAULT THEY DIDN'T.
SHE ISN'T VERY NICE.
SCATTER THE ASHES, DON'T SMEAR YOURSELF IN SOOT.
BUT SINCE WHEN HAS THAT MATTERED?

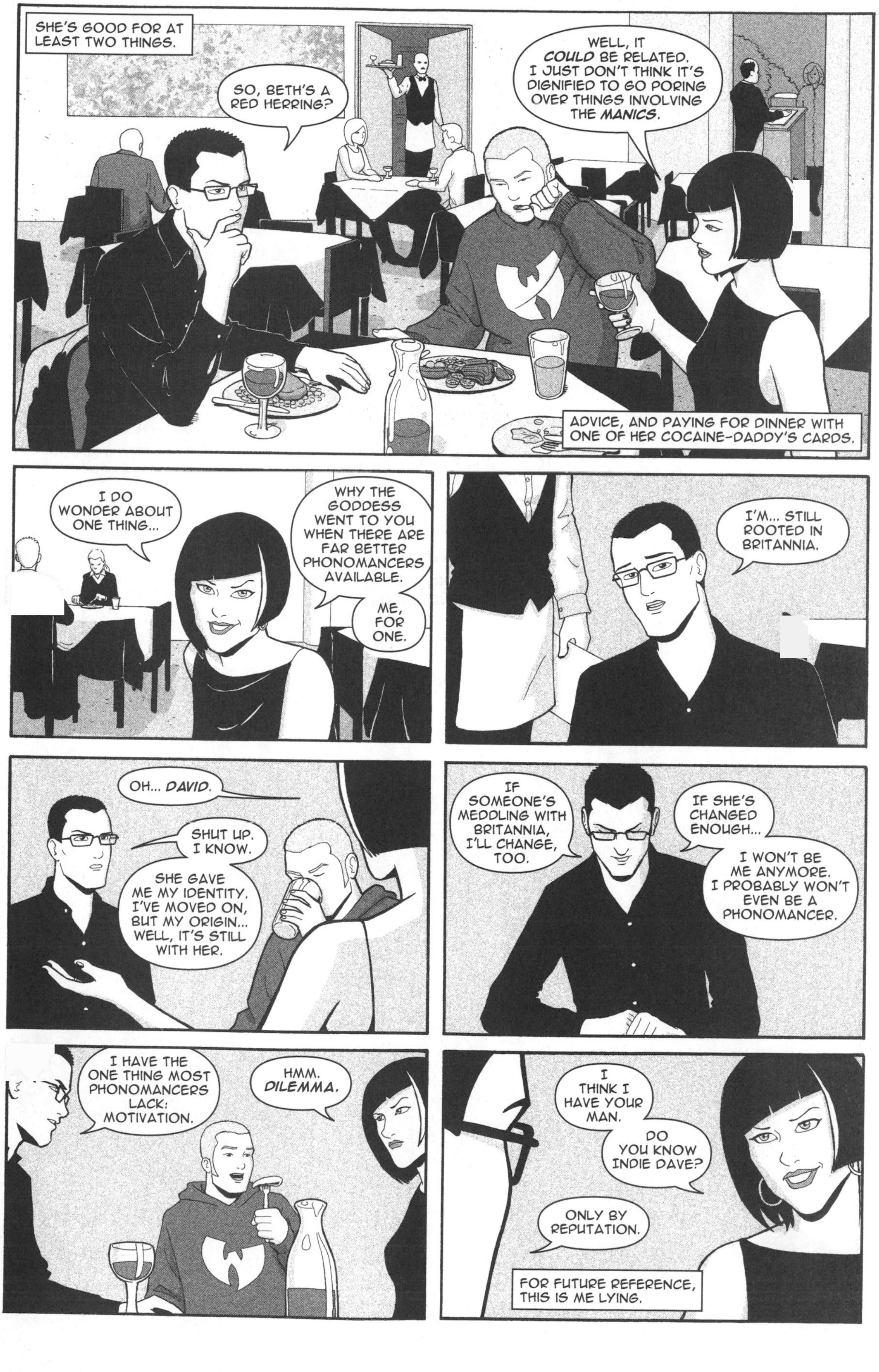
SHE'S GOOD FOR AT LEAST TWO THINGS.
SO, BETH'S A RED HERRING?
WELL, IT *COULD* BE RELATED. I JUST DON'T THINK IT'S DIGNIFIED TO GO PORING OVER THINGS INVOLVING THE *MANICS*.
ADVICE, AND PAYING FOR DINNER WITH ONE OF HER COCAINE-DADDY'S CARDS.
I DO WONDER ABOUT ONE THING...
WHY THE GODDESS WENT TO YOU WHEN THERE ARE FAR BETTER PHONOMANCERS AVAILABLE.
ME, FOR ONE.
I'M... STILL ROOTED IN BRITANNIA.
OH... *DAVID*.
SHUT UP. I KNOW.
SHE GAVE ME MY IDENTITY. I'VE MOVED ON, BUT MY ORIGIN... WELL, IT'S STILL WITH HER.
IF SOMEONE'S MEDDLING WITH BRITANNIA, I'LL CHANGE, TOO.
IF SHE'S CHANGED ENOUGH...
I WON'T BE ME ANYMORE. I PROBABLY WON'T EVEN BE A PHONOMANCER.
I HAVE THE ONE THING MOST PHONOMANCERS LACK: MOTIVATION.
HMM. *DILEMMA.*
I THINK I HAVE YOUR MAN.
DO YOU KNOW INDIE DAVE?
ONLY BY REPUTATION.
FOR FUTURE REFERENCE, THIS IS ME LYING.

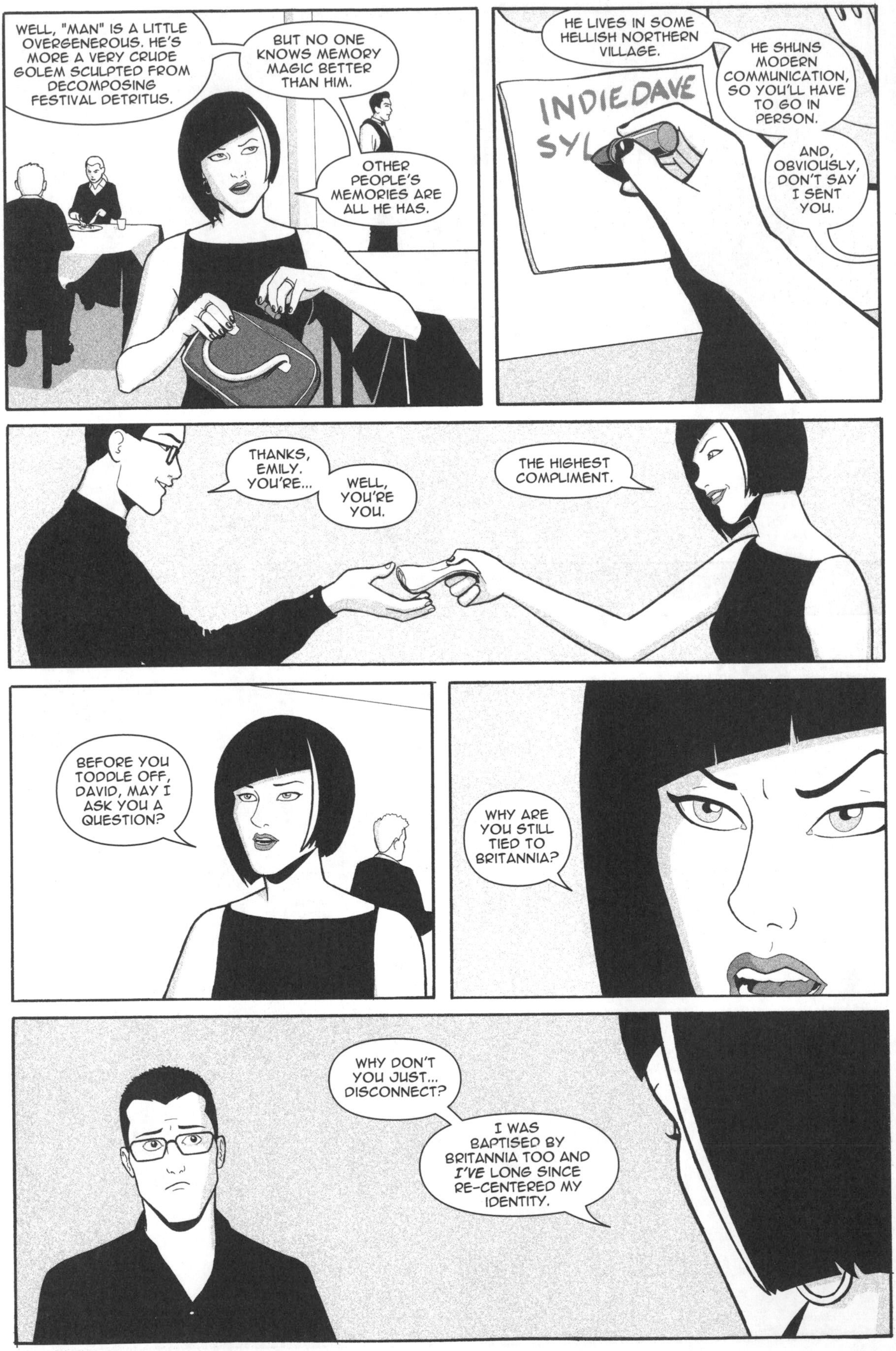
WELL, "MAN" IS A LITTLE OVERGENEROUS. HE'S MORE A VERY CRUDE GOLEM SCULPTED FROM DECOMPOSING FESTIVAL DETRITUS.
BUT NO ONE KNOWS MEMORY MAGIC BETTER THAN HIM.
OTHER PEOPLE'S MEMORIES ARE ALL HE HAS.
HE LIVES IN SOME HELLISH NORTHERN VILLAGE.
INDIE DAVE
SYL
HE SHUNS MODERN COMMUNICATION, SO YOU'LL HAVE TO GO IN PERSON.
AND, OBVIOUSLY, DON'T SAY I SENT YOU.
THANKS, EMILY. YOU'RE...
WELL, YOU'RE YOU.
THE HIGHEST COMPLIMENT.
BEFORE YOU TODDLE OFF, DAVID, MAY I ASK YOU A QUESTION?
WHY ARE YOU STILL TIED TO BRITANNIA?
WHY DON'T YOU JUST... DISCONNECT?
I WAS BAPTISED BY BRITANNIA TOO AND *I'VE* LONG SINCE RE-CENTERED MY IDENTITY.

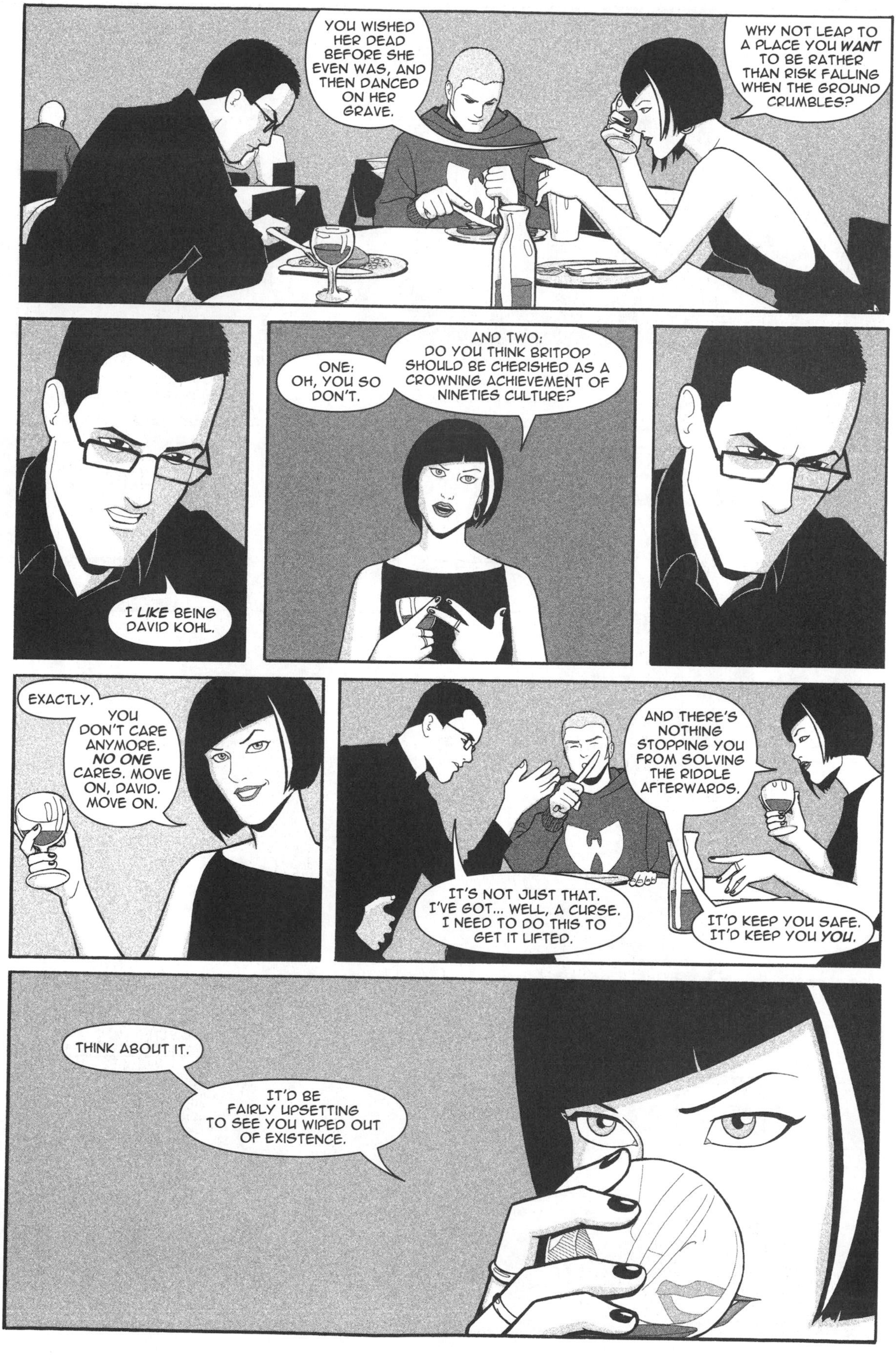
YOU WISHED HER DEAD BEFORE SHE EVEN WAS, AND THEN DANCED ON HER GRAVE.
WHY NOT LEAP TO A PLACE YOU WANT TO BE RATHER THAN RISK FALLING WHEN THE GROUND CRUMBLES?
I LIKE BEING DAVID KOHL.
ONE: OH, YOU SO DON'T.
AND TWO: DO YOU THINK BRITPOP SHOULD BE CHERISHED AS A CROWNING ACHIEVEMENT OF NINETIES CULTURE?
EXACTLY.
YOU DON'T CARE ANYMORE. NO ONE CARES. MOVE ON, DAVID. MOVE ON.
IT'S NOT JUST THAT. I'VE GOT... WELL, A CURSE. I NEED TO DO THIS TO GET IT LIFTED.
AND THERE'S NOTHING STOPPING YOU FROM SOLVING THE RIDDLE AFTERWARDS.
IT'D KEEP YOU SAFE. IT'D KEEP YOU YOU.
THINK ABOUT IT.
IT'D BE FAIRLY UPSETTING TO SEE YOU WIPED OUT OF EXISTENCE.

SMYTHE JEWELLERY
108

inadisc

Manetto's

HANDS OFF

I DON'T *KNOW* KNOW INDIE DAVE, BUT WE'VE CONSULTED OCCASIONALLY ON SHARED INTERESTS.

EXPERIMENTAL EXTRADIMENSIONAL PHONOMANTIC RITUALS AND HOW AWESOME KENICKIE WERE. THE USUAL.

BUT ASTER'S JEALOUS ENOUGH TO CARE THAT I'D DO THAT WITHOUT HER KNOWING.

PRIVATE

I.E. PERMISSION.

AND I'M MANIPULATIVE ENOUGH TO PRETEND I HAVEN'T.

AS WE PASS THROUGH BIRMINGHAM, I *THINK* I LIKE SLEEPER'S SECOND ALBUM.

BULLRING

AS WE ENTER YORKSHIRE, I START HUMMING SHED SEVEN SONGS TO MYSELF.

IT'S GETTING BAD QUICK.

STILL, NO KULA SHAKER YET.

KOHL, MAN. I DON'T GET INVOLVED IN YOUR SHIT BUT... WHAT IS THIS ABOUT?

IT'S ABOUT... WELL, IT'S ABOUT A GIRL.

HEH-HEH-HEH.

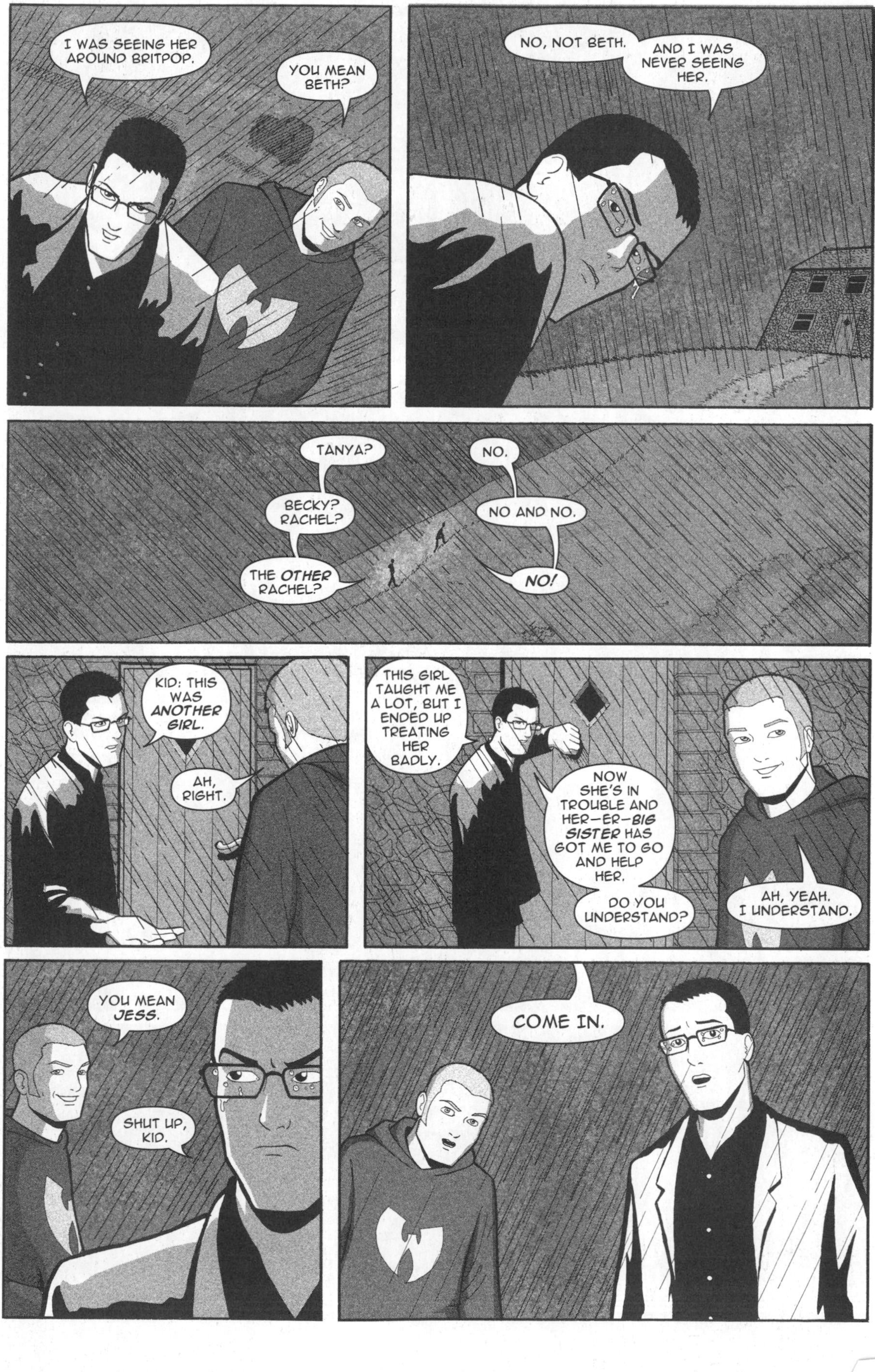

I WAS SEEING HER AROUND BRITPOP.
YOU MEAN BETH?
NO, NOT BETH.
AND I WAS NEVER SEEING HER.
TANYA?
NO.
BECKY? RACHEL?
NO AND NO.
THE *OTHER* RACHEL?
NO!
KID: THIS WAS ***ANOTHER GIRL***.
AH, RIGHT.
THIS GIRL TAUGHT ME A LOT, BUT I ENDED UP TREATING HER BADLY.
NOW SHE'S IN TROUBLE AND HER—ER—***BIG SISTER*** HAS GOT ME TO GO AND HELP HER.
DO YOU UNDERSTAND?
AH, YEAH. I UNDERSTAND.
YOU MEAN ***JESS***.
SHUT UP, KID.
COME IN.

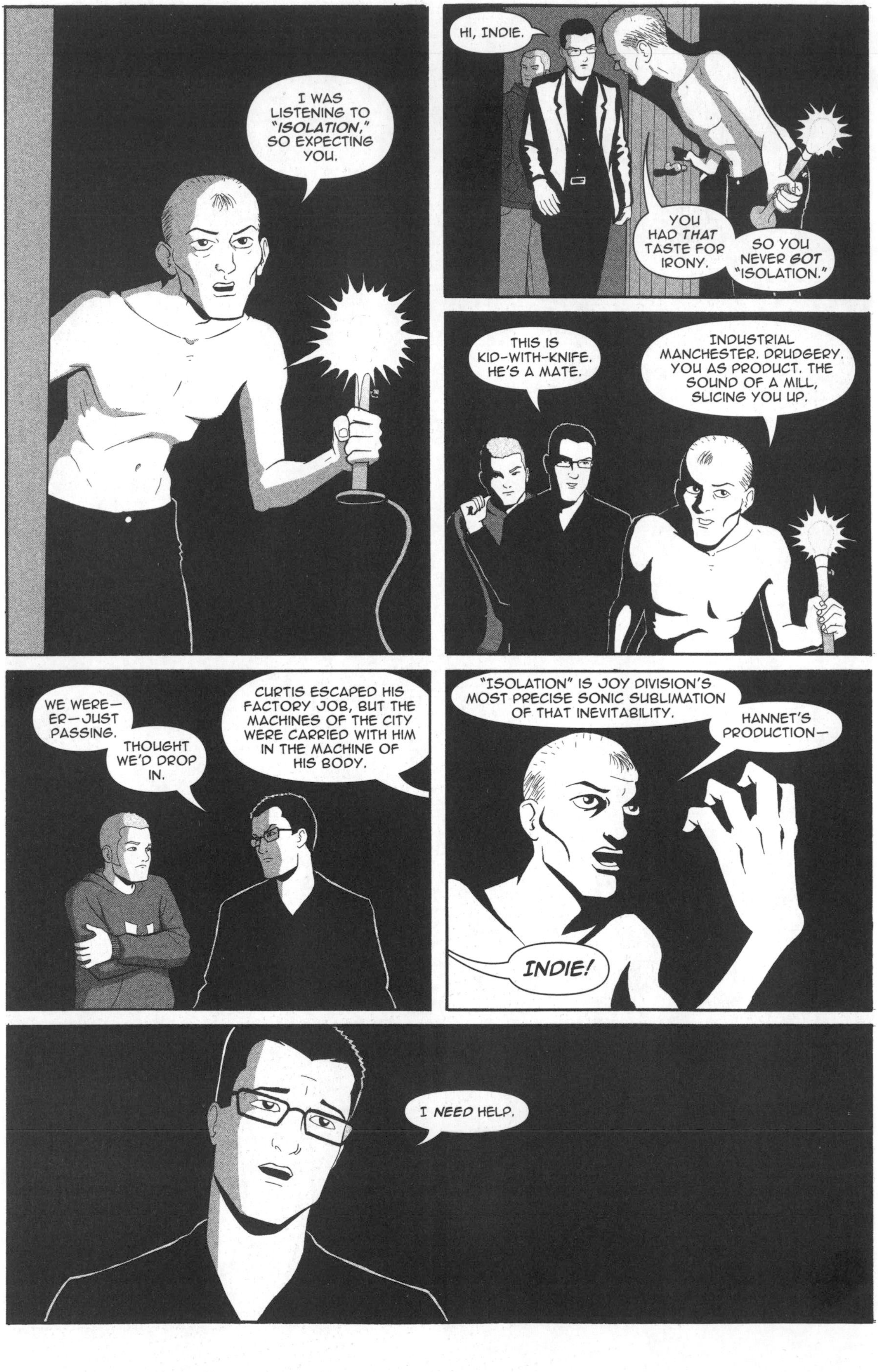
I WAS LISTENING TO "ISOLATION," SO EXPECTING YOU.
HI, INDIE.
YOU HAD THAT TASTE FOR IRONY.
SO YOU NEVER GOT "ISOLATION."
THIS IS KID-WITH-KNIFE. HE'S A MATE.
INDUSTRIAL MANCHESTER. DRUDGERY. YOU AS PRODUCT. THE SOUND OF A MILL, SLICING YOU UP.
WE WERE— ER—JUST PASSING.
THOUGHT WE'D DROP IN.
CURTIS ESCAPED HIS FACTORY JOB, BUT THE MACHINES OF THE CITY WERE CARRIED WITH HIM IN THE MACHINE OF HIS BODY.
"ISOLATION" IS JOY DIVISION'S MOST PRECISE SONIC SUBLIMATION OF THAT INEVITABILITY.
HANNET'S PRODUCTION—
INDIE!
I NEED HELP.

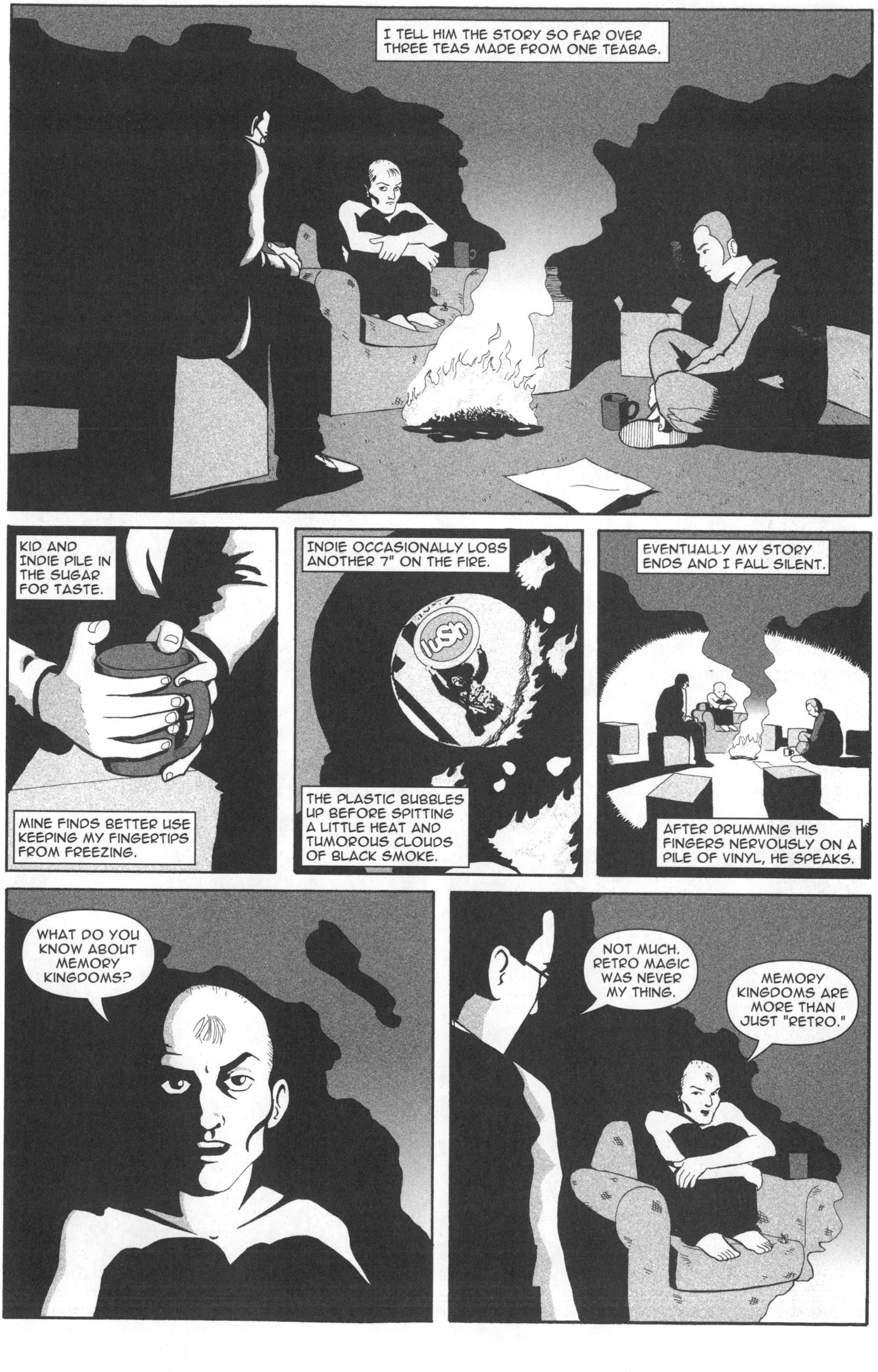
I TELL HIM THE STORY SO FAR OVER THREE TEAS MADE FROM ONE TEABAG.
KID AND INDIE PILE IN THE SUGAR FOR TASTE.
MINE FINDS BETTER USE KEEPING MY FINGERTIPS FROM FREEZING.
INDIE OCCASIONALLY LOBS ANOTHER 7" ON THE FIRE.
lush
THE PLASTIC BUBBLES UP BEFORE SPITTING A LITTLE HEAT AND TUMOROUS CLOUDS OF BLACK SMOKE.
EVENTUALLY MY STORY ENDS AND I FALL SILENT.
AFTER DRUMMING HIS FINGERS NERVOUSLY ON A PILE OF VINYL, HE SPEAKS.
WHAT DO YOU KNOW ABOUT MEMORY KINGDOMS?
NOT MUCH. RETRO MAGIC WAS NEVER MY THING.
MEMORY KINGDOMS ARE MORE THAN JUST "RETRO."

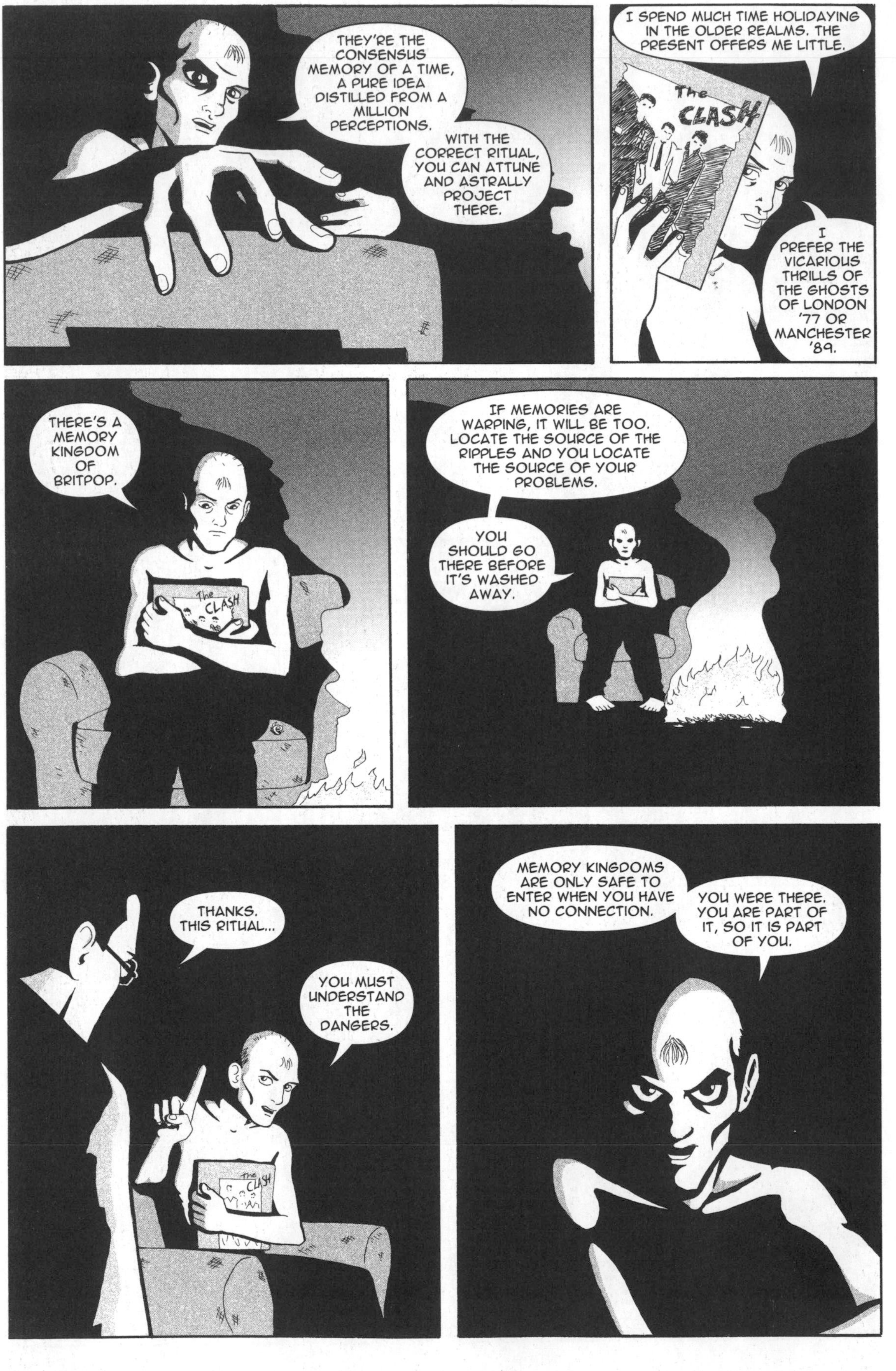
THEY'RE THE CONSENSUS MEMORY OF A TIME, A PURE IDEA DISTILLED FROM A MILLION PERCEPTIONS.
WITH THE CORRECT RITUAL, YOU CAN ATTUNE AND ASTRALLY PROJECT THERE.
I SPEND MUCH TIME HOLIDAYING IN THE OLDER REALMS. THE PRESENT OFFERS ME LITTLE.
The CLASH
I PREFER THE VICARIOUS THRILLS OF THE GHOSTS OF LONDON '77 OR MANCHESTER '89.
THERE'S A MEMORY KINGDOM OF BRITPOP.
The CLASH
IF MEMORIES ARE WARPING, IT WILL BE TOO. LOCATE THE SOURCE OF THE RIPPLES AND YOU LOCATE THE SOURCE OF YOUR PROBLEMS.
YOU SHOULD GO THERE BEFORE IT'S WASHED AWAY.
THANKS. THIS RITUAL...
YOU MUST UNDERSTAND THE DANGERS.
The CLASH
MEMORY KINGDOMS ARE ONLY SAFE TO ENTER WHEN YOU HAVE NO CONNECTION.
YOU WERE THERE. YOU ARE PART OF IT, SO IT IS PART OF YOU.

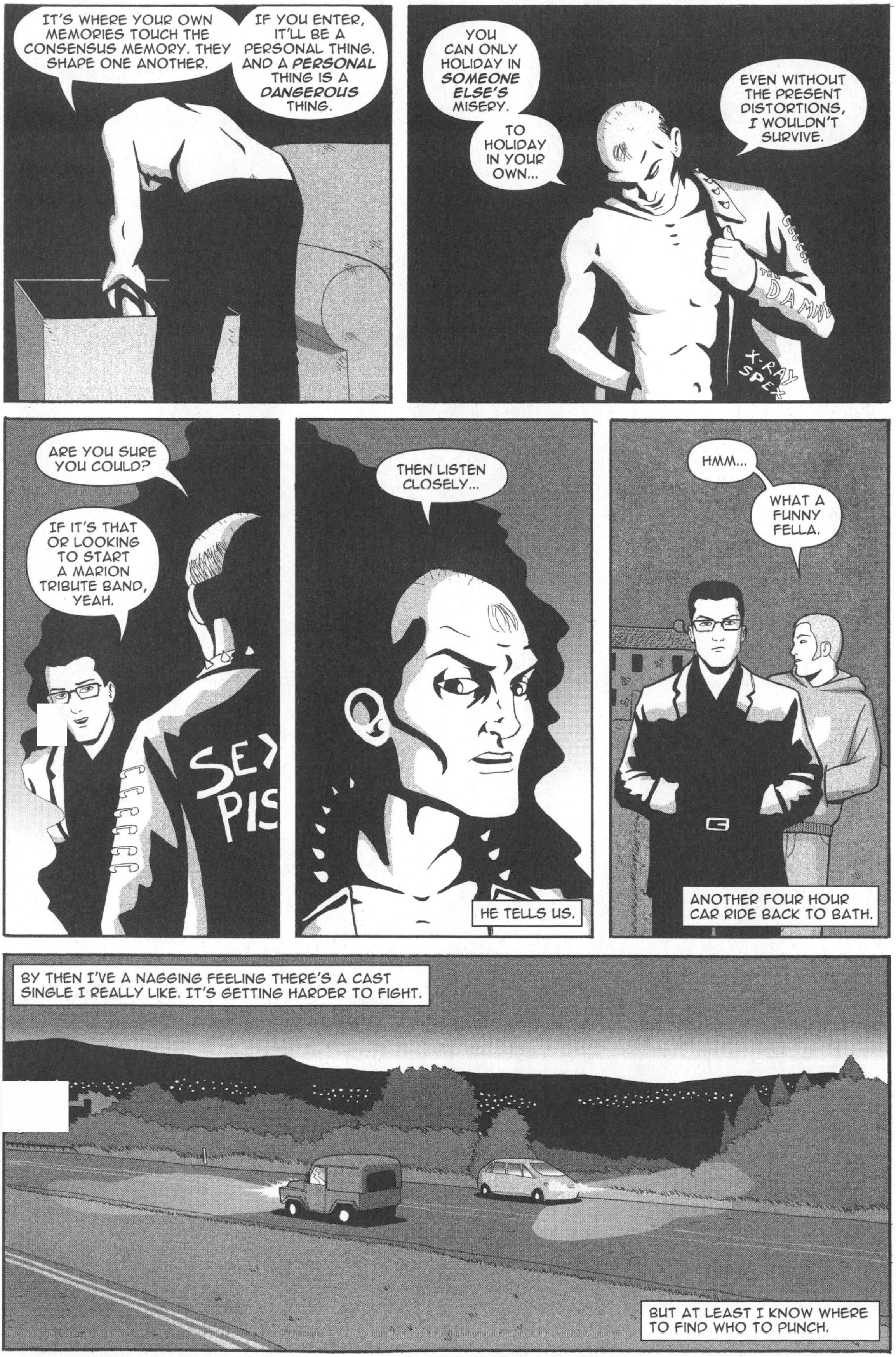
IT'S WHERE YOUR OWN MEMORIES TOUCH THE CONSENSUS MEMORY. THEY SHAPE ONE ANOTHER.
IF YOU ENTER, IT'LL BE A PERSONAL THING. AND A *PERSONAL* THING IS A *DANGEROUS* THING.
YOU CAN ONLY HOLIDAY IN *SOMEONE ELSE'S* MISERY.
TO HOLIDAY IN YOUR OWN...
EVEN WITHOUT THE PRESENT DISTORTIONS, *I* WOULDN'T SURVIVE.
THE DAMNED
X-RAY SPEX
ARE YOU SURE YOU COULD?
IF IT'S THAT OR LOOKING TO START A MARION TRIBUTE BAND, YEAH.
SEX PIS
THEN LISTEN CLOSELY...
HE TELLS US.
HMM...
WHAT A FUNNY FELLA.
ANOTHER FOUR HOUR CAR RIDE BACK TO BATH.
BY THEN I'VE A NAGGING FEELING THERE'S A CAST SINGLE I REALLY LIKE. IT'S GETTING HARDER TO FIGHT.
BUT AT LEAST I KNOW WHERE TO FIND WHO TO PUNCH.

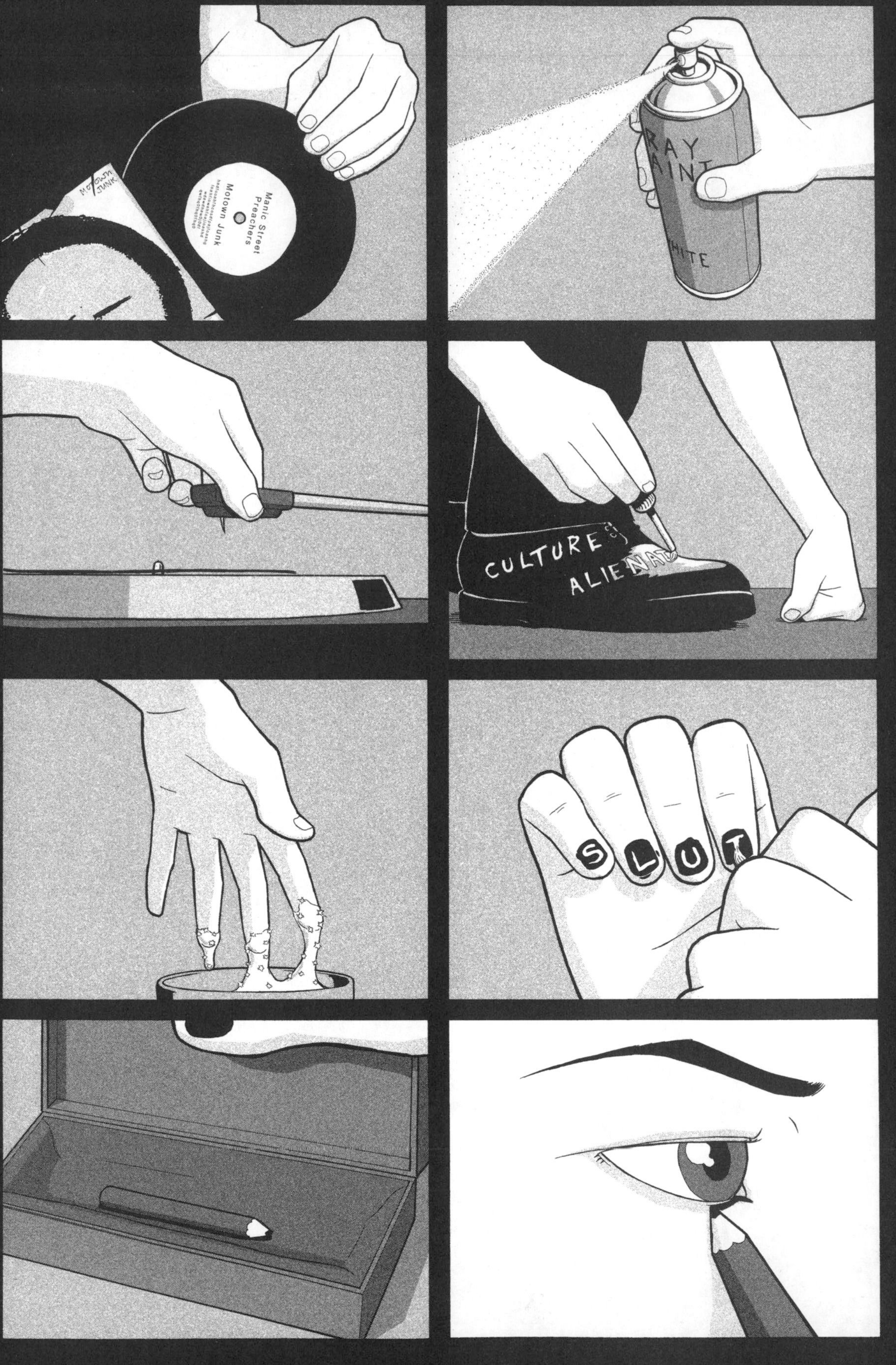
Manic Street Preachers
Motown Junk
MOTOWN JUNK
RAY AINT
HITE
CULTURE ALIENAT
SLUT

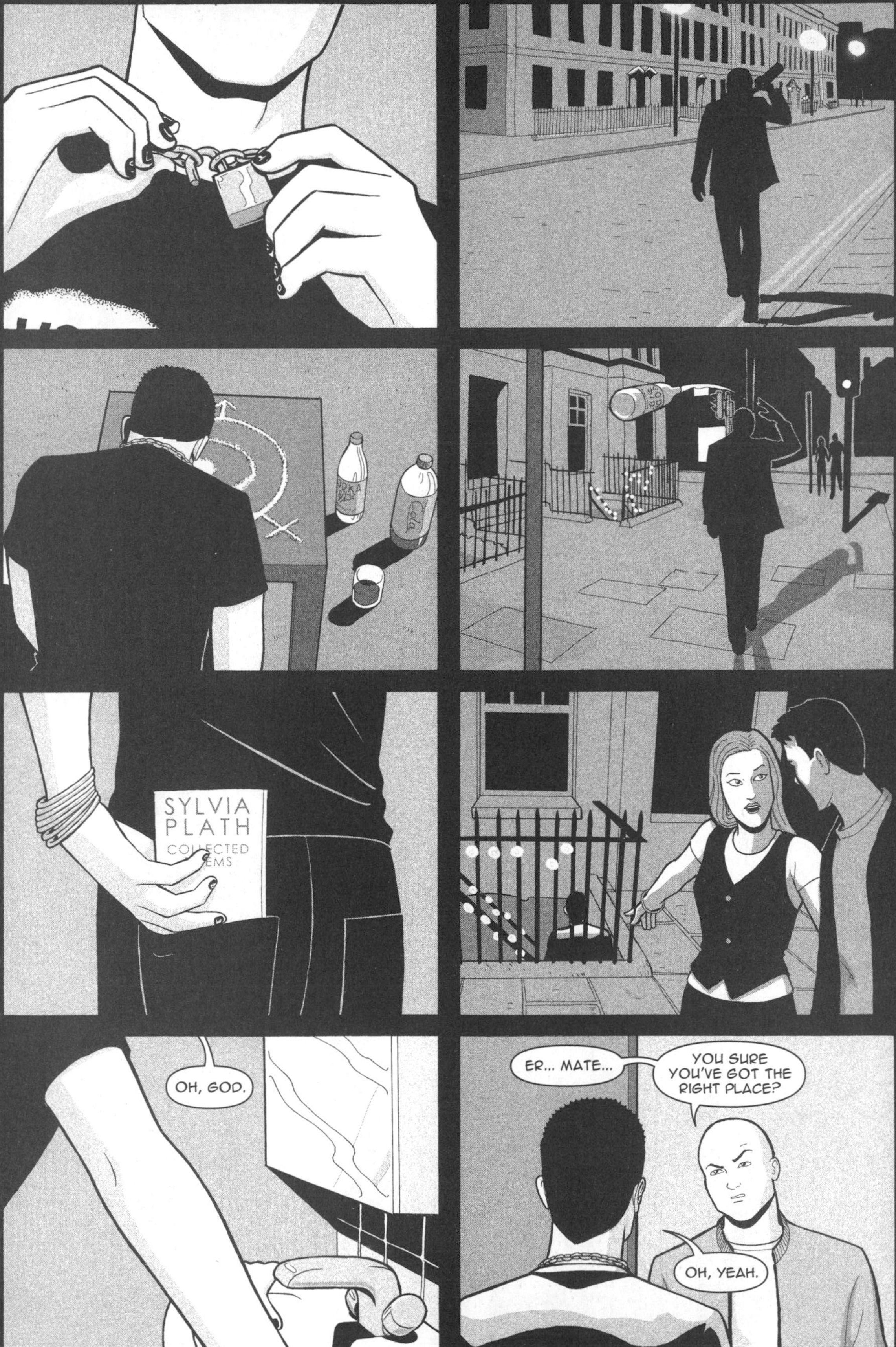
SYLVIA PLATH
COLLECTED
OH, GOD.
ER... MATE...
YOU SURE YOU'VE GOT THE RIGHT PLACE?
OH, YEAH.

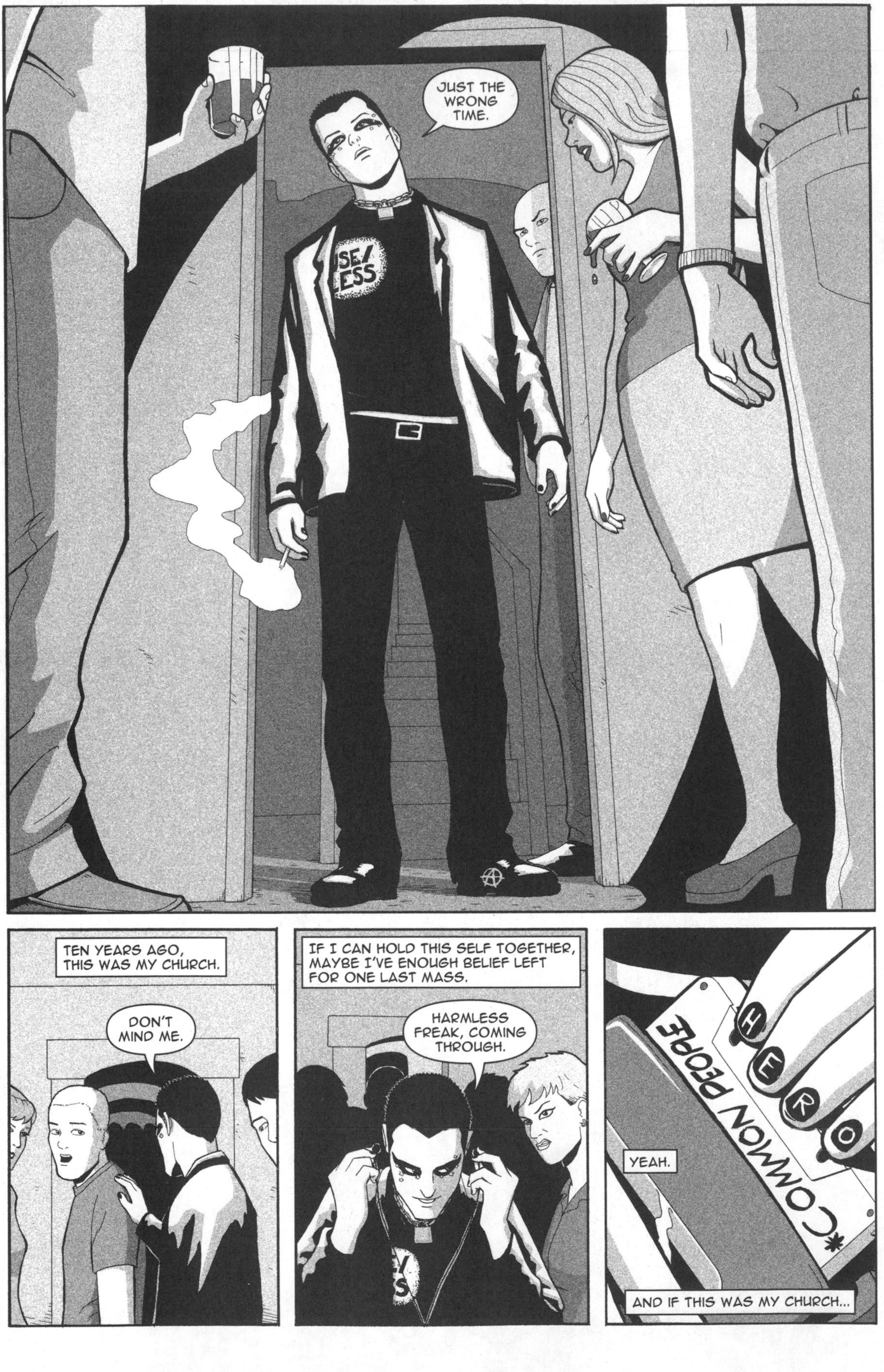
JUST THE WRONG TIME.
USE/LESS
TEN YEARS AGO, THIS WAS MY CHURCH.
DON'T MIND ME.
IF I CAN HOLD THIS SELF TOGETHER, MAYBE I'VE ENOUGH BELIEF LEFT FOR ONE LAST MASS.
HARMLESS FREAK, COMING THROUGH.
HERO
COMMON PEOPLE
YEAH.
AND IF THIS WAS MY CHURCH...

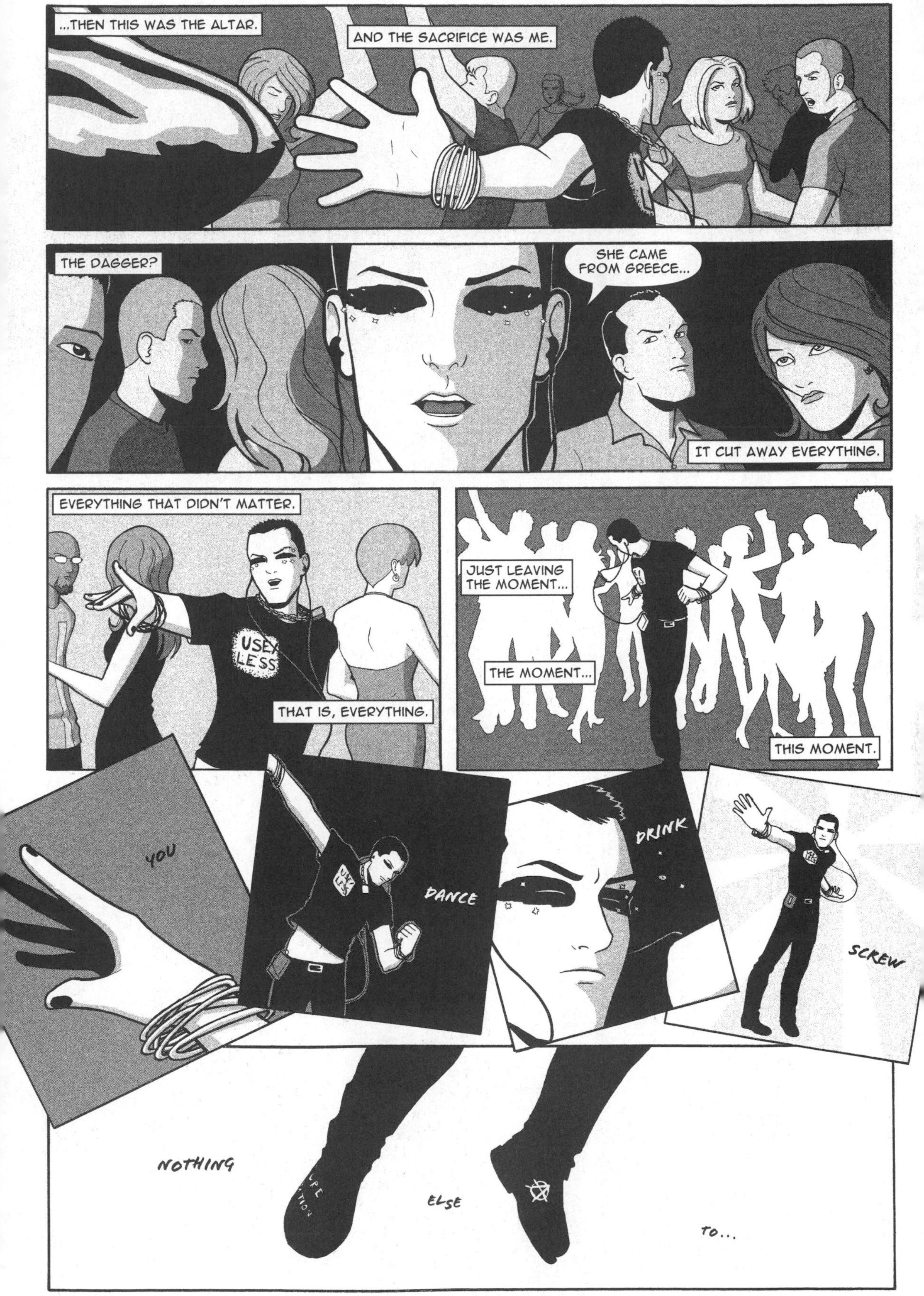
...THEN THIS WAS THE ALTAR.
AND THE SACRIFICE WAS ME.
THE DAGGER?
SHE CAME FROM GREECE...
IT CUT AWAY EVERYTHING.
EVERYTHING THAT DIDN'T MATTER.
USE-LESS
THAT IS, EVERYTHING.
JUST LEAVING THE MOMENT...
THE MOMENT...
THIS MOMENT.
YOU
DANCE
DRINK
SCREW
NOTHING
ELSE
TO...

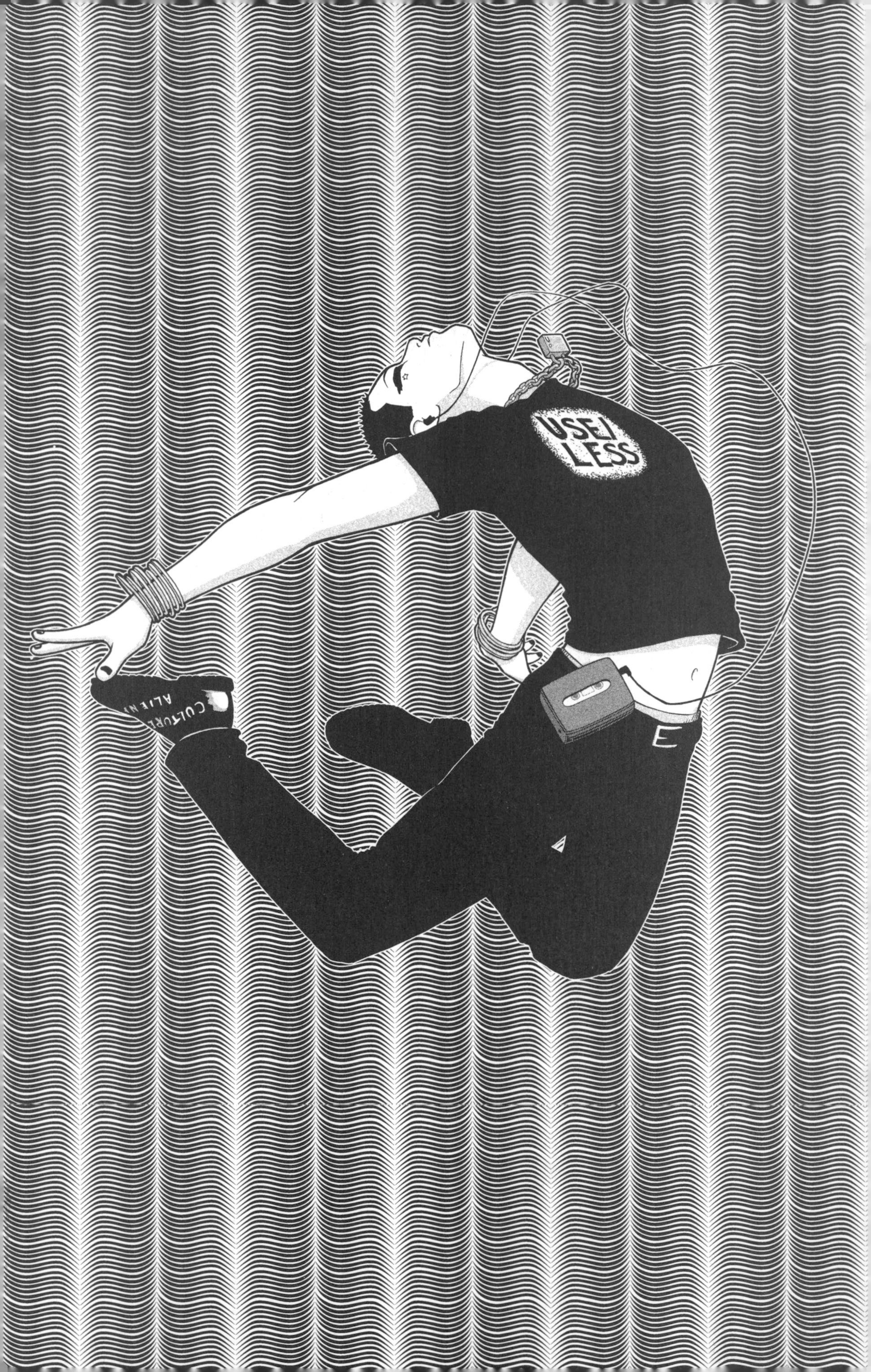
USE
LESS
CULTURE
ALIEN

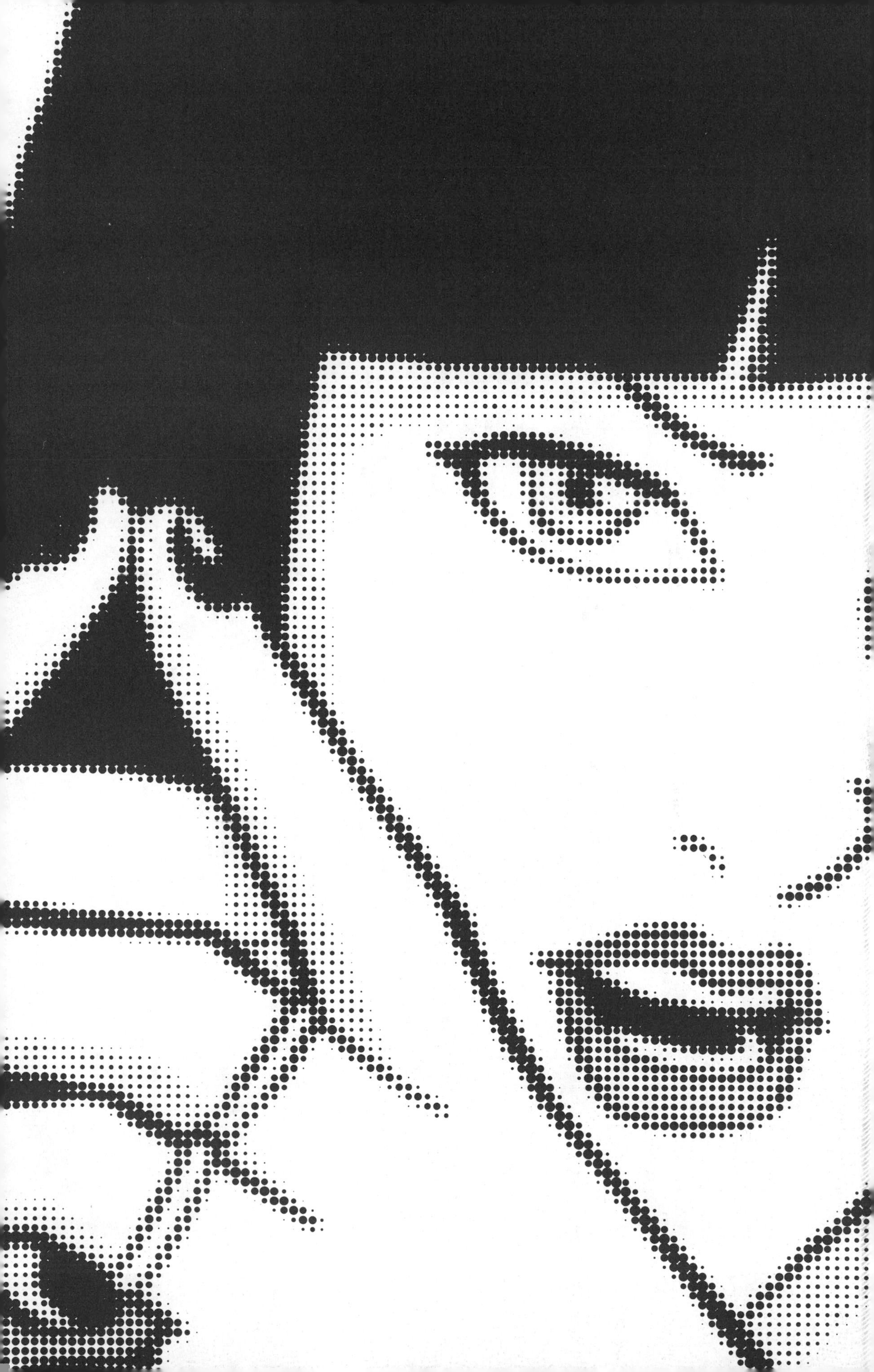

CHAPTER FOUR

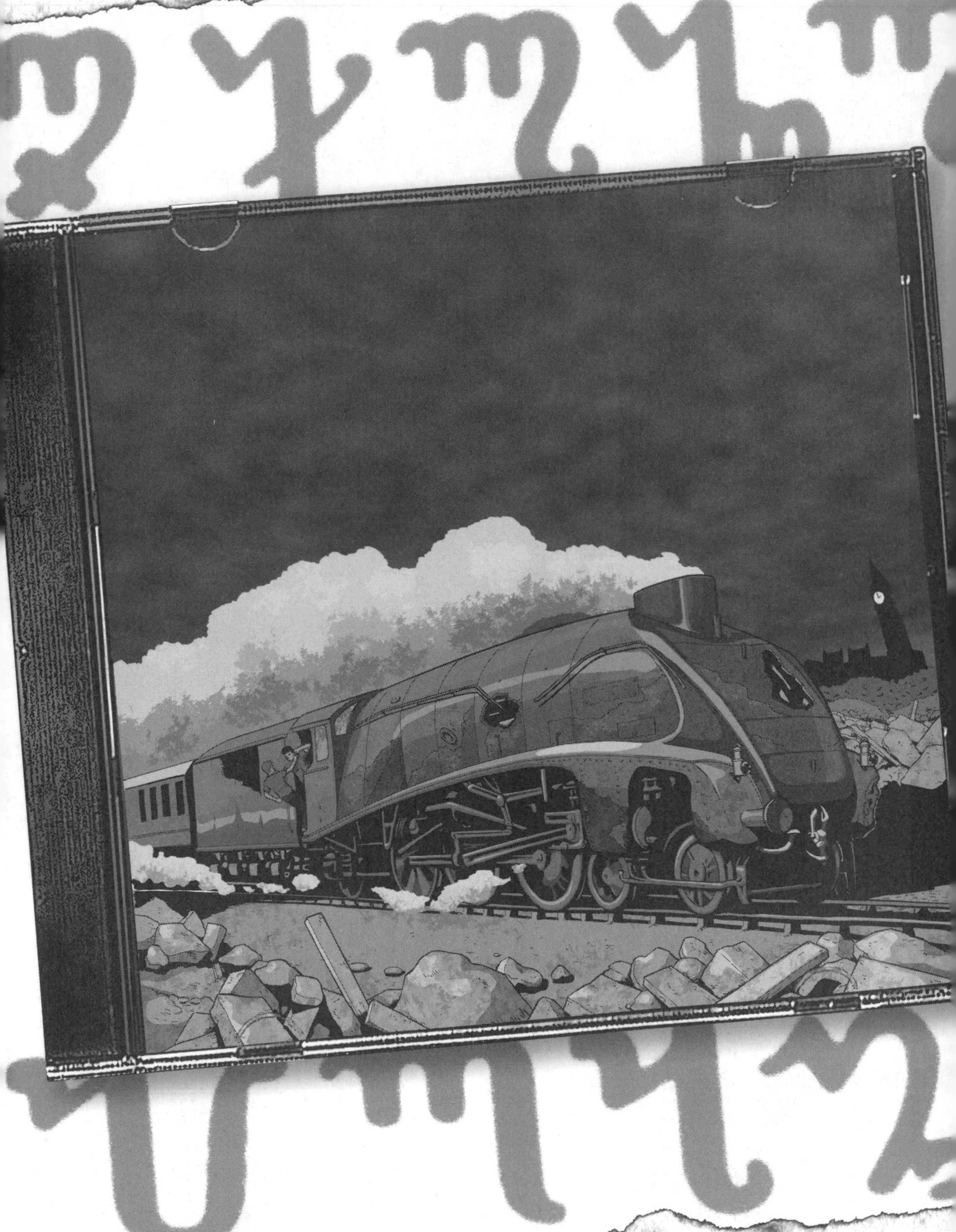

MURDER PARK

AND...

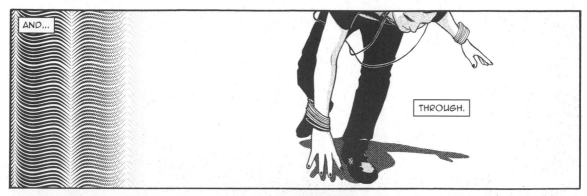

THROUGH.

JUST REMEMBER: THIS ISN'T REAL.

IT'S A MEMORY KINGDOM.

WHATEVER'S REWRITING EVERYONE'S RECOLLECTIONS IS HERE.

YOUR PLAYLIST FOR THE EVENING:

FIND IT.

GET OUT.

I REPEAT: IT'S JUST THE ECHO OF A TIME LONG GONE. IT CAN'T TOUCH YOU.

BECAUSE YOU'RE DAVID KOHL *NOW* NOT DAVID KOHL *THEN*.

HELL, JUST MEMORIES.

CAN'T TOUCH YOU.

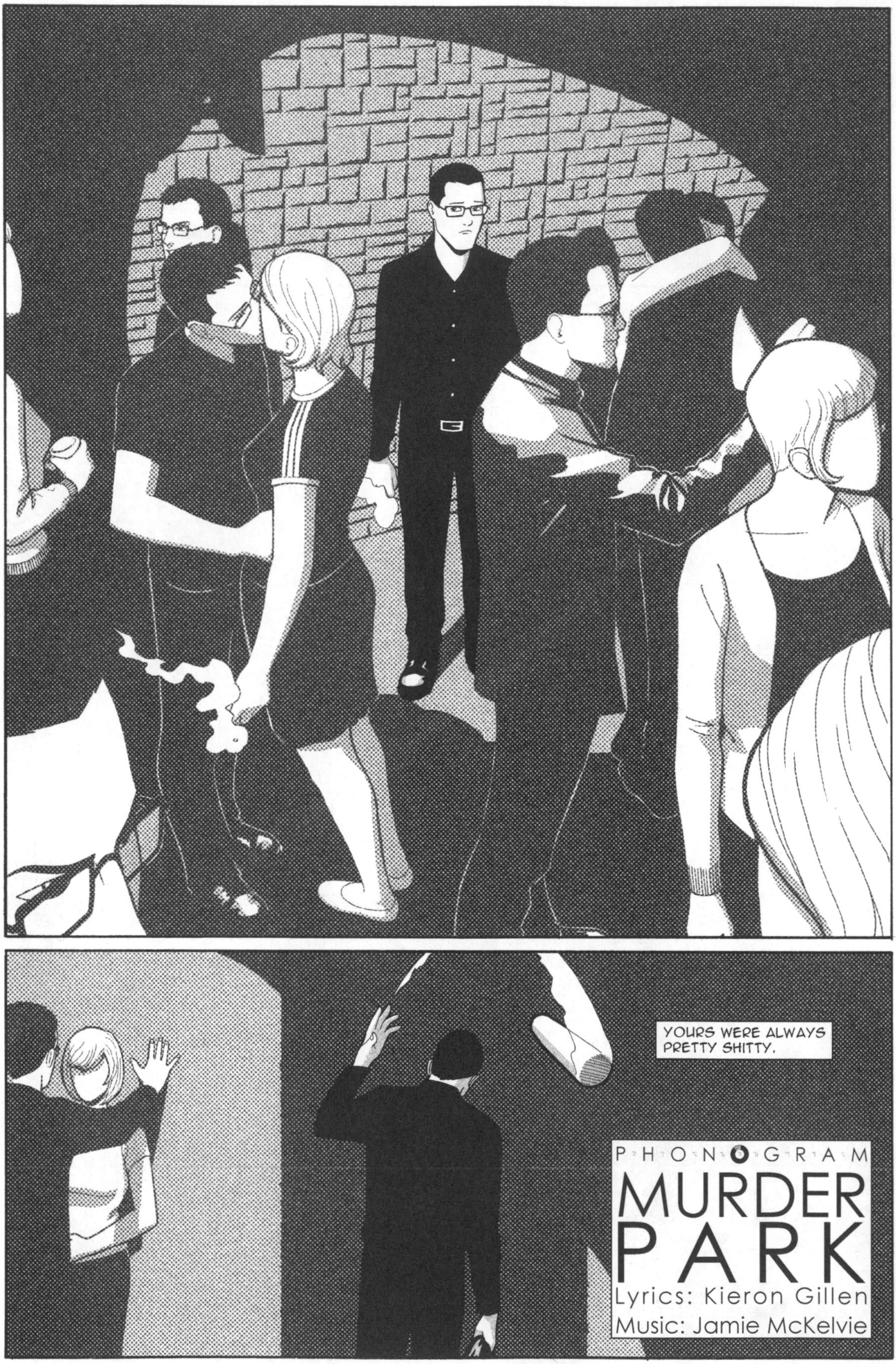
YOURS WERE ALWAYS PRETTY SHITTY.
PHONOGRAM
MURDER PARK
Lyrics: Kieron Gillen
Music: Jamie McKelvie

YOU! HELP ME WITH THIS.

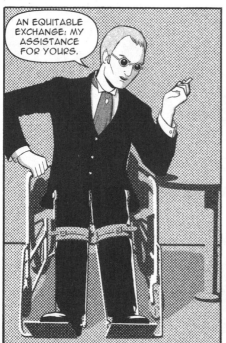

AN EQUITABLE EXCHANGE: MY ASSISTANCE FOR YOURS.

AREN'T YOU...

SHUSH! NO NAMES. JUST FIGURE OUT WHAT I'M MISSING.

AN "I" AND "O".

THAT? THAT'S WHAT I'M MISSING?

HMM.

YOU KNOW, I DON'T THINK I'M ACTUALLY MISSING THAT AT ALL.

HOWEVER, I OWE A DEBT WHICH MUST BE REPAID FORTHWITH. I'LL BE YOUR GUIDE IN THIS TWILIGHT OF ENGLAND'S DREAMING.

BUT WHAT TO SHOW?

The Kingdom falls to
Byzantine days.

'Tis Long since
Britannia return'd.

Prophecy fulfilled!
Fulfilled in Glory!

King And Regent
Crown'd He whom
Goddess awoke.

Founds his New
Camelot in this, their
New Jerusalem.

Wins a Queen of
highest standing
from rivals' arms.

Assembles She living
miracles from limbs
long dead.

Assembles He a court
of e'er growing glory.

The harvest of glory
reaps also doom.

It comes as a
swaggering
Necromancer,

His Golem, base yet
rare, cruel yet fair,

And their conceptions
diff'rent of Kingdoms'
nature.

King's ire sparks. A
challenge offers,
sallies forth.

Wins a battle.
Loses a War.

For petitions for
Britannic favour
goes awry.

Forced to choose, she
chooses the comers new.

The losses of war:
Britannia's Heart.
Britannia's Will.

Goddess grows grey
and wan and soon
is gone.

She lies still beneath
Primrose Hill

O'er which squats
the fallen court.

They lick red wounds
and delve the pit.

The King turns to
enemies sworn to
find an escape.

The Queen in torpor
sits; experiments
discarded.

Decadence Victorious.

Britannia's choice
mourns not; he
prefers her dead.

Instead, the
Necromancer seeks
his own escape;

A tower.

A tower of people;
the people,
his people.

Great attentions
wander, great
wonders rot.

A litany of horror
writ in their place.

From Ghouls who
feed on the open
guts of men

Whose crime was to
ignore the time to...

OH, DID ANYONE *EVER*
REALLY THINK THIS
TWADDLE HAD THE
MAKINGS OF A MYTH?

BUT STILL: WHATEVER
YOU WISH TO SEE, I
CAN SHOW YOU.

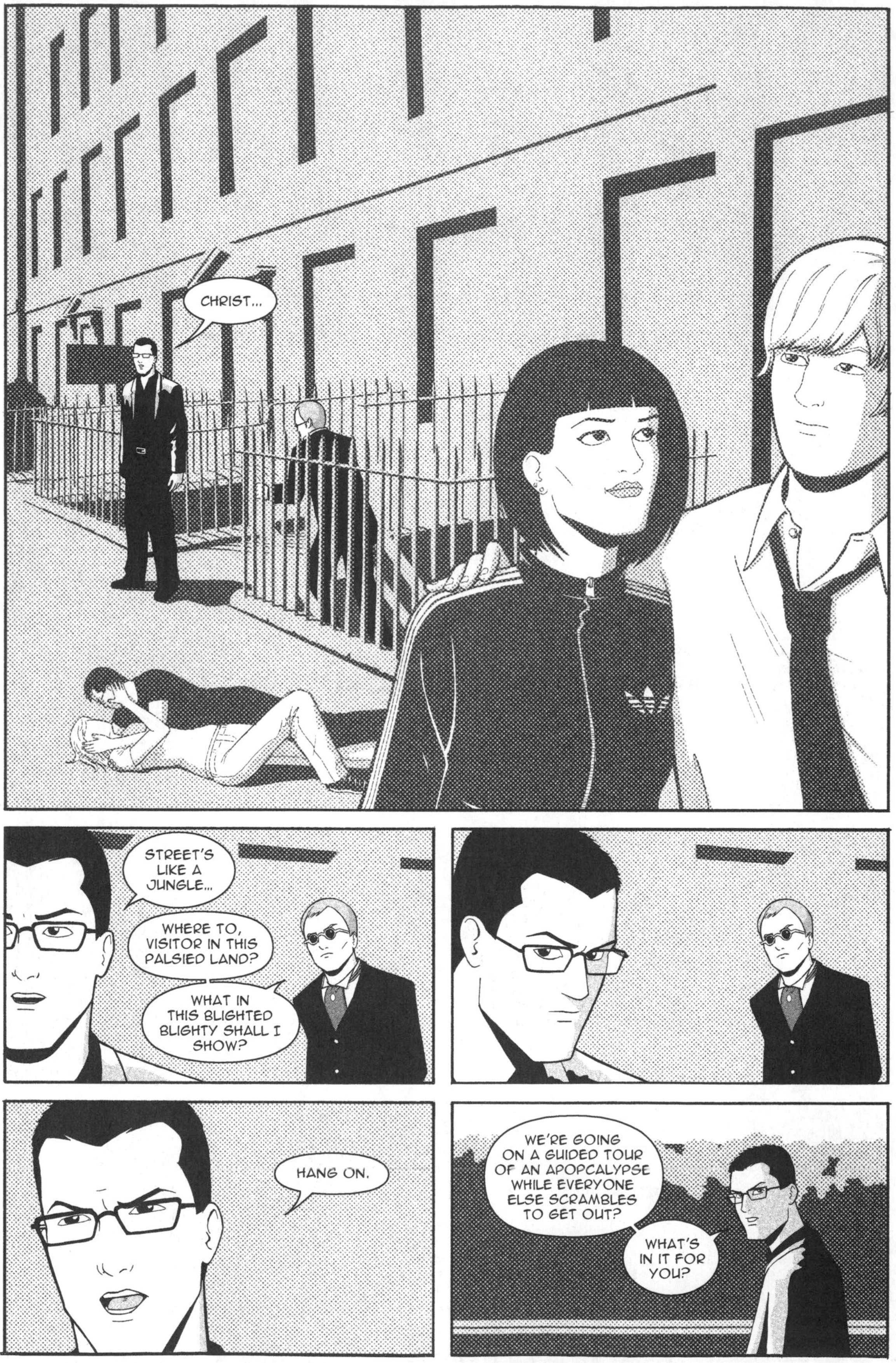
CHRIST...
STREET'S LIKE A JUNGLE...
WHERE TO, VISITOR IN THIS PALSIED LAND?
WHAT IN THIS BLIGHTED BLIGHTY SHALL I SHOW?
HANG ON.
WE'RE GOING ON A GUIDED TOUR OF AN APOPCALYPSE WHILE EVERYONE ELSE SCRAMBLES TO GET OUT?
WHAT'S IN IT FOR YOU?

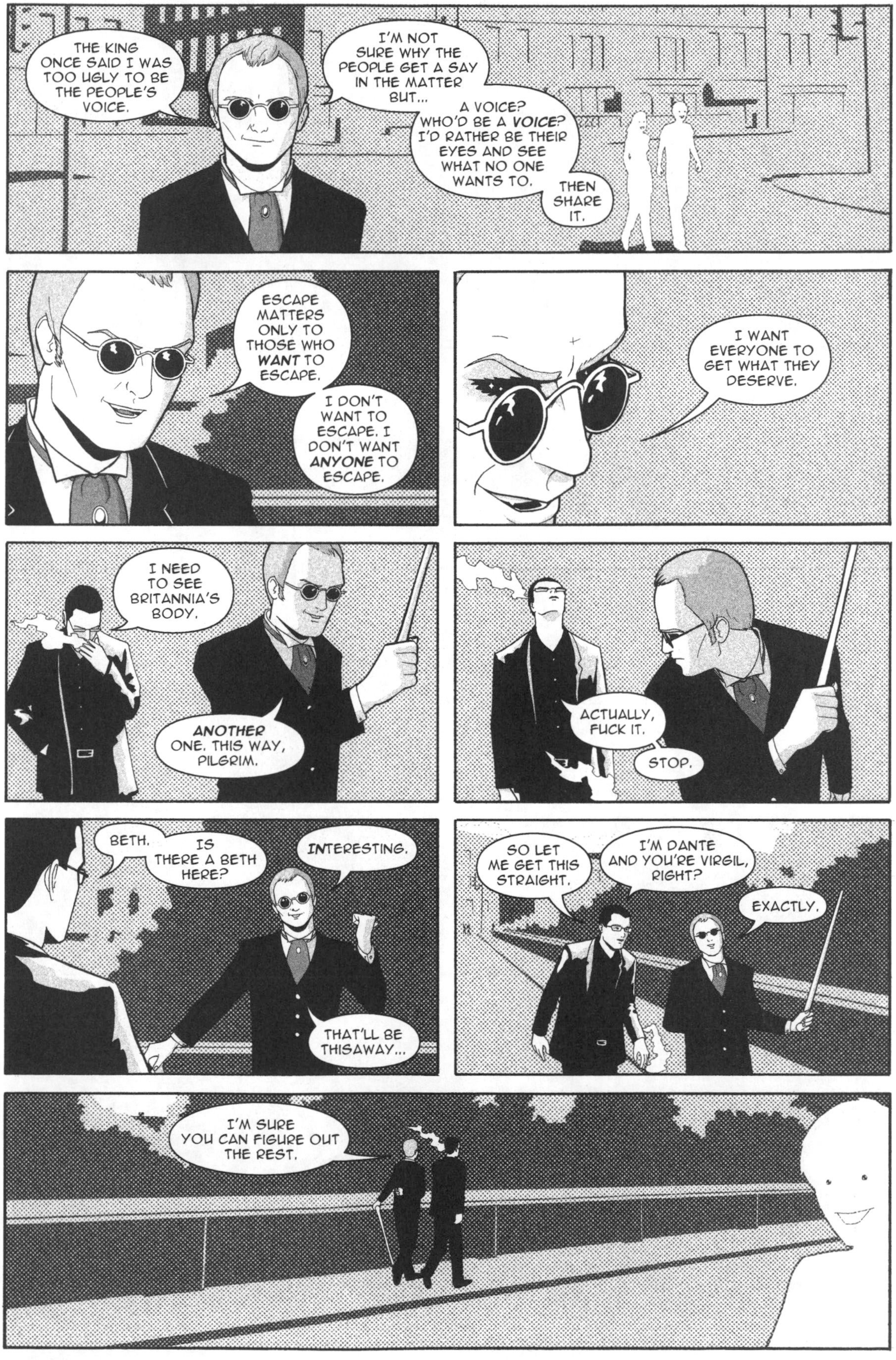

THE KING ONCE SAID I WAS TOO UGLY TO BE THE PEOPLE'S VOICE.
I'M NOT SURE WHY THE PEOPLE GET A SAY IN THE MATTER BUT...
A VOICE? WHO'D BE A VOICE? I'D RATHER BE THEIR EYES AND SEE WHAT NO ONE WANTS TO.
THEN SHARE IT.
ESCAPE MATTERS ONLY TO THOSE WHO WANT TO ESCAPE.
I DON'T WANT TO ESCAPE. I DON'T WANT ANYONE TO ESCAPE.
I WANT EVERYONE TO GET WHAT THEY DESERVE.
I NEED TO SEE BRITANNIA'S BODY.
ANOTHER ONE. THIS WAY, PILGRIM.
ACTUALLY, FUCK IT.
STOP.
BETH.
IS THERE A BETH HERE?
INTERESTING.
THAT'LL BE THISAWAY...
SO LET ME GET THIS STRAIGHT.
I'M DANTE AND YOU'RE VIRGIL, RIGHT?
EXACTLY.
I'M SURE YOU CAN FIGURE OUT THE REST.

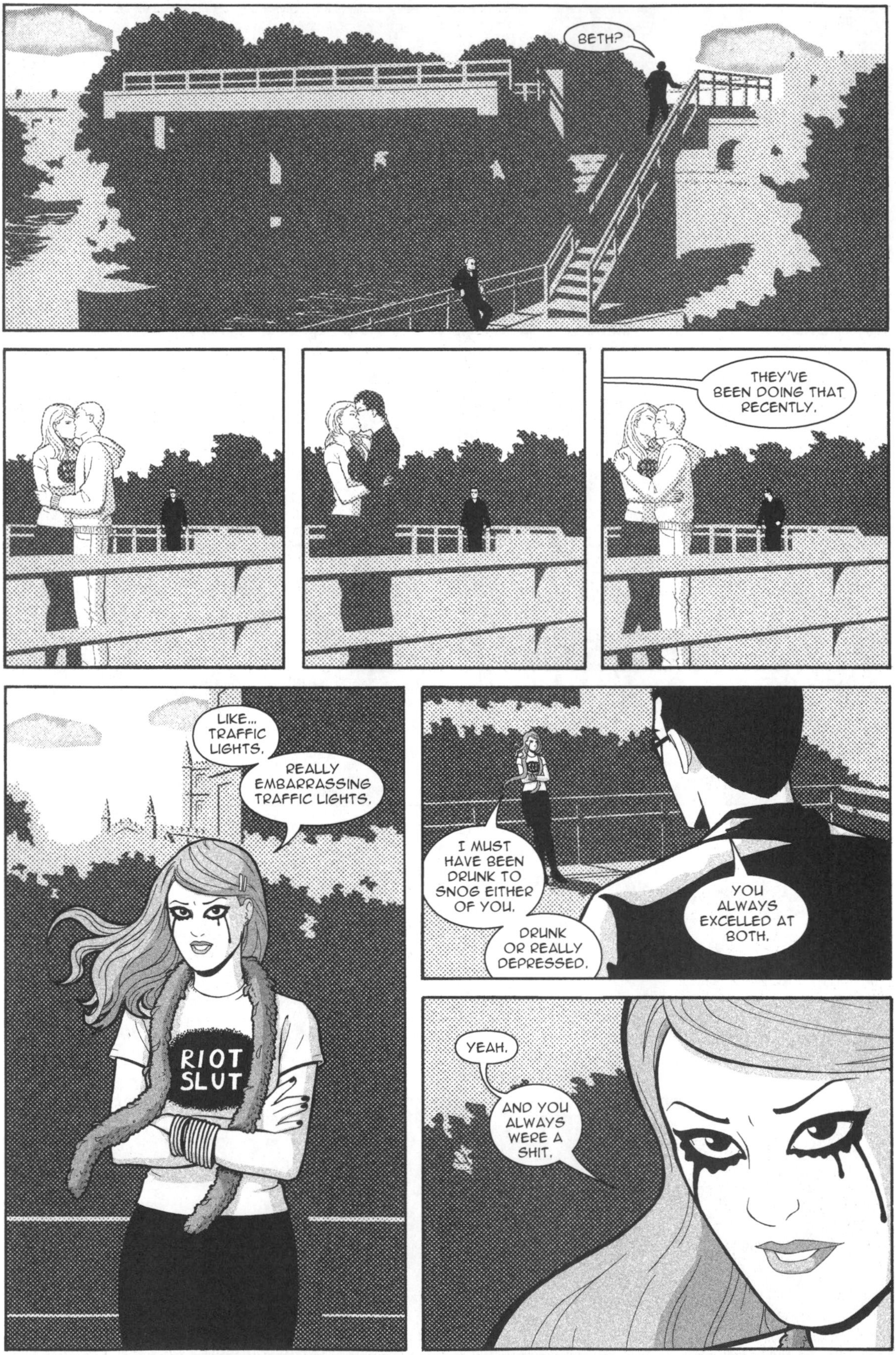
BETH?
THEY'VE BEEN DOING THAT RECENTLY.
LIKE... TRAFFIC LIGHTS.
REALLY EMBARRASSING TRAFFIC LIGHTS.
RIOT SLUT
I MUST HAVE BEEN DRUNK TO SNOG EITHER OF YOU.
DRUNK OR REALLY DEPRESSED.
YOU ALWAYS EXCELLED AT BOTH.
YEAH.
AND YOU ALWAYS WERE A SHIT.

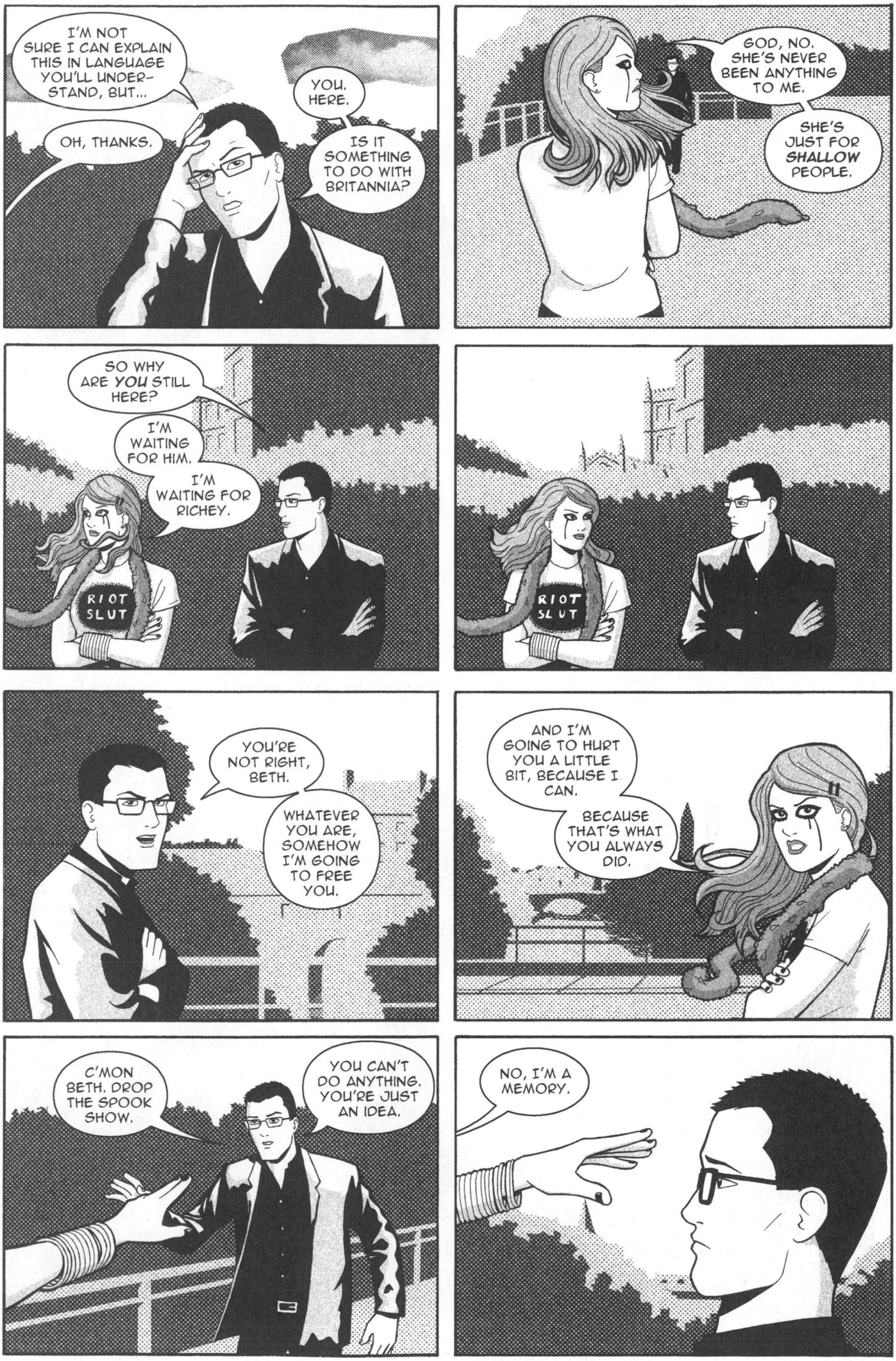
I'M NOT SURE I CAN EXPLAIN THIS IN LANGUAGE YOU'LL UNDER-STAND, BUT...
OH, THANKS.
YOU. HERE.
IS IT SOMETHING TO DO WITH BRITANNIA?
GOD, NO. SHE'S NEVER BEEN ANYTHING TO ME.
SHE'S JUST FOR SHALLOW PEOPLE.
SO WHY ARE YOU STILL HERE?
I'M WAITING FOR HIM.
I'M WAITING FOR RICHEY.
RIOT SLUT
RIOT SLUT
YOU'RE NOT RIGHT, BETH.
WHATEVER YOU ARE, SOMEHOW I'M GOING TO FREE YOU.
AND I'M GOING TO HURT YOU A LITTLE BIT, BECAUSE I CAN.
BECAUSE THAT'S WHAT YOU ALWAYS DID.
C'MON BETH. DROP THE SPOOK SHOW.
YOU CAN'T DO ANYTHING. YOU'RE JUST AN IDEA.
NO, I'M A MEMORY.

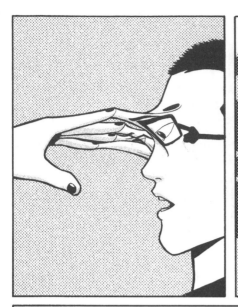

THE ONLY THING THAT ALWAYS HURTS.

...NO.

I THOUGHT I'D LIKE THAT, BUT... NO.

IT'S JUST SHITTY.

RIOT LUT

GOD, I HOPE I DON'T END UP LIKE YOU.

YOU DON'T GET IT. EVERYTHING'S CHANGING HERE. IT'S MIXING UP.

IMAGINE IT... SWAPPING AROUND. I COULD BE YOU.

AND YOU... YOU'D BE THE ONE STARING AT MY HOUSE LIGHTS AT 1 AM.

YOUR NAILS BITING INTO YOUR PALMS AS YOU WATCH ME DANCE.

YOU WRITING LETTERS THAT NEVER GET SENT. YOU CRYING. YOU DRINKING. YOU CRYING SOME MORE.

MAYBE YOU'LL BE THE NOTHING.

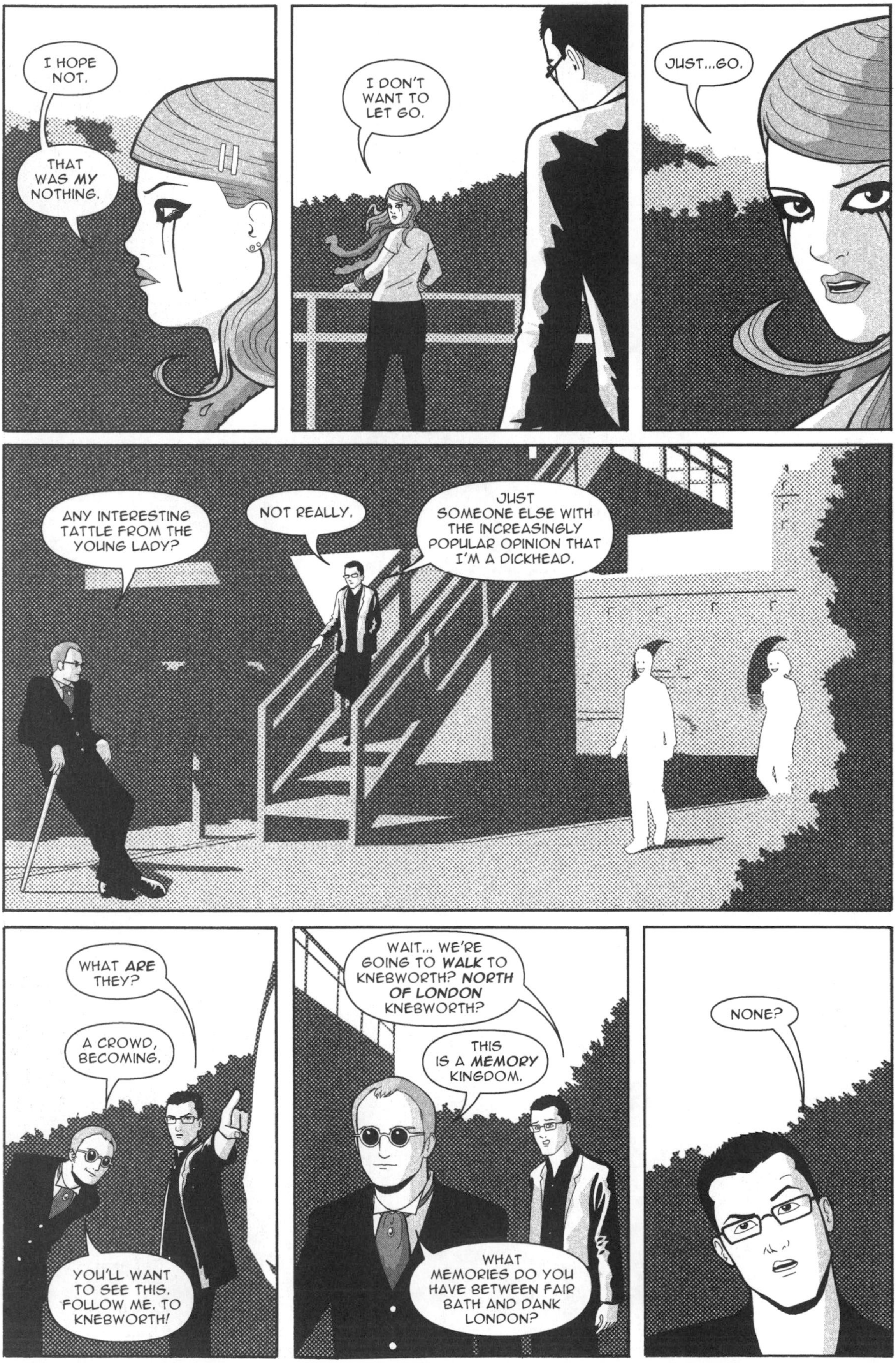
I HOPE NOT.
THAT WAS MY NOTHING.
I DON'T WANT TO LET GO.
JUST...GO.
ANY INTERESTING TATTLE FROM THE YOUNG LADY?
NOT REALLY.
JUST SOMEONE ELSE WITH THE INCREASINGLY POPULAR OPINION THAT I'M A DICKHEAD.
WHAT ARE THEY?
A CROWD, BECOMING.
YOU'LL WANT TO SEE THIS. FOLLOW ME. TO KNEBWORTH!
WAIT... WE'RE GOING TO WALK TO KNEBWORTH? NORTH OF LONDON KNEBWORTH?
THIS IS A MEMORY KINGDOM.
WHAT MEMORIES DO YOU HAVE BETWEEN FAIR BATH AND DANK LONDON?
NONE?

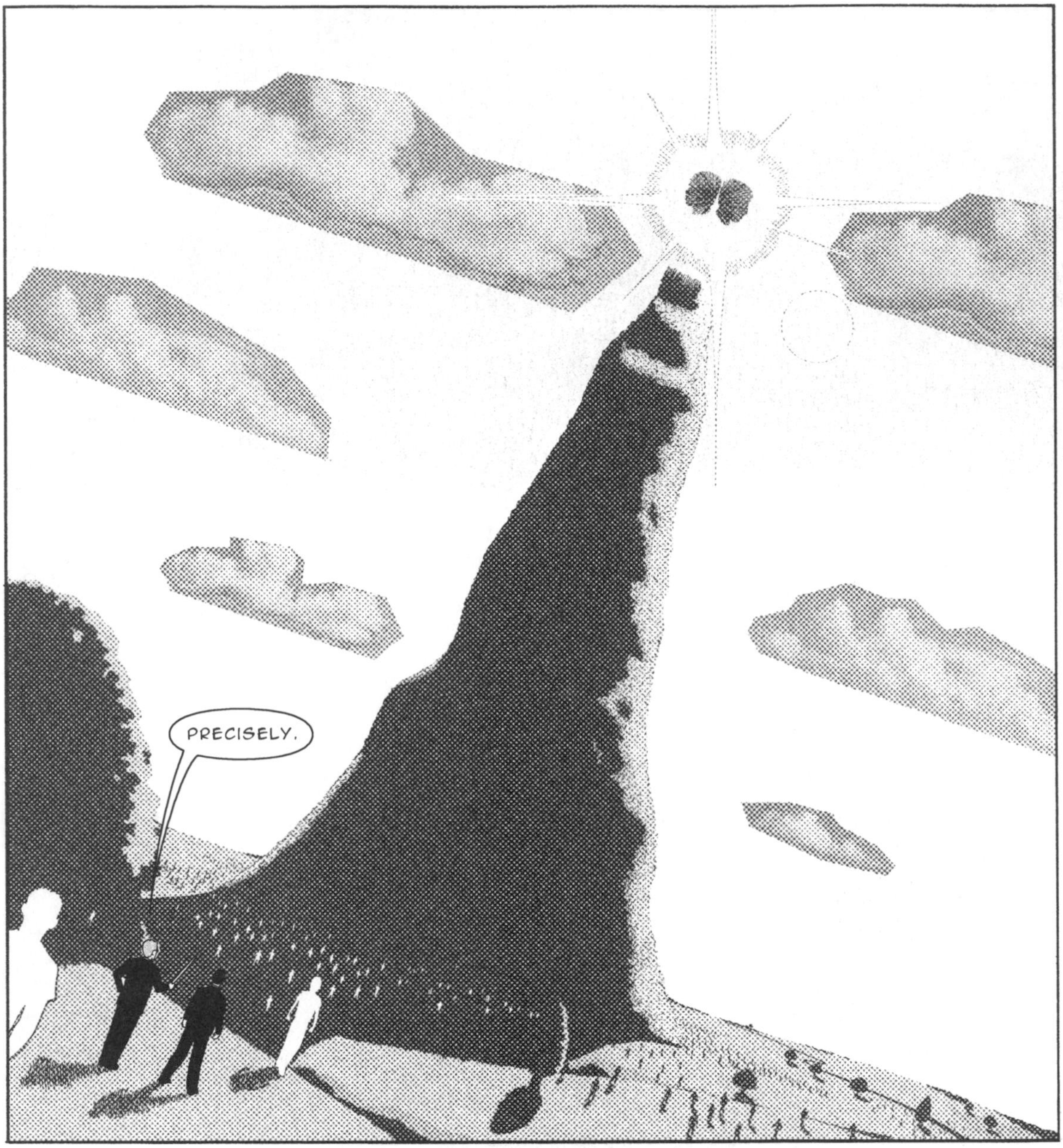
PRECISELY.

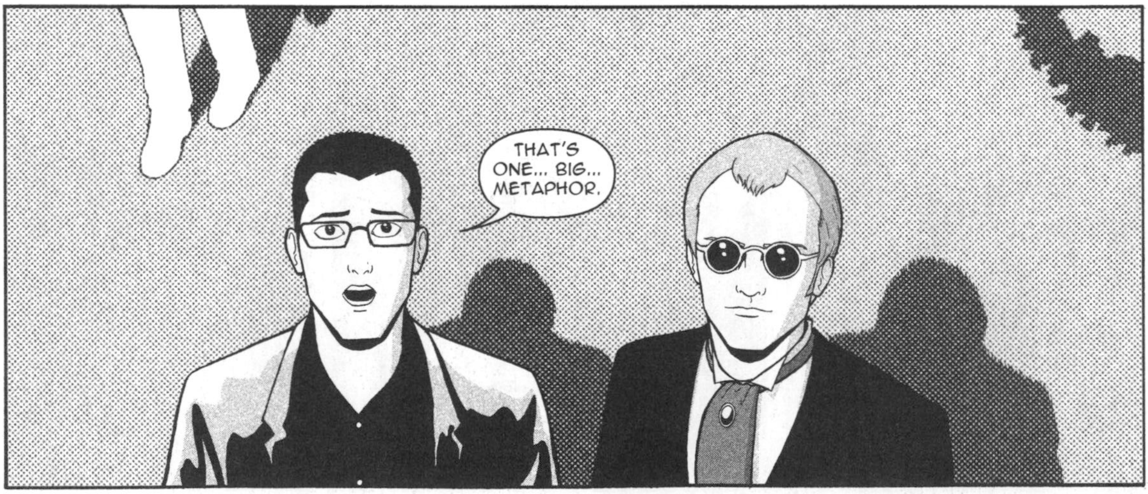
THAT'S ONE... BIG... METAPHOR.

WHAT'S THE STORY?

OH, *PLEASE.*

IT'S THE NECROMANCER'S GREAT WORK, TO GET WHAT HE'S ALWAYS WANTED.

OUT, OF WHEREVER HE IS.

STAND ON ENOUGH SHOULDERS AND HE'LL BE CLEAR OF THE REALM...

BUT PEOPLE AREN'T SUFFICIENT FOR SUCH AN ENDEAVOUR. YOU NEED A CROWD.

SO HE MADE ONE.

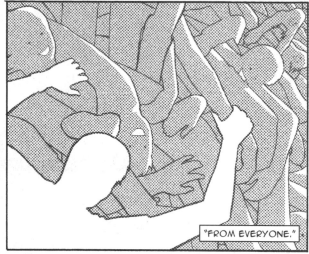

"FROM EVERYONE."

"A PRECARIOUS BUSINESS WITH THAT GOLEM OF HIS AROUND."

"BUT FOR NOW THERE'S ALWAYS MORE."

THEY CAN'T HELP BUT STARE AND COME HITHER.

AND WHO'D TRY TO STOP THEM?

HEY!

HELLO?
HELLO!
FUCKING STOP!
GOOD. NOW... WHAT ARE YOU DOING?
WE WERE MORE THAN JUST CROWDS. STOP IT.
WHA...
NO... NO.

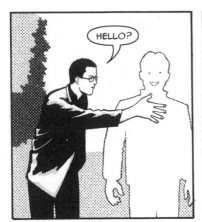

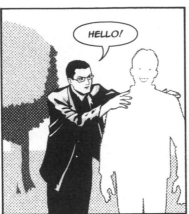

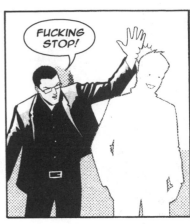

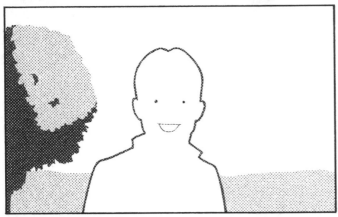

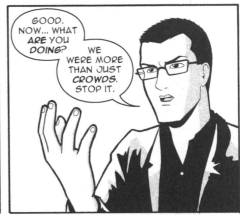

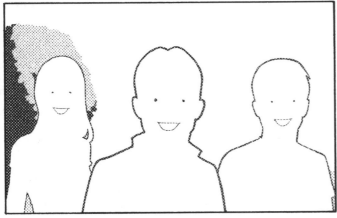

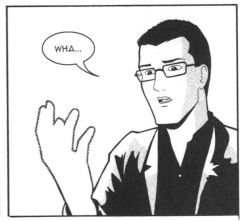

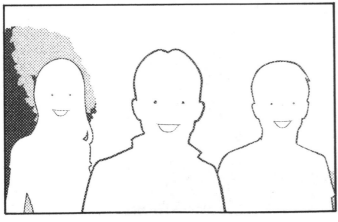

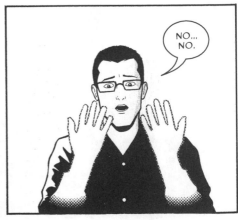

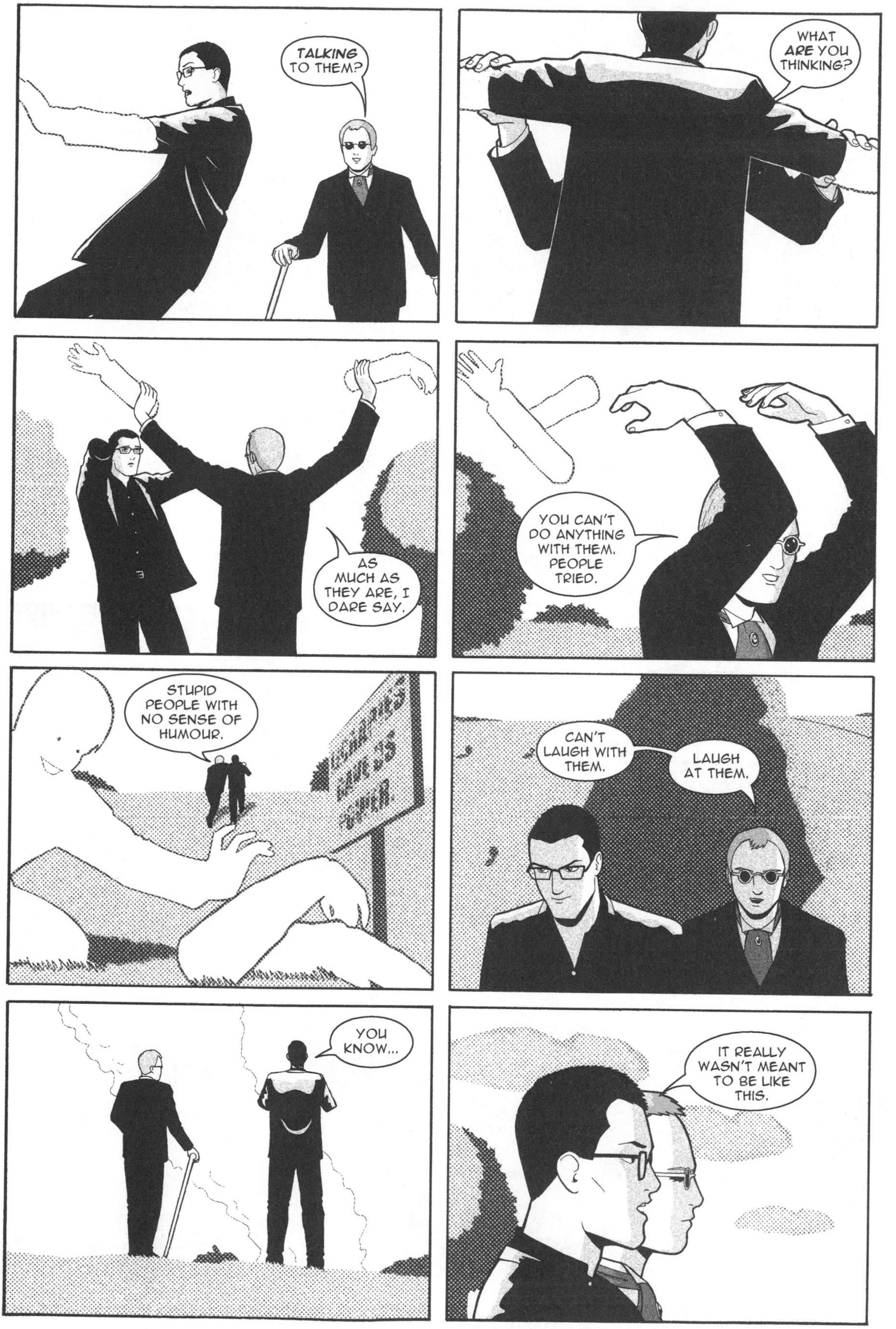

TALKING TO THEM?
WHAT *ARE* YOU THINKING?
AS MUCH AS THEY ARE, I DARE SAY.
YOU CAN'T DO ANYTHING WITH THEM. PEOPLE TRIED.
STUPID PEOPLE WITH NO SENSE OF HUMOUR.
CAN'T LAUGH WITH THEM.
LAUGH AT THEM.
YOU KNOW...
IT REALLY WASN'T MEANT TO BE LIKE THIS.

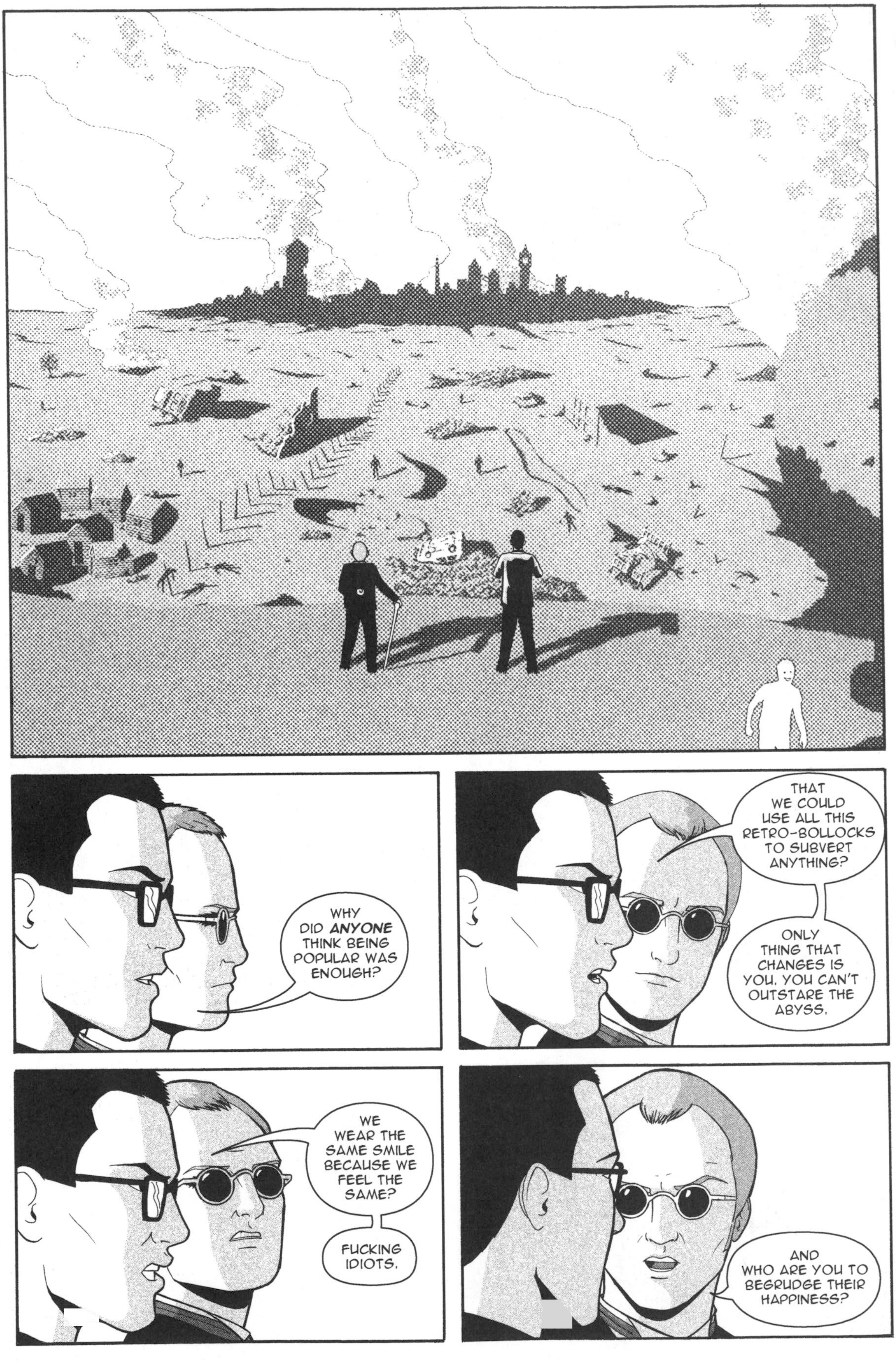
WHY DID ANYONE THINK BEING POPULAR WAS ENOUGH?
THAT WE COULD USE ALL THIS RETRO-BOLLOCKS TO SUBVERT ANYTHING?
ONLY THING THAT CHANGES IS YOU. YOU CAN'T OUTSTARE THE ABYSS.
WE WEAR THE SAME SMILE BECAUSE WE FEEL THE SAME?
FUCKING IDIOTS.
AND WHO ARE YOU TO BEGRUDGE THEIR HAPPINESS?

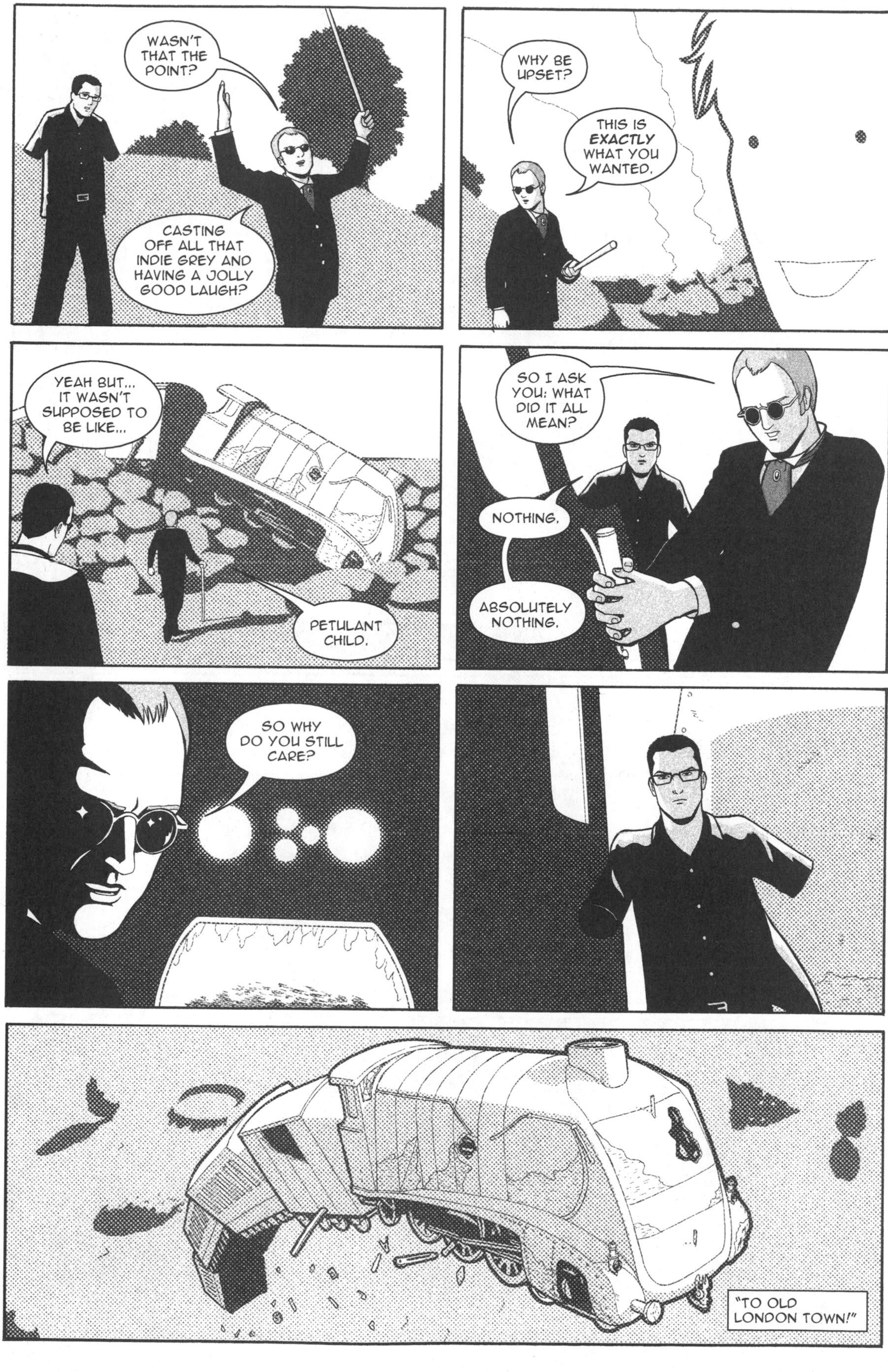
WASN'T THAT THE POINT?
CASTING OFF ALL THAT INDIE GREY AND HAVING A JOLLY GOOD LAUGH?
WHY BE UPSET?
THIS IS EXACTLY WHAT YOU WANTED.
YEAH BUT... IT WASN'T SUPPOSED TO BE LIKE...
PETULANT CHILD.
SO I ASK YOU: WHAT DID IT ALL MEAN?
NOTHING.
ABSOLUTELY NOTHING.
SO WHY DO YOU STILL CARE?
"TO OLD LONDON TOWN!"

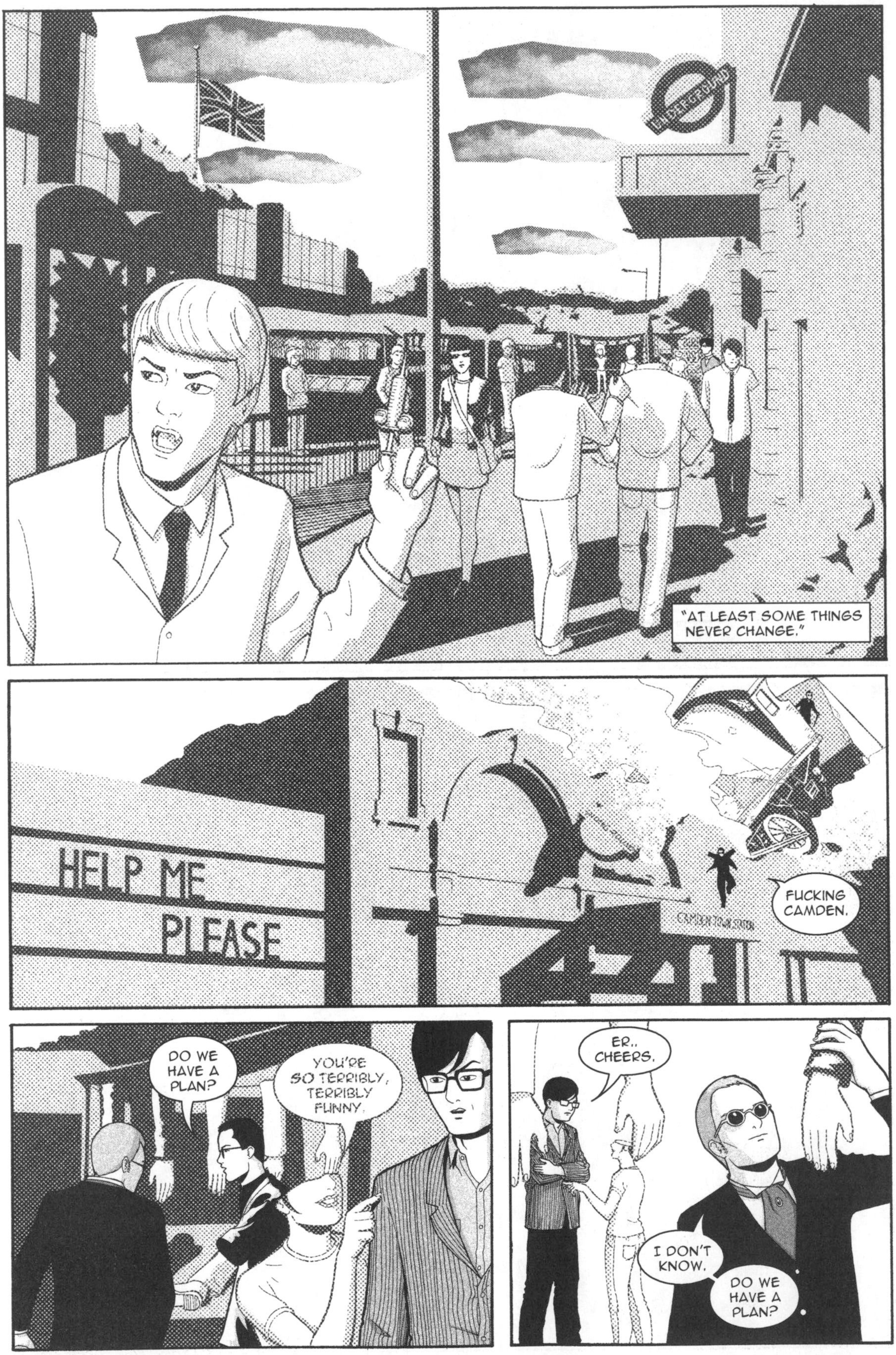
"AT LEAST SOME THINGS NEVER CHANGE."
HELP ME PLEASE
CAMDEN TOWN STATION
FUCKING CAMDEN.
DO WE HAVE A PLAN?
YOU'RE SO TERRIBLY, TERRIBLY FUNNY.
ER.. CHEERS.
I DON'T KNOW.
DO WE HAVE A PLAN?

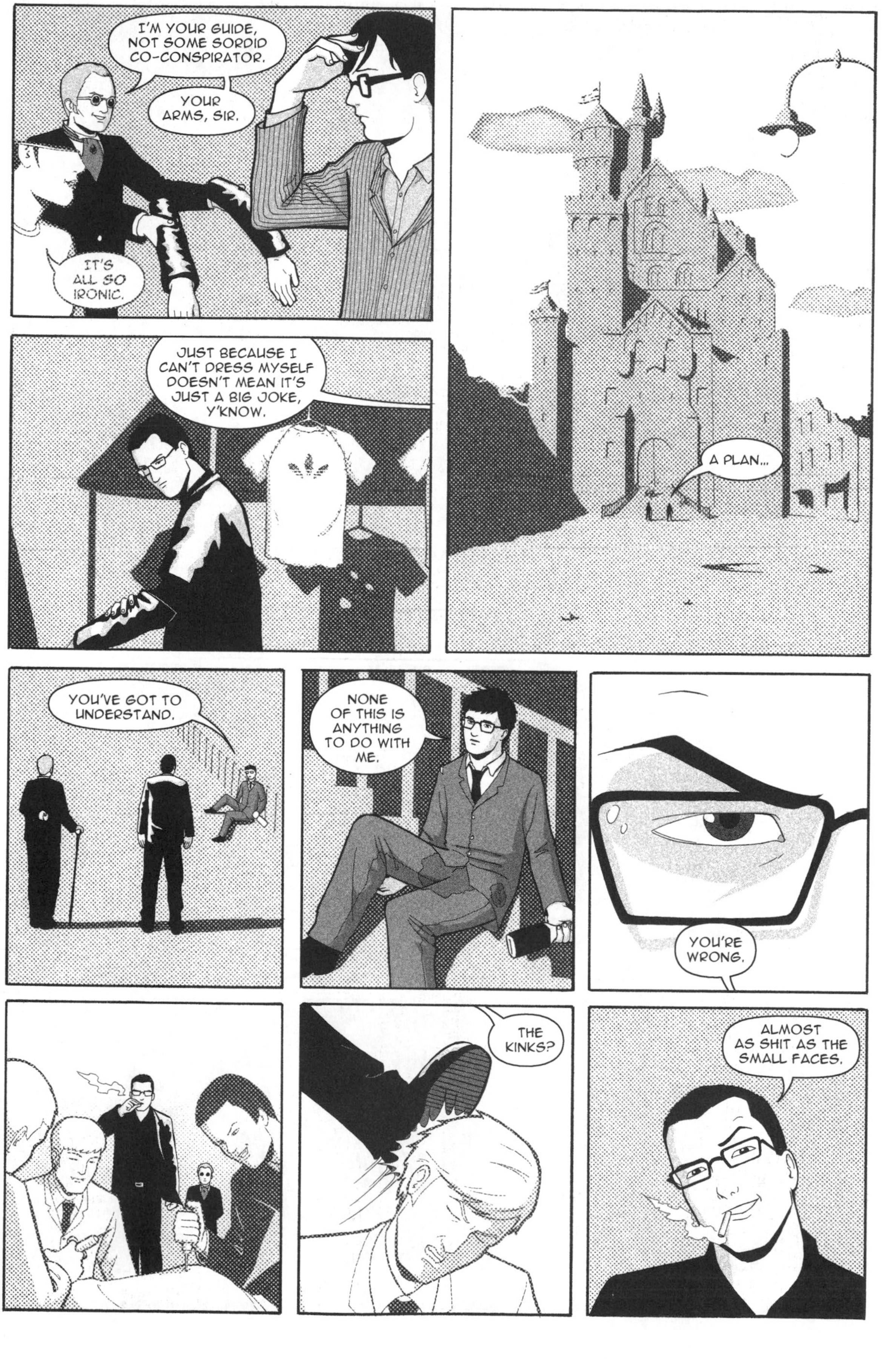
I'M YOUR GUIDE, NOT SOME SORDID CO-CONSPIRATOR.
YOUR ARMS, SIR.
IT'S ALL SO IRONIC.
JUST BECAUSE I CAN'T DRESS MYSELF DOESN'T MEAN IT'S JUST A BIG JOKE, Y'KNOW.
A PLAN...
YOU'VE GOT TO UNDERSTAND.
NONE OF THIS IS ANYTHING TO DO WITH ME.
YOU'RE WRONG.
THE KINKS?
ALMOST AS SHIT AS THE SMALL FACES.

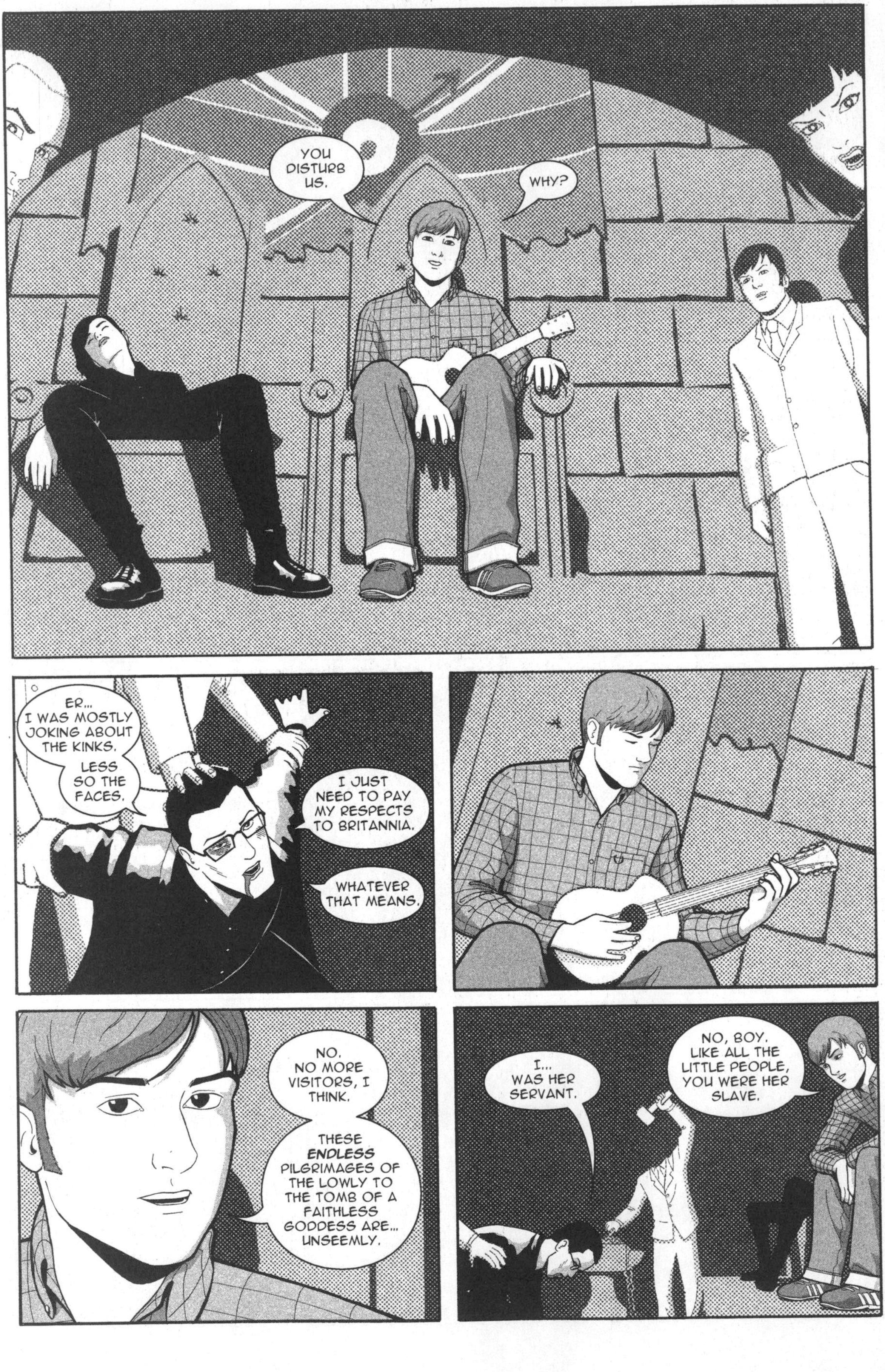
YOU DISTURB US.
WHY?
ER... I WAS MOSTLY JOKING ABOUT THE KINKS.
LESS SO THE FACES.
I JUST NEED TO PAY MY RESPECTS TO BRITANNIA.
WHATEVER THAT MEANS.
NO. NO MORE VISITORS, I THINK.
THESE *ENDLESS* PILGRIMAGES OF THE LOWLY TO THE TOMB OF A FAITHLESS GODDESS ARE... UNSEEMLY.
I... WAS HER SERVANT.
NO, BOY. LIKE ALL THE LITTLE PEOPLE, YOU WERE HER SLAVE.

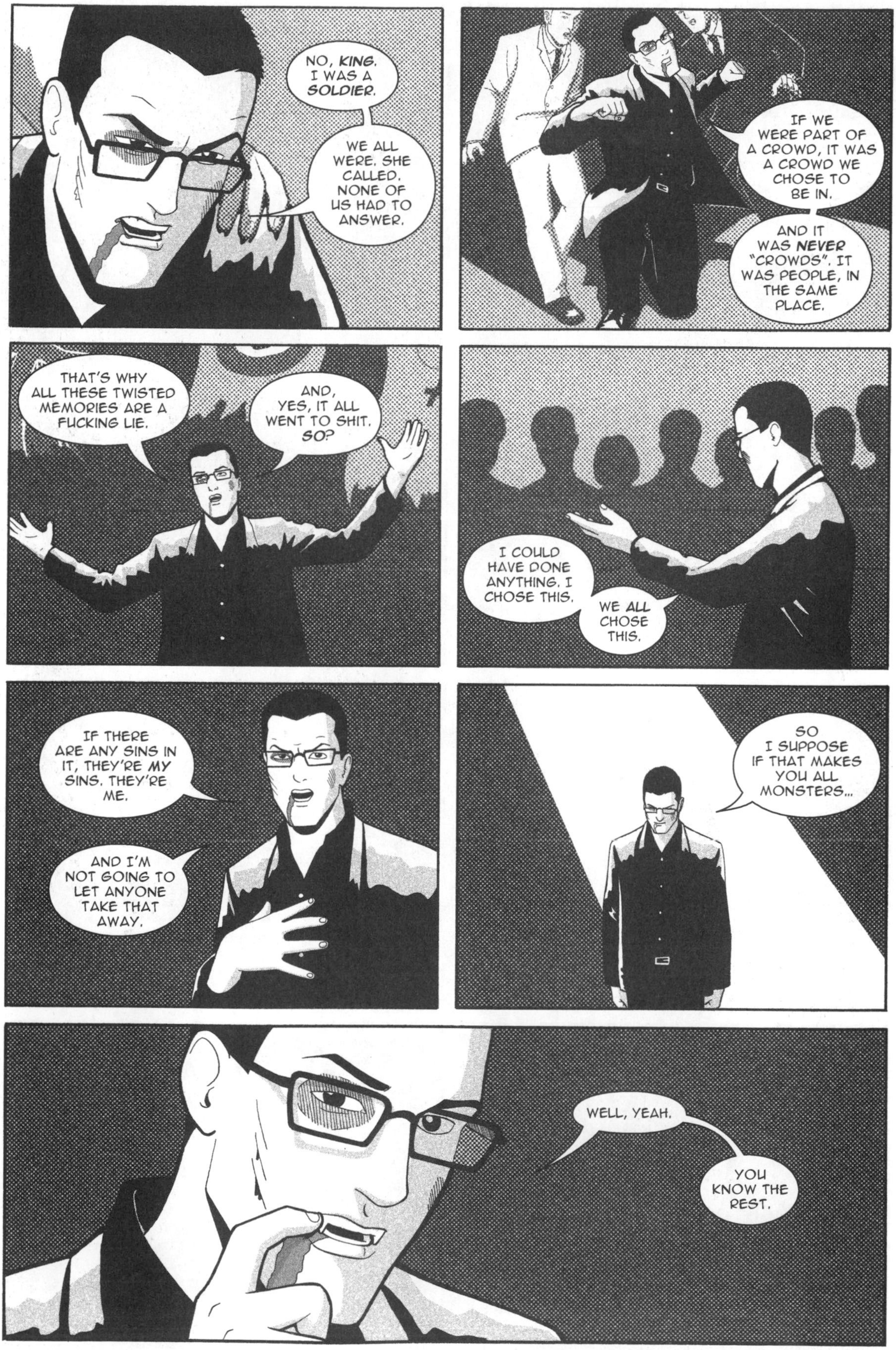
NO, KING. I WAS A SOLDIER.
WE ALL WERE. SHE CALLED. NONE OF US HAD TO ANSWER.
IF WE WERE PART OF A CROWD, IT WAS A CROWD WE CHOSE TO BE IN.
AND IT WAS NEVER "CROWDS". IT WAS PEOPLE, IN THE SAME PLACE.
THAT'S WHY ALL THESE TWISTED MEMORIES ARE A FUCKING LIE.
AND, YES, IT ALL WENT TO SHIT. SO?
I COULD HAVE DONE ANYTHING. I CHOSE THIS.
WE ALL CHOSE THIS.
IF THERE ARE ANY SINS IN IT, THEY'RE MY SINS. THEY'RE ME.
AND I'M NOT GOING TO LET ANYONE TAKE THAT AWAY.
SO I SUPPOSE IF THAT MAKES YOU ALL MONSTERS...
WELL, YEAH.
YOU KNOW THE REST.

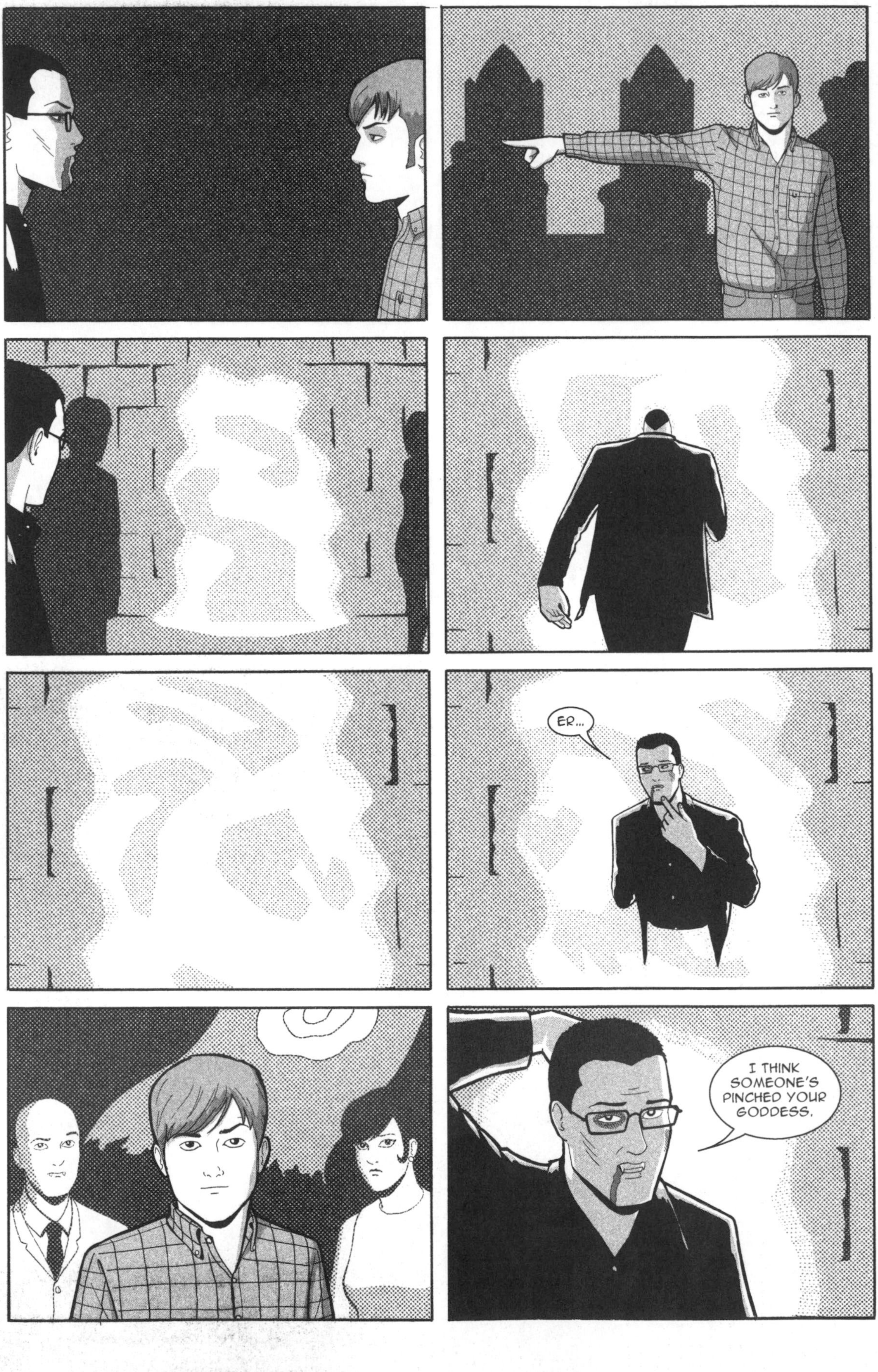
ER...
I THINK SOMEONE'S PINCHED YOUR GODDESS.

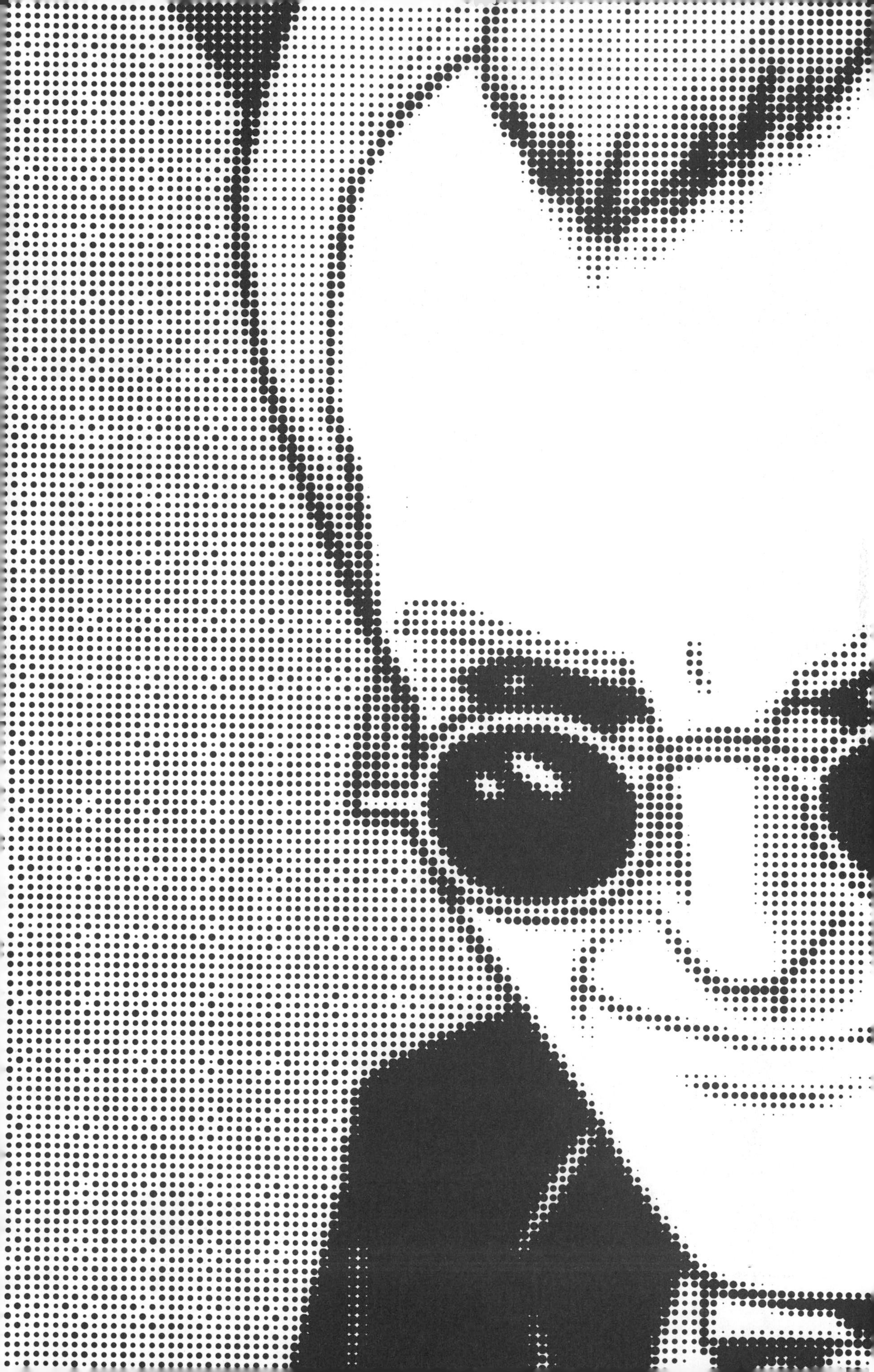

CHAPTER FIVE

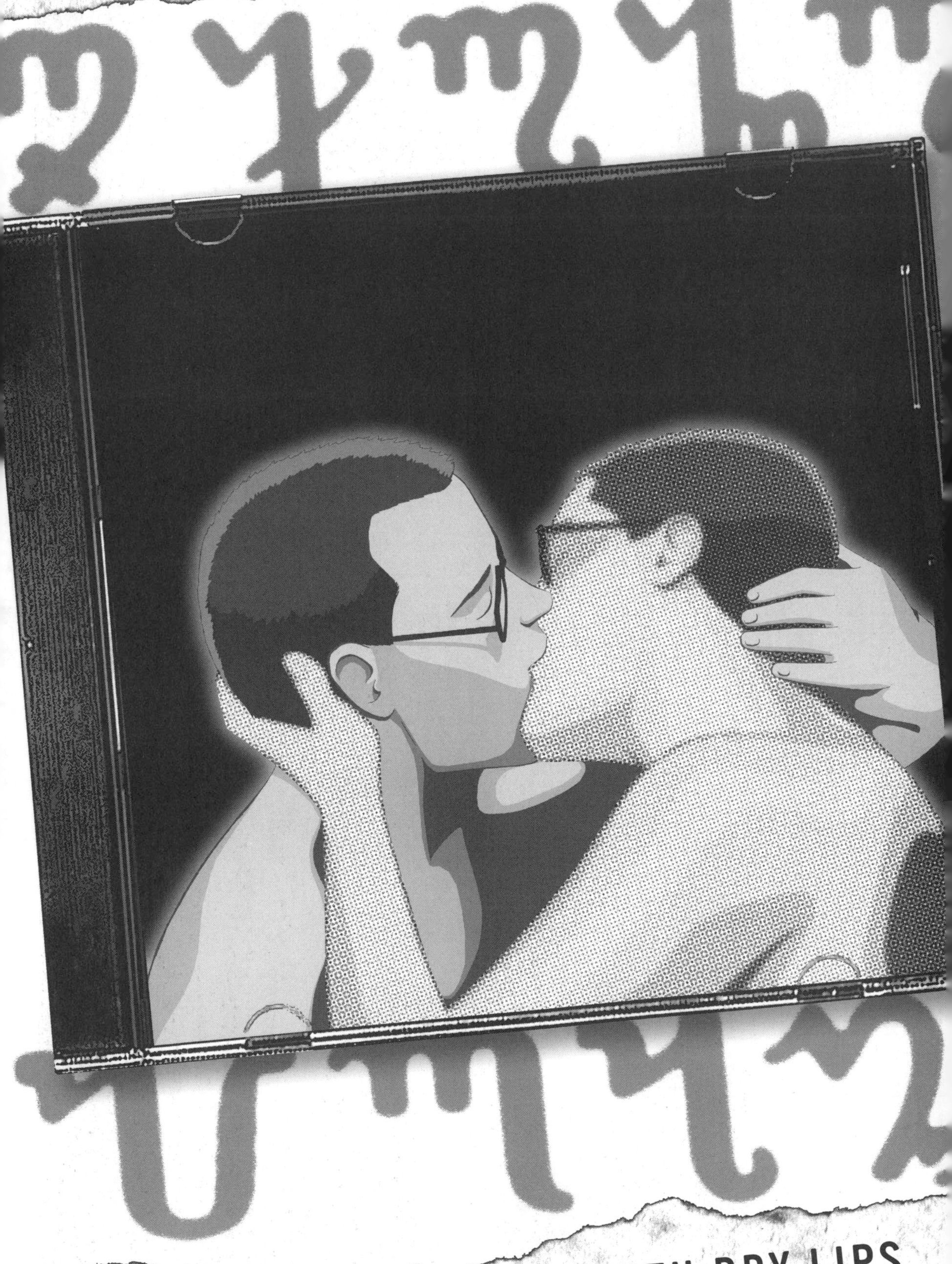

KISSING WITH DRY LIPS

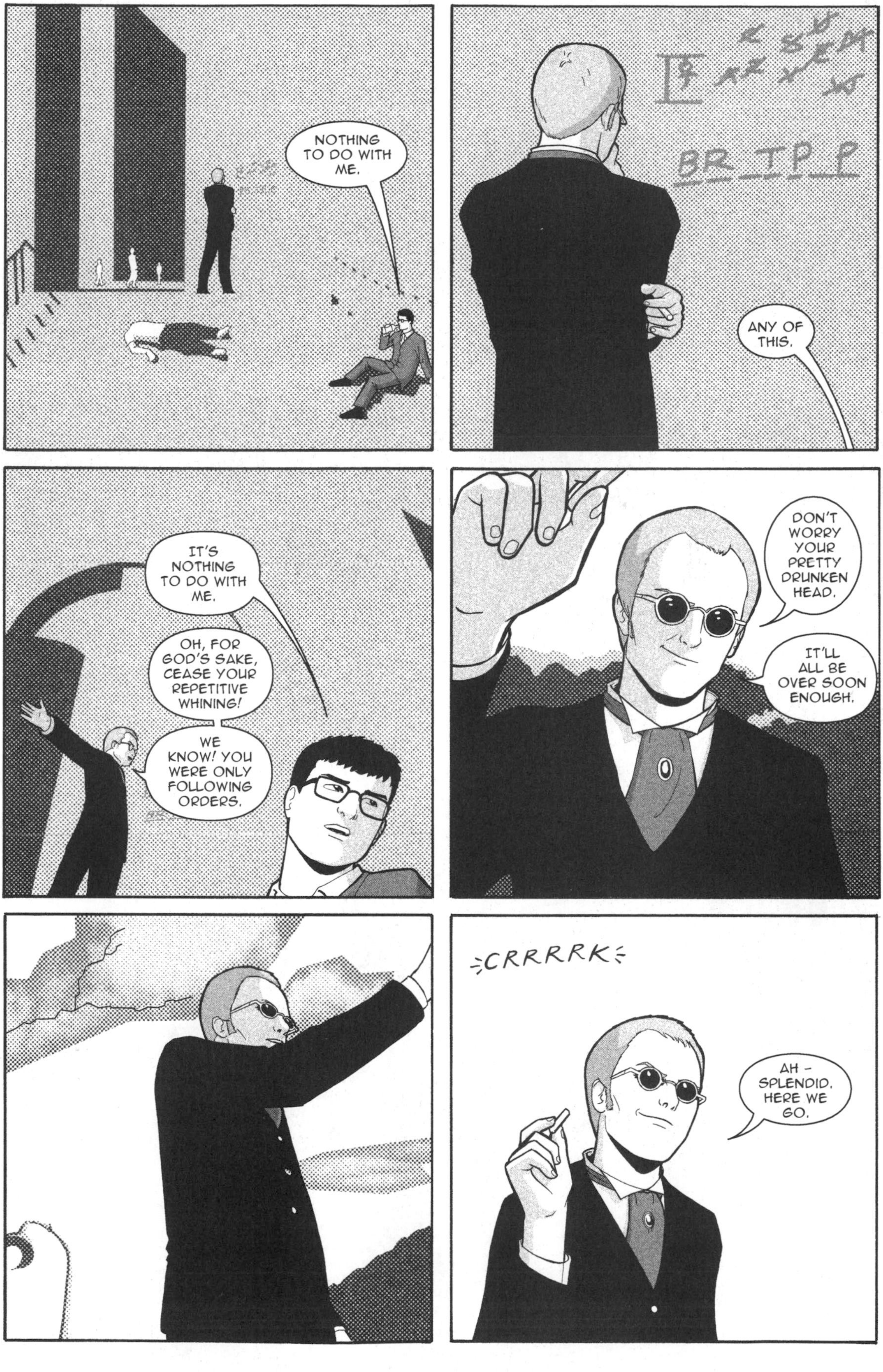
NOTHING TO DO WITH ME.
ANY OF THIS.
BR TP P
IT'S NOTHING TO DO WITH ME.
OH, FOR GOD'S SAKE, CEASE YOUR REPETITIVE WHINING!
WE KNOW! YOU WERE ONLY FOLLOWING ORDERS.
DON'T WORRY YOUR PRETTY DRUNKEN HEAD.
IT'LL ALL BE OVER SOON ENOUGH.
CRRRRK
AH - SPLENDID. HERE WE GO.

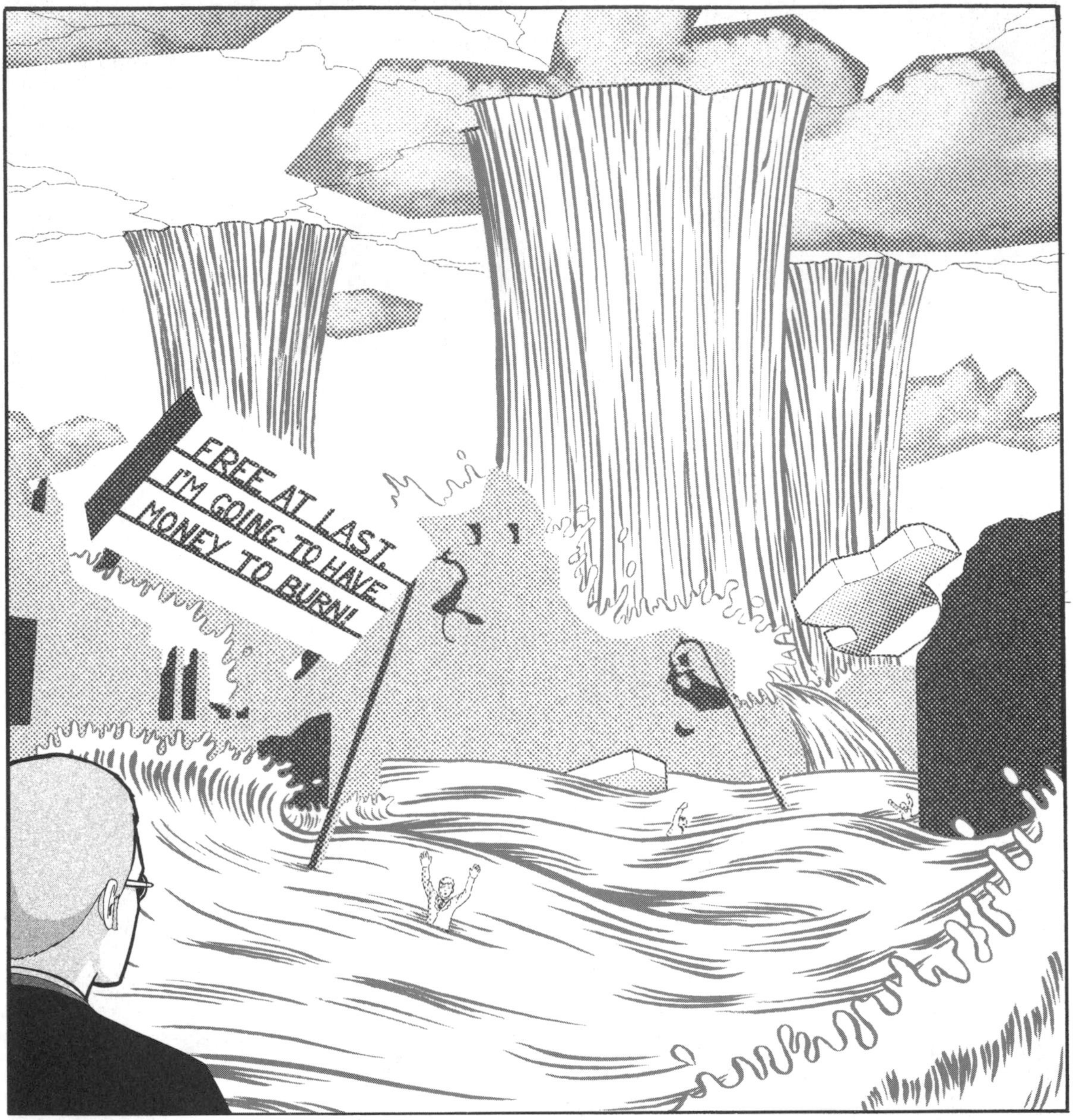
FREE AT LAST.
I'M GOING TO HAVE
MONEY TO BURN!

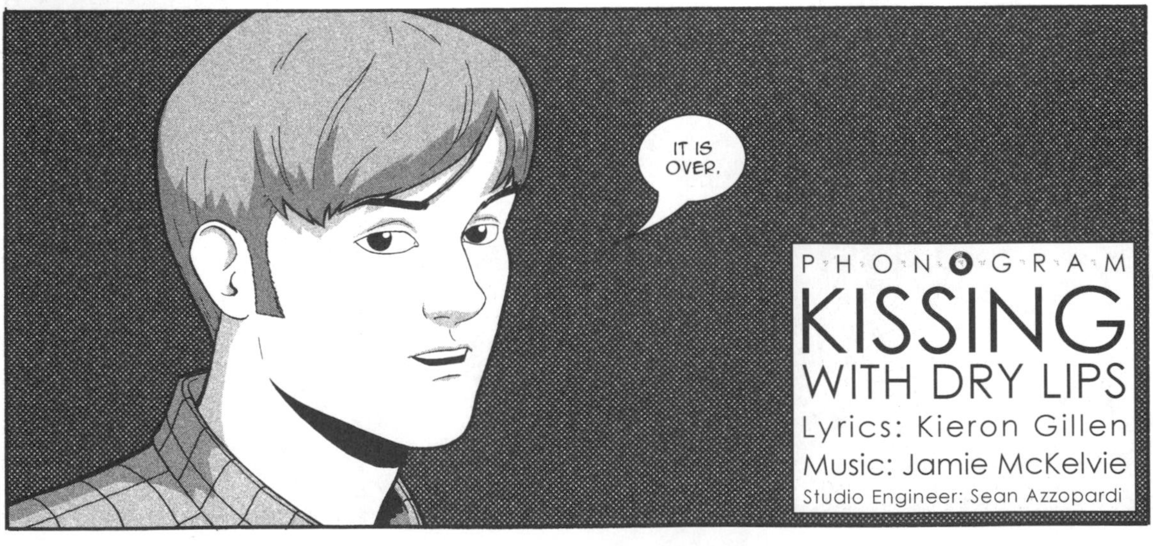
IT IS OVER.
PHONOGRAM
KISSING WITH DRY LIPS
Lyrics: Kieron Gillen
Music: Jamie McKelvie
Studio Engineer: Sean Azzopardi

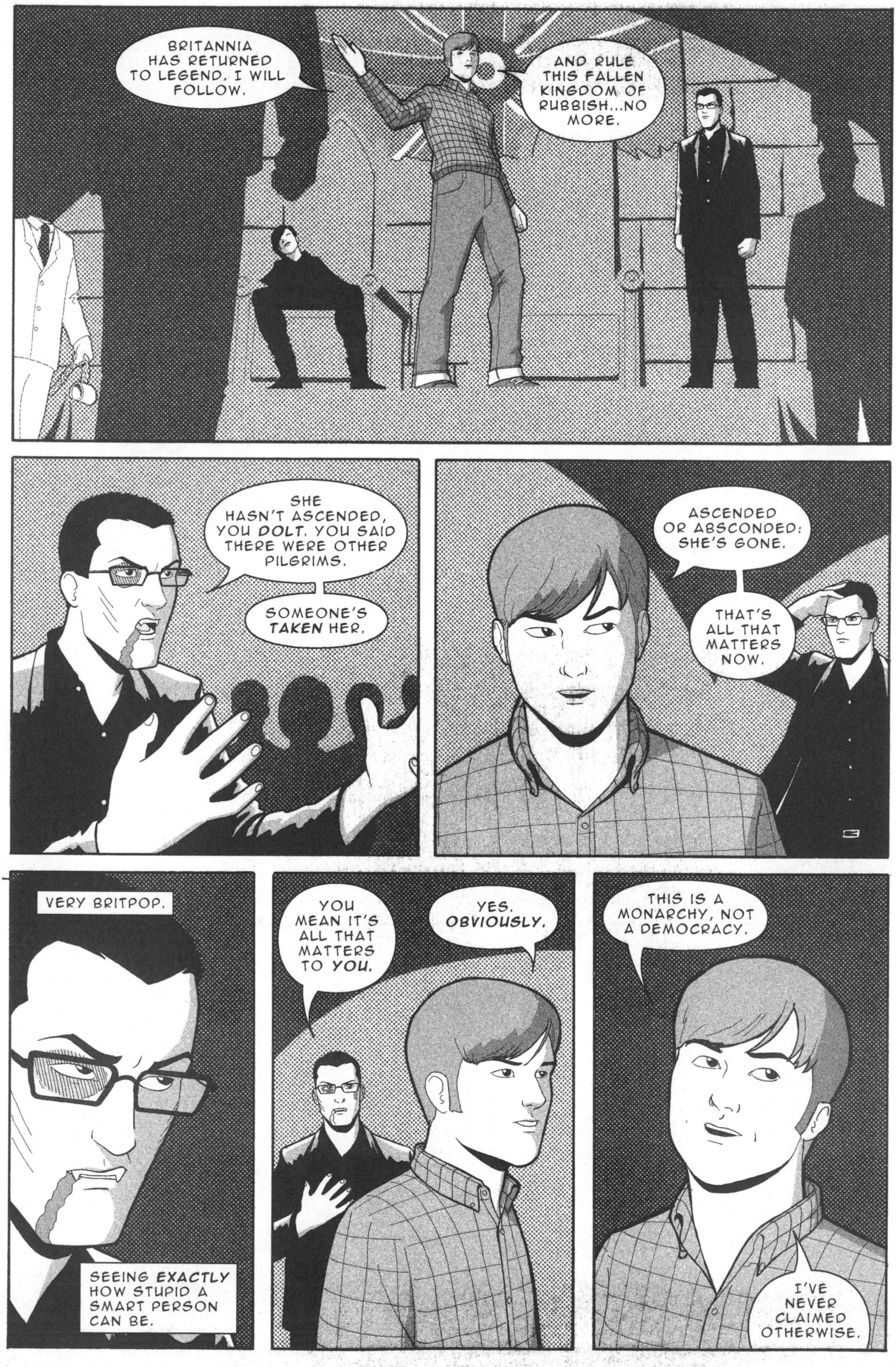
BRITANNIA HAS RETURNED TO LEGEND. I WILL FOLLOW.
AND RULE THIS FALLEN KINGDOM OF RUBBISH...NO MORE.
SHE HASN'T ASCENDED, YOU DOLT. YOU SAID THERE WERE OTHER PILGRIMS.
SOMEONE'S TAKEN HER.
ASCENDED OR ABSCONDED: SHE'S GONE.
THAT'S ALL THAT MATTERS NOW.
VERY BRITPOP.
SEEING EXACTLY HOW STUPID A SMART PERSON CAN BE.
YOU MEAN IT'S ALL THAT MATTERS TO YOU.
YES. OBVIOUSLY.
THIS IS A MONARCHY, NOT A DEMOCRACY.
I'VE NEVER CLAIMED OTHERWISE.

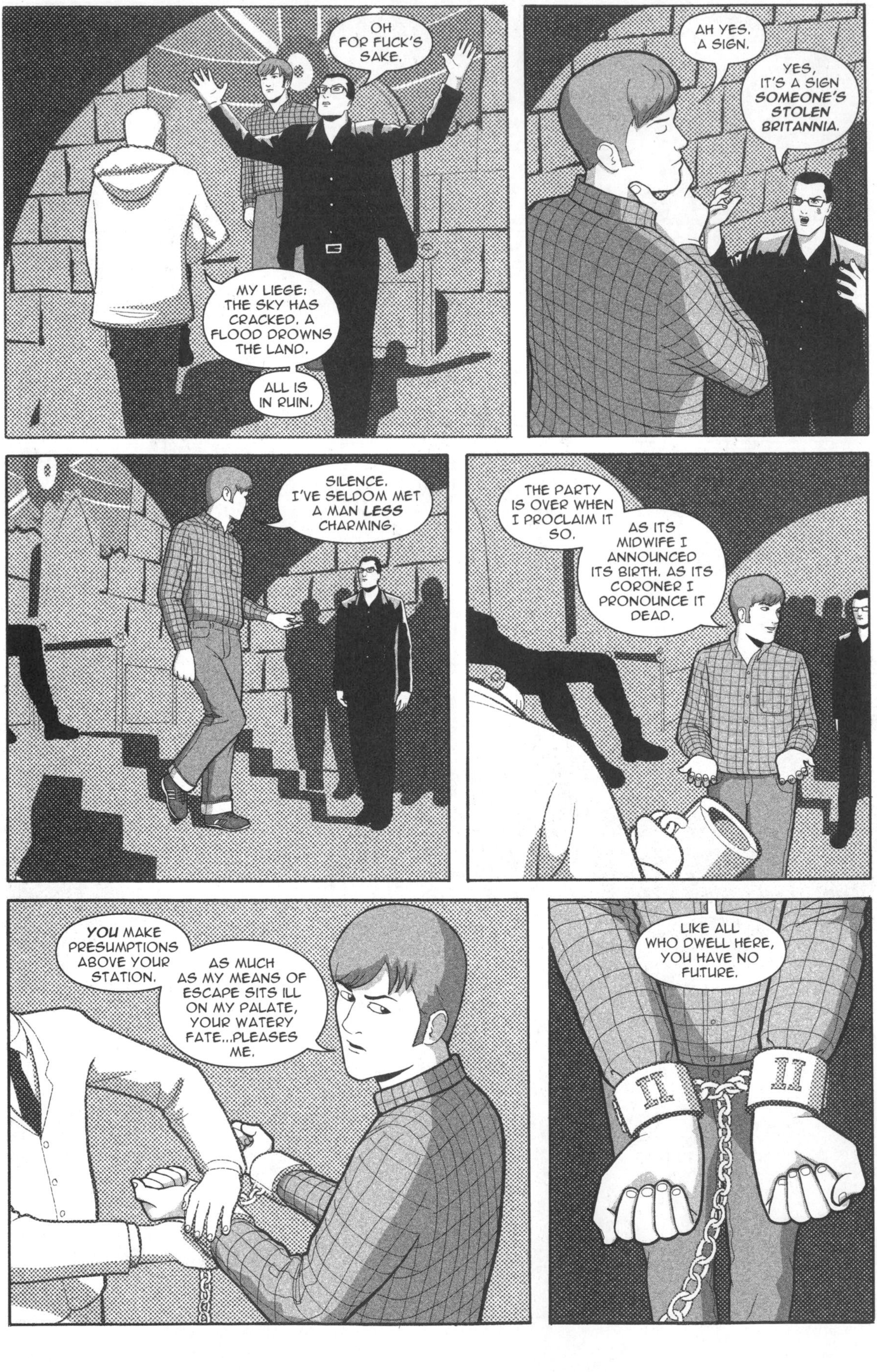
OH FOR FUCK'S SAKE.
MY LIEGE: THE SKY HAS CRACKED. A FLOOD DROWNS THE LAND.
ALL IS IN RUIN.
AH YES. A SIGN.
YES, IT'S A SIGN SOMEONE'S STOLEN BRITANNIA.
SILENCE. I'VE SELDOM MET A MAN LESS CHARMING.
THE PARTY IS OVER WHEN I PROCLAIM IT SO.
AS ITS MIDWIFE I ANNOUNCED ITS BIRTH. AS ITS CORONER I PRONOUNCE IT DEAD.
YOU MAKE PRESUMPTIONS ABOVE YOUR STATION.
AS MUCH AS MY MEANS OF ESCAPE SITS ILL ON MY PALATE, YOUR WATERY FATE...PLEASES ME.
LIKE ALL WHO DWELL HERE, YOU HAVE NO FUTURE.

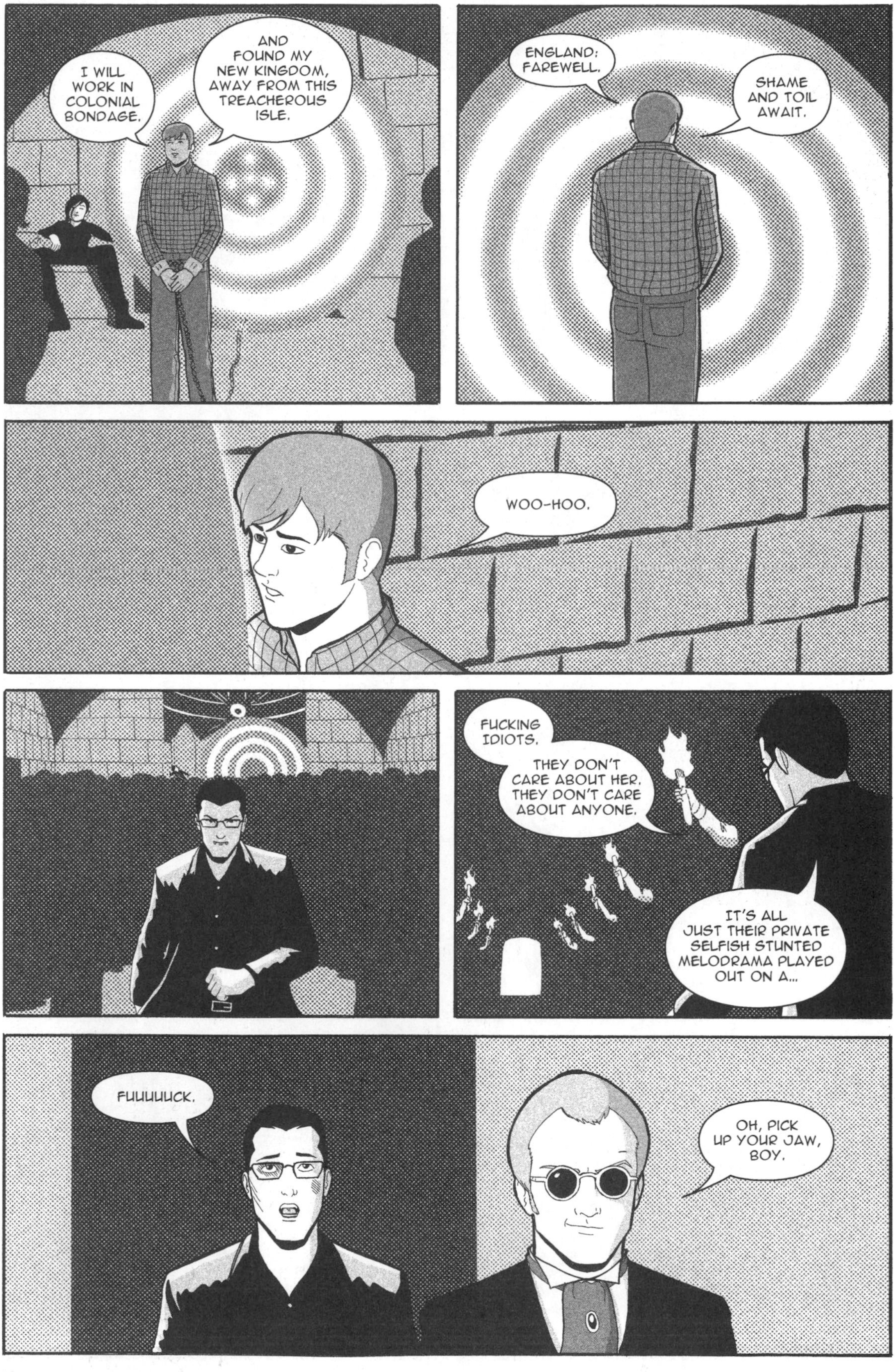
I WILL WORK IN COLONIAL BONDAGE.
AND FOUND MY NEW KINGDOM, AWAY FROM THIS TREACHEROUS ISLE.
ENGLAND: FAREWELL.
SHAME AND TOIL AWAIT.
WOO-HOO.
FUCKING IDIOTS.
THEY DON'T CARE ABOUT HER. THEY DON'T CARE ABOUT ANYONE.
IT'S ALL JUST THEIR PRIVATE SELFISH STUNTED MELODRAMA PLAYED OUT ON A...
FUUUUUCK.
OH, PICK UP YOUR JAW, BOY.

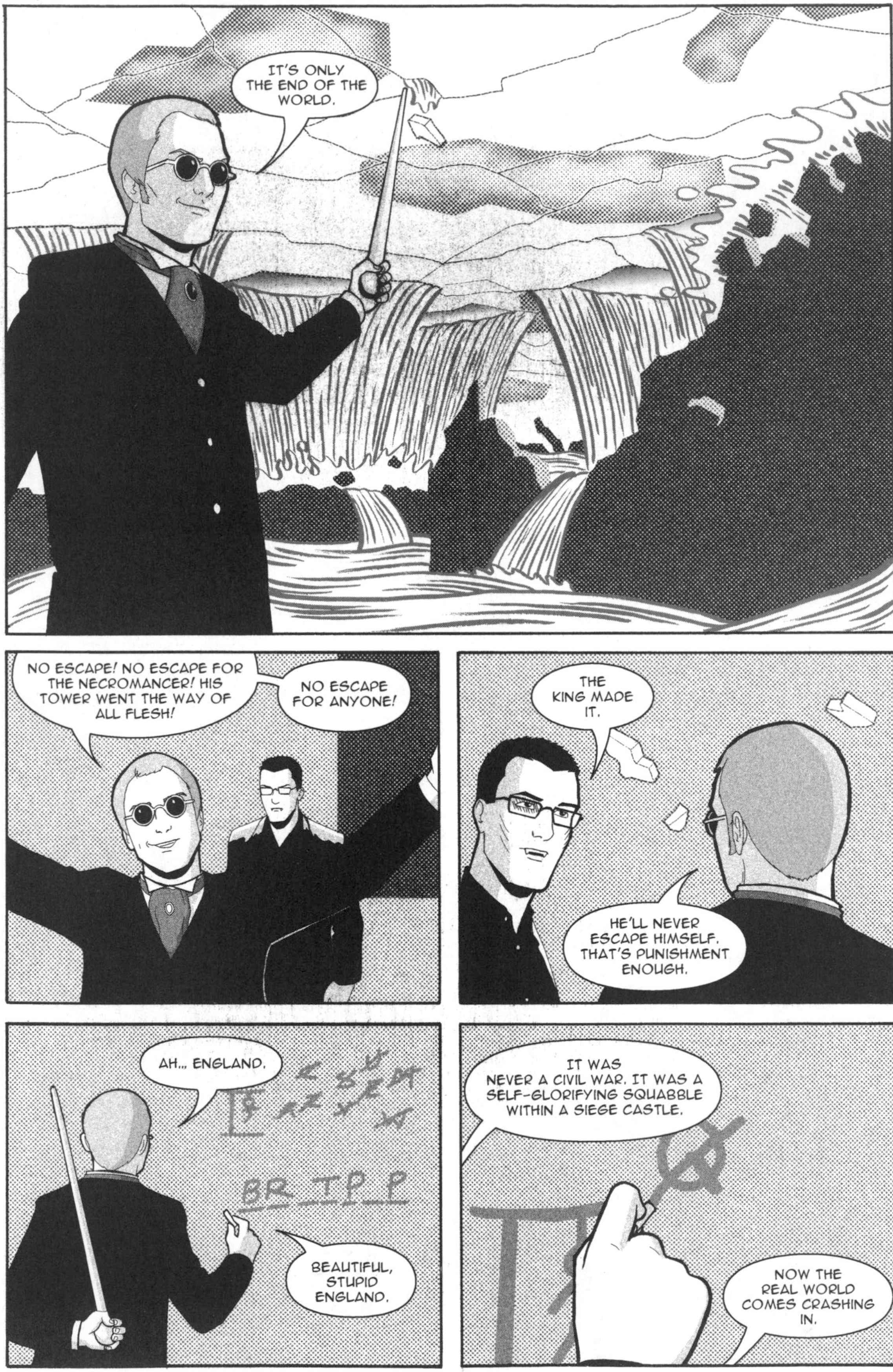
IT'S ONLY THE END OF THE WORLD.
NO ESCAPE! NO ESCAPE FOR THE NECROMANCER! HIS TOWER WENT THE WAY OF ALL FLESH!
NO ESCAPE FOR ANYONE!
THE KING MADE IT.
HE'LL NEVER ESCAPE HIMSELF. THAT'S PUNISHMENT ENOUGH.
AH... ENGLAND.
BR TP P
BEAUTIFUL, STUPID ENGLAND.
IT WAS NEVER A CIVIL WAR. IT WAS A SELF-GLORIFYING SQUABBLE WITHIN A SIEGE CASTLE.
NOW THE REAL WORLD COMES CRASHING IN.

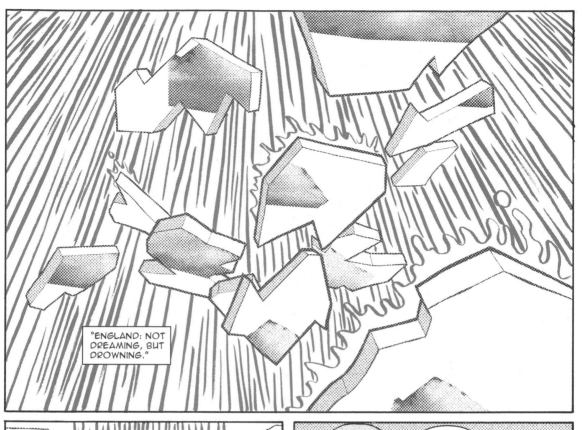

"ENGLAND: NOT DREAMING, BUT DROWNING."

OH GOD.

DAVID?

WHO WOULD WANT TO POSSESS THE *IDEA* OF A DEAD GODDESS?

AND UPON POSSESSING SUCH A THING, WHATEVER WOULD THEY DO WITH IT?

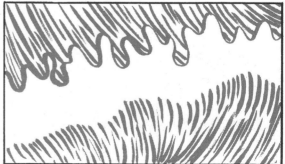

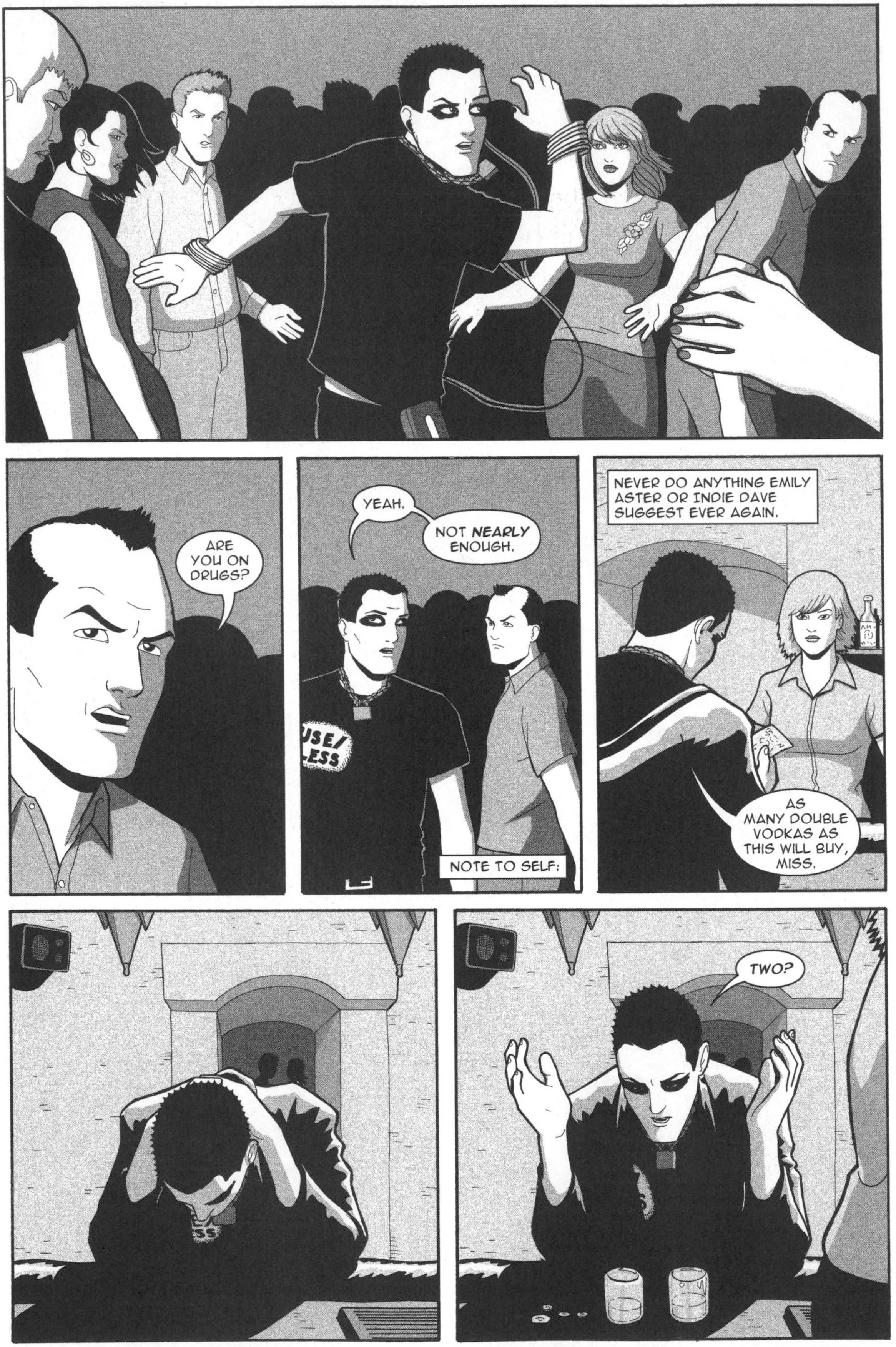
ARE YOU ON DRUGS?
YEAH.
NOT NEARLY ENOUGH.
USE/
LESS
NOTE TO SELF:
NEVER DO ANYTHING EMILY ASTER OR INDIE DAVE SUGGEST EVER AGAIN.
AS MANY DOUBLE VODKAS AS THIS WILL BUY, MISS.
TWO?

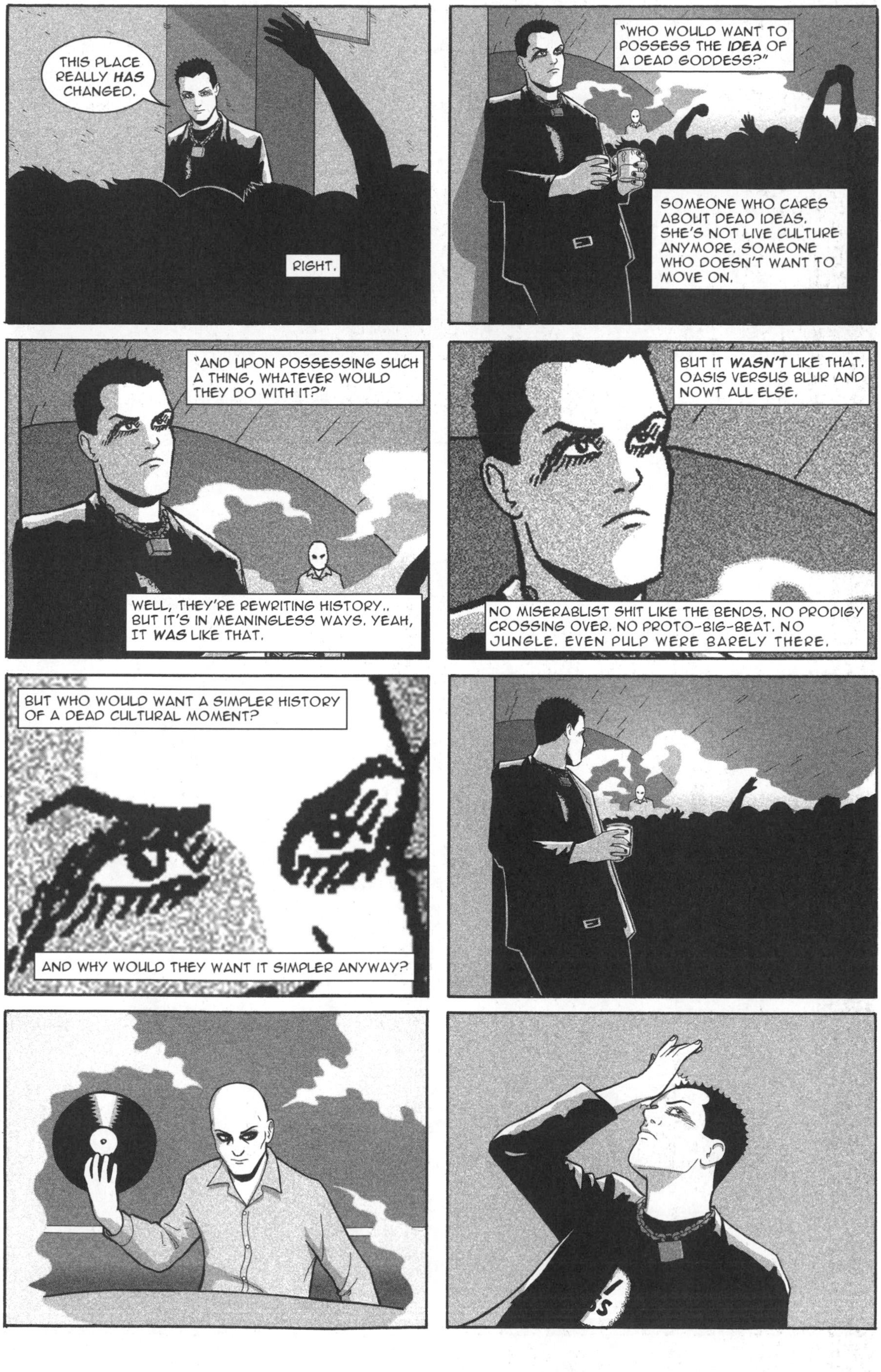
THIS PLACE REALLY HAS CHANGED.
RIGHT.
"WHO WOULD WANT TO POSSESS THE IDEA OF A DEAD GODDESS?"
SOMEONE WHO CARES ABOUT DEAD IDEAS. SHE'S NOT LIVE CULTURE ANYMORE. SOMEONE WHO DOESN'T WANT TO MOVE ON.
"AND UPON POSSESSING SUCH A THING, WHATEVER WOULD THEY DO WITH IT?"
WELL, THEY'RE REWRITING HISTORY.. BUT IT'S IN MEANINGLESS WAYS. YEAH, IT WAS LIKE THAT.
BUT IT WASN'T LIKE THAT. OASIS VERSUS BLUR AND NOWT ALL ELSE.
NO MISERABLIST SHIT LIKE THE BENDS. NO PRODIGY CROSSING OVER. NO PROTO-BIG-BEAT. NO JUNGLE. EVEN PULP WERE BARELY THERE.
BUT WHO WOULD WANT A SIMPLER HISTORY OF A DEAD CULTURAL MOMENT?
AND WHY WOULD THEY WANT IT SIMPLER ANYWAY?

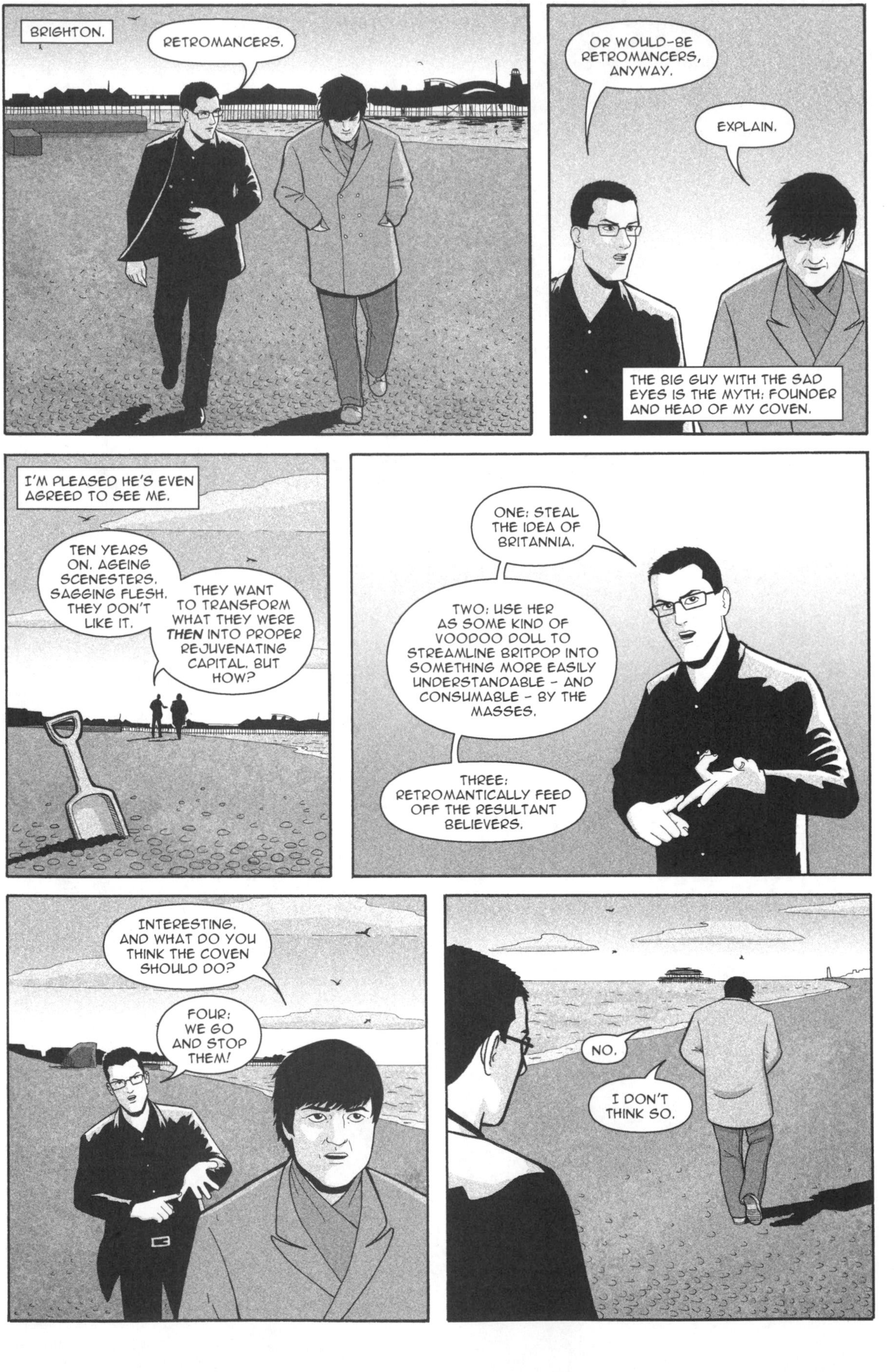
BRIGHTON.
RETROMANCERS.
OR WOULD-BE RETROMANCERS, ANYWAY.
EXPLAIN.
THE BIG GUY WITH THE SAD EYES IS THE MYTH: FOUNDER AND HEAD OF MY COVEN.
I'M PLEASED HE'S EVEN AGREED TO SEE ME.
TEN YEARS ON. AGEING SCENESTERS. SAGGING FLESH. THEY DON'T LIKE IT.
THEY WANT TO TRANSFORM WHAT THEY WERE *THEN* INTO PROPER REJUVENATING CAPITAL. BUT HOW?
ONE: STEAL THE IDEA OF BRITANNIA.
TWO: USE HER AS SOME KIND OF VOODOO DOLL TO STREAMLINE BRITPOP INTO SOMETHING MORE EASILY UNDERSTANDABLE - AND CONSUMABLE - BY THE MASSES.
THREE: RETROMANTICALLY FEED OFF THE RESULTANT BELIEVERS.
INTERESTING. AND WHAT DO YOU THINK THE COVEN SHOULD DO?
FOUR: WE GO AND STOP THEM!
NO.
I DON'T THINK SO.

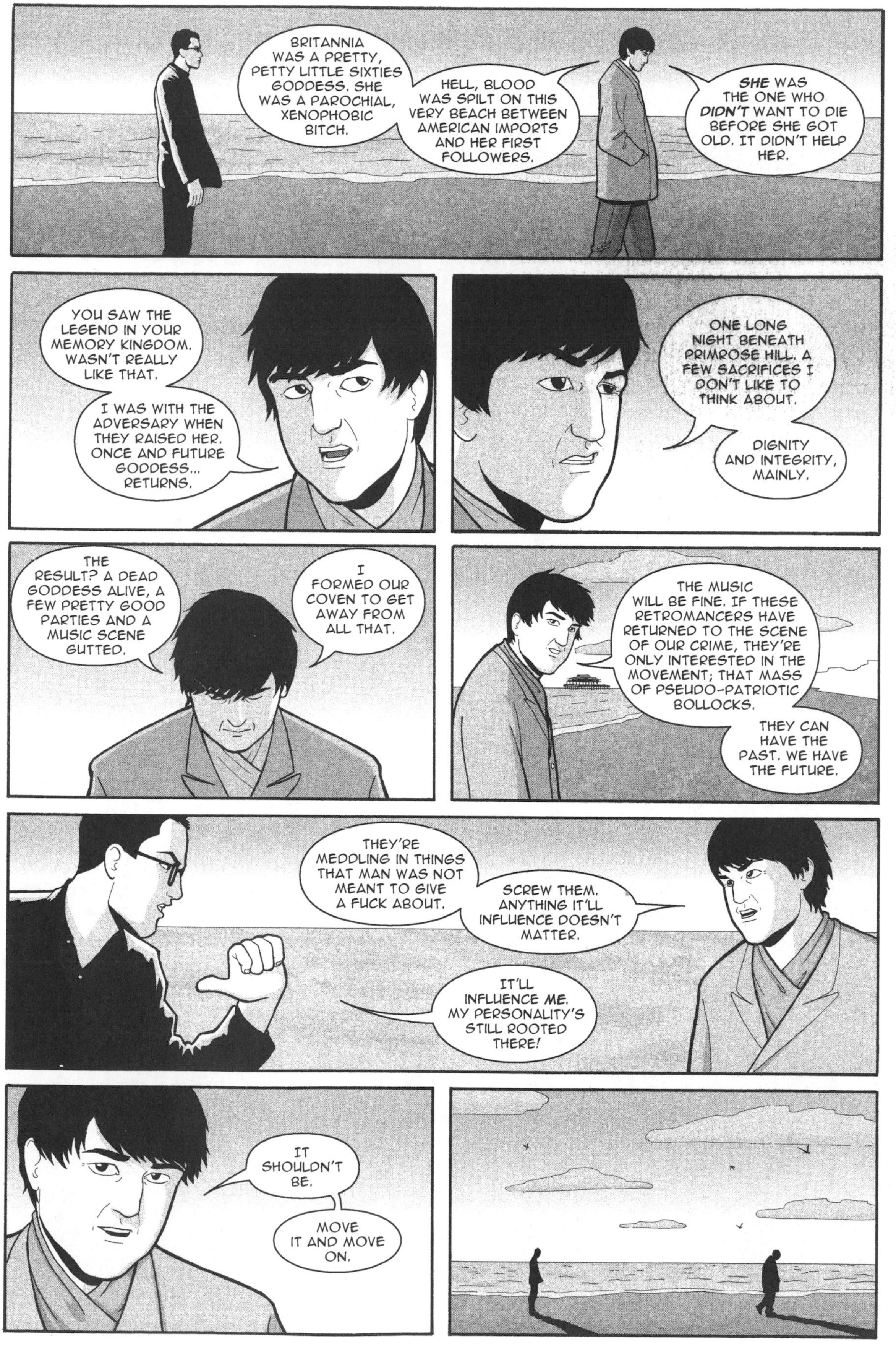
BRITANNIA WAS A PRETTY, PETTY LITTLE SIXTIES GODDESS. SHE WAS A PAROCHIAL, XENOPHOBIC BITCH.
HELL, BLOOD WAS SPILT ON THIS VERY BEACH BETWEEN AMERICAN IMPORTS AND HER FIRST FOLLOWERS.
SHE WAS THE ONE WHO DIDN'T WANT TO DIE BEFORE SHE GOT OLD. IT DIDN'T HELP HER.
YOU SAW THE LEGEND IN YOUR MEMORY KINGDOM. WASN'T REALLY LIKE THAT.
I WAS WITH THE ADVERSARY WHEN THEY RAISED HER. ONCE AND FUTURE GODDESS... RETURNS.
ONE LONG NIGHT BENEATH PRIMROSE HILL. A FEW SACRIFICES I DON'T LIKE TO THINK ABOUT.
DIGNITY AND INTEGRITY, MAINLY.
THE RESULT? A DEAD GODDESS ALIVE, A FEW PRETTY GOOD PARTIES AND A MUSIC SCENE GUTTED.
I FORMED OUR COVEN TO GET AWAY FROM ALL THAT.
THE MUSIC WILL BE FINE. IF THESE RETROMANCERS HAVE RETURNED TO THE SCENE OF OUR CRIME, THEY'RE ONLY INTERESTED IN THE MOVEMENT; THAT MASS OF PSEUDO-PATRIOTIC BOLLOCKS.
THEY CAN HAVE THE PAST. WE HAVE THE FUTURE.
THEY'RE MEDDLING IN THINGS THAT MAN WAS NOT MEANT TO GIVE A FUCK ABOUT.
SCREW THEM. ANYTHING IT'LL INFLUENCE DOESN'T MATTER.
IT'LL INFLUENCE ME. MY PERSONALITY'S STILL ROOTED THERE!
IT SHOULDN'T BE.
MOVE IT AND MOVE ON.

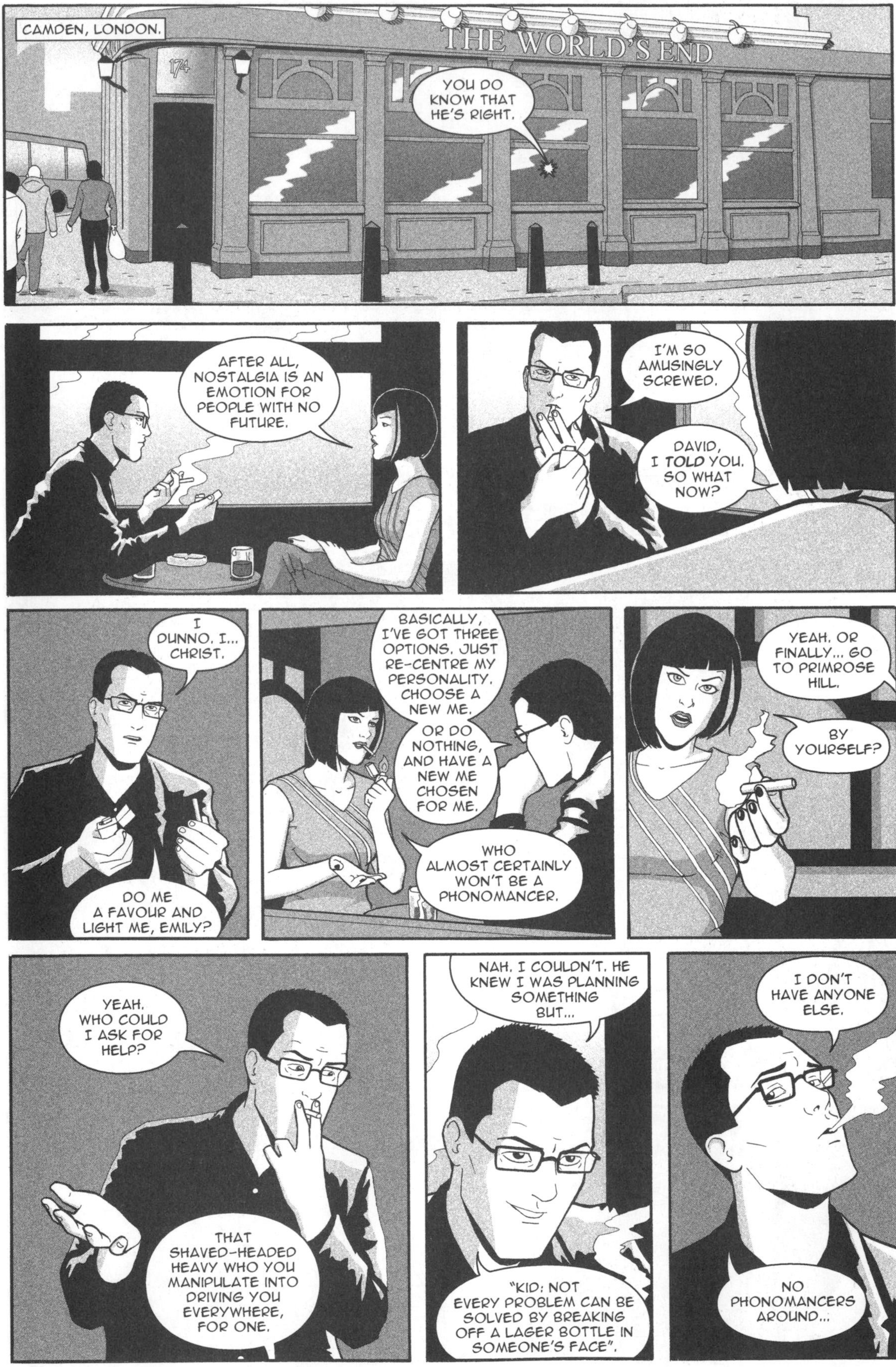
CAMDEN, LONDON.
THE WORLD'S END
174
YOU DO KNOW THAT HE'S RIGHT.
AFTER ALL, NOSTALGIA IS AN EMOTION FOR PEOPLE WITH NO FUTURE.
I'M SO AMUSINGLY SCREWED.
DAVID, I *TOLD* YOU. SO WHAT NOW?
I DUNNO. I... CHRIST.
DO ME A FAVOUR AND LIGHT ME, EMILY?
BASICALLY, I'VE GOT THREE OPTIONS. JUST RE-CENTRE MY PERSONALITY, CHOOSE A NEW ME.
OR DO NOTHING, AND HAVE A NEW ME CHOSEN FOR ME.
WHO ALMOST CERTAINLY WON'T BE A PHONOMANCER.
YEAH. OR FINALLY... GO TO PRIMROSE HILL.
BY YOURSELF?
YEAH. WHO COULD I ASK FOR HELP?
THAT SHAVED-HEADED HEAVY WHO YOU MANIPULATE INTO DRIVING YOU EVERYWHERE, FOR ONE.
NAH. I COULDN'T. HE KNEW I WAS PLANNING SOMETHING BUT...
"KID: NOT EVERY PROBLEM CAN BE SOLVED BY BREAKING OFF A LAGER BOTTLE IN SOMEONE'S FACE".
I DON'T HAVE ANYONE ELSE.
NO PHONOMANCERS AROUND...

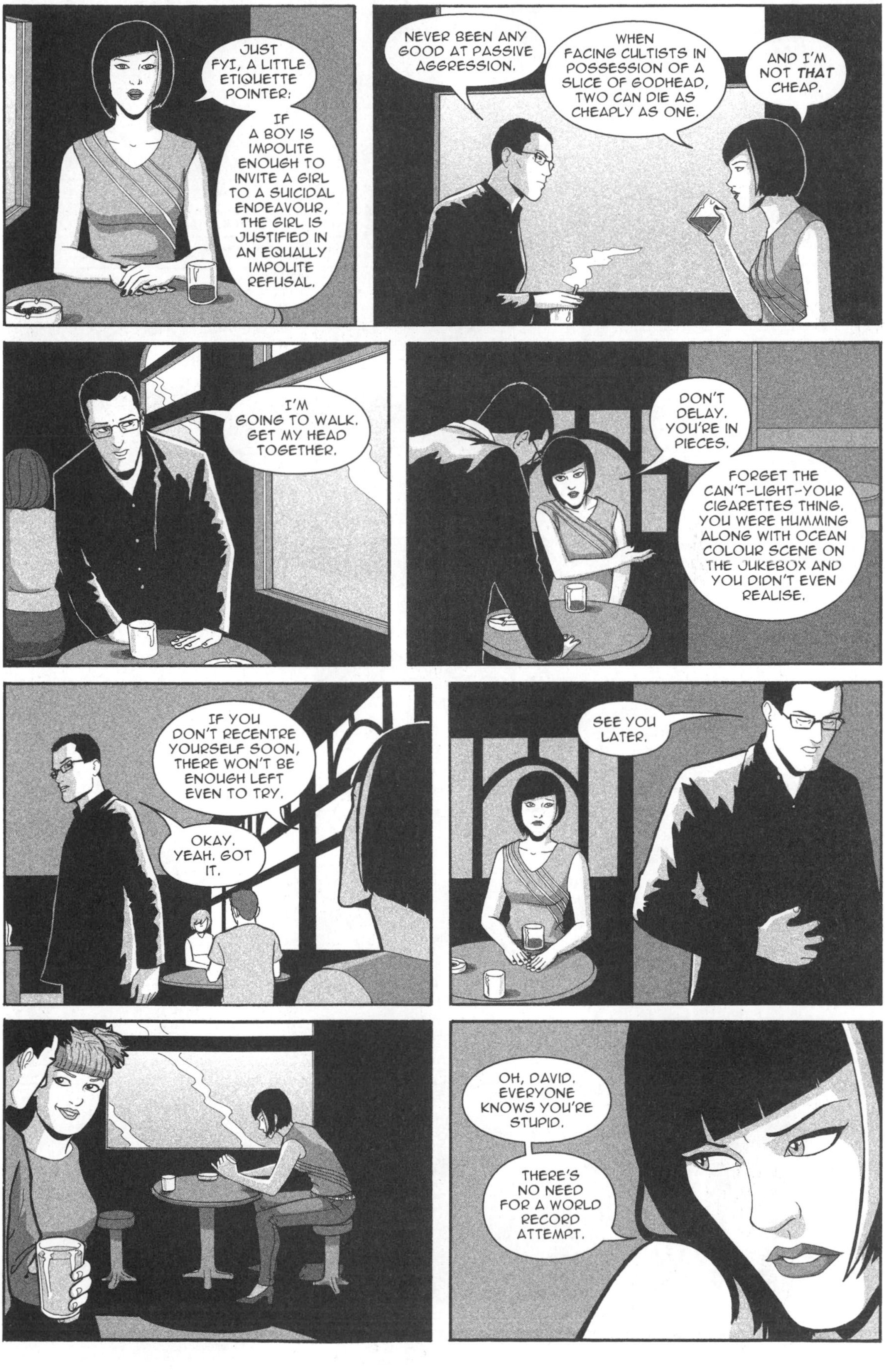
JUST FYI, A LITTLE ETIQUETTE POINTER:
IF A BOY IS IMPOLITE ENOUGH TO INVITE A GIRL TO A SUICIDAL ENDEAVOUR, THE GIRL IS JUSTIFIED IN AN EQUALLY IMPOLITE REFUSAL.
NEVER BEEN ANY GOOD AT PASSIVE AGGRESSION.
WHEN FACING CULTISTS IN POSSESSION OF A SLICE OF GODHEAD, TWO CAN DIE AS CHEAPLY AS ONE.
AND I'M NOT *THAT* CHEAP.
I'M GOING TO WALK. GET MY HEAD TOGETHER.
DON'T DELAY. YOU'RE IN PIECES.
FORGET THE CAN'T-LIGHT-YOUR CIGARETTES THING. YOU WERE HUMMING ALONG WITH OCEAN COLOUR SCENE ON THE JUKEBOX AND YOU DIDN'T EVEN REALISE.
IF YOU DON'T RECENTRE YOURSELF SOON, THERE WON'T BE ENOUGH LEFT EVEN TO TRY.
OKAY. YEAH. GOT IT.
SEE YOU LATER.
OH, DAVID. EVERYONE KNOWS YOU'RE STUPID.
THERE'S NO NEED FOR A WORLD RECORD ATTEMPT.

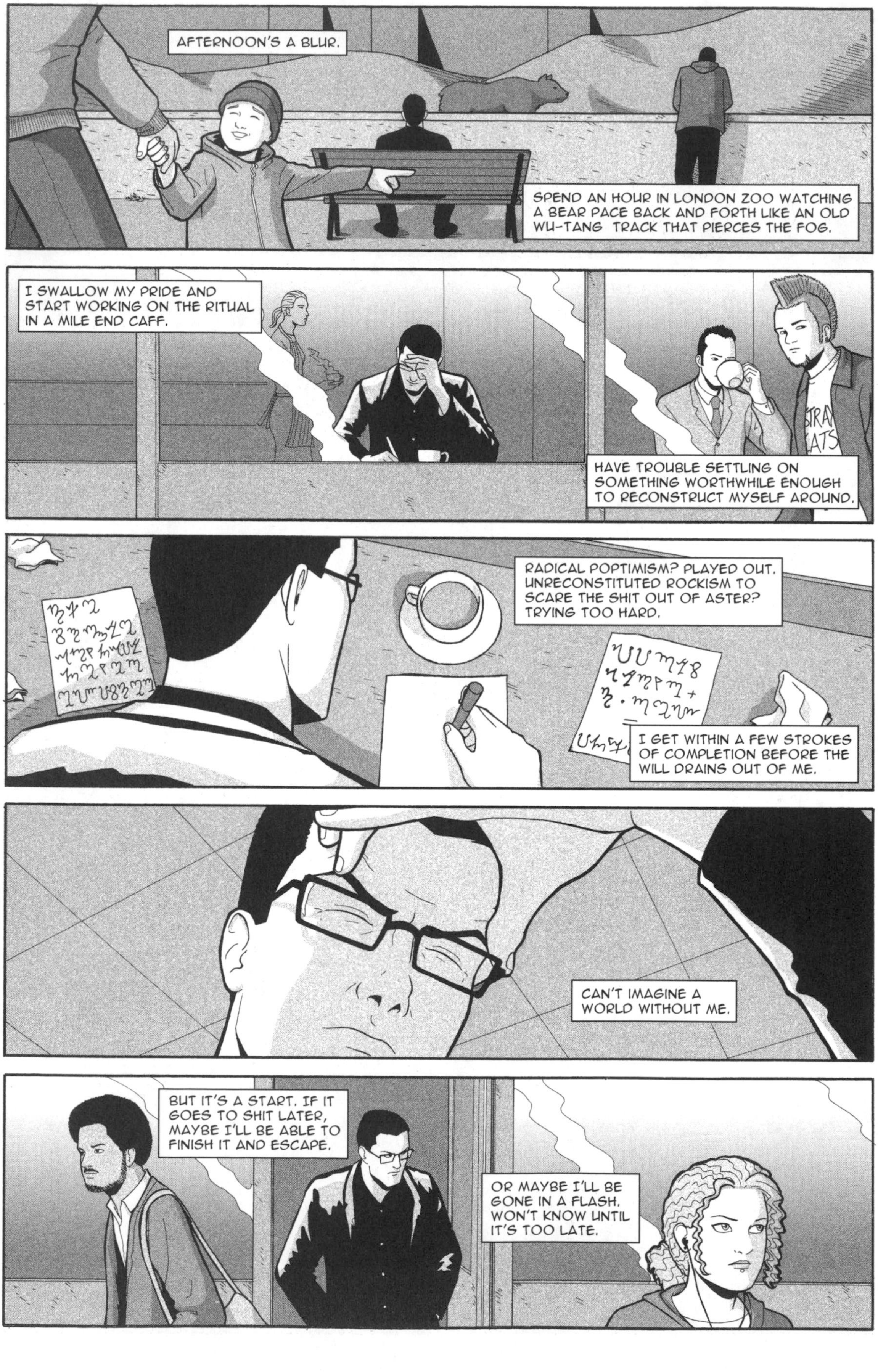
AFTERNOON'S A BLUR.
SPEND AN HOUR IN LONDON ZOO WATCHING A BEAR PACE BACK AND FORTH LIKE AN OLD WU-TANG TRACK THAT PIERCES THE FOG.
I SWALLOW MY PRIDE AND START WORKING ON THE RITUAL IN A MILE END CAFF.
HAVE TROUBLE SETTLING ON SOMETHING WORTHWHILE ENOUGH TO RECONSTRUCT MYSELF AROUND.
RADICAL POPTIMISM? PLAYED OUT. UNRECONSTITUTED ROCKISM TO SCARE THE SHIT OUT OF ASTER? TRYING TOO HARD.
I GET WITHIN A FEW STROKES OF COMPLETION BEFORE THE WILL DRAINS OUT OF ME.
CAN'T IMAGINE A WORLD WITHOUT ME.
BUT IT'S A START. IF IT GOES TO SHIT LATER, MAYBE I'LL BE ABLE TO FINISH IT AND ESCAPE.
OR MAYBE I'LL BE GONE IN A FLASH. WON'T KNOW UNTIL IT'S TOO LATE.

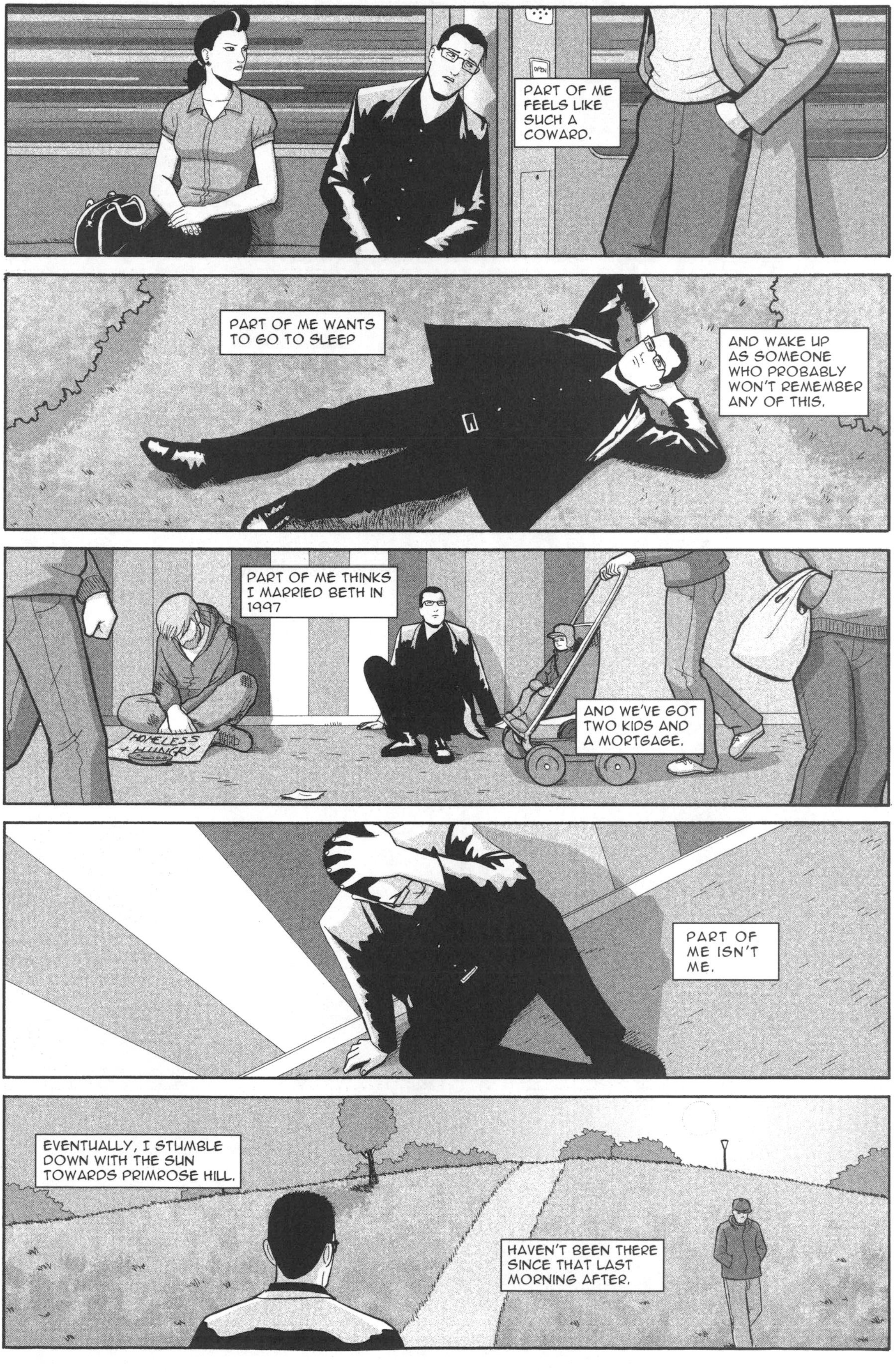

PART OF ME FEELS LIKE SUCH A COWARD.
PART OF ME WANTS TO GO TO SLEEP
AND WAKE UP AS SOMEONE WHO PROBABLY WON'T REMEMBER ANY OF THIS.
PART OF ME THINKS I MARRIED BETH IN 1997
HOMELESS + HUNGRY
AND WE'VE GOT TWO KIDS AND A MORTGAGE.
PART OF ME ISN'T ME.
EVENTUALLY, I STUMBLE DOWN WITH THE SUN TOWARDS PRIMROSE HILL.
HAVEN'T BEEN THERE SINCE THAT LAST MORNING AFTER.

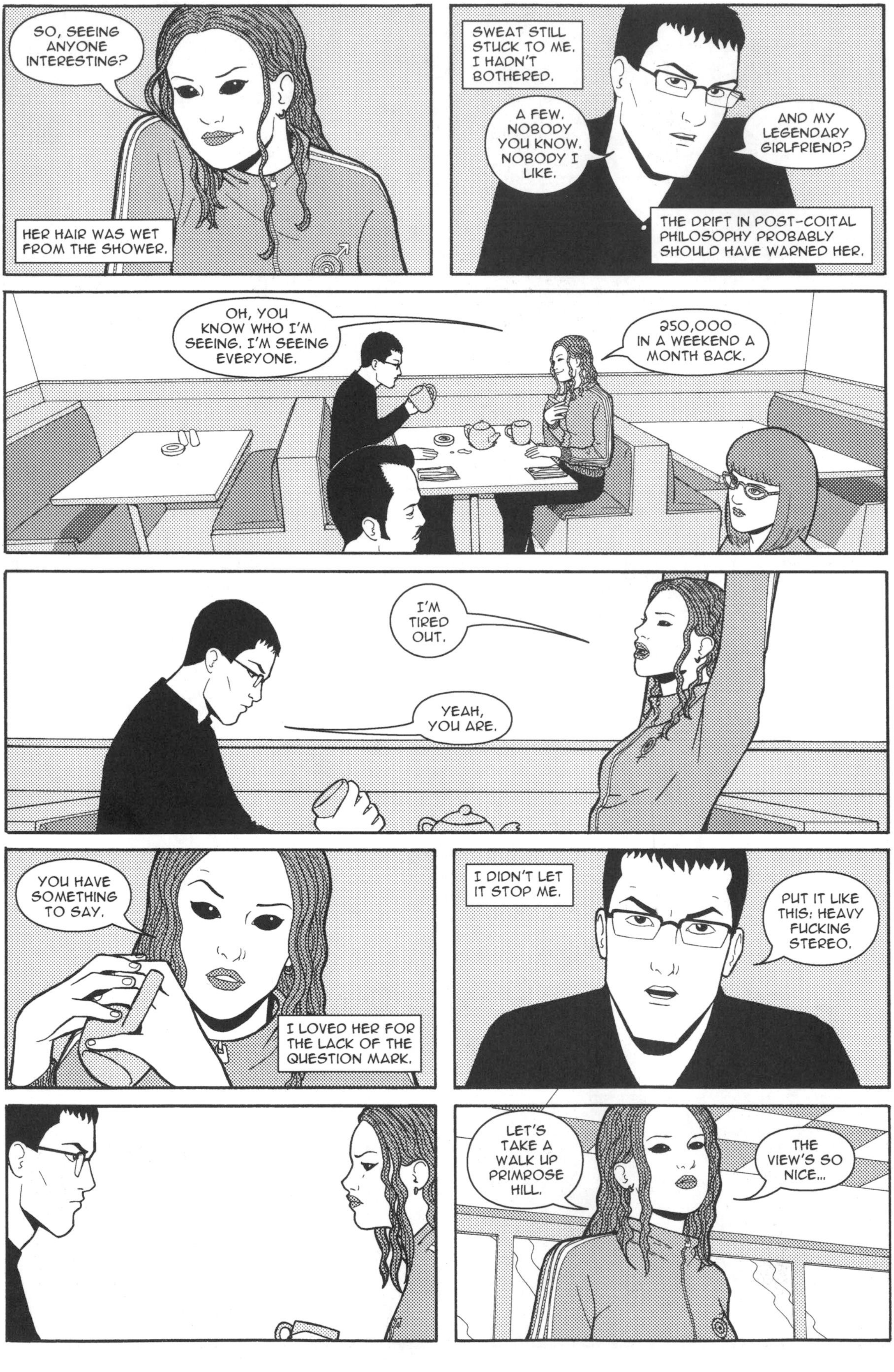
SO, SEEING ANYONE INTERESTING?
HER HAIR WAS WET FROM THE SHOWER.
SWEAT STILL STUCK TO ME. I HADN'T BOTHERED.
A FEW. NOBODY YOU KNOW. NOBODY I LIKE.
AND MY LEGENDARY GIRLFRIEND?
THE DRIFT IN POST-COITAL PHILOSOPHY PROBABLY SHOULD HAVE WARNED HER.
OH, YOU KNOW WHO I'M SEEING. I'M SEEING EVERYONE.
250,000 IN A WEEKEND A MONTH BACK.
I'M TIRED OUT.
YEAH, YOU ARE.
YOU HAVE SOMETHING TO SAY.
I LOVED HER FOR THE LACK OF THE QUESTION MARK.
I DIDN'T LET IT STOP ME.
PUT IT LIKE THIS: HEAVY FUCKING STEREO.
LET'S TAKE A WALK UP PRIMROSE HILL.
THE VIEW'S SO NICE...

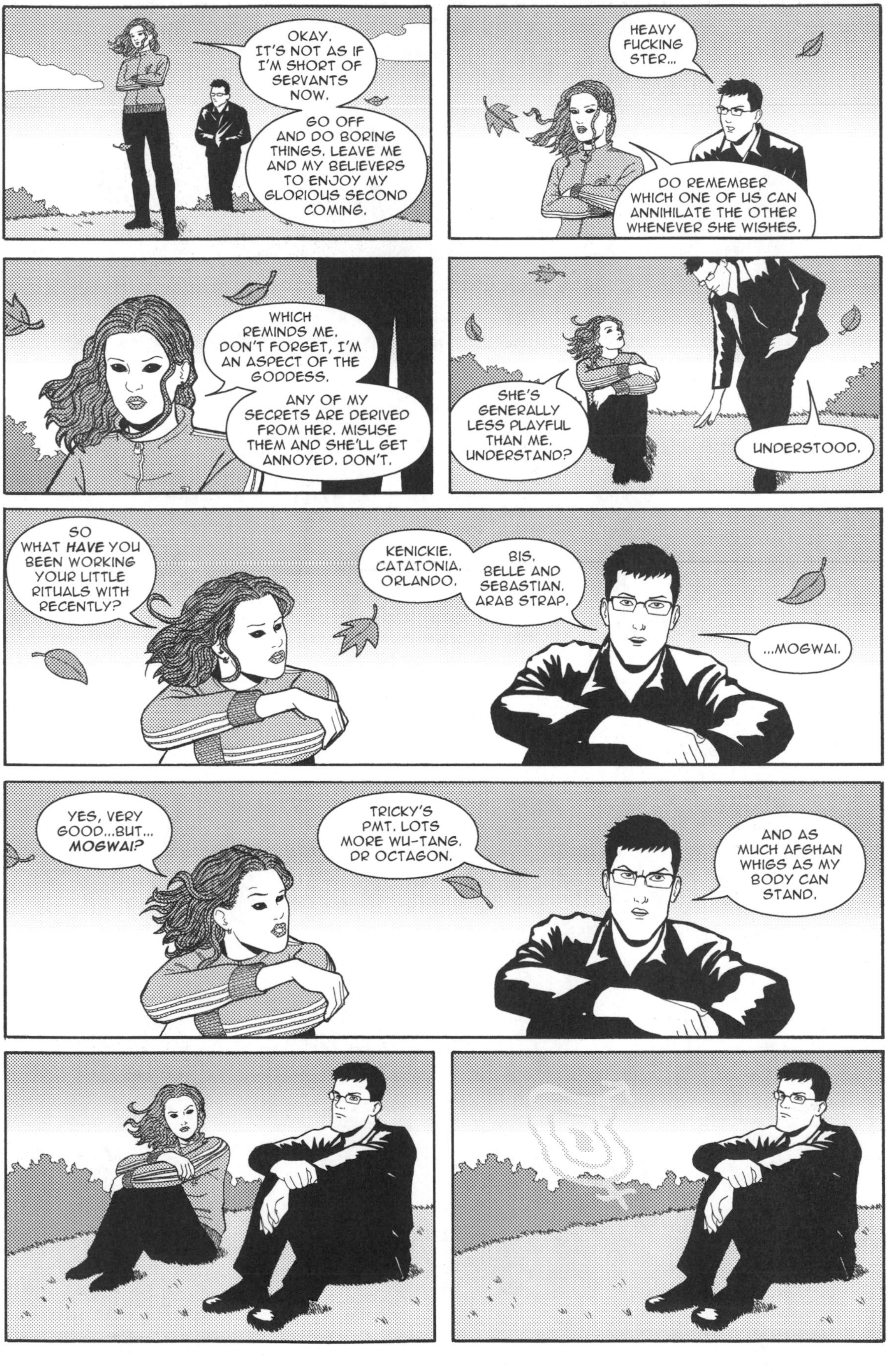
OKAY. IT'S NOT AS IF I'M SHORT OF SERVANTS NOW.
GO OFF AND DO BORING THINGS. LEAVE ME AND MY BELIEVERS TO ENJOY MY GLORIOUS SECOND COMING.
HEAVY FUCKING STER...
DO REMEMBER WHICH ONE OF US CAN ANNIHILATE THE OTHER WHENEVER SHE WISHES.
WHICH REMINDS ME. DON'T FORGET, I'M AN ASPECT OF THE GODDESS.
ANY OF MY SECRETS ARE DERIVED FROM HER. MISUSE THEM AND SHE'LL GET ANNOYED. DON'T.
SHE'S GENERALLY LESS PLAYFUL THAN ME. UNDERSTAND?
UNDERSTOOD.
SO WHAT **HAVE** YOU BEEN WORKING YOUR LITTLE RITUALS WITH RECENTLY?
KENICKIE. CATATONIA. ORLANDO.
BIS. BELLE AND SEBASTIAN. ARAB STRAP.
...MOGWAI.
YES, VERY GOOD...BUT... ***MOGWAI?***
TRICKY'S PMT. LOTS MORE WU-TANG. DR OCTAGON.
AND AS MUCH AFGHAN WHIGS AS MY BODY CAN STAND.

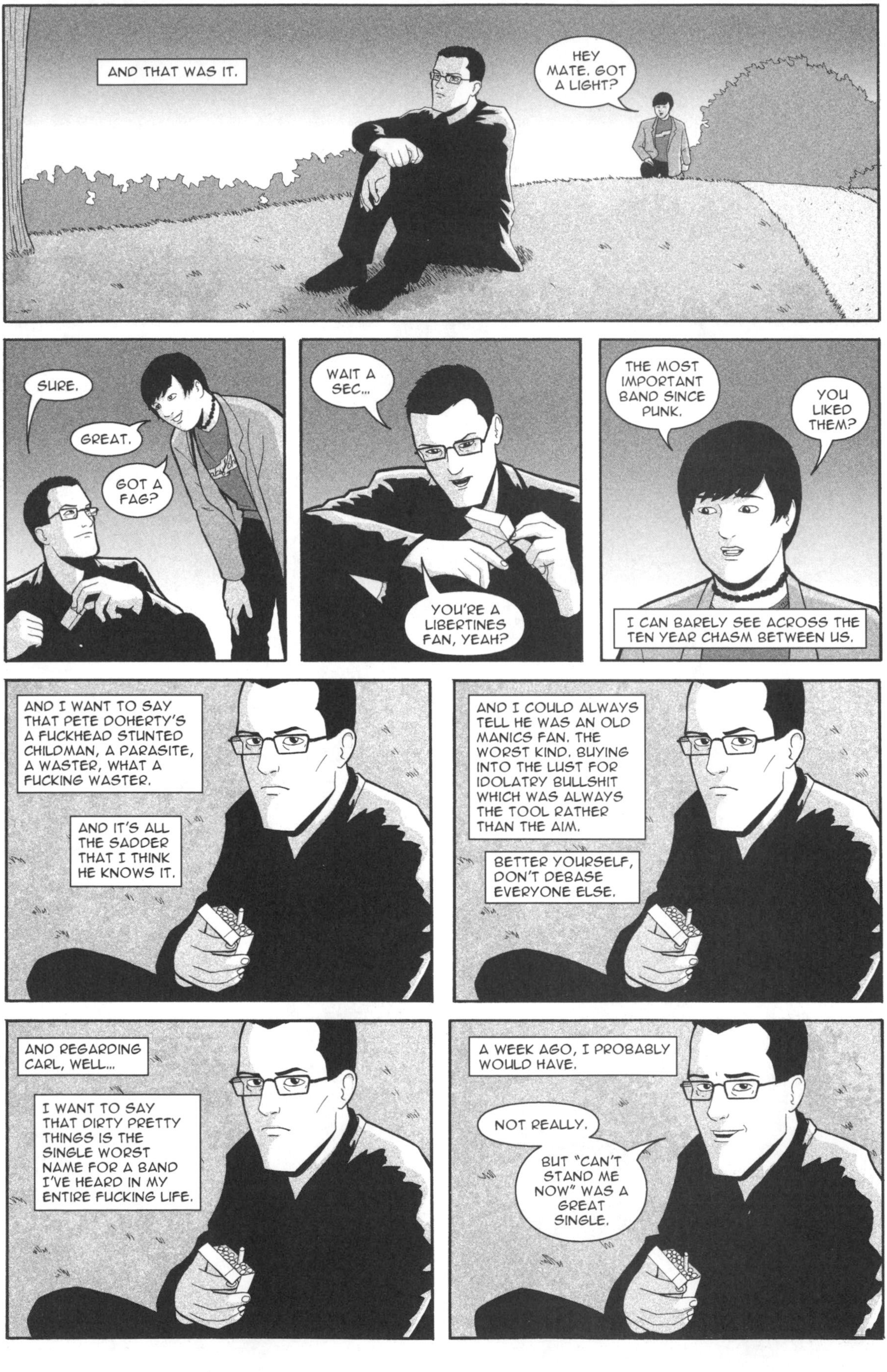
AND THAT WAS IT.
HEY MATE. GOT A LIGHT?
SURE.
GREAT.
GOT A FAG?
WAIT A SEC...
YOU'RE A LIBERTINES FAN, YEAH?
THE MOST IMPORTANT BAND SINCE PUNK.
YOU LIKED THEM?
I CAN BARELY SEE ACROSS THE TEN YEAR CHASM BETWEEN US.
AND I WANT TO SAY THAT PETE DOHERTY'S A FUCKHEAD STUNTED CHILDMAN, A PARASITE, A WASTER, WHAT A FUCKING WASTER.
AND IT'S ALL THE SADDER THAT I THINK HE KNOWS IT.
AND I COULD ALWAYS TELL HE WAS AN OLD MANICS FAN. THE WORST KIND. BUYING INTO THE LUST FOR IDOLATRY BULLSHIT WHICH WAS ALWAYS THE TOOL RATHER THAN THE AIM.
BETTER YOURSELF, DON'T DEBASE EVERYONE ELSE.
AND REGARDING CARL, WELL...
I WANT TO SAY THAT DIRTY PRETTY THINGS IS THE SINGLE WORST NAME FOR A BAND I'VE HEARD IN MY ENTIRE FUCKING LIFE.
A WEEK AGO, I PROBABLY WOULD HAVE.
NOT REALLY.
BUT "CAN'T STAND ME NOW" WAS A GREAT SINGLE.

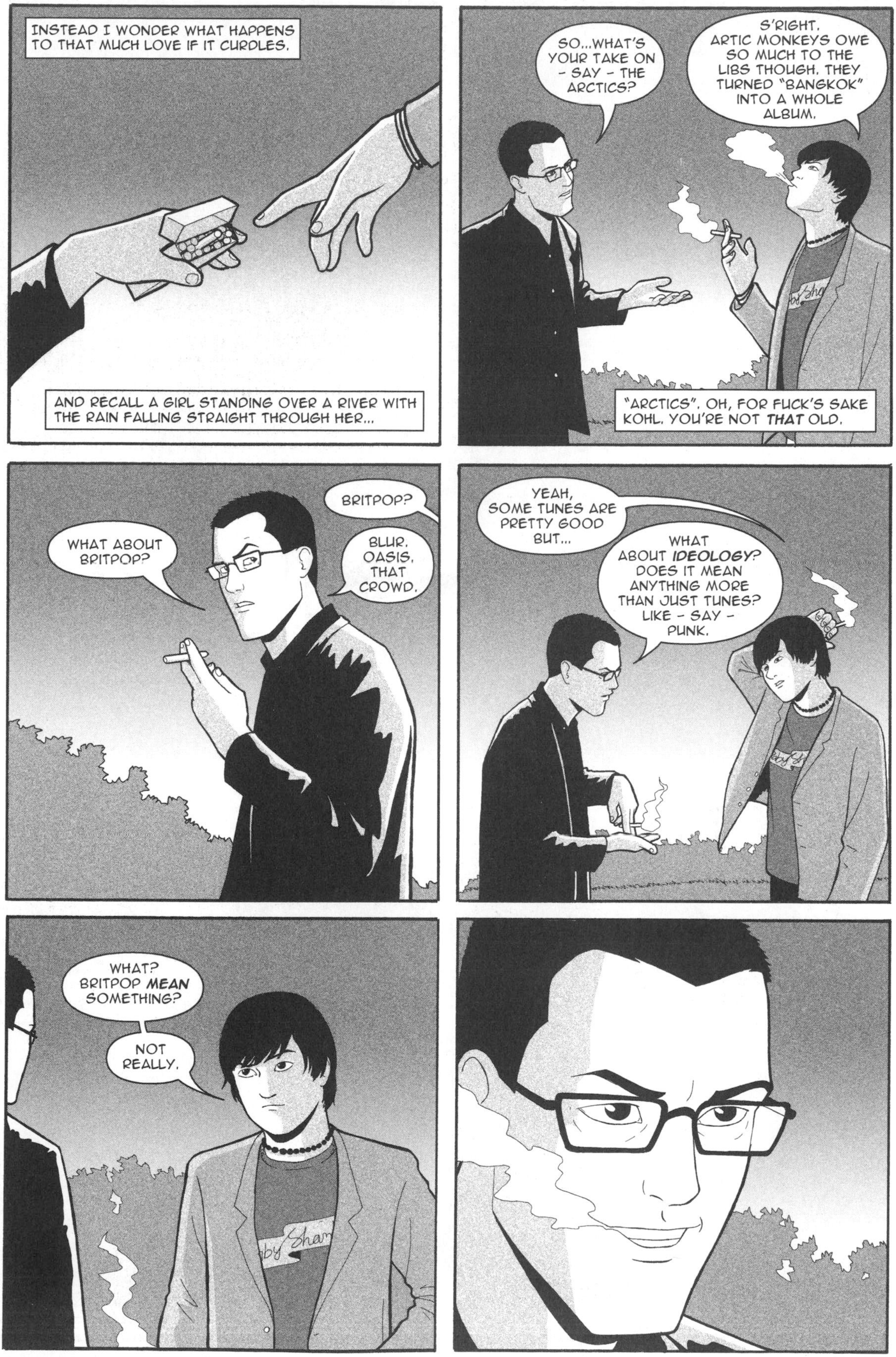
INSTEAD I WONDER WHAT HAPPENS TO THAT MUCH LOVE IF IT CURDLES.
AND RECALL A GIRL STANDING OVER A RIVER WITH THE RAIN FALLING STRAIGHT THROUGH HER...
SO...WHAT'S YOUR TAKE ON - SAY - THE ARCTICS?
S'RIGHT. ARTIC MONKEYS OWE SO MUCH TO THE LIBS THOUGH. THEY TURNED "BANGKOK" INTO A WHOLE ALBUM.
"ARCTICS". OH, FOR FUCK'S SAKE KOHL. YOU'RE NOT **THAT** OLD.
WHAT ABOUT BRITPOP?
BRITPOP?
BLUR. OASIS. THAT CROWD.
YEAH, SOME TUNES ARE PRETTY GOOD BUT...
WHAT ABOUT ***IDEOLOGY***? DOES IT MEAN ANYTHING MORE THAN JUST TUNES? LIKE - SAY - PUNK.
WHAT? BRITPOP **MEAN** SOMETHING?
NOT REALLY.

SO YOU THINK BRITPOP **SHOULD** MEAN SOMETHING TO ME?

NAH. I AGREE ENTIRELY.

LET'S SEE IF WE CAN KEEP IT THAT WAY.

SURE, HE'S STUPID AND HAS NO TASTE.

GREAT. HE'S GOT A RIGHT TO BE STUPID.

EVERYONE HAS.

U ΓΥΓϜ⅄ ϡϜ ϡϜ ϞͰϞϹϚ⅄ ϞͰϼ⅄ϞϹ⅄

THEIR OWN STUPID, UNBLEMISHED BY ANY OF MINE.

IF THEY FINISH WHATEVER THEY'RE DOING DOWN THERE, IT WON'T BE.

ϟϞϞϜϚϡ ΓϜΓϜϜ⅄ ϡϜ ϞϞϞϟϞϞϞϞϞϞϪϡϜ⅄

ANYTHING MIXING GUITARS AND BRITAIN WILL CARRY OUR TAINT. IT'LL BE JUST A WEAKER ECHO, A REVIVAL OF A REVIVAL.

THE LAST THING I EXPECTED: A REASON TO FIGHT OTHER THAN MY OWN ARSE.

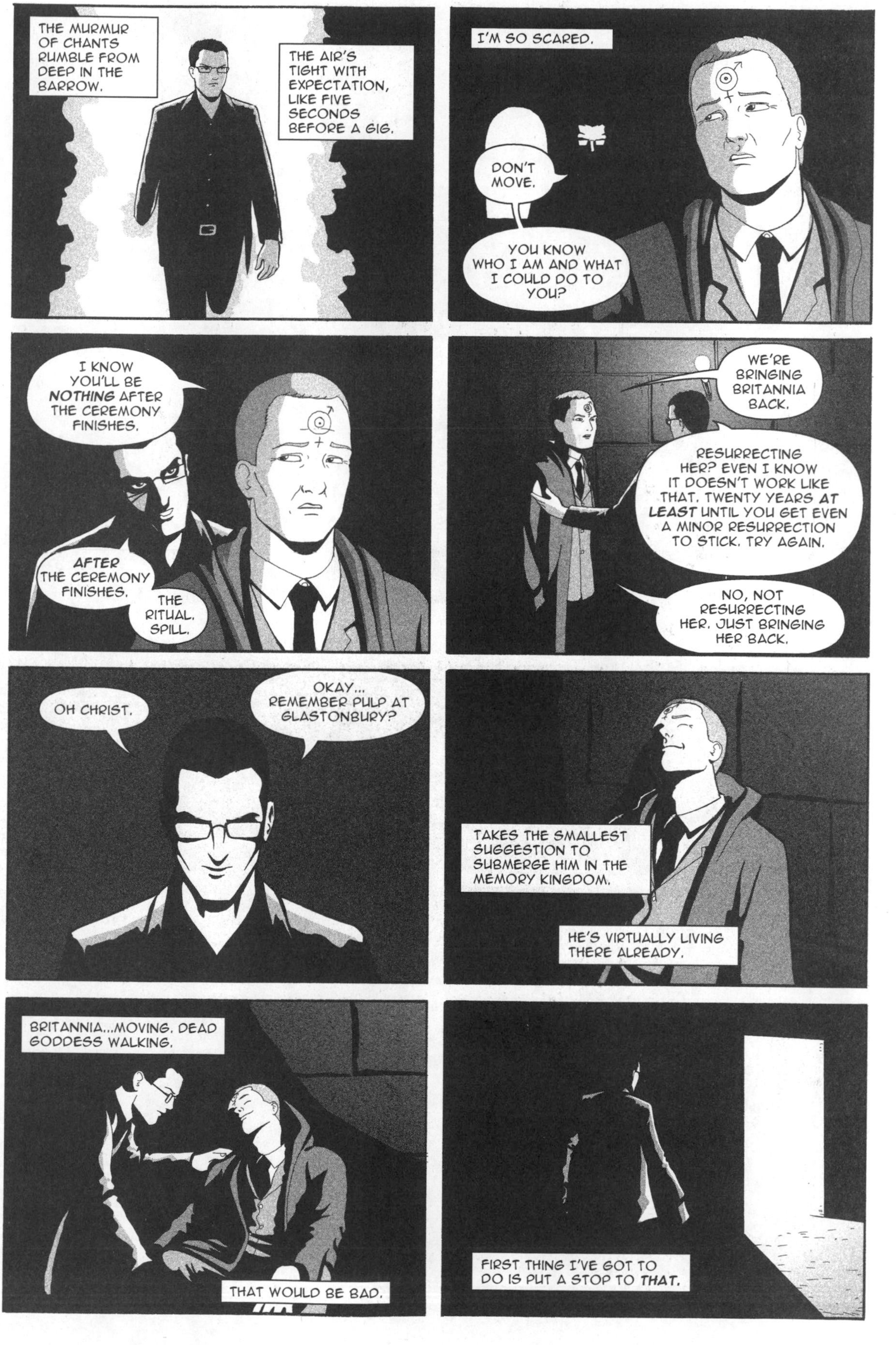
THE MURMUR OF CHANTS RUMBLE FROM DEEP IN THE BARROW.
THE AIR'S TIGHT WITH EXPECTATION, LIKE FIVE SECONDS BEFORE A GIG.
I'M SO SCARED.
DON'T MOVE.
YOU KNOW WHO I AM AND WHAT I COULD DO TO YOU?
I KNOW YOU'LL BE *NOTHING* AFTER THE CEREMONY FINISHES.
AFTER THE CEREMONY FINISHES.
THE RITUAL. SPILL.
WE'RE BRINGING BRITANNIA BACK.
RESURRECTING HER? EVEN I KNOW IT DOESN'T WORK LIKE THAT. TWENTY YEARS **AT *LEAST*** UNTIL YOU GET EVEN A MINOR RESURRECTION TO STICK. TRY AGAIN.
NO, NOT RESURRECTING HER. JUST BRINGING HER BACK.
OH CHRIST.
OKAY... REMEMBER PULP AT GLASTONBURY?
TAKES THE SMALLEST SUGGESTION TO SUBMERGE HIM IN THE MEMORY KINGDOM.
HE'S VIRTUALLY LIVING THERE ALREADY.
BRITANNIA...MOVING. DEAD GODDESS WALKING.
THAT WOULD BE BAD.
FIRST THING I'VE GOT TO DO IS PUT A STOP TO ***THAT.***

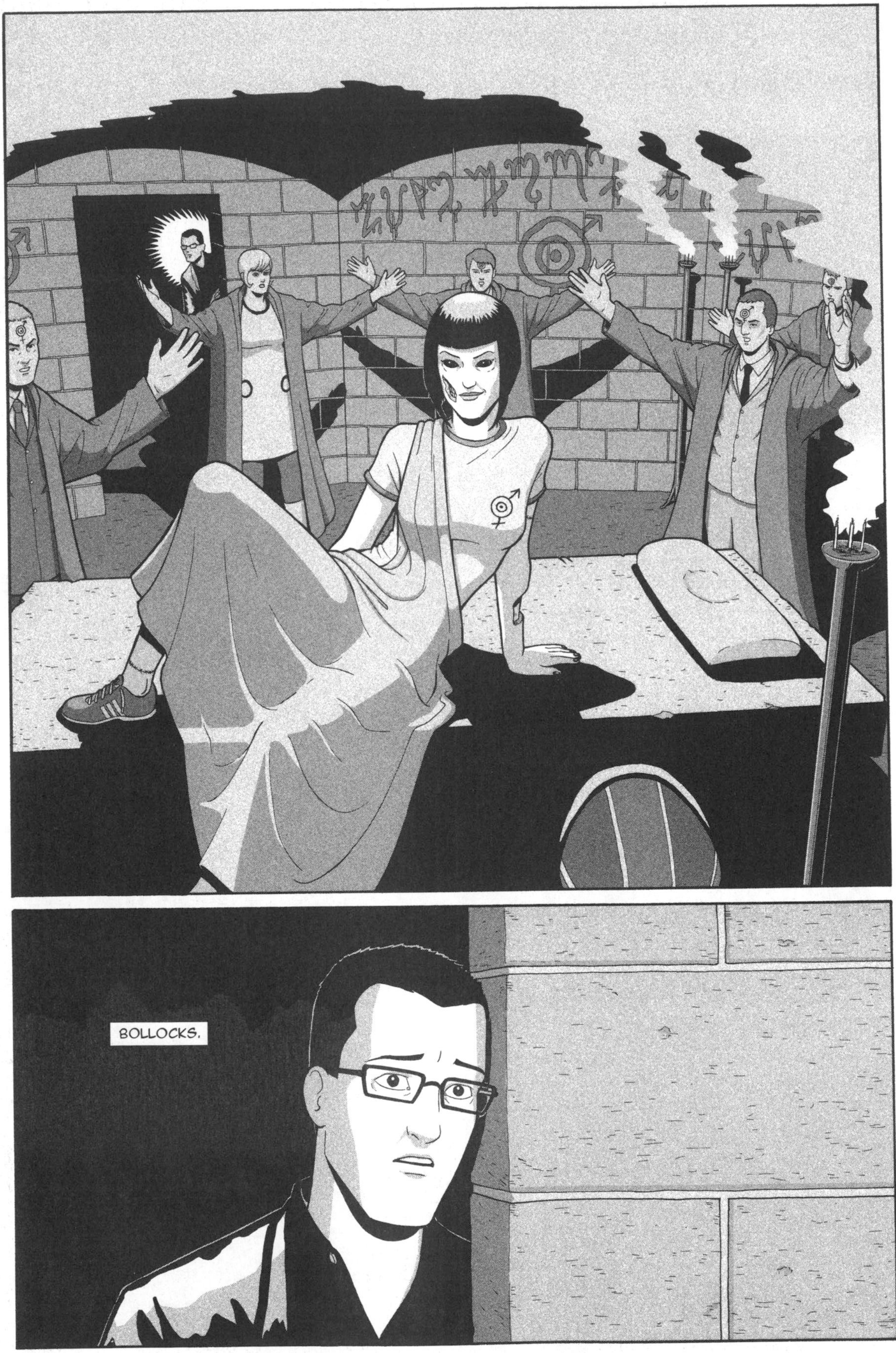
BOLLOCKS.

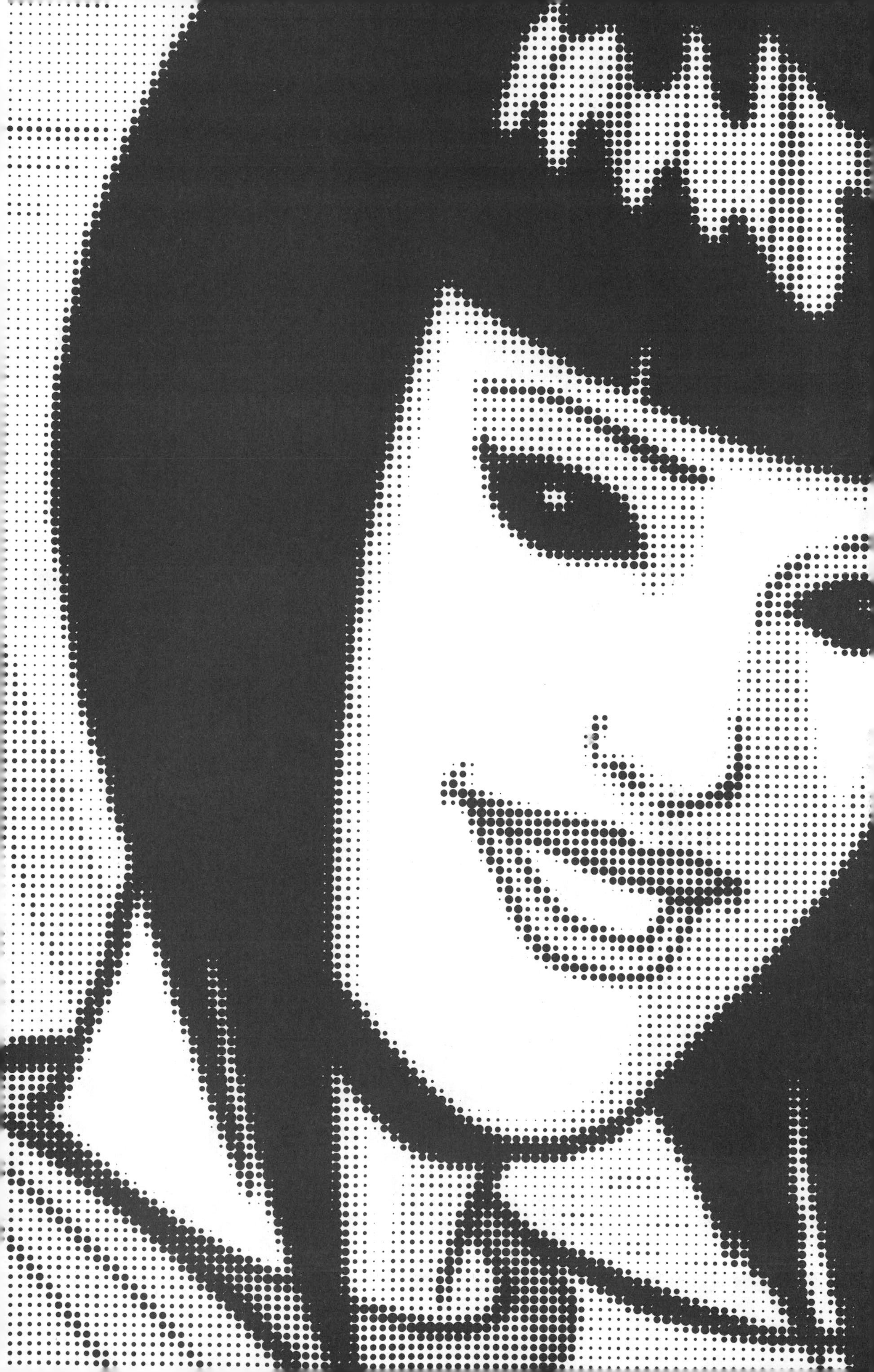

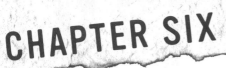

CHAPTER SIX

LIVE FORƎVEƎ
A GODDESS WALKS
WHEƎEIN:
AN AƎGUMENT IS POSED TO A GODDESS, WHO MAKES A DECISION.
AN AƎGUMENT IS POSED TO A GHOST, WHO DOES LIKEWISE.
AND A MAN DECIDES WHAT HE BELIEVES IN IS NOTHING,
BUT IT'S HIS NOTHING.

LIVE FOREVER

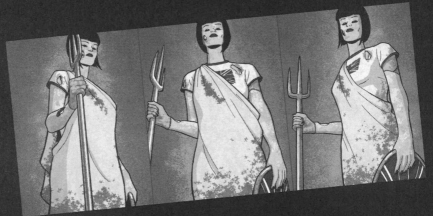

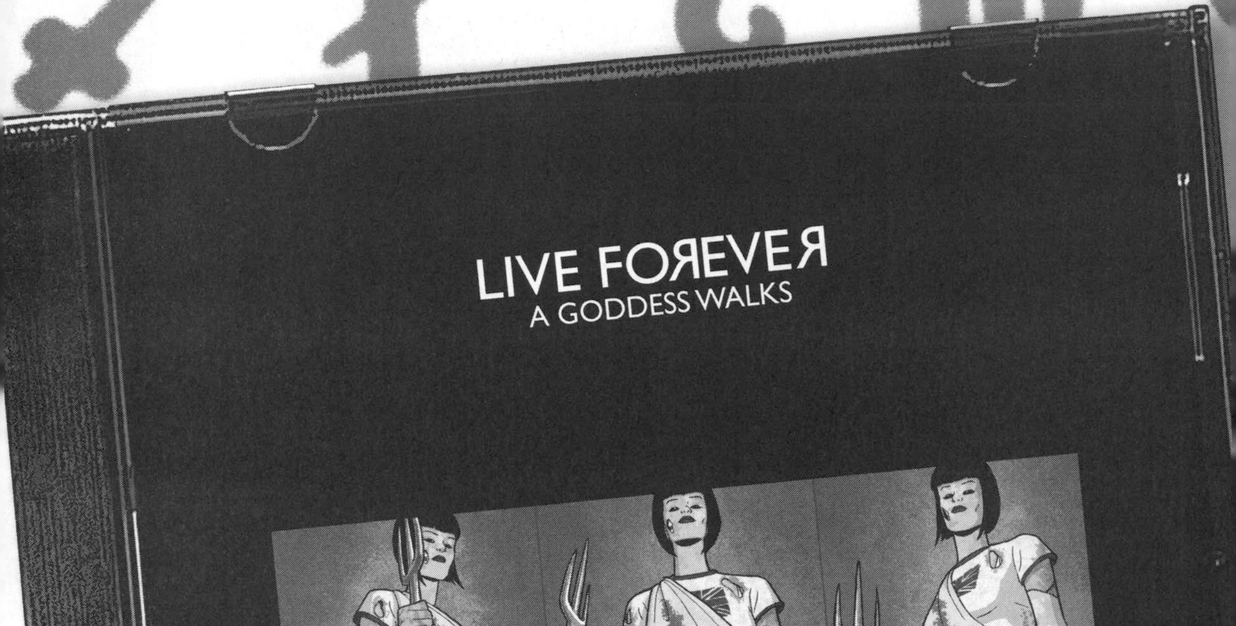

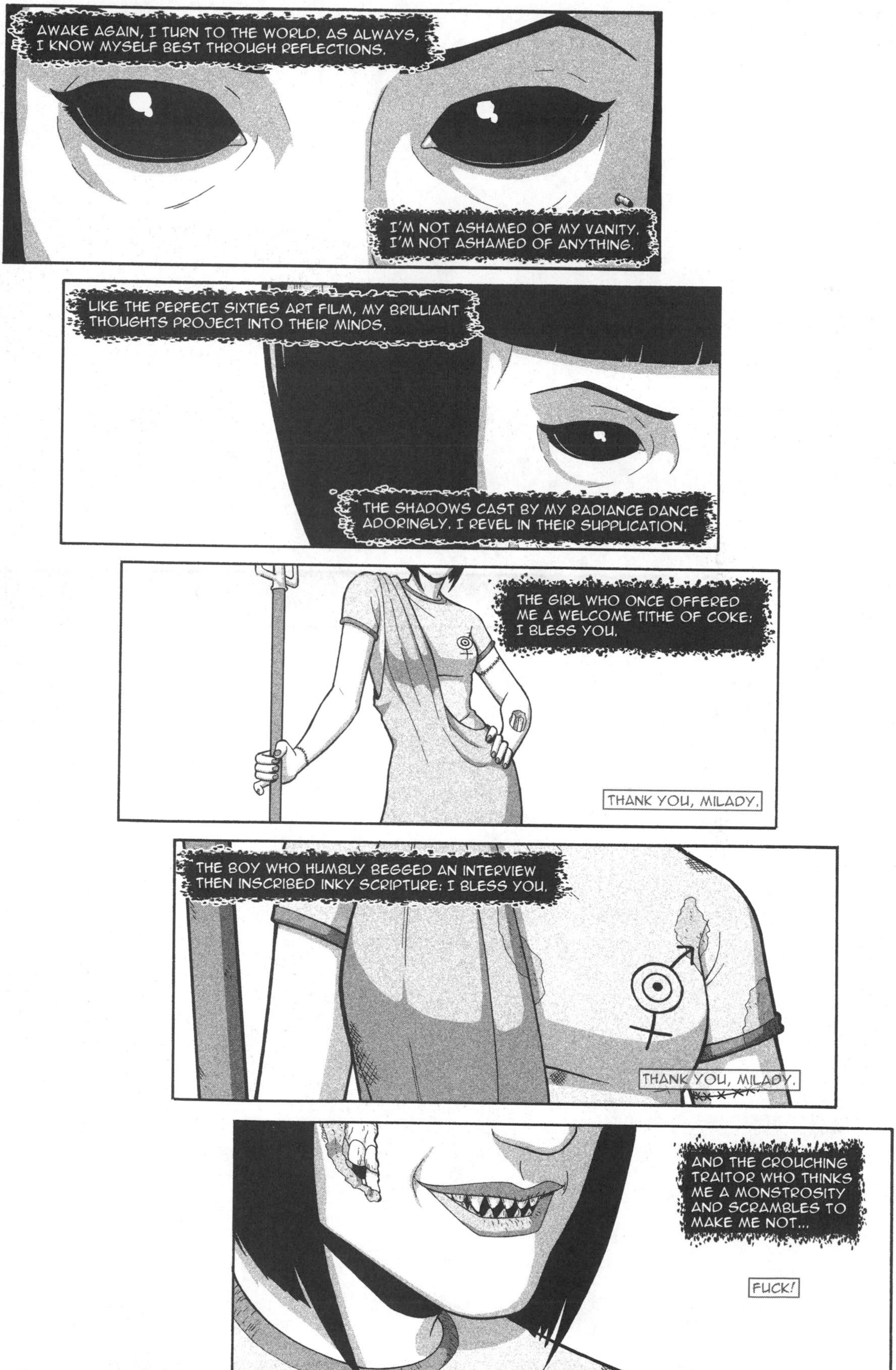
AWAKE AGAIN, I TURN TO THE WORLD. AS ALWAYS, I KNOW MYSELF BEST THROUGH REFLECTIONS.
I'M NOT ASHAMED OF MY VANITY. I'M NOT ASHAMED OF ANYTHING.
LIKE THE PERFECT SIXTIES ART FILM, MY BRILLIANT THOUGHTS PROJECT INTO THEIR MINDS.
THE SHADOWS CAST BY MY RADIANCE DANCE ADORINGLY. I REVEL IN THEIR SUPPLICATION.
THE GIRL WHO ONCE OFFERED ME A WELCOME TITHE OF COKE: I BLESS YOU.
THANK YOU, MILADY.
THE BOY WHO HUMBLY BEGGED AN INTERVIEW THEN INSCRIBED INKY SCRIPTURE: I BLESS YOU.
THANK YOU, MILADY.
AND THE CROUCHING TRAITOR WHO THINKS ME A MONSTROSITY AND SCRAMBLES TO MAKE ME NOT...
FUCK!

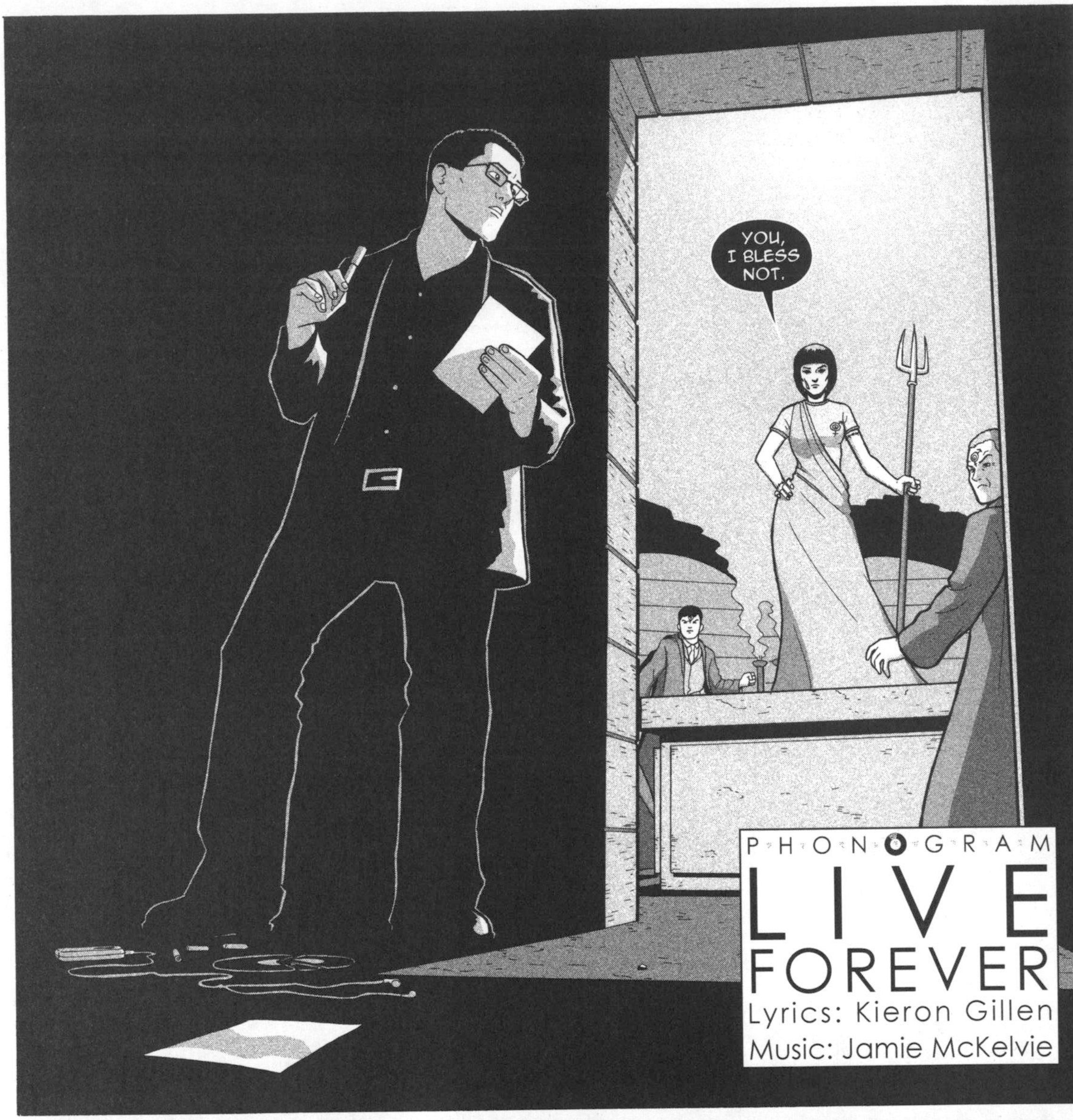
YOU, I BLESS NOT.
PHONOGRAM
LIVE FOREVER
Lyrics: Kieron Gillen
Music: Jamie McKelvie

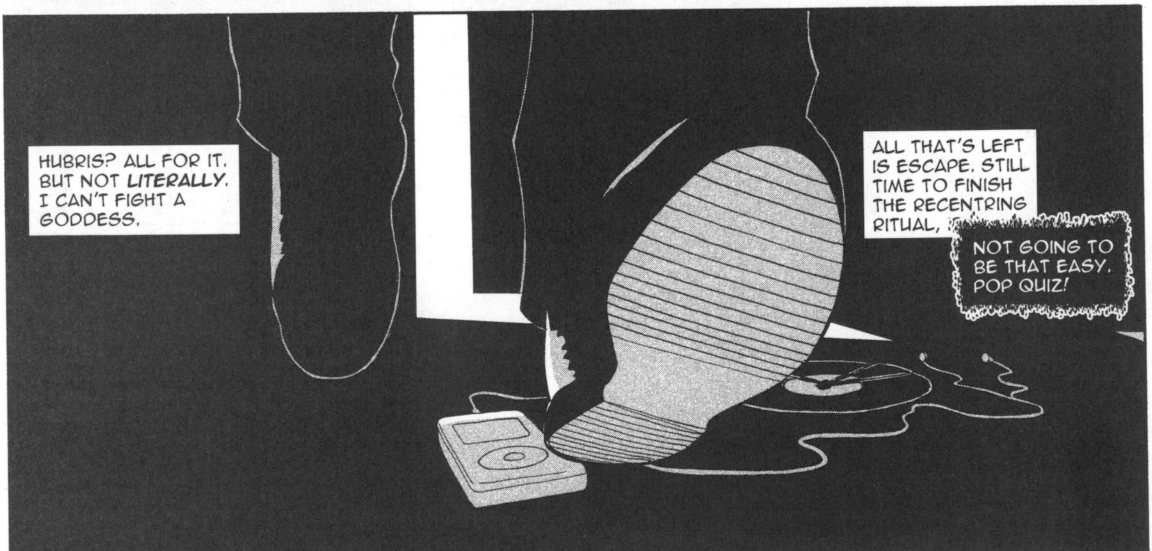
HUBRIS? ALL FOR IT. BUT NOT LITERALLY. I CAN'T FIGHT A GODDESS.
ALL THAT'S LEFT IS ESCAPE. STILL TIME TO FINISH THE RECENTRING RITUAL,
NOT GOING TO BE THAT EASY. POP QUIZ!

WHO RECORDED "GIRL FROM MARS" AND "KUNG-FU"?

NO DISTRACTIONS. NO DISTRACTIONS. DON'T THINK OF...

...ASH.

YOU SEE, DAVID?

EVEN NOW YOU CAN'T COMPLETELY LET GO OF THE PAST.

AND THE PAST WON'T LET GO OF YOU.

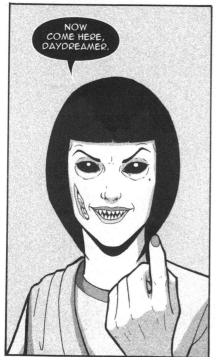

NOW COME HERE, DAYDREAMER.

MY LATEST RESURRECTION PROMISES TO BE SIMPLY THE MOST SUPER YET.

IT'S A RARE LEGEND WHO GETS TO SEE IF THE THIRD TIME REALLY IS THE CHARM.

NOW: SIT STILL AND STOP YOUR PRATTLING.

MY *FAITHFUL* SERVANTS NEED ATTENTION.

WE HAVE TENDED YOUR LEGEND, MILADY. WE BROUGHT YOU BACK.

ALL WE ASK IS TO SHARE YOUR VICTORY.

WE WISH ONLY A CLOSER UNION.

HMM.

  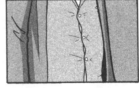 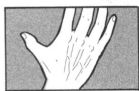

  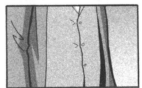 

 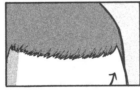 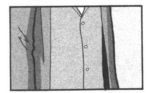 

IT IS DONE.

A BOND UNBREAKABLE.

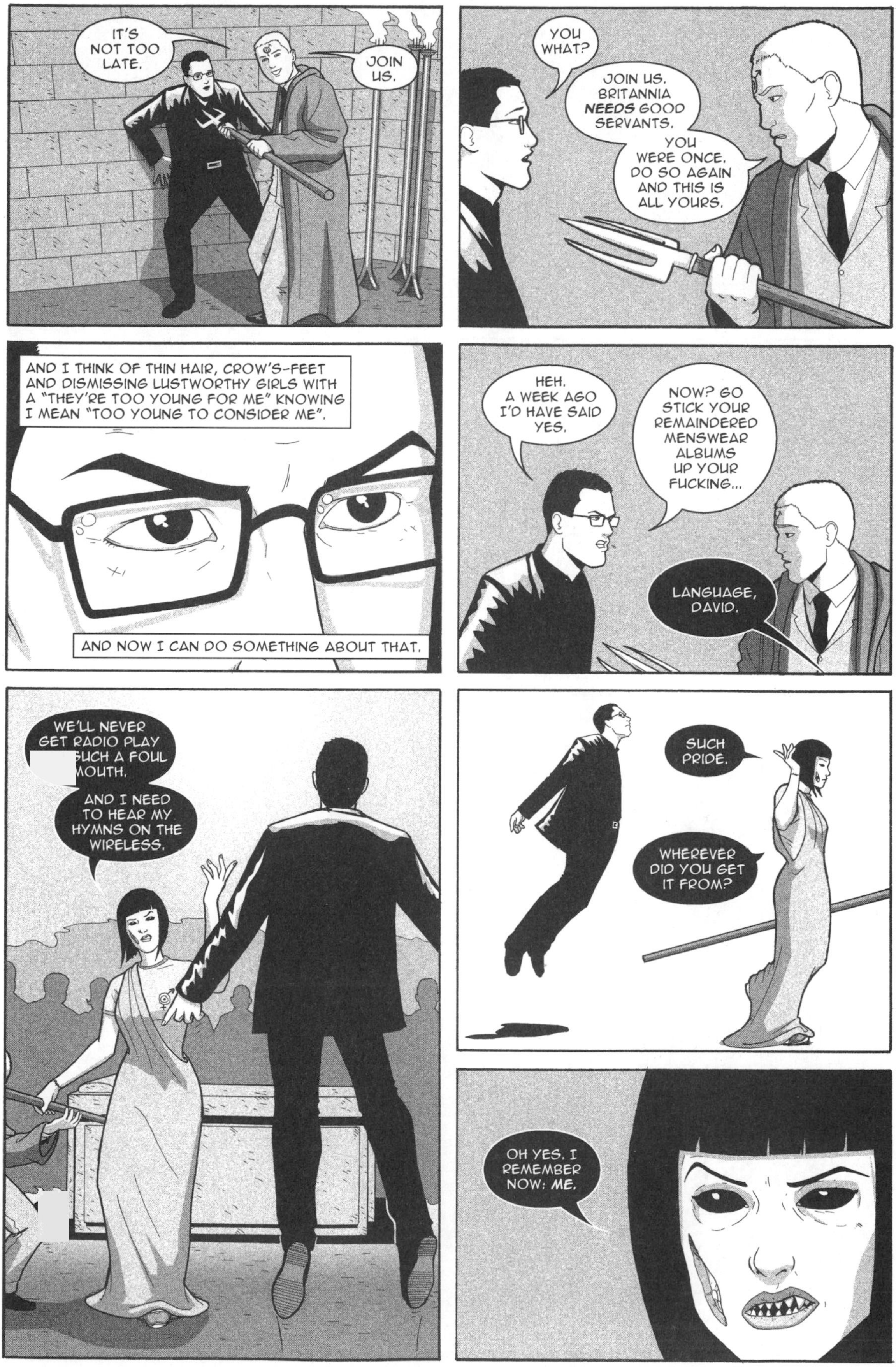

IT'S NOT TOO LATE.
JOIN US.
YOU WHAT?
JOIN US. BRITANNIA **NEEDS** GOOD SERVANTS.
YOU WERE ONCE. DO SO AGAIN AND THIS IS ALL YOURS.
AND I THINK OF THIN HAIR, CROW'S-FEET AND DISMISSING LUSTWORTHY GIRLS WITH A "THEY'RE TOO YOUNG FOR ME" KNOWING I MEAN "TOO YOUNG TO CONSIDER ME".
AND NOW I CAN DO SOMETHING ABOUT THAT.
HEH. A WEEK AGO I'D HAVE SAID YES.
NOW? GO STICK YOUR REMAINDERED MENSWEAR ALBUMS UP YOUR FUCKING...
LANGUAGE, DAVID.
WE'LL NEVER GET RADIO PLAY SUCH A FOUL MOUTH.
AND I NEED TO HEAR MY HYMNS ON THE WIRELESS.
SUCH PRIDE.
WHEREVER DID YOU GET IT FROM?
OH YES. I REMEMBER NOW: ***ME.***

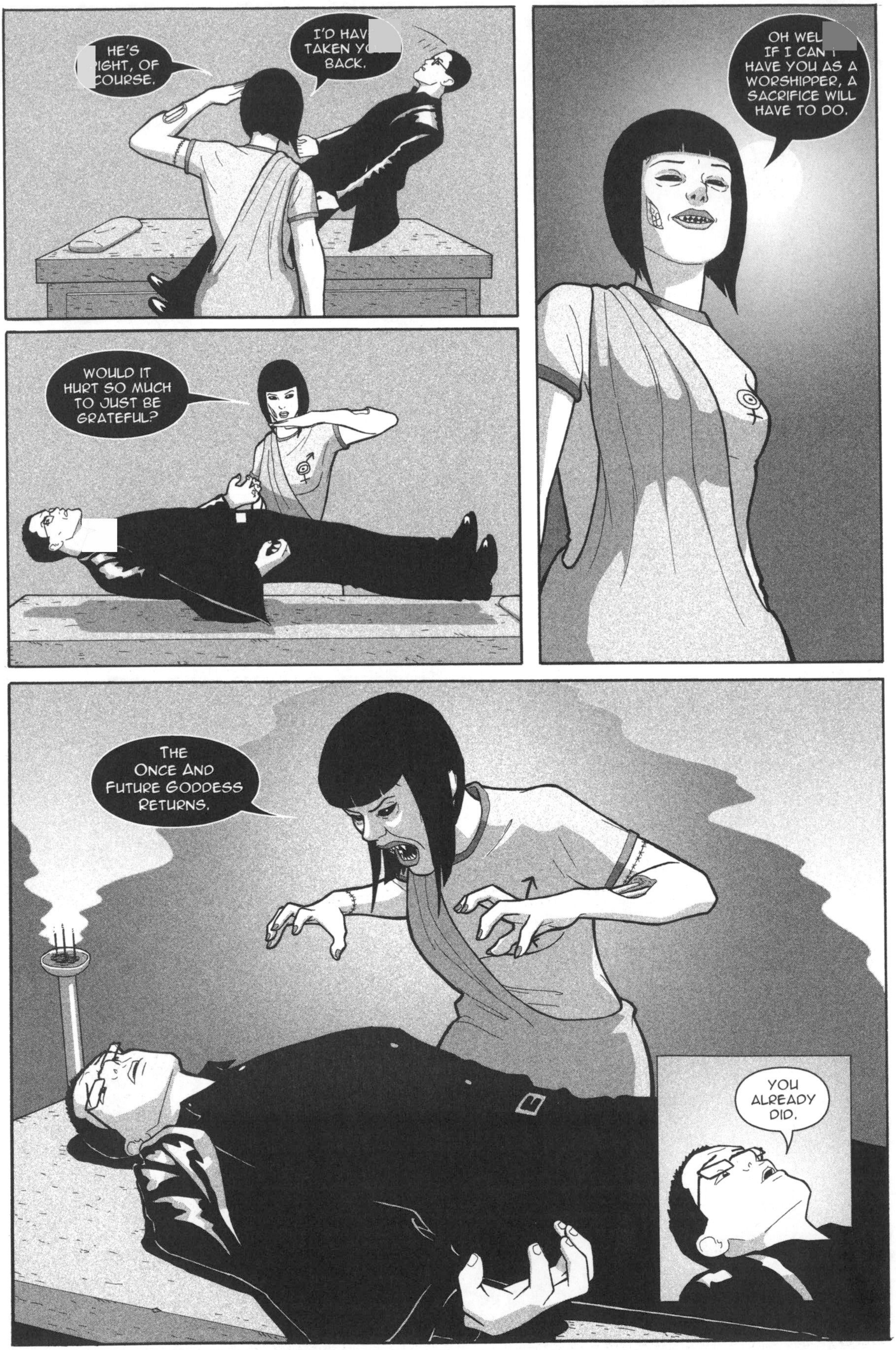
HE'S IGHT, OF COURSE.
I'D HAV TAKEN YO BACK.
OH WEL IF I CAN HAVE YOU AS A WORSHIPPER, A SACRIFICE WILL HAVE TO DO.
WOULD IT HURT SO MUCH TO JUST BE GRATEFUL?
THE ONCE AND FUTURE GODDESS RETURNS.
YOU ALREADY DID.

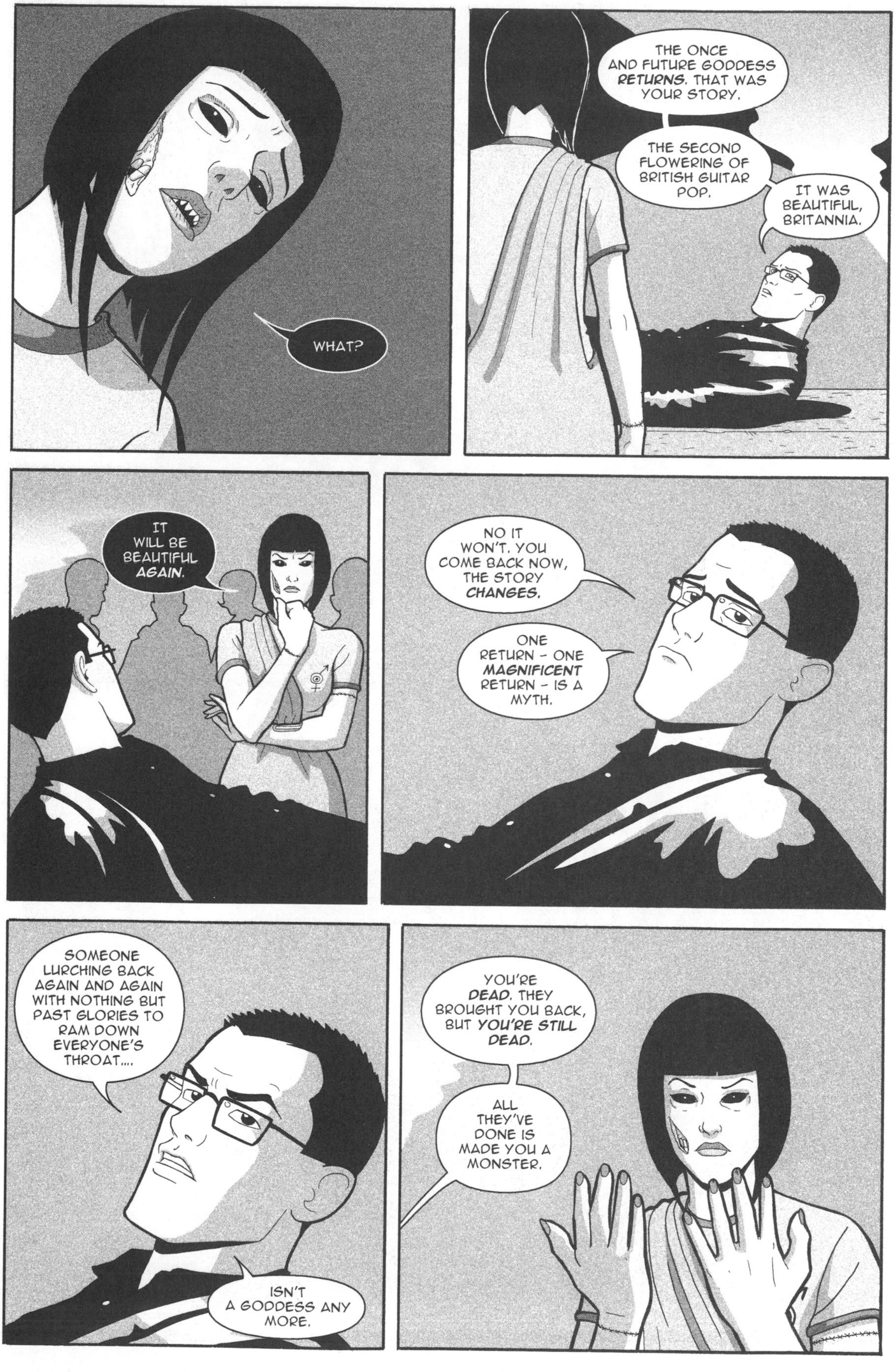
WHAT?
THE ONCE AND FUTURE GODDESS RETURNS. THAT WAS YOUR STORY.
THE SECOND FLOWERING OF BRITISH GUITAR POP.
IT WAS BEAUTIFUL, BRITANNIA.
IT WILL BE BEAUTIFUL AGAIN.
NO IT WON'T. YOU COME BACK NOW, THE STORY CHANGES.
ONE RETURN – ONE MAGNIFICENT RETURN – IS A MYTH.
SOMEONE LURCHING BACK AGAIN AND AGAIN WITH NOTHING BUT PAST GLORIES TO RAM DOWN EVERYONE'S THROAT....
ISN'T A GODDESS ANY MORE.
YOU'RE DEAD. THEY BROUGHT YOU BACK, BUT YOU'RE STILL DEAD.
ALL THEY'VE DONE IS MADE YOU A MONSTER.

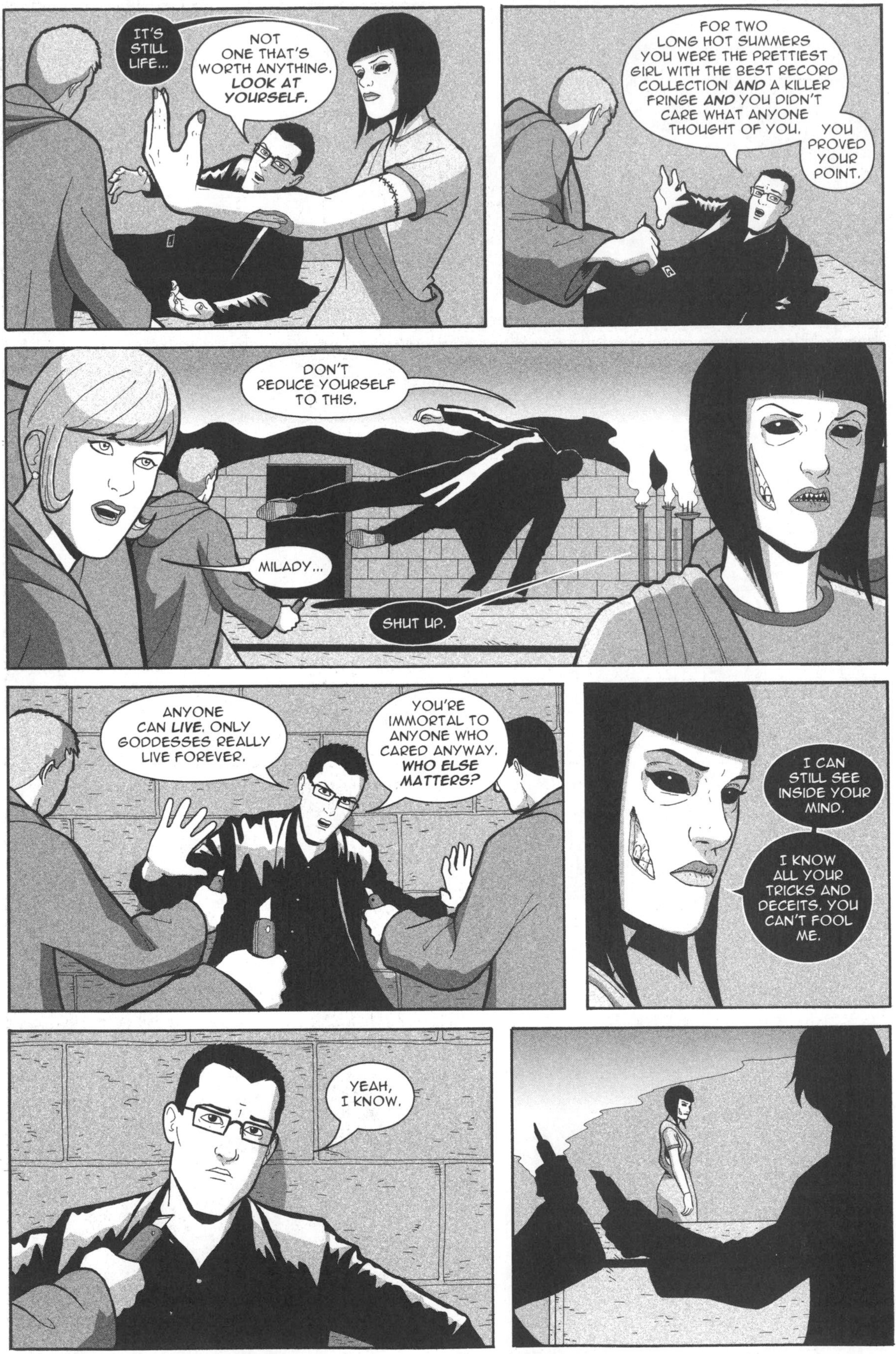

IT'S STILL LIFE...
NOT ONE THAT'S WORTH ANYTHING. **LOOK AT YOURSELF.**
FOR TWO LONG HOT SUMMERS YOU WERE THE PRETTIEST GIRL WITH THE BEST RECORD COLLECTION **AND** A KILLER FRINGE **AND** YOU DIDN'T CARE WHAT ANYONE THOUGHT OF YOU.
YOU PROVED YOUR POINT.
DON'T REDUCE YOURSELF TO THIS.
MILADY...
SHUT UP.
ANYONE CAN **LIVE**. ONLY GODDESSES REALLY LIVE FOREVER.
YOU'RE IMMORTAL TO ANYONE WHO CARED ANYWAY. **WHO ELSE MATTERS?**
I CAN STILL SEE INSIDE YOUR MIND.
I KNOW ALL YOUR TRICKS AND DECEITS. YOU CAN'T FOOL ME.
YEAH, I KNOW.

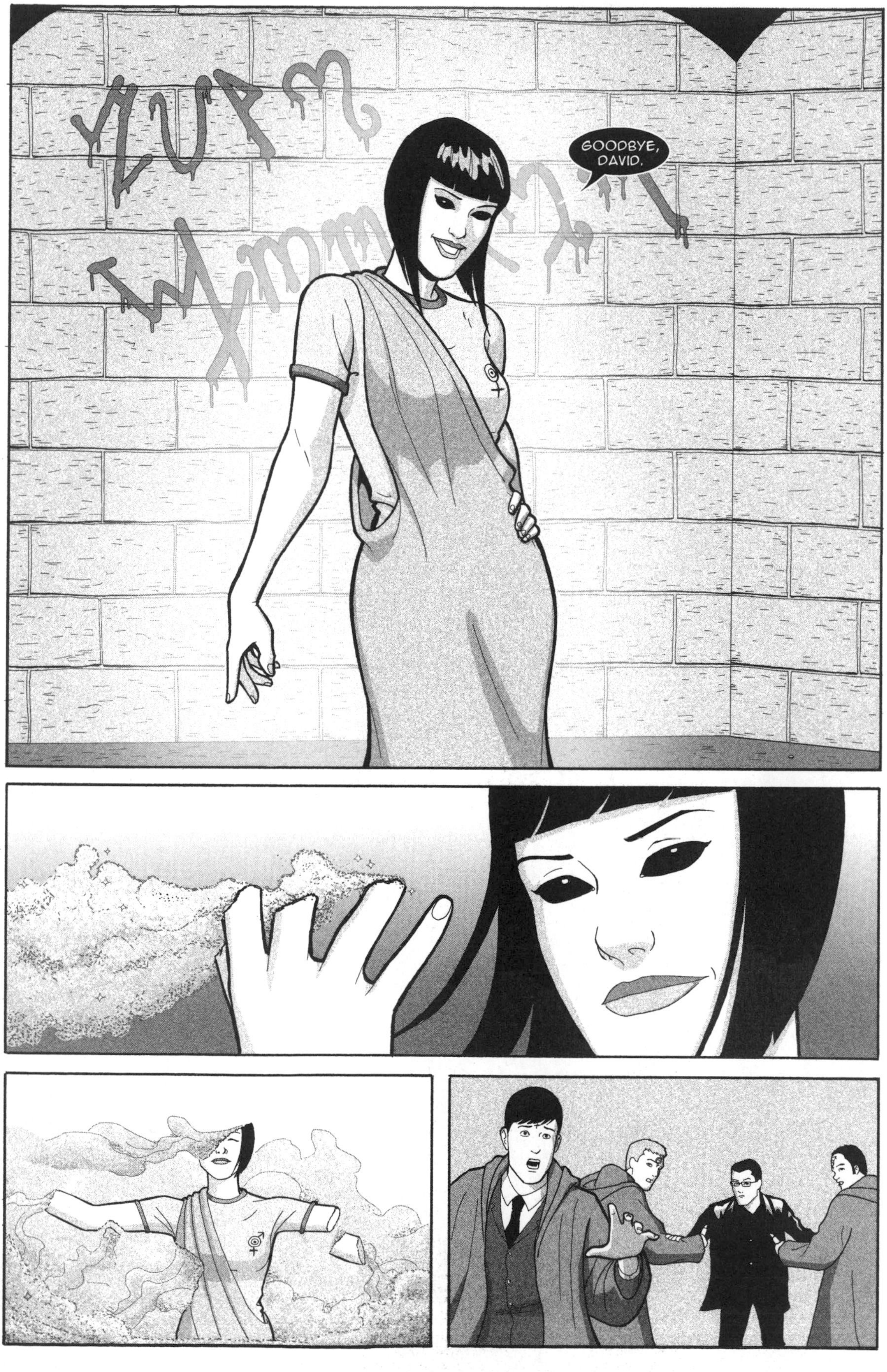
GOODBYE, DAVID.

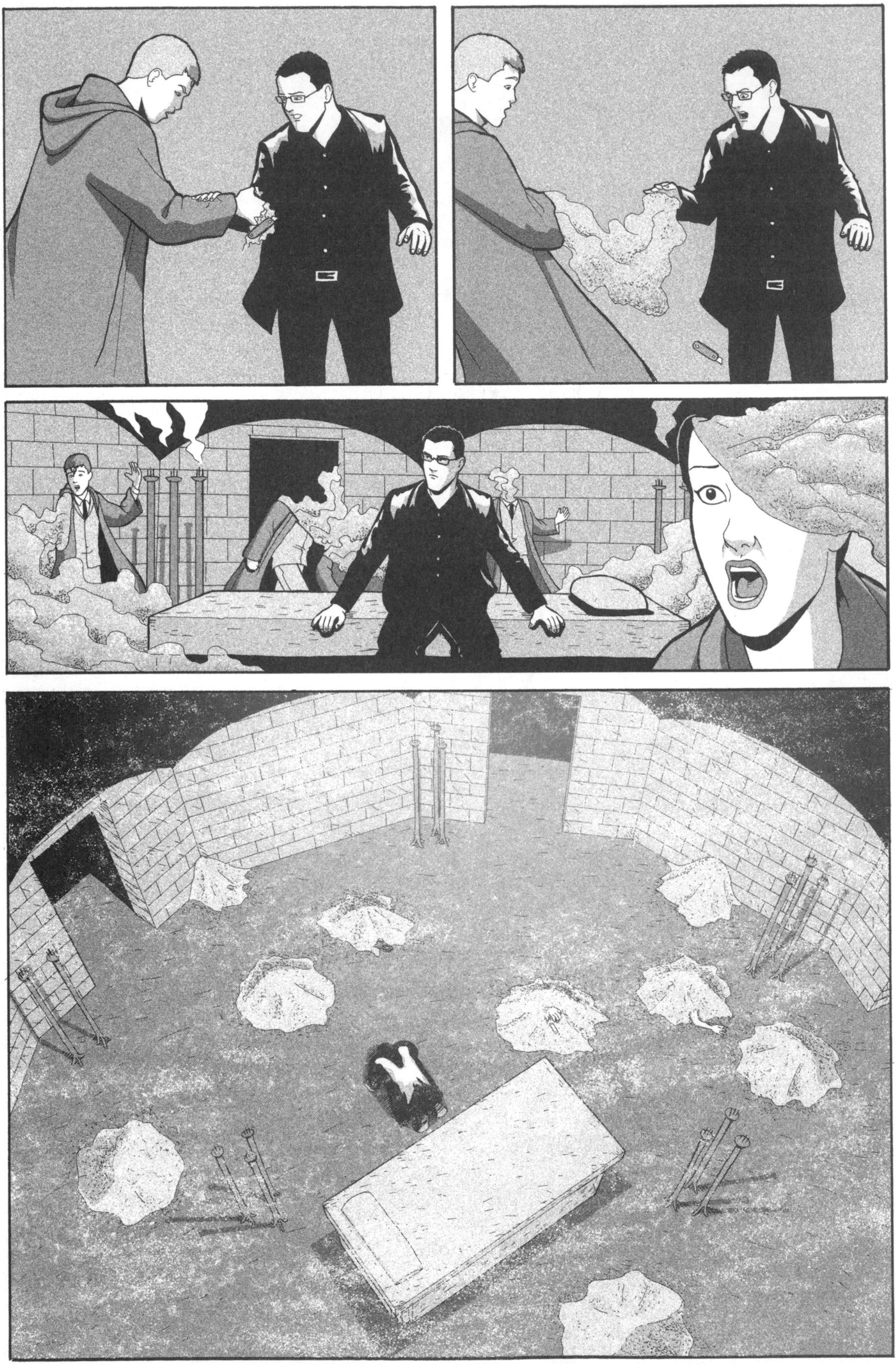

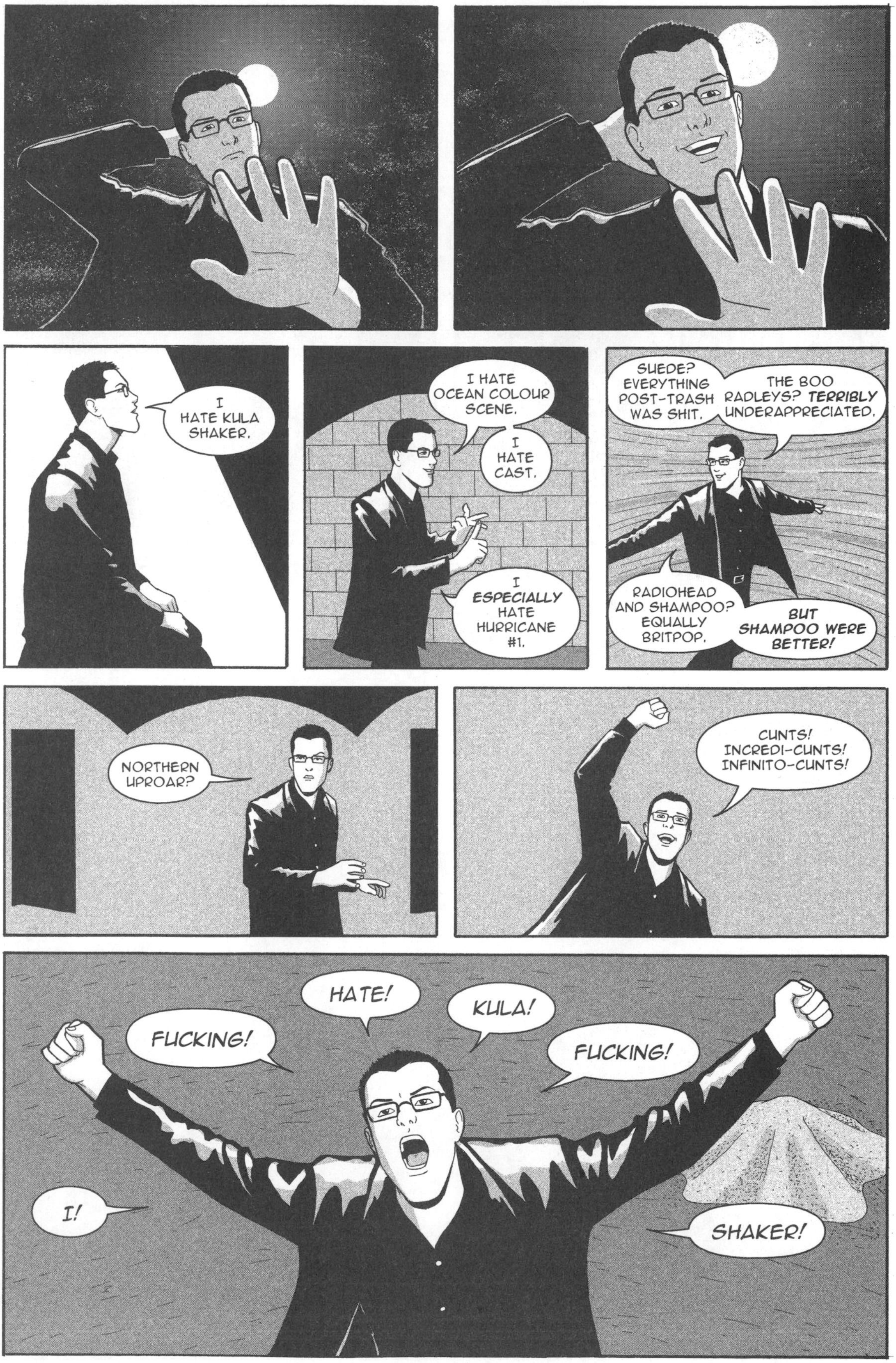
I HATE KULA SHAKER.
I HATE OCEAN COLOUR SCENE.
I HATE CAST.
I ESPECIALLY HATE HURRICANE #1.
SUEDE? EVERYTHING POST-TRASH WAS SHIT.
THE BOO RADLEYS? TERRIBLY UNDERAPPRECIATED.
RADIOHEAD AND SHAMPOO? EQUALLY BRITPOP.
BUT SHAMPOO WERE BETTER!
NORTHERN UPROAR?
CUNTS! INCREDI-CUNTS! INFINITO-CUNTS!
I!
FUCKING!
HATE!
KULA!
FUCKING!
SHAKER!

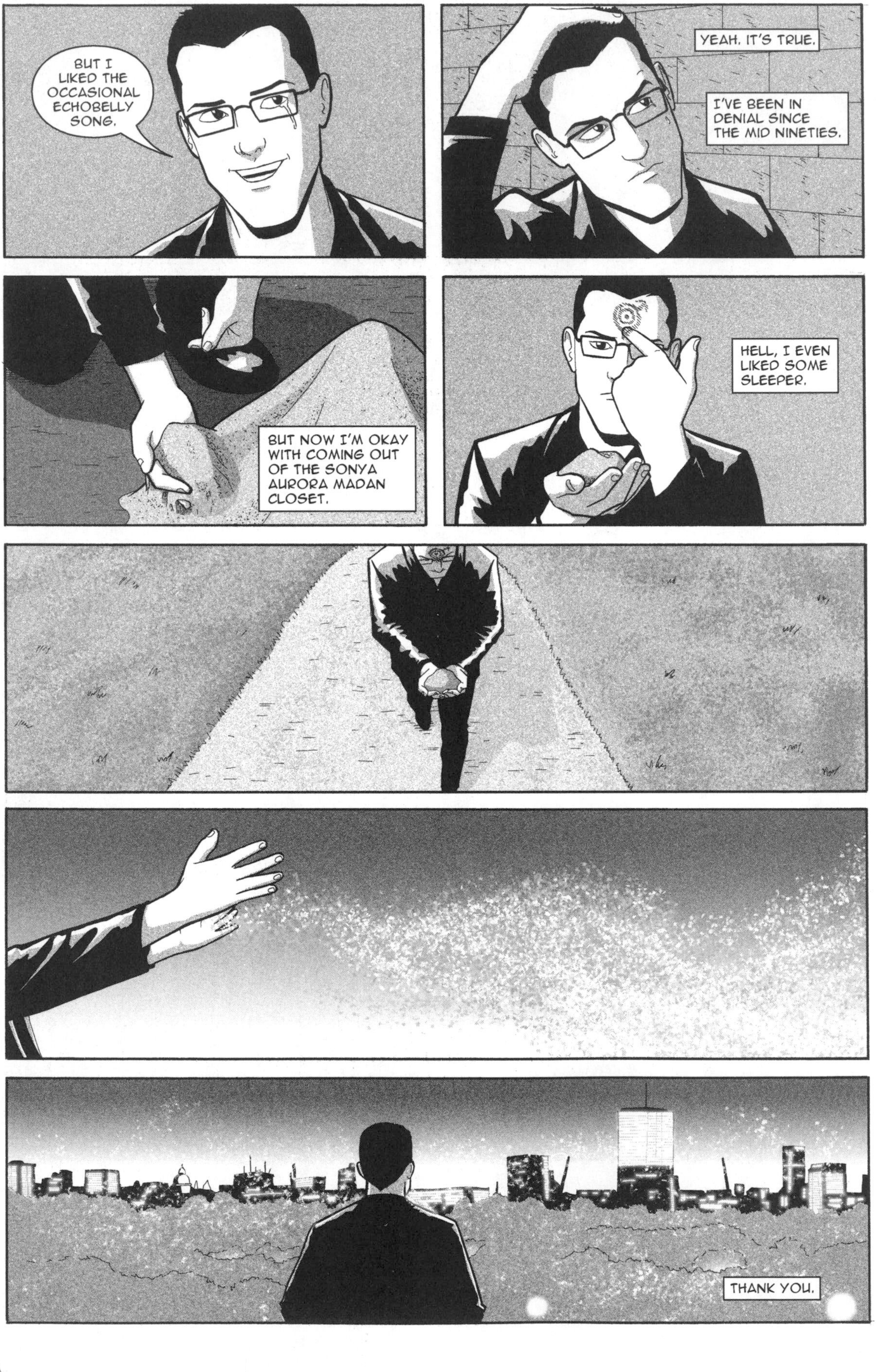

BUT I LIKED THE OCCASIONAL ECHOBELLY SONG.
YEAH. IT'S TRUE.
I'VE BEEN IN DENIAL SINCE THE MID NINETIES.
BUT NOW I'M OKAY WITH COMING OUT OF THE SONYA AURORA MADAN CLOSET.
HELL, I EVEN LIKED SOME SLEEPER.
THANK YOU.

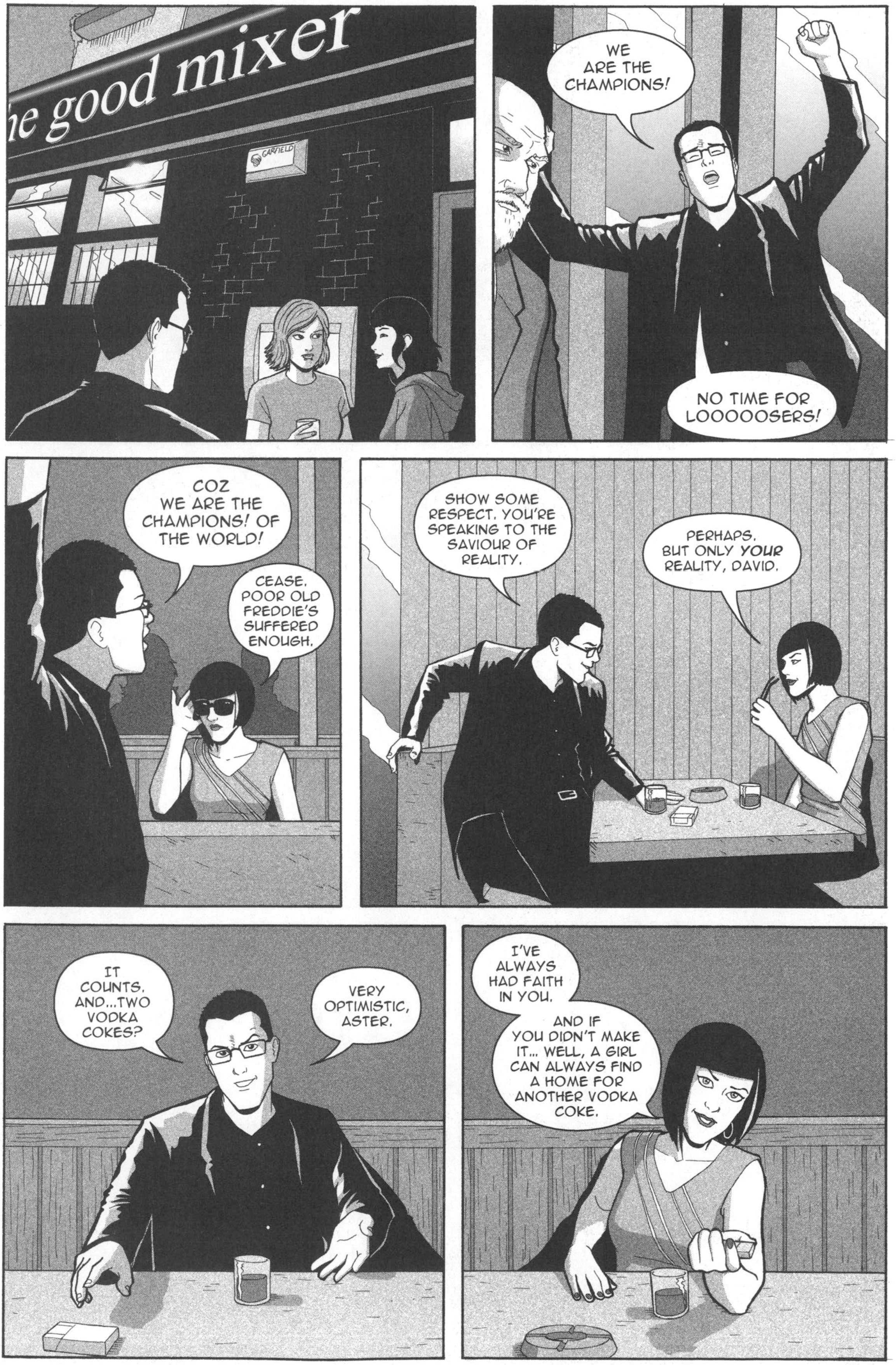
the good mixer
GARFIELD
WE ARE THE CHAMPIONS!
NO TIME FOR LOOOOOSERS!
COZ WE ARE THE CHAMPIONS! OF THE WORLD!
CEASE. POOR OLD FREDDIE'S SUFFERED ENOUGH.
SHOW SOME RESPECT. YOU'RE SPEAKING TO THE SAVIOUR OF REALITY.
PERHAPS. BUT ONLY YOUR REALITY, DAVID.
IT COUNTS. AND...TWO VODKA COKES?
VERY OPTIMISTIC, ASTER.
I'VE ALWAYS HAD FAITH IN YOU.
AND IF YOU DIDN'T MAKE IT... WELL, A GIRL CAN ALWAYS FIND A HOME FOR ANOTHER VODKA COKE.

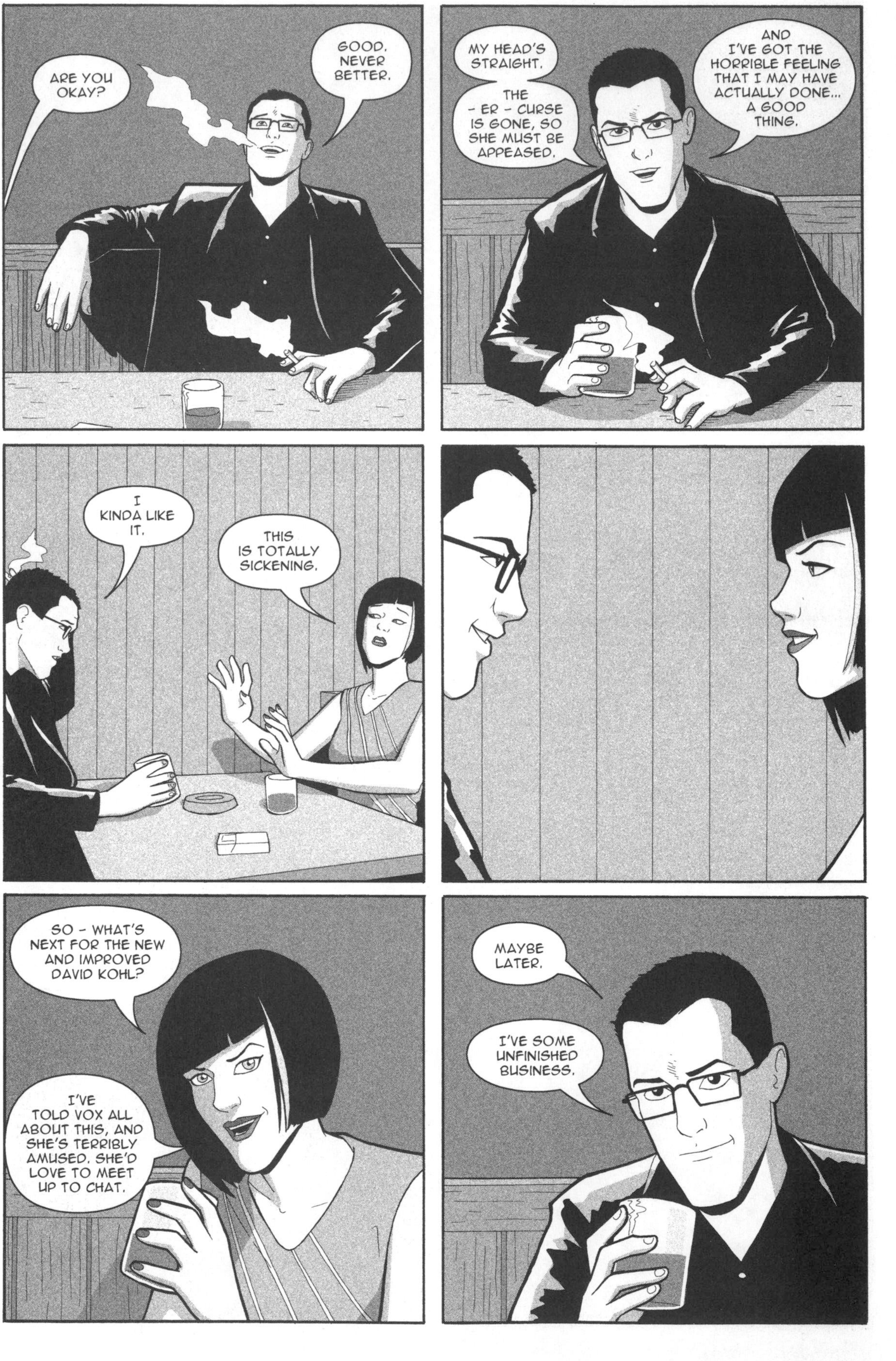
ARE YOU OKAY?
GOOD, NEVER BETTER.
MY HEAD'S STRAIGHT.
THE - ER - CURSE IS GONE, SO SHE MUST BE APPEASED.
AND I'VE GOT THE HORRIBLE FEELING THAT I MAY HAVE ACTUALLY DONE... A GOOD THING.
I KINDA LIKE IT.
THIS IS TOTALLY SICKENING.
SO - WHAT'S NEXT FOR THE NEW AND IMPROVED DAVID KOHL?
I'VE TOLD VOX ALL ABOUT THIS, AND SHE'S TERRIBLY AMUSED. SHE'D LOVE TO MEET UP TO CHAT.
MAYBE LATER.
I'VE SOME UNFINISHED BUSINESS.

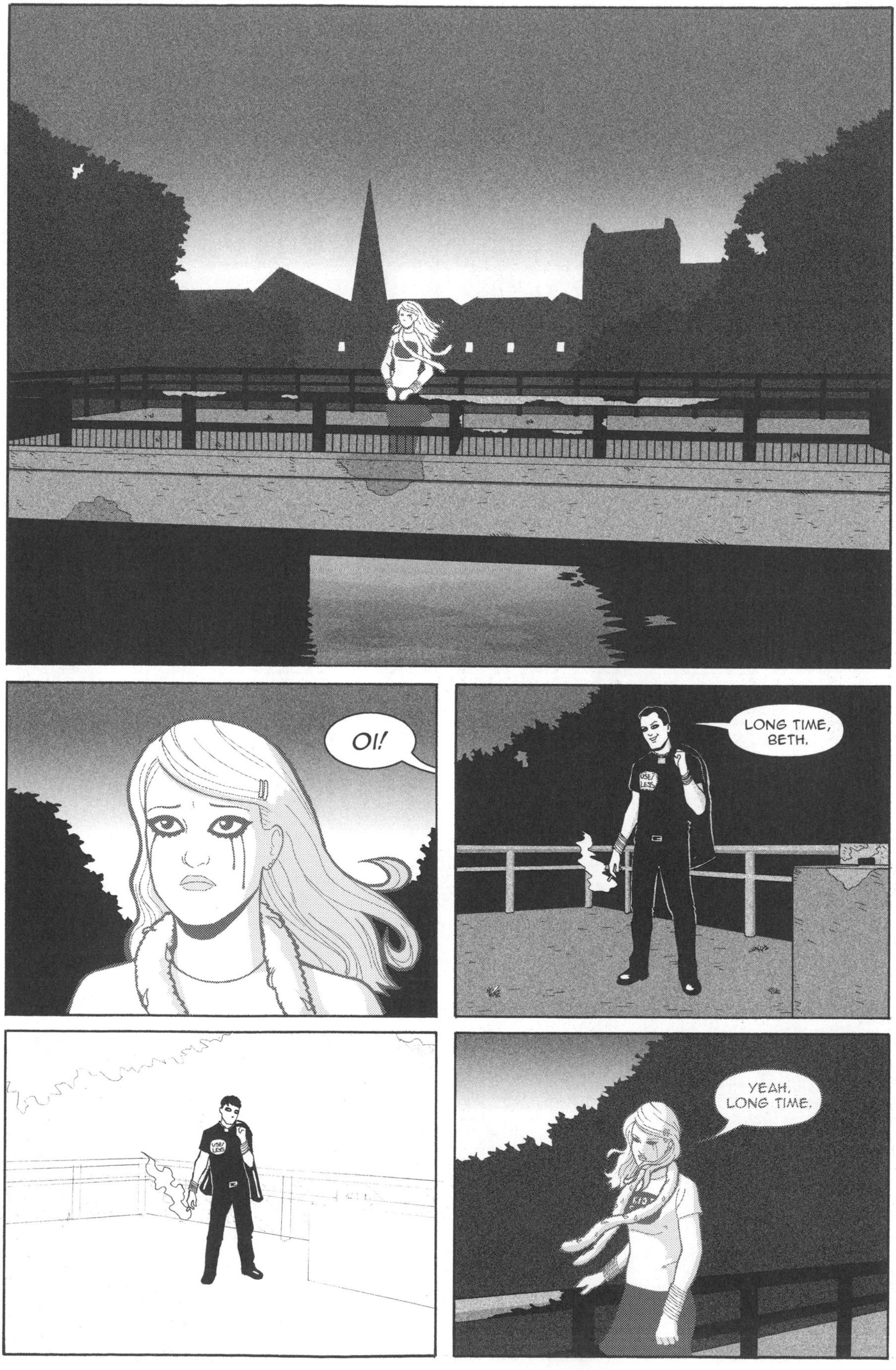
OI!
LONG TIME, BETH.
USE/LESS
YEAH. LONG TIME.

BEEN THINKING.
WHY DIDN'T ANYTHING REALLY HAPPEN BETWEEN US?
BECAUSE I DIDN'T LIKE YOU THAT WAY.
USE LESS
RIOT SLUT
SO WHY DID YOU TAKE IT AS FAR AS YOU DID?
RIOT SLUT
BECAUSE I DIDN'T LIKE MYSELF THAT MUCH EITHER.
YEAH.
ME TOO.
SO...
RIOT SLUT
WANT ME TO TAKE YOU AFTER RICHEY?

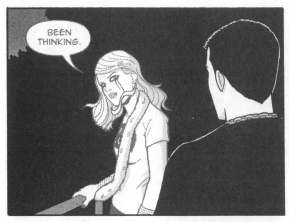

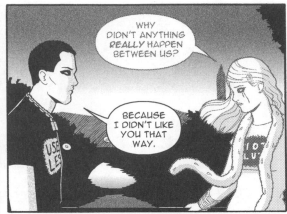

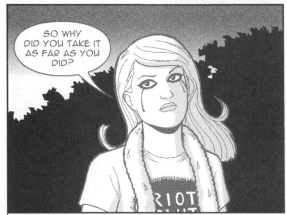

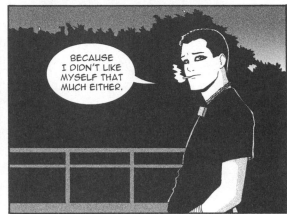

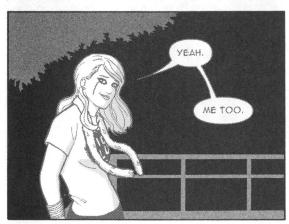

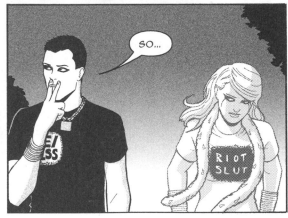

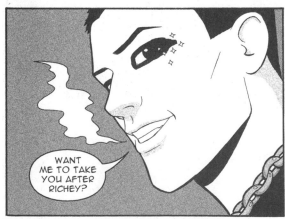

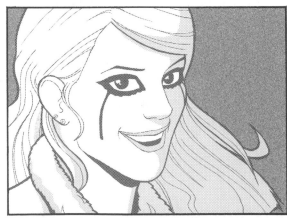

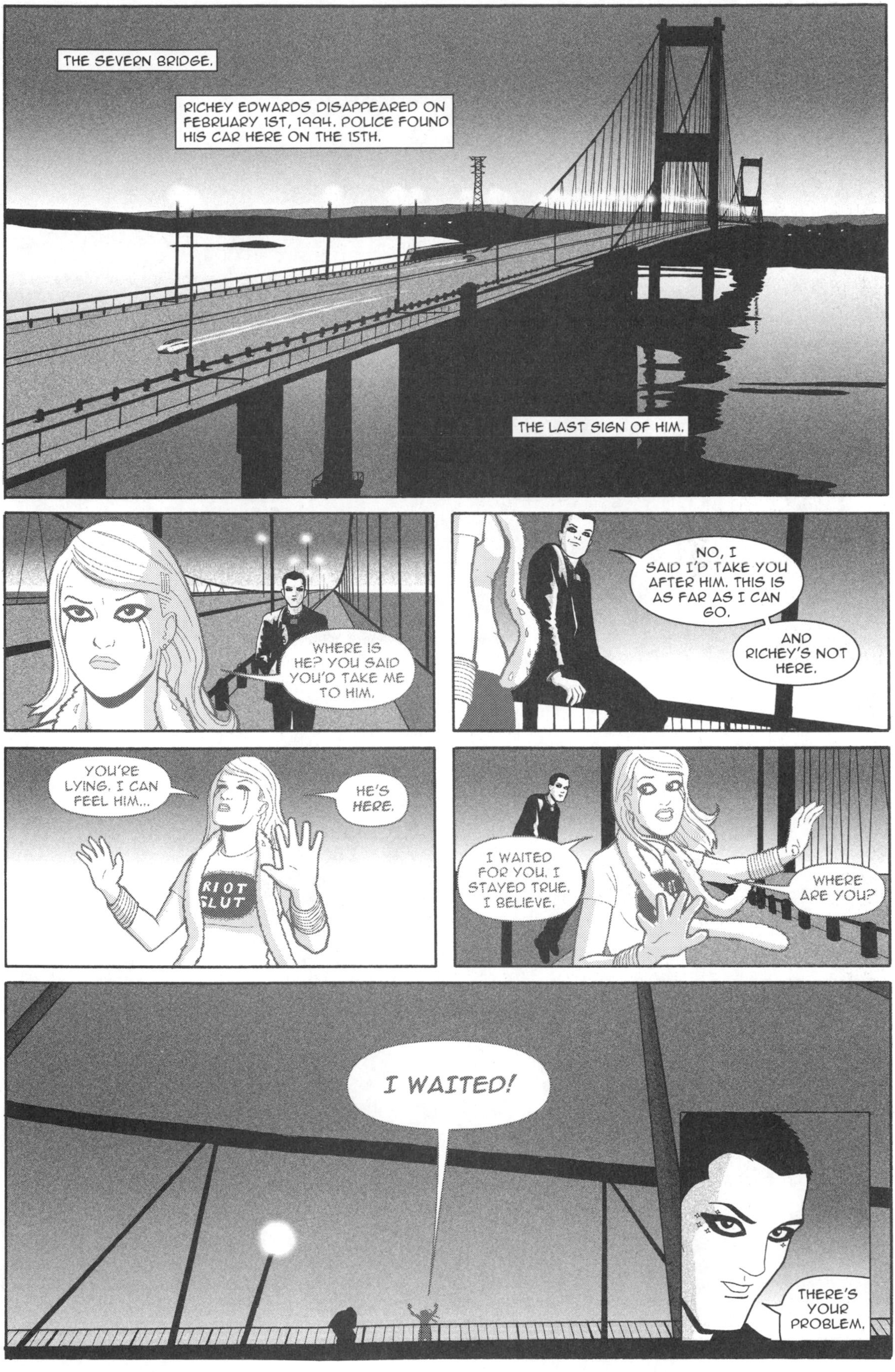
THE SEVERN BRIDGE.
RICHEY EDWARDS DISAPPEARED ON FEBRUARY 1ST, 1994. POLICE FOUND HIS CAR HERE ON THE 15TH.
THE LAST SIGN OF HIM.
WHERE IS HE? YOU SAID YOU'D TAKE ME TO HIM.
NO, I SAID I'D TAKE YOU AFTER HIM. THIS IS AS FAR AS I CAN GO.
AND RICHEY'S NOT HERE.
YOU'RE LYING. I CAN FEEL HIM...
HE'S *HERE*.
RIOT SLUT
I WAITED FOR YOU. I STAYED TRUE. I BELIEVE.
WHERE ARE YOU?
I WAITED!
THERE'S YOUR PROBLEM.

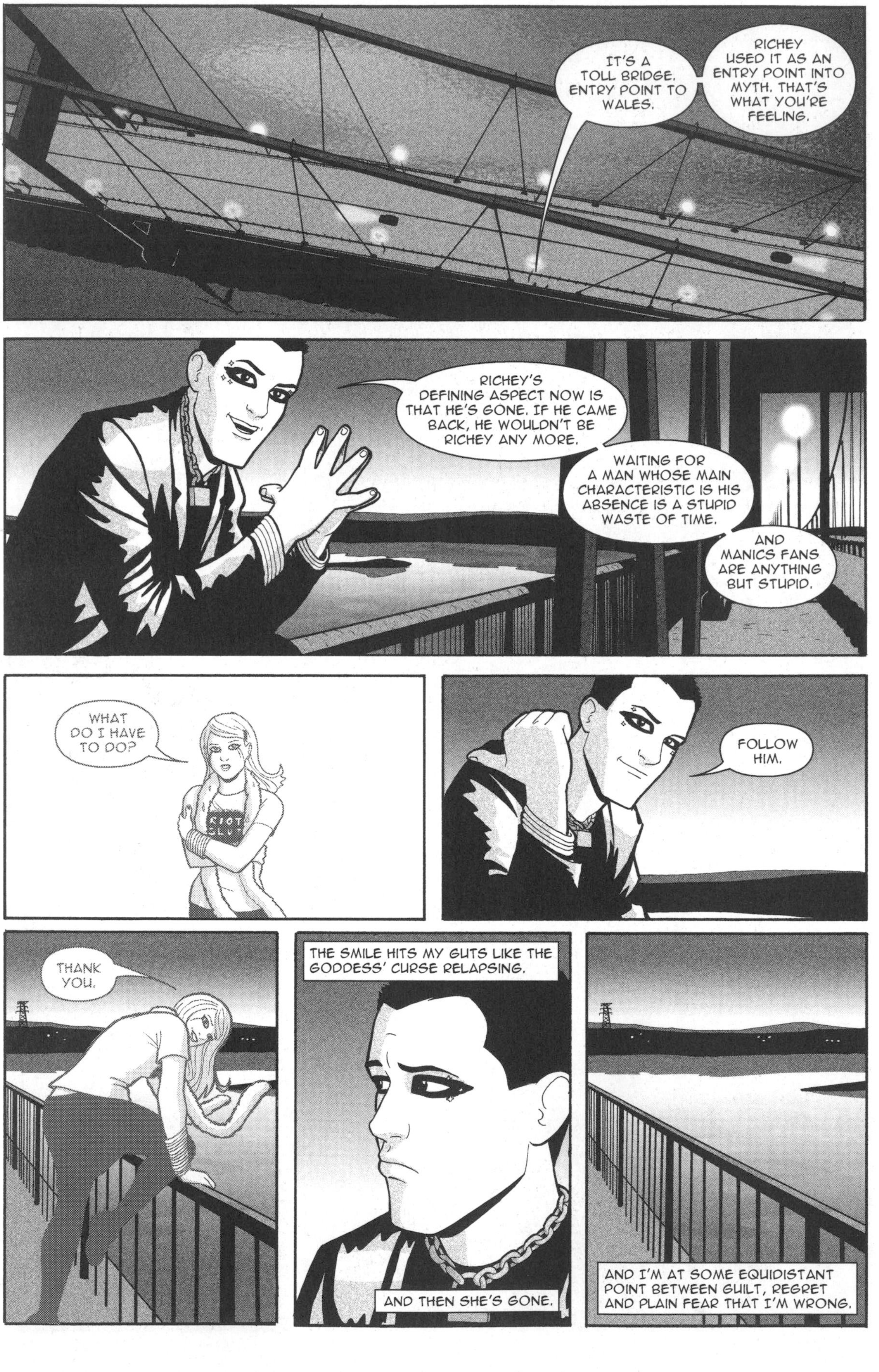
IT'S A TOLL BRIDGE. ENTRY POINT TO WALES.
RICHEY USED IT AS AN ENTRY POINT INTO MYTH. THAT'S WHAT YOU'RE FEELING.
RICHEY'S DEFINING ASPECT NOW IS THAT HE'S GONE. IF HE CAME BACK, HE WOULDN'T BE RICHEY ANY MORE.
WAITING FOR A MAN WHOSE MAIN CHARACTERISTIC IS HIS ABSENCE IS A STUPID WASTE OF TIME.
AND MANICS FANS ARE ANYTHING BUT STUPID.
WHAT DO I HAVE TO DO?
FOLLOW HIM.
THANK YOU.
THE SMILE HITS MY GUTS LIKE THE GODDESS' CURSE RELAPSING.
AND THEN SHE'S GONE.
AND I'M AT SOME EQUIDISTANT POINT BETWEEN GUILT, REGRET AND PLAIN FEAR THAT I'M WRONG.

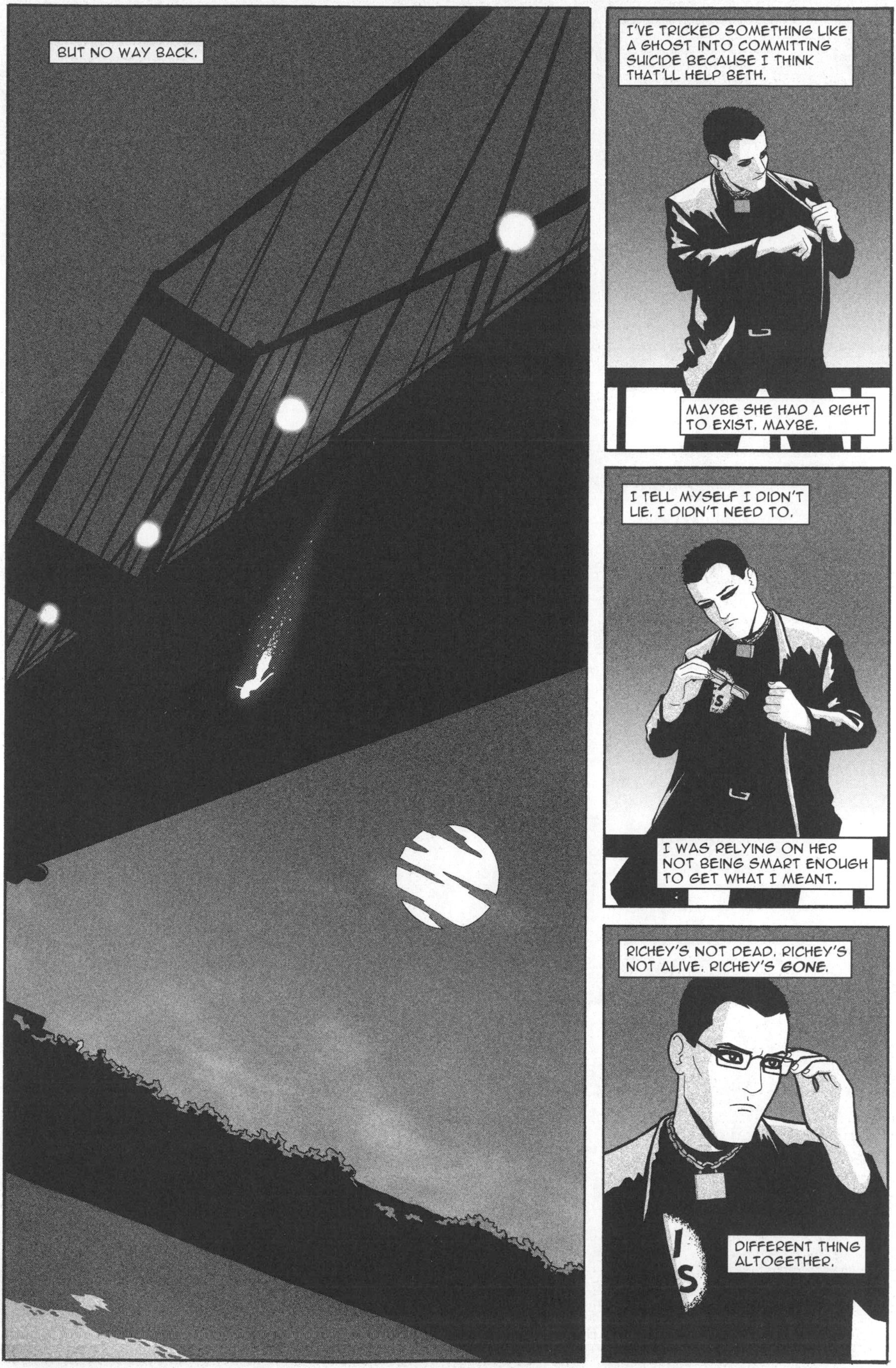
BUT NO WAY BACK.
I'VE TRICKED SOMETHING LIKE A GHOST INTO COMMITTING SUICIDE BECAUSE I THINK THAT'LL HELP BETH.
MAYBE SHE HAD A RIGHT TO EXIST. MAYBE.
I TELL MYSELF I DIDN'T LIE. I DIDN'T NEED TO.
I WAS RELYING ON HER NOT BEING SMART ENOUGH TO GET WHAT I MEANT.
RICHEY'S NOT DEAD. RICHEY'S NOT ALIVE. RICHEY'S *GONE*.
DIFFERENT THING ALTOGETHER.

ROCK IMMORTALITY. HOW DO YOU OBTAIN IT? BY BEING MEMORABLE. AN UNTIMELY DEATH JUST DOESN'T CUT IT ANY MORE.

YOU NEED SOMETHING A LITTLE MORE UNPRECEDENTED TO BECOME EVER-LIVING NARRATIVE.

DID HE DO IT DELIBERATELY? DOESN'T MATTER.

ALL THAT MATTERS IS THE ACT WAS ENOUGH TO MAKE THE IDEA OF RICHEY INTO A GOD.

THE PRICE WAS SUICIDE WITHOUT A NOTE OR A DISAPPEARANCE WITHOUT SAYING HE WAS ALIVE.

THE PRICE WAS BEING A SHIT.

HE DIDN'T OWE US ANYTHING – AND VICE VERSA. THAT'S HOW POP WORKS. POP IS FOR *YOU.*

BUT HIS ASCENSION PUT THE PEOPLE WHO LOVED HIM – REALLY LOVED HIM – THROUGH A LIVING HELL.

BELIEF IS ALL-IMPORTANT IN WHAT WE DO.

YOU BELIEVE, IT BURNS, FLICKERS AND DIES. THE ASHES MIX WITH THE SOIL AND WE CALL THEM MEMORIES.

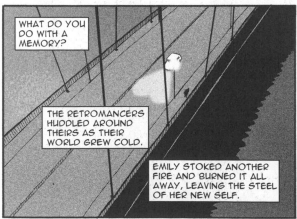

WHAT DO YOU DO WITH A MEMORY?

THE RETROMANCERS HUDDLED AROUND THEIRS AS THEIR WORLD GREW COLD.

EMILY STOKED ANOTHER FIRE AND BURNED IT ALL AWAY, LEAVING THE STEEL OF HER NEW SELF.

AND, YEAH, EVEN *I* WORKED OUT THAT NO MATTER HOW BAD IT OBJECTIVELY WAS...

IT'S HOW I WAS MADE. AND AFTER A FEW DRINKS, YOU MAY EVEN GET ME TO ADMIT IT.

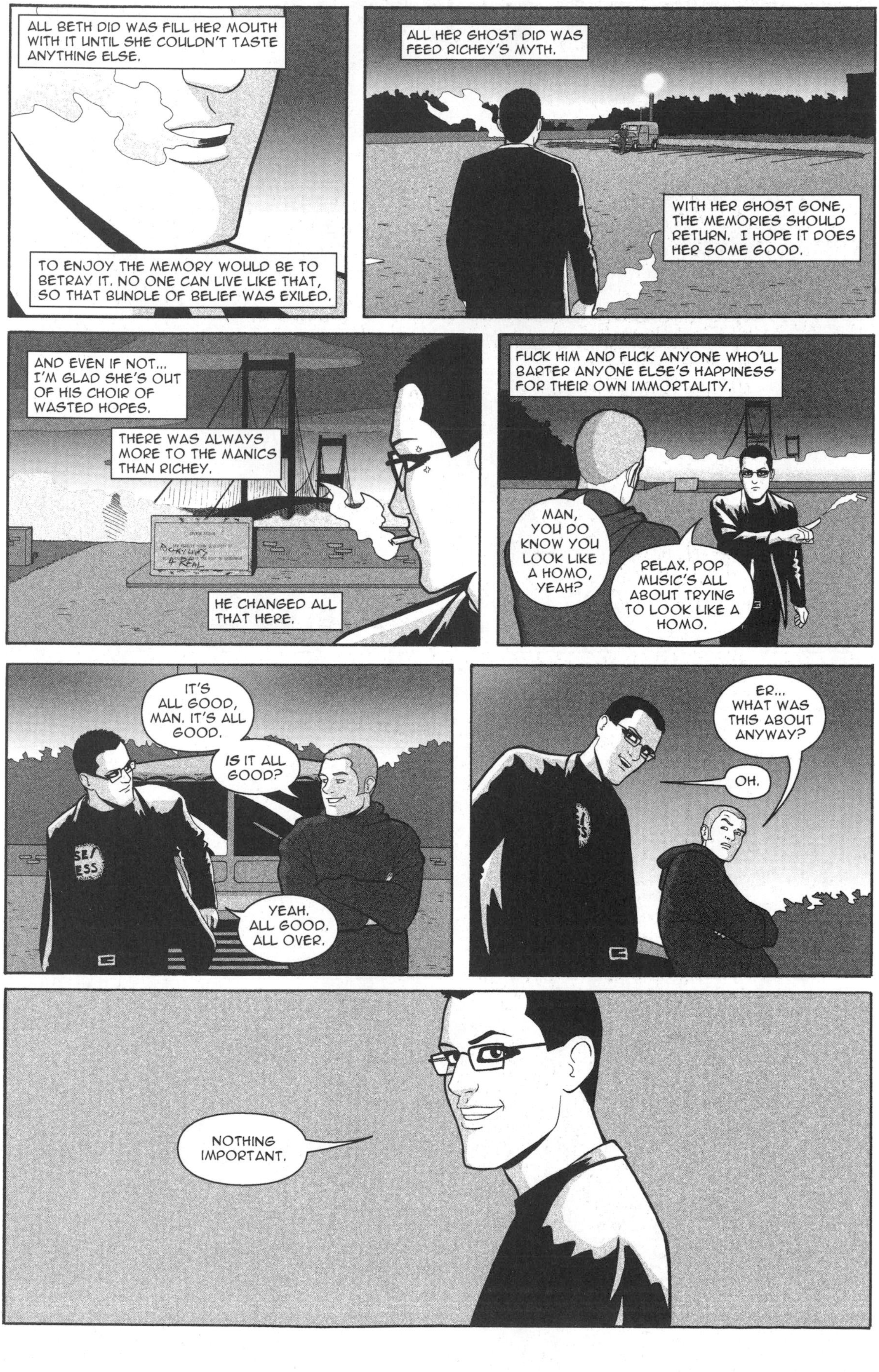
ALL BETH DID WAS FILL HER MOUTH WITH IT UNTIL SHE COULDN'T TASTE ANYTHING ELSE.
TO ENJOY THE MEMORY WOULD BE TO BETRAY IT. NO ONE CAN LIVE LIKE THAT, SO THAT BUNDLE OF BELIEF WAS EXILED.
ALL HER GHOST DID WAS FEED RICHEY'S MYTH.
WITH HER GHOST GONE, THE MEMORIES SHOULD RETURN. I HOPE IT DOES HER SOME GOOD.
AND EVEN IF NOT... I'M GLAD SHE'S OUT OF HIS CHOIR OF WASTED HOPES.
THERE WAS ALWAYS MORE TO THE MANICS THAN RICHEY.
RICHY LIVES 4 REAL
HE CHANGED ALL THAT HERE.
FUCK HIM AND FUCK ANYONE WHO'LL BARTER ANYONE ELSE'S HAPPINESS FOR THEIR OWN IMMORTALITY.
MAN, YOU DO KNOW YOU LOOK LIKE A HOMO, YEAH?
RELAX. POP MUSIC'S ALL ABOUT TRYING TO LOOK LIKE A HOMO.
IT'S ALL GOOD, MAN. IT'S ALL GOOD.
IS IT ALL GOOD?
YEAH. ALL GOOD. ALL OVER.
ER... WHAT WAS THIS ABOUT ANYWAY?
OH.
NOTHING IMPORTANT.

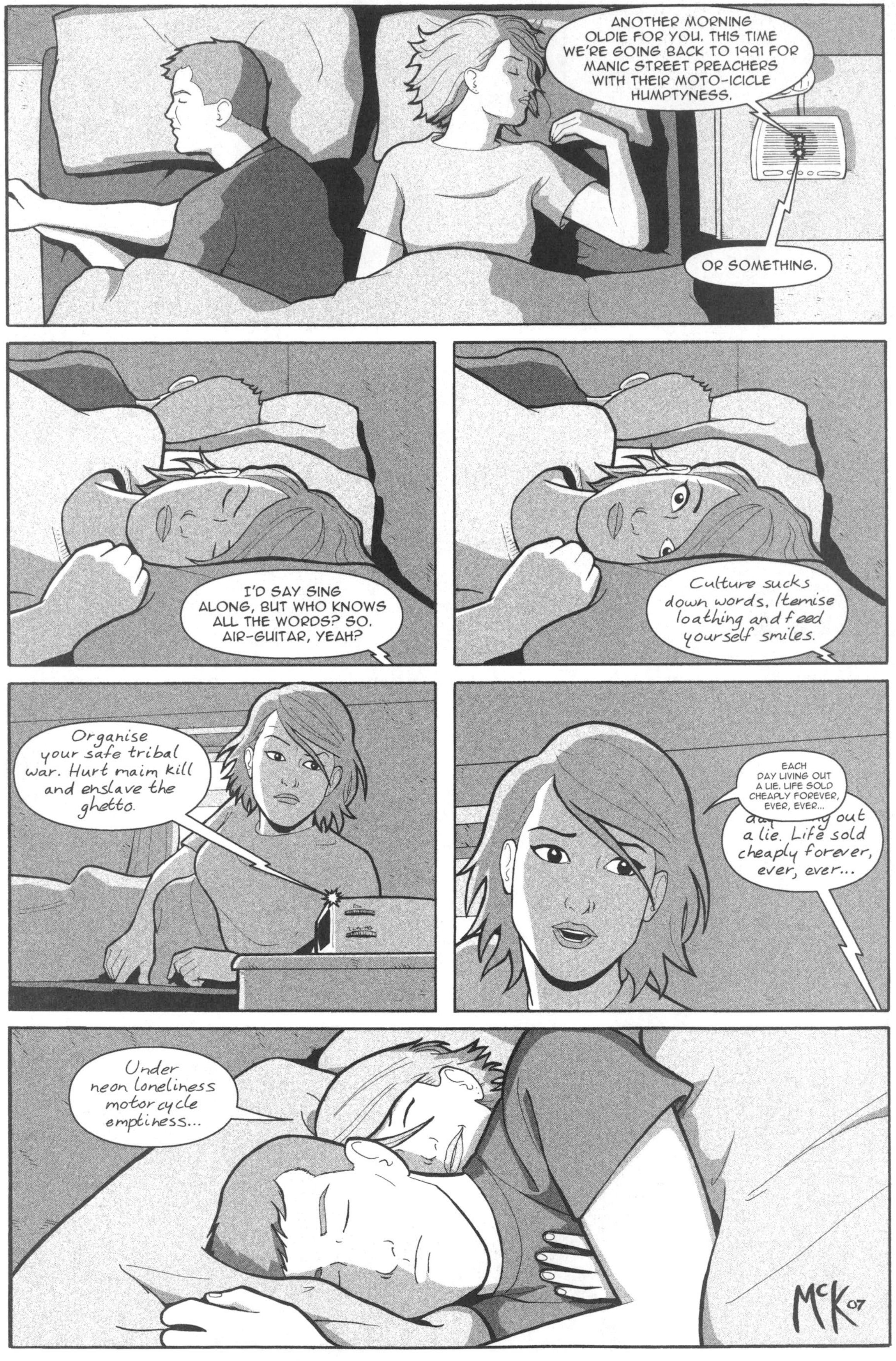
ANOTHER MORNING OLDIE FOR YOU. THIS TIME WE'RE GOING BACK TO 1991 FOR MANIC STREET PREACHERS WITH THEIR MOTO-ICICLE HUMPTYNESS.
OR SOMETHING.
I'D SAY SING ALONG, BUT WHO KNOWS ALL THE WORDS? SO. AIR-GUITAR, YEAH?
Culture sucks down words. Itemise loathing and feed yourself smiles.
Organise your safe tribal war. Hurt maim kill and enslave the ghetto.
EACH DAY LIVING OUT A LIE. LIFE SOLD CHEAPLY FOREVER, EVER, EVER...
a lie. Life sold cheaply forever, ever, ever...
Under neon loneliness motorcycle emptiness...
McK 07

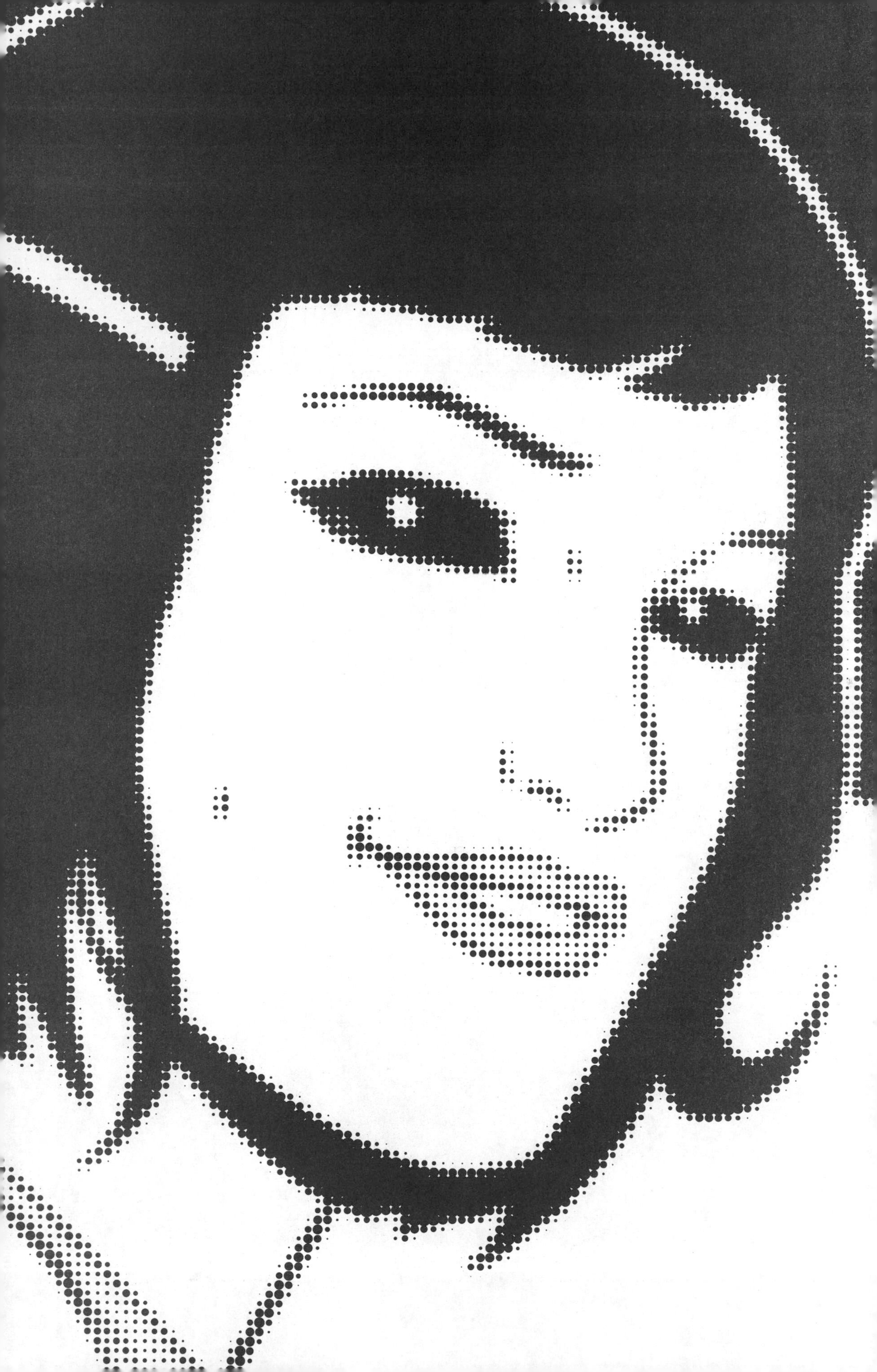

GLOSSARY

We dropped one of these in every single issue of the original run of Phonogram. We put the same proviso here as there. None of this is necessary to understand the story. Everything you need to know about a band is right there in the narrative, and should be able to be grasped from the context it's in. By how Kohl sneers at - say - Kula Shaker, you know it's some terrible band. You know what it's like to hate a band. That said, it is all based on the real world. You may wish to know more, and where to start listening, so we do this glossary for your amusement and elucidation. And we make jokes, or at least the approximation thereof.

So… non-essential but fun. Local colour. Geddit? Goddit. Good.

"250,000 in a weekend a month back.": A reference to Oasis' Knebworth gigs. Get thee to their own entry.

AFGHAN WHIGS: Nineties Cincinnati rock band with lashings of guilt-ridden soul. If you're a girl, they're everything Mum warned you men were. Beware. Start with *Gentlemen*.

ARAB STRAP: Glasgow post-rock/mumbling duo. Bad Sex and Good Songs. Start with *Philophobia*, though *The Week Never Starts Around Here* is closer to the period.

ARCTIC MONKEYS, THE: Probably, in the final analysis, the NME hype-band of recent years who deserved it. Sample their social-observation garage-pop in *Whatever People Say I Am, That's What I'm Not*.

ASH: Northern Irish three-piece-turned-four-piece. Play both kinds of music: Punk and Pop. Britpop era album would be *1977*.

AUTEURS, THE: Acerbic, literate British guitar pop formed around the gloriously bitter arch-curmudgeon Luke Haines. Period album is *After Murder Park*.

BANGKOK: Libertines B-side from the back of their *Time For Heroes* single. Bit like the Arctic Monkeys, apparently.

BENDS, THE: Radiohead's second album. The one where they went from one-hit-wonders to perennial pseudish-student favourites. Actually, damn good.

BELLE AND SEBASTIAN: Classic Glaswegian sixties-esque jangle. Music for people with diaries. Brilliant. True period stuff would be *Tigermilk* but start with *If You're Feeling Sinister*.

"BIG BEAT": Populist dance genre with aforementioned beats which are big. Heavenly Social, breaking down, building up, whatever. The Chemical Brothers' *Exit Planet Dust* would be a relevant start.

BIS: Glasgow pop-irritant who quietly precipitated a fanzine boom. The mass catalyst was their *Secret Vampire Soundtrack* EP.

BLUR: From their origins as Colchester's answer to the indie-dance of Madchester they reinvented themselves as militant retro-mods against the perfidious United States, inventing Britpop in the process. *Modern Life is Rubbish*, *Parklife* and *The Great Escape* vary in quality, but are all definitive period portraits.

BR_T P_P: In a Christmas Select magazine advert the Auteurs' Luke Haines was pictured playing Hangman with himself. This was the word he was trying to get. Bitter is fun.

BRIGHTON BEACH: A beach, in Brighton. Site of legendary sixties battles between Mods and Rockers. See *Quadrophenia* already.

BRITPOP: Mid-nineties manufactured guitar pop movement based around explicit rejection of U.S. grunge in favour of homegrown influences. Subject of some graphic novel or another.

BOO RADLEYS, THE: Liverpool Shoegazing band who blossomed into proto-Britpop expansive Beatles-inspired glory with their *Giant Steps*. Their *Wake Up!* album was a key Britpop development, the failure of their *C'mon Kids* a key sign of its demise.

BUZZCOCKS: Manchester pop/punk band whose *Spiral Scratch* EP begat the whole post-punk Indie DIY explosion in the late seventies. Start with their singles, collected on *Going Steady*.

CAST: The Las-influenced guitar band formed by the Ex-Las bassist, the lovely John Powers. Not terribly good. Key Britpop album: *All Change*.

CAMDEN: Seedy area in North London which acted as the unlikely cultural capital of Britpop.

"Can't Imagine The World Without Me": Neat title of early Echobelly single. Song couldn't match it. What song could?

"Can't Stand Me Now": Auto-eulogic single by The Libertines from second album, and pretty much their epitaph.

CATATONIA: Welsh indie dream-pop formed around the bar-room charm of Cerys Matthews. Their real success came later, but Kohl's talking about debut *Way Beyond Blue*.

CARL: Carl Barât, the creative half of the Libertines who you don't read about on the front of the English tabloids most mornings.

"Classy": Kenickie album track about Going